Also by CHRIS JORDAN

TORN
TRAPPED
TAKEN

CHRIS JORDAN

MEASURE
OF
DARKNESS

MIRA®

MIRA

Recycling programs
for this product may
not exist in your area.

ISBN-13: 978-0-7783-1258-1

MEASURE OF DARKNESS

For questions and comments about the quality of this book please contact us at
Customer_eCare@Harlequin.ca.

www.Harlequin.com

Printed in U.S.A.

For Lynn, forever and always.

Little Gull Cottage
Prides Crossing, Massachusetts

Being a genius isn't terribly useful when you're five years old. Joey understands chord progressions, he sees the shape of music way better than most adults, but has very little understanding of evil in the shape of man. And yet he senses that something is wrong. The bad man has never touched or threatened the boy—all communication comes through the woman—but the man's very presence makes Joey regress to his old habit of sucking his thumb. A habit he long ago—a year at least—abandoned to please his mother.

Mi Ma. Mommy. Joey last saw his mother two weeks ago, and he worries incessantly that he may never see her again, despite more or less constant reassurance from the woman who is taking care of him.

"Where's my real mommy?" he asks. It's his most frequent question, and the only one that matters.

"I told you, sweetie, she had to go away to the hospital."

Joey nods, his eyes big. "Real Mommy's okay?"

"She's fine. She'll be back in a few days, as soon as she's all the way better. Okay?"

"Okay," he says.

"You want to play some more? How about your Mozart, you love Mozart."

On the verge of tears he shakes his head.

"How about a story. *The Phantom Tollbooth?* You like that one, don't you?"

Weeping silently, the boy sucks his thumb and nods.

The scary man has many names. Just lately he's been calling himself Kidder. He thinks of himself as having a sense of humor, although others might disagree. If the ability to kill without remorse is funny—and it does sometimes make him laugh out loud—then he has a great sense of humor. His present assignment involves keeping an eye on a very special little boy and his caregiver. Great location. A private, oceanfront estate with absentee owners. Less than an hour from the city and yet it's country quiet, with total privacy and a lovely view of the sea. Easy duty for him, not so much for the woman, who gets all in a tizzy when the boy whines for his real mother.

Kidder doesn't get it, why the kid won't stop whining. The little brat has a new mommy, one focused solely on his welfare—a definite improvement on the old one, no question there. He has his special kid-size piano keyboard and his headphones, where he can practice for hours at a time—and only when he wants to, it's not like anybody makes him. If he's bored with music he has all the toys in the world, pizza whenever he wants and a big-screen TV loaded with DVDs of his favorite shows. Not exactly a torture situation. More like a trip to his own personal Disney World.

At the moment New Mommy is reading him a story,

and when she gets to the end she starts all over again, keeps it up until the brat finally falls asleep.

Kidder thinks it's funny that when New Mommy puts the kid to bed she calls it "putting him down." Like he's a dog at the pound being put to sleep forever. Not that New Mommy would ever do such a thing. She's all soft and weepy and worried, totally clueless about the real nature of the operation, and comes to Kidder with her eyes wet, like she caught tears from the kid.

"How much longer?" she asks.

"A day. A week. Forever."

"That's not funny!"

"It is if I say it is," Kidder says.

"How long?" she insists.

"Not my call. When Shane says so, that's when. You know how he is."

"I need to speak to him," she says, her voice choking. "I need to talk to Shane. Please?"

He shakes his head, grinning. "You knew it was a one-way deal when you signed up. No calls to him. Not from me, not from you, not from anybody. That's the only way to keep the boy safe. I explained all that."

"I know, I know, but it's making me crazy."

"Yeah? I'll make you crazy. Me and Wee Willie Winkie. Come on over here and sit on my lap."

"You're disgusting!"

That makes Kidder laugh. He makes the same sound when killing, a jagged, high-pitched giggle as sharp and sudden as a bag of razor blades. Not that he's going to kill the woman or the brat.

Not yet anyway. Not today.

When it does happen, he'll try to make it fun for everyone.

Part 1.
The Last Kid Finder

Chapter One

The Trunk Thing

The killer came to us in the trunk of a Lincoln Town Car, and stayed just long enough to wreck the house. By that I mean the pile of brick that Naomi Nantz uses as her personal residence as well as for the business of solving unsolvable cases, assisting the helpless and generally amusing herself by being difficult, if not impossible.

My name is Alice Crane, and I serve as Ms. Nantz's recording secretary and chief factotum. In case you don't know—I had to look it up when she hired me—a factotum is an employee or assistant employed in a wide range of capacities. I mean, come on, this is the twenty-first century, who uses fusty old words like that anymore?

My boss, Naomi Nantz, that's who.

The Nantz residence takes up most of a block in the Back Bay area of Boston. Don't bother trying to find us, we're camouflaged as two—or is it three?—typical Victorian brick town houses located somewhere between Storrow Drive to the north, Boylston Street to the south, Arlington Street to the east and Charlesgate to the west. Check your map and you'll see that pretty much covers the neighborhood. On the outside we're staid and rather ordinary, the kind of staid and ordinary that only money

can buy. On the inside, which was gutted and rebuilt a
few years before I entered the picture, it's clean and sleek
and modern, except for the Zen sand garden that takes
up part of the ground floor. Boss lady often meditates in
the garden, drawing what look to me like meaningless
lines in the sand, saying it helps her to think.

Like several of the staff, I live in. At the time of hire,
it wasn't a choice for me because my adorable husband
had suddenly vanished along with all of my money, and
it was either the Nantz residence or my sister's place in
Malden. The choice was Back Bay, with twelve-foot ceilings, an exquisitely furnished suite, or Malden, a paneled
basement with a cat-scented futon. Not a tough decision.
There are days when boss lady drives me nuts, but my
sister has the same ability, and she doesn't pay. Whereas
Naomi Nantz pays very well indeed, with benefits that
include room and board, full medical and dental, as well
as the occasional opportunity to right wrongs, dodge bullets, tilt at windmills and rescue kidnapped children.

I'd like to say there's never a dull moment, but that
wouldn't be true. There are many dull moments, for
which I'm thankful. Twenty-nine years on this planet
have taught me that dull moments are to be savored.
Dull moments fortify the soul, because without them life
would just be one thing after another, blurred together
like the windows on a passing subway car.

In my opinion the best dull moments occur around the
kitchen table. In this case a ten-foot-long pickled-white
oak table situated in the southeast corner of Mrs. Beasley's basement kitchen. If Beasley has a first name, she's
not inclined to share it, nor any information about what
might have happened to Mr. Beasley, if ever he existed.
She's not much for conversation, preferring to let her
food do the talking. Her food, be assured, is eloquent on

many subjects. For most people "fruit plate" suggests a cafeteria serving, but then most people have never had the experience of a Beasley Breakfast Fruit Plate. Farm fresh local strawberries dusted with one of her secret ingredients—could it be some exotic formulation of cinnamon? Perfectly ripened peaches that have doubtless been airlifted in from Georgia (Beasley has many connections) and sliced into mouth-size morsels. A single Medjool date stuffed with diced pecans. A chilled pear compote, lightly gingered. Honeyed bran muffins straight from the oven, slathered with hand-churned apricot butter that will make your eyes roll back in pleasure. And Mrs. Beasley's famous French press coffee, which makes your favorite Starbucks taste like thin dishwater.

There are only three at the table this morning because young Teddy Boyle, our spiky-haired live-in computer guru, has not yet emerged from his dungeon. Too much late-night fun, apparently. Well, he's of a late-night age, either twenty-one (so he says) or eighteen (so Naomi thinks) or barely sixteen (my theory). Whatever, he's missing the muffins, so to speak.

For the better part of half an hour there are no more than a dozen words exchanged between us. Naomi, never a casual conversationalist, concentrates on her morning papers: the *Boston Herald, Boston Globe, New York Times* and *Wall Street Journal,* which she studies in exactly that order. Nothing casual about it, although she seems to enjoy the process as she scans and absorbs the text. Among her many talents, virtual retention of everything she sees, hears and reads. Not word-for-word, but the essence thereof. On many a case her remarkable memory has dredged up some small, useful item of information from weeks or months or even years ago. A notice of alternate parking on a particular street in the South

End. Who was third runner-up in a celebrity fishing
tournament in Nantucket. A warehouse fire in Jamaica
Plain. A hit-and-run in Chelsea. Lives have been saved
because of what she remembers, villains apprehended.
In one very disturbing case a prominent sociopath took
his own life—and if you knew the circumstances, and
the unspeakable crime he committed, you'd undoubtedly
agree he made the right choice.

While Naomi reads, uploading data, Mrs. Beasley,
silent as usual, methodically fills in Sudoku squares
using a felt-tip pen, never lifting her eyes from the page.
Left to myself I'd probably have the TV on to one of the
morning chat shows, but there are house rules about television, so I content myself with the *Globe's* entertainment section, improving my cultural awareness about
the hottest new reality show.

"Beasley, do you mind a question?"

Beasley looks up from her puzzle, shrugs.

"Okay, here goes. Say you're a celebrity chef who has
to prepare tarantula for eight—you're in a Central American jungle, campfire but no stove—could you make it
taste good?"

"No," she says, after giving it some thought. "Not ta-
rantulas. I could do something with jumping spiders."

I'm pretty sure she's kidding, but can't be certain because that happens to be the moment when dapper Jack
Delancey, our chief investigator, strolls in and makes the
request that will soon result in us being invaded and the
house, or part of it, being wrecked.

"Sorry to interrupt, but this is an emergency situation," he announces, his lean, athletic figure ramrod
straight in a gorgeously tailored dark gray suit, a look
that gets him dubbed "Gentleman Jack" in the tabloids.
"I need your help."

"You, specifically?" Naomi asks, instantly alert.

"A friend."

Naomi's eyes drift back to the *Journal*. "Go through proper channels," she says. "Being an employee doesn't mean we drop everything to assist some crony of yours, Jack, certainly not before we've finished coffee. Run it by Dane, that's the way it's done."

Jack, normally a very cool customer, responds with an unexpected edge to his mellifluous baritone. "In about three seconds you'll be removing your foot from your mouth. The man in trouble is Randall Shane."

The name is not familiar to me, but evidently it is to Naomi because she pushes back her chair and goes, "Why didn't you say so? Where is he?"

Jack grins handsomely. "Little problem there."

The Nantz residential garage is located on one of the so-called "public alleys" that bisect the blocks here in the Back Bay. The idea was that tradesmen would approach from the rear, skulking through alleys, rather than contaminating the formal entrances of the main streets. Nowadays there are more green Dumpsters than tradesmen in the alleys, but those town houses fortunate enough to have garages typically face them on the alley. It's all part of being discreet—there's no good coming from advertising where the BMWs are hiding. Also handy for smuggling in witnesses or suspects when you don't want them to be seen entering your domicile.

There are three narrow bays in the Nantz garage, and one of them is filled to overflowing by Jack Delancey's nearly new Lincoln Town Car. To my way of thinking, Townies have that airport limo look, but Jack favors them for ride and size, and the dapper investigator would never be mistaken for a limo driver, not unless you want to find yourself cuffed to the bumper, admiring his chrome.

Supposedly he hasn't done that to anyone since he resigned from the FBI and went to work for Naomi, but I
wouldn't advise testing the guy. My read on Gentleman
Jack is that he can be charming when he wants to be, and
dangerous when it suits him, as many a bad actor has discovered to his or her own chagrin. "Bad actor" is Jack
talk for criminal. Most of the time he talks like a cop,
except on those rare occasions when he's relaxed enough
to discuss the fine points of professional baseball, when
he sounds like just another statistically obsessed Red
Sox fan from the North Shore. Jack's a Gloucester boy,
in accent if not at heart. Gloucester being more famous
for craggy fishermen in slickers than lightly tanned investigators who favor two-thousand-dollar Italian suits
and metrosexual manicures. Probably pedicures, too, although his fourth wife will be happy to hear I've never
seen him with his socks off.

"There's a good chance that we're already under surveillance," Jack tells Naomi as we enter the garage. "So
I did the trunk thing."

Trunk thing? I start to ask what that means, exactly,
when Jack presses his key fob and pops the lid, and out
from the voluminous trunk unfolds a man who towers
over us all. It's a very neat unfolding, limbs and knees
deployed, a muscular torso rising, and turning into the
light a large round head with close-cropped hair and
deep-set eyes in need of sleep. A head that keeps rising
until it brushes the ceiling.

Randall Shane. Yards of him.

"I really messed up this time," Shane says, looking
forlorn. "I may have killed an innocent man."

"We'll see about that," Naomi says. "My office. Now."

What Naomi calls her office is really our command
center. Think mission control, without all the giant

screens, but with a similar sense of purpose, and the ability to communicate with just about anybody, anywhere, over any system, as well as extract data, voluntary or not. The style is spare and cool. Lots of dark laminates, cove lighting, discreetly recessed panels, stacks and servers hidden away. There's never any doubt about who is in command, either. You can tell because she gets the pivoting seat behind the big curved desk with all the touch screens and gizmos, and we peons get the straight-back chairs with the wide unpadded armrests that are adequate for a laptop or a notebook, or in my case an unfinished cup of Beasley's coffee and a legal pad.

Randall Shane wouldn't fit in the peon chairs without a very large shoehorn, so he roams the big high-ceilinged room and finally, at boss lady's insistence, parks on the far edge of the command desk, his long chino-clad legs crossed at the ankle and his large, muscular arms folded across his very substantial chest. Not a weightlifter type, from the lean-waisted look of him, just built to a larger scale than most. Making all six feet of Jack Delancey seem short and slight in comparison. The neatly trimmed salt-and-pepper Van Dyke beard gives Shane the look of a supersize jazz musician. The watery blue eyes are soulful, but pure cop, always watching.

"Heard of you," the big man says, focusing on Naomi. "Jack says you're the best, and that includes me."

Naomi smiles, shrugs. "We do different things. Or do things differently. Probably both." After a moment's pause, she begins again. "Normally when interviewing a potential client I'd wait for the rest of my team to be assembled and then record a formal statement, but since this is hardly a standard situation, please go ahead. We'll do the legal stuff later, when our attorney is present."

"There isn't much time," Shane responds, fidgeting, his big hands busy making fists. "This won't be a normal arrest," he cautions. "Once they take me, I'll likely be transferred to an undisclosed location for interrogation. A form of in-country rendition. No lawyers, no communication. That's how they do it."

"Who are 'they,' Mr. Shane? Please be specific."

"Randall, please, or just plain Shane."

"'They'?" Naomi persists. "Explain. Elaborate."

"Sorry. Whatever covert agency is about to frame me for the murder of my client."

"Your client?"

He nods, looking mournful. "Joseph Keener, MIT professor. His son, Joey, is missing, that's why he contracted me. In all likelihood I'm responsible for Professor Keener's death. I didn't kill him, but they'll make it look that way. The evidence will be rock solid."

"What covert agency?"

Shane shakes his head. "I'm not sure," he begins, "but my best guess is an agency associated with the Department of Defense. Or possibly Homeland Security. My client was working on a top-secret project, and it's possible that—"

And that's when the windows explode, covering us all in diamonds of shattered safety glass. The security alarms start to whoop but there's no time to react, let alone flee to the safe room. Through the sudden breach swing half a dozen gun-wielding thugs wearing black ski masks. In less than a heartbeat there's a second explosion and somehow a wire net engulfs Randall Shane, and they take him down like a wild animal, hitting him with several tranquilizer darts through the net, until he sighs and stops struggling.

Unconscious, maybe dead.

That's all I can see from under my little desk, face burrowing into the thick carpet. That and the shiny black boots standing an inch from my head.

Chapter Two

Tea & Sympathy, Not

The first time I ever laid eyes on Naomi Nantz she had a bad toothache. I was the office manager for an association of dentists in Cambridge and she came in as an emergency appointment. Barely got through the door before fainting from the pain. By which I mean she stated her name and then her eyes rolled up and she dropped to the floor. Apparently she'd been ignoring a deep abscess in a lower left premolar for a couple of weeks, due to being involved in a case, and finally her body said that's enough, we're turning off the lights. That's how Dr. Pavi, our really excellent oral surgeon, explained the situation when she regained consciousness. Then he ever so gently put her back under, did whatever he needed to do, successfully and with a minimum of fuss. From then on Naomi Nantz was one of our loyal patients. Came in every three months for a deep cleaning and, because she misses nothing, apparently took notice of how I managed the office. One time her appointment coincided with me having red eyes from days (and nights) of crying and she asked what was wrong and for some reason I told her, which was strictly against the office rules (written by me) of sharing personal or family troubles with patients (we were there to serve, not kvetch), and Naomi said she'd see what she could do, and I said my husband has vanished and my savings account is empty, what can you possibly do?

She'd smiled and said, let me get back to you.

Two days later she called me into the Back Bay residence—sent a driver for me, actually—had me take a seat and then proceeded to explain, very calmly and deliberately, that my husband wasn't the man I thought he was, and for that matter my marriage had never been legal. The man I knew as Robinson "Robbie" Reynolds was in reality a handsome, charismatic con artist born William J. Crockett—"Wedding Willy" to the bunco squads—who wooed and married two or three victims at a time, then drained their assets. My assets had been a personal savings account (fairly substantial because I'm very careful with money and always keep to a budget) and my parents' four-bedroom home in Newton, which I'd been managing as a rental since Mom died, the income being split between my sister and me. Somehow or other Robbie had got my signature on a legal document and he'd sold the big house in Newton, as well as our small but very comfortable condo in Arlington, cleared the bank accounts and then vanished. Leaving me more or less homeless and with my sister ready to kill me because she'd "always known Robbie was bad news," although I'd never noticed that, what with her giggly jokes that were variations on "if you ever get sick of my little sister, you know where to find me!" Can't blame her, really, Robbie was irresistible. I'm the living proof.

Anyhow, Naomi saw to it that he'd been arrested in Toronto on a similar charge—yet another "marriage"— where he's currently serving time and supposedly writing a book about his exploits. None of the money was ever recovered because aside from his habit of proposing to foolish females who had a few bucks socked away, Robbie liked to trade on the currency markets, highly leveraged, and he lost every penny.

So, that's my sad little story, and the upshot is that Naomi offered me a job managing *her* office, at twice the salary and double the benefits, and that's how I happened to find myself face to the floor, and boss lady somewhere above me demanding, "Show us the warrant! Where's the paper?"

During and after the snatch-and-grab of Randall Shane, Naomi Nantz is highly indignant, demanding legal justification for the home invasion. None is forthcoming, because no one on the assault squad ever says a word. They simply do not respond. Not a word. Not to Naomi, not to anyone. That kind of black-masked silence is truly scary, in a way much scarier than the invasion itself.

The only good thing about the whole awful mess is that it's over in less than two minutes. They break in through the windows, seize our client and seemingly vanish into thin air, back out the same way they came in. By the time we call Beacon Hill Security and tell them not to bother sending a car, the crisis is already over.

As the security alarms cease whooping, I get up from the floor, still shaking. "Where'd they go? For that matter, where'd they come from?"

When Jack Delancey finally speaks—not a peep of protest out of him during the snatch, and no show of resistance—he says, tersely, "Had to be stealth helicopters. No other explanation."

Naomi grunts, as if she hates the very idea.

"Hey! What happened?"

Standing in the doorway, looking as befuddled as a child, is our resident computer genius, Teddy Boyle, his ungelled Mohawk sadly drooping. Apparently he fell asleep wearing headphones and consequently didn't hear a thing.

"Sorry I missed all the fun," he says, convincing no one.

Mrs. Beasley, coming up to see what set off the alarms, glances at the wreckage of the command center, shakes her head and issues a command of her own. "Tea and scones, kitchen table."

Like obedient children we all follow her down to the kitchen.

When angry I tend to raise my voice. Naomi gets all quiet and focused. Gave me chills at first, watching her cool down over a case. Wouldn't want to be the object of her wrath, because she never, ever gives up. If she fails, and supposedly it has happened now and then—not on my watch, not so far—it's usually because the bad guy has already died, taking essential secrets to his grave. "His" because most of our cases involve males, from my experience, although boss lady has no problem going after female criminals whenever they make the mistake of crossing her path.

Utterly calm, she begins to lay out assignments while we dutifully sip Beasley's perfectly brewed tea and munch on her crumbly, jam-smeared scones. "Jack, everything you know. In order, please."

Our chief investigator takes a moment, gathering his thoughts. "I was awakened by a phone call at 6:15 a.m. Shane needs my help, can I meet him in Kendall Square? There was the usual early-commuter traffic, so by the time I found him it was 7:10."

"This was at the crime scene?"

Jack shakes his head. "No. Shane had fled the crime scene. His client, the professor, lives somewhere in Cambridge, not far from MIT."

Naomi nods, and subtly checks to be sure I'm taking notes, which of course I am. "Joey Keener, the missing child. Any idea how old he is?"

Jack shrugs. "I think Shane said he was five. I'll confirm when I get the murder location from Cambridge P.D."

"Your friend Shane thinks he's being framed by a 'covert agency,' possibly part of the Department of Defense or the Department of Homeland Security. Apparently having to do with the fact that his client was working on a top-secret project. Did he give you any hint what that project was about?"

"No. He just said the guy was a genius. Not what he was working on."

"What made him suspect he was being framed?"

"His gun was missing."

"Ah," she says, pursing her lips as she registers the information. "A missing gun. That explains his suspicion about being framed, perhaps, but not why he believes a government agency is responsible."

Again with the uncomfortable shrug from Jack. He loathes being asked to speculate when he's unsure of the facts. "There wasn't a lot of time for conversation. Shane said words to the effect of his client was a genius— something to do with physics, I think—and somebody must have wanted to shut him up." Jack clears his throat, meets her eyes. "I'll know a lot more in a couple of hours. After I've got background on the murder and the missing kid."

Naomi studies him. "In other words you've got more

but you'd rather not share it until you've collected pertinent data, confirming your suspicions."

He nods.

"Fine, we'll get your full report this evening. Plenty
for us to do in the meantime."

Jack gives her a tight smile, thanks Beasley and exits
the kitchen, snapping open his cell phone as he goes.

Naomi turns to our young hacker, who looks sleepy
no longer. Looking, for that matter, more than a little
shell-shocked by what has so suddenly transpired, and
having barely touched his scone, much to our chef's
clucking disapproval. Six months ago young Mr. Boyle
was operating out of a Newbury Street coffeehouse,
hacking for cash and sleeping in shelters and all-night
cybercafés. All he owned in the world was a battered,
customized laptop and the clothes on his back. Oh, and
various body piercings of dubious quality, at least one of
which looked like an ordinary paper clip hanging from
his lower lip. Despite that, or maybe because of it, Naomi
had taken notice. She tried him on a fairly easy assignment, and then a more difficult case that involved bending a truly frightening number of laws, and then one day
she'd announced that the scruffy teenage hacker would
be joining the household on a permanent basis. It was
rough for a while—despite his innate politeness, the boy
has a feral quality and hates to be confined—but just
lately he seems to be acclimating, even blooming under
her tutelage. Today his wrinkled black T-shirt says it all:
LIFE IS A BITCH—I KNOW BECAUSE I WORK FOR
HER. A gift from Naomi, who is not without a sense of
humor.

"Teddy, I want to know everything there is to know
about Randall Shane, his alleged victim, Joseph Keener,
and the son, Joey. Public, private, personal, professional.

Shane is a legendary kid finder and has worked a number of high-profile cases, so there will be a lot of hits. The juicy stuff will likely be in secure files, and that means take precautions."

When Teddy rolls his eyes, Naomi hones in with a certain tone. "Young man, I'm aware you take pride in your ability to access data and remain undetected. Pride is good, and you're a valued member of this team because of your talent and your tenacity. But given what just happened here—a man was snatched from this very house by persons unknown, in broad daylight, with clockwork efficiency—a little paranoia is more than justified. We don't yet know who we're dealing with, but make no mistake, there will be people with your skill set on the other side. If you get careless or arrogant or overconfident you could be the next one seized by men in ski masks. Is that understood?"

Teddy nods, looking just a little skinnier and even more tightly wound.

Naomi drains her cup and stands up. "Beasley, you're on standby. No formal lunch today. Sandwiches on request to the library, which will serve as a temporary command center." She turns to me. "Alice, make arrangements for repairs, completed by end of day if possible. Or, failing that, closed to the weather. And deal with the cops."

"What cops?"

"The ones who will soon be at the front entrance, wanting to know what happened."

"What shall I tell them?"

"Whatever you like," she says. "Just keep them out of my hair and out of my house."

Right on cue, the doorbell rings, followed shortly thereafter by the pounding of a fist.

Chapter Three

The Very Private Investigator

"A movie, huh?" the young patrolwoman says. "So where are they?"

"It was just the one scene. They needed the exterior shot."

"The witness report said helicopter, unmarked, low altitude. Men swarming down ropes. Some kind of assault type of situation."

"Stuntmen. Fortunately no one was hurt, and they're paying for the repairs. Part of the contract."

The patrolwoman makes a note, looks at me doubtfully. "There's nothing about a film permit for this block."

"Not my department. Up to the movie people."

"You got a name for the production company?"

"Not me. The property manager might."

"Name and number?"

I hand her our attorney's card. A perfect endless loop, as the young patrolwoman will discover, if she bothers to follow up. Doubtful, since we're not filing a complaint.

"There's glass all over the sidewalk," she points out.

"I'll get my broom."

More notes. The cop gives me a long look, as if trying

to decide if I'm fronting for some criminal activity even now taking place inside the residence. "Must charge a lot, a place like this, to let 'em bust your windows."

"Again, not my department. But I assume it was a generous offer."

"What is your department, Ms. Crane?"

"Alice. I'm the caretaker."

"Uh-huh. Is the owner in residence?"

"As I understand it, the property is owned by a real estate holding company."

"So this is like, what, an investment kind of deal?"

"Apparently. As I say, I'm only the—"

"Caretaker. Yeah, I got it." The notebook snaps shut. "We're done. Have a nice day. My advice, take care of the glass. This city, somebody'll sue ya."

"Thanks, Officer."

All of the above is conducted on the sidewalk, below the entrance, which rises seven steps from the pavement. Naomi's rules forbid law enforcement officers from entering the premises unless invited. She calls it the vampire rule. Plenty of cops have been invited, over the years, and a chosen few have stayed for dinner, but this is the first full-scale invasion without a warrant. And it wasn't cops this time, not exactly. And maybe not even slightly. More like a paramilitary mission executed with stopwatch precision.

Next task, fix the building. We have a standing arrangement with Danny Bechst. You've probably seen his vans around town, with the Bechst of Boston logo wrapped around the vehicles. The deal is, when we call Danny he drops everything and works the problem until it is completed, around the clock if necessary. For this he gets a very handsome annual retainer plus double the normal hourly rate, so Danny Boy *loves* it when we call.

Included in the compensation package is an understanding that all work be conducted with the utmost regard to privacy and security. His men, and they're all men except for a couple of females on his interior painting crew, are not to stray unchaperoned anywhere on the premises. As far as Danny's crew are aware, the owner is a rich eccentric who treasures her privacy, only the last of which happens to be true, technically. It helps that most of his guys don't speak English and wouldn't know who Naomi Nantz is if they tripped over her, which Danny makes sure they don't. Trip over her, that is.

I punch Danny's number and in less than an hour a couple of his men, working from the outside, have screwed temporary plywood panels to the broken windows, and Danny himself is inside the command center taking measurements.

"No problem," he promises. "End of day it'll look like new, only better."

There are a few more things you need to know about boss lady before we can proceed. What I said about how she treasures her privacy, believe me, that's understating. When Naomi Nantz calls herself a "Very Private Investigator" she's not kidding, and she'll do almost anything to keep it that way. Also true, that she's neither rich nor eccentric. Brilliant and difficult is not the same as eccentric. Eccentric is dressing your pets in period costumes; brilliant and difficult means you know exactly how to go about saving an innocent life and/or bringing the guilty to justice, and you don't much care who might get offended or insulted along the way.

The assumption that she must be rich, to live in such a place and undertake cases of her choosing, regardless of recompense, is understandable, but mistaken. I'm in charge of the operating budget, paying the staff and so on, and I happen to know that she draws a salary like everyone else. Okay, more than everyone else, but still. Nor was I fibbing about the residence being owned by some sort of holding company, and legally managed through a law firm. So it is. As to who is really paying the bills and underwriting the whole enterprise—we call him (or it could be a her) the Benefactor—only Naomi knows the truth of the matter. Or so we all assume. When something extraordinary happens, she's the one who makes contact, so she must know who it is, right?

As to the woman herself, for the past three years I've been working closely with her on a daily basis, and yet I know nothing for certain about her personal history, her family or how she came to be here, doing what she does. I'm not even sure if Naomi Nantz is her birth name. Boss lady is pretty much off grid and I'm inclined to respect that choice.

Up to a point.

With the repairs sorted out, I head down the hall to the library, a large room with tall built-in bookcases on three walls. There's one corner window where if I stand on my tippy-toes I can just glimpse the Charles River. Other than the roof deck and Beasley's kitchen, this is my favorite place in the residence, mostly because it's so rarely used that I usually have it to myself. Not today. Naomi has taken possession of the leather-covered magazine table, setting up a laptop, a broadband phone with a couple of open lines and a secure line hardwired into a satellite phone antenna. I let her know where we stand, cop-wise and repair-wise, and she motions to a rail-back chair as she finishes her call.

"You'll be writing up your notes for the daily meeting, of course."

"Of course. That's why you pay me the big bucks."

"Probably don't have a lot to write up, just yet."

"Not just yet. There'll be a lot more when Jack and Teddy report."

Naomi nods to herself, musing, and I can almost hear her brain humming as she shifts through scenarios and alternatives. "This is a bit delicate, but there's something we need to keep in mind." She hesitates.

"Shoot," I urge her. "I'm a big girl, I can take it."

"My concern is with Jack Delancey. He'll be our main investigator on this case—he expects no less—but the circumstances are such that he may be compromised."

"Excuse me?"

"Friendship can do that. He and Shane go way back, and Jack holds him in the highest regard. Clearly he can't bring himself to consider the possibility that Randall Shane might be playing us."

"Wait. You really think he killed this professor guy?"

"I've no idea, but I'm keeping an open mind. The facts must lead us, not our hearts."

"So why aren't you telling this to Jack instead of me?"

Naomi grimaces slightly, as if made uneasy by what she's about to say. "Because I want you to keep your eyes open. If you think Jack misses something crucial, whether accidentally or on purpose, you will report to me."

I'm astonished. "You want me to rat out Jack Delancey?"

"An unfortunate phrase. But yes, if the situation warrants it, that's exactly what I expect."

Chapter Four

The Rest of Forever

Gradually he awakens, becomes aware on some primitive level that is sentient. At first there is no sense of self. He's no more than an assemblage of pain, nerves firing from various locations on his large body, defining a vague shape. Hands painfully cramped, feet aching, joints smoldering. Something in the middle makes itself known, unpleasantly. A sack of bubbling acid? No, a stomach, seething. At one end, pounding, a brain held like a bruised yolk inside a damaged shell.

He has a name, if only he can find it.

Halfway to forever, the name finally surfaces, drifting lazily around the brain. He claims it, holds it tight. At some point Shane realizes that his eyes are open and the darkness is an actual darkness. His limbs are restrained by something soft and unyielding. He's strapped down, elaborately, on a padded table. Testing the restraints, he measures his own unnatural weakness and surmises that he's been heavily drugged, possibly with muscle relaxants. They'll be watching, whoever "they" are. Darkness being no barrier with the right equipment. He stops struggling and waits, knowing they will come, eventually, and that he must prepare himself.

The rest of forever goes by. As more memories surface he replays recent conversations, examines decisions, finds himself wanting. How could he have been so wrong?

At last, from deep inside the darkness, a voice. "Joseph Keener."

Behind him somewhere, and then closer, much closer. Close enough to feel the air move in a reedy whisper. "Professor Joseph Keener. What did he know?"

Shane attempts to speak, discovers that his tongue will not respond.

Louder. *"What did Joe know?"*

Eventually it becomes a kind of chant.

Chapter Five

Free Thought Radicals

At 6:00 p.m. precisely we convene in the library for the first case briefing, which is always a big deal. Naomi is a stickler for being on time, so the protocol is to show up a minute or two early, take your seat and try to sit up straight. Boss lady is never there to begin with; she always makes an entrance, and this evening is no exception. The other notable entrance of the evening belongs to Dane Porter, our attorney. Dane is five foot nothing, but feisty, and has a legal mind that's the antidote to every blond joke. How many blond lawyers does it take to keep Naomi Nantz and her team out of jail when they overstep the bounds? Exactly one.

"Sorry I missed all the excitement," Dane says, sauntering in on spike heels that should be registered as weapons. She's wearing a hand-tailored power suit— wide pinstripes on a dark blue background, trim lapels, a tight-vested waist—and a custom-made handbag given to her by a female hip-hop artist (a famous one, who shall remain nameless here because she likes handguns) who happens to dance to the same music as the lovely lawyer.

"Was it really a helicopter attack? Men on ropes?" she asks Jack, who is busy examining his well-buffed nails.

"That's affirmative," he says.

"Alice?" Dane says, flashing me a radiant smile. "Tell me lover boy is joking."

"Never saw the helicopter," I say, "but there were definitely men on ropes. With guns."

"How exciting!"

"Good evening, Counselor," says Naomi, entering with laptop in hand. She takes the temporary command seat, directly across the table from me.

As usual it will be my job to take meticulous notes in my personal shorthand, in a form known only to myself, and to keep a precise chronology of the ongoing investigation, updated on a daily and sometimes hourly basis. The active case briefings are never, ever electronically recorded for a variety of reasons, legal and otherwise. The idea is to prevent criminals we might be investigating—or interested law enforcement agencies—from hacking into our system and determining what we know at any given moment. It's not paranoia, because it actually happened on an earlier case, hence the precautions.

"We convene this evening in extraordinary circumstances," Naomi begins. "A man was kidnapped from this premises by agents unknown, possibly for the purposes of enhanced interrogation. We have as yet no clue as to his whereabouts, his state of health or who, exactly, is holding him. This is intolerable, and tonight we begin the process of finding out what happened and why. Teddy, you'll present first. Start with the murder victim."

Teddy's hands shake slightly as he presses a key on his laptop. An image lights up the screen. "Joseph Vincent Keener," he announces, gathering confidence. "Age forty-two. Born, Hanover, New Hampshire."

We're looking at a head shot of Joseph Keener, wearing an ill-fitting suit and tie. A round, unremarkable face.

Heavy black-rimmed glasses and just a hint of jowls, despite a scrawny neck that doesn't quite fill his shirt collar. High forehead with the beginnings of pattern baldness thinning his light brown hair. His ears stick out, making him look oddly vulnerable. He's not smiling and was glancing to the side and slightly down when the shutter clicked. Even in a formal head shot with studio lighting he seems to be lost in a world of his own.

There's a moment of awkward silence. We're looking at a dead man.

Teddy says, "Keener was a ward of the state—his parents, both talented musicians, died in an accident—and he was raised in a succession of foster homes from infancy. Somehow he managed to get himself enrolled at Caltech, age fifteen, which pretty much says it all. Language skills pretty average, but mathematical concepts and theoretical geometry are off the charts. When Shane called him a genius he wasn't exaggerating. After Caltech, Joseph Keener came back East to pursue doctoral studies in quantum physics at MIT and was eventually made a full professor. There's no mention of a marriage, or indeed of any family at all. Professor Keener is widely published, and considered something of a recluse with a possible social interaction deficit, but at MIT that's not exactly unusual. His lectures are well attended, and despite a shyness that causes him to avert his eyes while in conversation, Professor Keener is able to take questions and lead discussions with his brilliant and often challenging students. That's a quote, more or less."

"A quote," Jack says, puzzled. "Where'd you get it? You didn't leave the residence, correct? Didn't interview any associates?"

"There's a site for student evals."

"Evals?"

"Evaluations," Teddy explains. "Some were real flamers, others seemed fair and balanced. But they all commented on Professor Keener's social awkwardness, one way or another."

Jack nods, gives him a thumbs-up. "Way to go, kid. That would have taken me at least a day's worth of shoe leather."

Teddy tries to hide his grin, but it doesn't take a rocket scientist (or a physicist for that matter) to see that he's pleased. For the first month or so on the job he was so intimidated by the former FBI agent that he avoided him whenever possible. To be fair it took dapper Jack a while to get used to Teddy's fashion statements, in particular the piercings, which he refers to as "staples," as in, hey kid, what's with the staple in your cheek? Lately they seem to have entered a zone of mutual tolerance and now, perhaps, collegial respect.

"In addition to teaching full-time at MIT, Professor Keener helped found QuantaGate, an R & D firm in Waltham, out on 128."

"Sounds familiar," Naomi muses. "A defense contractor, I believe."

Teddy looks startled. "Correct. Something to do with developing a quantum computer, which as far as I know is pretty much still theoretical. The stuff on the Net is very vague, mostly PR postings about the founding of the company. If we want more specifics on what exactly they're working on, or how far they've gotten, I'd have to get into the DOD."

Naomi's eyes glint. "You will absolutely not attempt to hack into the Department of Defense, is that understood?"

"Oh yeah, understood," Teddy says, without really

backing down. "I understand I could do it, but you don't want me to."

Naomi says, "A quantum computer, theoretical or not, would be of interest to any number of covert agencies from any number of countries. It's probable that's what Shane referred to as a top-secret project. We'll come back to that, but for now let's stick with the victim's bio. You say you found no mention of Professor Keener being the father of a five-year-old boy?"

"No," Teddy says. "Not by the students or the staff. They pretty much peg him as an SWG. That's, um, Single White Geek in eval shorthand. Professor Keener's biweekly deduction for the university medical is for a single plan, and there are no births registered naming him as a father in any databases. From what I can tell this kid is so missing he doesn't exist."

"Sounds like your shoe leather might be useful after all, Jack," Naomi suggests. "Who were his parents, how did they die, what was his experience in foster care? Maybe somebody from his past would know about personal things, like having a child out of wedlock."

"I'll get on it," he says, making an entry in his notebook.

"Let's move on to Randall Shane," Naomi suggests.

The photo of the victim is replaced by a recent snapshot of Randall Shane, seen from the waist up and looking very purposeful and muscular. Teddy says, "This was posted on the Facebook page of a woman whose daughter was recovered by Mr. Shane, and who was effusive in her praise. He's camera-shy and asked her to take it down, which she did, but it wasn't deleted from the cache."

We learn that Shane, 46, graduated from a public high school in East Hampstead, Long Island, and eventually from Rochester Institute of Technology in Rochester,

New York, with a degree in computer science. While at Rochester he met the woman he would eventually marry. Recruited as a civilian software engineer by the FBI to help modernize their fingerprint database, he'd eventually applied to and been accepted as a special agent, in which capacity he continued until the deaths of his wife and daughter, after which he resigned from the FBI.

"That's the standard bio on the guy," Teddy says. "There's more, of course."

"Hold on, cowboy," Dane says. "Are you telling us that bad boy is a computer geek? With those guns?"

"Guns?" Naomi asks, puzzled. "He was unarmed."

"Muscles, silly." Dane poses, cocking her right arm. "Biceps."

"Ah," says Naomi, satisfied. "Continue."

Teddy is new enough to the team to still be made uneasy by the frequent, challenging interruptions, encouraged by boss lady, who believes that banter and peer pressure create what she calls "free thought radicals." The back-and-forth is all part of her method, which can be difficult for a person as naturally shy as Teddy. He swallows hard, takes a deep breath, finds his place. "In those days Shane was kind of a geek at heart, if not in appearance. That's how the FBI used him, too. He spent about half his career testifying or lecturing on methods of forensic identification, not out in the field. He was basically an expert with a cool badge. They still use his program for the fingerprint database."

Naomi interrupts, as is her wont: "Jack? Does that accord with your personal knowledge?"

"Yep," says Jack, adjusting the crease of his slacks. "The kid has it right."

Naomi's attention returns to Teddy. "Continue."

He takes a breath, nods. "So everything changes one

rainy Sunday night in New Jersey. Shane and his wife and kid are driving back from D.C. to New York. Mr. Shane at this time works out of the FBI field office in Manhattan."

"They're in Washington why?"

"Um, school project for the daughter. Visiting the Smithsonian."

"Keep going."

"Jersey Turnpike. Shane's feeling sleepy, so his wife takes over the driving. He nods off, and at some point the vehicle is sideswiped by a freight truck. When he wakes up in the wreckage, wife and daughter are both dead. As you might expect, the man himself was a wreck for a while. He resigns from the Bureau and eventually establishes himself as a legendary finder of lost children, but he retains a number of key contacts who still work for the FBI, including the current Assistant Director of Counterterrorism."

"A-Dick," Jack says, smiling, throwing it out there.

"What?"

"That's what they call an assistant director. An AD or A-Dick. Not necessarily a term of affection."

"As I was saying," Teddy says, elbowing his way back into the conversation, "there's some indication that Assistant Director Bevins is a friend with benefits."

"They sleep together?"

"Past tense, if it happened. But they're still close."

"Jack?"

"A matter of speculation," he admits with an indifferent shrug. "Nobody knew for sure and they certainly weren't saying."

"Okay. The counterterrorism connection is interesting, given what's happened," Naomi points out. "Let's keep that in mind as we move on."

"How did he first get in the business of rescuing kidnapped kids?" Dane wants to know. "Was that part of his purview at the Bureau?"

"No. Later, after the accident, while he was undergoing therapy for a sleep disorder. An acquaintance asked for help, he managed to recover the child and found a new calling."

"Back up there," Naomi says. "Sleep disorder?"

"Yeah. I don't know if it's weird or ironic or what, but ever since he woke up from the accident, Mr. Shane has suffered from a peculiar, possibly unique sleep disorder. Like they've studied him, written articles about it."

"Ironic would not be the correct term," Naomi suggests. "Tragic would be the correct term. Is that agreed?"

"Great song, though," Dane interjects airily.

"Nuts," Jack says, suddenly animated. "If you don't know what ironic means, don't use it in the lyrics. Rain on a wedding day isn't irony, it's bad weather. It sucks, but it isn't ironic."

Naomi interjects, "Enough on the golden-oldie lyrics. Back to subject, please. Teddy?"

"A death row pardon two minutes too late is definitely ironic," Teddy points out, in a small, hesitant voice.

"Teddy!"

"Okay, okay. Took a while to separate the facts from the legend, but despite or possibly because of his sleep disorder, which means he sometimes stays awake for days at a time and eventually hallucinates, Randall Shane is considered to be among the best solo operatives who specialize in child recovery."

"Not among," Jack says, arms folded. "The best, period. Randall Shane is the last of the real kid finders. They broke the mold."

Teddy shrugs his narrow shoulders, as if to concede

the point. "Unlike many in the field, which can be pretty shady, monetary gain does not seem to be his primary motivation. For him it's a calling."

"Most of his cases are pro bono," Jack concedes.

"Seventy percent," Teddy says.

"Whatever, Shane ain't about the money. He can't even afford to drive a decent car," Jack says.

Teddy suddenly has a mischievous glint in his eyes. "Current ride, a five-year-old Townie, previously registered to John B. Delancey of Gloucester, Mass."

Jack shrugs his wide, well-tailored shoulders, but he's no doubt impressed. "Donation to a good cause. And no, I didn't get a tax deduction because Shane has never registered as a nonprofit, although he should."

Teddy keeps going. "Current residence, Humble, New York. Small town in the general vicinity of Rochester."

"Humble?" Dane says, grinning. "Is *that* ironic?"

Naomi sighs loudly, which effectively stops the banter. "You have more?" she asks.

"Tons," says Teddy. "I found more than a hundred references to the so-called Shane's Sleep Disorder Syndrome. Plus interesting facts on a variety of his cases."

"Excellent, but hold for now," Naomi says. "Jack, can you bring us up to speed on the murder investigation?"

Jack flips open his small reporter's notebook. Strictly a prop, in my opinion, but he's never without it. "So far everything Shane told me checks out. Cambridge homicide detectives are investigating the death by gunshot of Joseph Keener at his residence on Putnam Avenue, approximately two miles from the campus. The murder happened early this morning. State police are assisting—that means they'll eventually run the investigation, in all probability—and the FBI is all over the scene."

"Anybody you know?"

"Cambridge, affirmative, Staties, affirmative. I'm meeting with my state police source this evening. Hopefully he'll have more to add."

"Anything from your old colleagues in the FBI?"

"As you know, my former associates are mostly in the Boston field office, and normally the locals would be responding, assuming the murder has some federal connection. But this is a special team sent in directly from Justice. Unknown to me on a personal level."

"You make yourself known?"

He shakes his head. "Not yet. Just to my guy in the Cambridge Major Crimes Unit and he won't mention our interest unless I ask him to. He knows the deal."

"Good," Naomi says. "Let's stay at arm's length from our friends in federal law enforcement until we've had a peek at the big picture. That being said, did you get any sense they're aware that Randall Shane has been seized and/or arrested by agents unknown?"

"The opposite. There's an APB out on him as a so-called 'person of interest.' He's their prime suspect and they think he's in the wind."

"Set the scene," Naomi suggests. "Shower us with details."

"There's not all that much, I'm afraid. Cambridge police were alerted by a 911 call that originated from the Keener residence at 5:42 a.m. The caller would not give his name, but stated a man had been killed. That was Shane, so they'll have him on digital audio making the call, for whatever that's worth. The first mobile unit responded to the scene in ten minutes or less, found the front door open and the victim facedown in a pool of blood in the hallway, a few yards from the front door. Major Crimes and forensic units arrive, as well as the medical examiner. The M.E. determines the victim died of a single shot to the back of the head. Clotting and body temp suggest he'd been dead for no more than an hour or so before the call was made. No weapon recovered at the scene. Detectives did a canvas and his neighbors described him as the usual: shy type, kept to himself, very quiet. No one heard the gunshot."

"Any indication of a child in the home?"

Jack shakes his head. "The investigating detective told me it was the residence of a single man, living alone. Cambridge police are unaware of any missing child connected with the victim. No such report was ever filed. There is no indication of a child in the home, not even a photo. No toys, no games, no bedroom set up for a kid, nothing."

"No sign of a child," Naomi muses, keenly interested. "How very odd. Two possibilities immediately present themselves. Either the victim has a child and all evidence has been removed from the home—surely he'd have pictures even if the mother has custody?—or the victim never had a child, certainly not a missing child, and Shane was somehow duped for reasons unknown."

"To set him up for murder," Jack suggests.

Naomi nods to herself, tapping her pen, wheels turning. "Okay, fine, that's our theory of the moment, in deference to your relationship with the suspect—but he remains a prime suspect unless or until the evidence leads us elsewhere."

"He didn't do it."

"You're a friend. I need more."

"Fine," Jack says, with a steely edge to his voice.

"Now please explain the discrepancy," she suggests.

"What discrepancy?" Jack says, all innocence.

"You rendezvous with your buddy Randall Shane at 7:00 a.m. and yet you don't show up here until 8:30 a.m.

Kendall Square is at most fifteen minutes from this location. Where did you go? What did you do?"

Jack sighs. "We attempted to break into a motel."

"A motel located where?"

"The Residence Inn off Kendall Square. Shane thought it likely that he'd been lured to the victim's home so that evidence could be planted in his room."

"That's his theory."

"Yes."

Silence. Everybody fidgets, including Jack. Uncomfortable moments accumulate. Finally I stick my oar in and go, "Um, *attempted* to break in?"

"I know," Jack says with a sigh. "Embarrassing. Two former special agents, and we couldn't manage to break into a motel room. We had the key card, so it wasn't even a break-in, technically. My only excuse, the place was being staked out by state police detectives, and they happened to be good."

"They must have been very good," Naomi suggests.

"More stubborn than good, but still. The plan was, Shane creates a diversion, I slip into his room and check it out for planted evidence."

"What kind of diversion?"

"An exploding vehicle just around the corner from the motel. Specifically a small GMC pickup truck with a full tank of gas."

"Failed to explode?"

"Oh, it exploded," Jack says with some satisfaction. "The cab went fifty yards in one direction, the chassis in another, mostly straight up. Produced a very impressive fireball and a really nice mushroom cloud of black smoke. But the damn Staties didn't move. It was like they were expecting a diversion and determined not to budge.

No way I could get into the room undetected, which had been the whole point."

Dane stirs, says, "Hey, I don't get it. How'd they know to stake out Shane's motel room less than an hour after the crime was reported? How did they even know he was involved at that point? The Cambridge cops had barely taken possession of the scene, let alone been in a position to identify suspects, or pass it on to the state police."

"Good question," Jack says. "Shane told me the motel must have been under surveillance before he called 911. He gets back to the vicinity of the motel ten minutes after he makes the call, the state police were already in place, well established. That's when he knows for sure he's being set up and that's when he calls me."

"And you responded, even though you may have been assisting in the commission of a felony murder."

"Damn right. I've known the guy since the Academy. No way did he murder a client."

"And did detectives recover a murder weapon?"

Jack shakes his head. "Not yet, and not from the motel room."

"So your working theory was mistaken and nothing was planted to incriminate Shane?"

"I didn't say that. The detectives found a bloodstained shirt under the bathroom sink in his room."

"Ah. You're assuming that's the forensic link. Shane's DNA on the shirt, blood matched to the professor?"

"That's my assumption."

"But the murder weapon is still out there."

"So far."

Naomi announces, "Excellent case briefing."

To an outside observer she might seem inordinately pleased, considering the subject matter, but that's the way she rolls. "We'll assume for now that Shane is alive and being held in some unknown location for purposes of interrogation, pretty much as he predicted. If they'd wanted to kill him they would have done so, rather than go to the trouble of seizing him from this residence. Dane, you'll work your sources at the Justice Department, see if there's any scuttlebutt on Randall Shane, or any known involvement by a covert security agency."

"Whatever this is, it's buried deeper than deep," Dane says. "I think a personal appearance is warranted. Show the flag."

"Agreed," Naomi says. "Take the shuttle."

Dane pouts. "I was thinking the Gulfstream."

Naomi, very firm: "Not warranted."

"But the Benefactor is always very generous with his—"

"Shuttle. End of discussion."

"Yes, ma'am," says Dane, crossing her arms across her chest. "Ma'am" being what she calls boss lady when she doesn't get her way.

Naomi ignores the attorney being spoiled and childish—the Benefactor's personal Gulfstream is indeed at our disposal, but only for exigent circumstances—and turns to the elder male in our presence, the handsome alpha dog.

"Jack, you'll turn up whatever you can on additional background on the victim and his theoretical son. And see about infiltrating QuantaGate."

"Budget considerations?" he asks, looking up from his notebook with a furtive glance at the still-pouting Dane.

"Whoever it takes."

"Great. I'll go with the Invisible Man. Assuming he's available."

The Invisible Man is an operative Jack has used in the

past. None of us have ever seen him. I'm assuming he's not actually invisible.

"Use whatever operatives you see fit," Naomi says. "And there may be another line of inquiry worth pursuing. As I recall, QuantaGate was financed by local venture capitalist Jonny Bing. Who I believe is an acquaintance of yours, Dane."

Dane, startled, bursts out laughing. "You recalled or you Googled?"

"I recall," Naomi says firmly. "Am I wrong?"

"We partied once or twice a few years ago," Dane admits. "You remember Sasha? The party planner? When Sash and I were having our little thing, one of her top clients was Jonny Bing. Sash always called him Jonny Bling, which I thought was pretty cute. Of course at the time I thought everything she did and said was cute. Anyhow, Jonny had these amazing parties on his yacht. Looked more like a cruise ship to me, but you know how that goes. For an egocentric billionaire, he's really kind of cool. Wild sense of humor, and he likes to see that a good time is had by all. If you want, I can call his people, see if he'll consent to an interview."

"Absolutely. Do it," Naomi says. "Are the assignments clear? Dane? Jack? Alice? Yes? Teddy, you will continue to mine data but will steer clear of the Department of Defense. I remind you all that certain agencies within the national security community have been known to run covert operations under the Patriot Act, answerable to basically no one. At this time we'll continue to keep a low profile with local law enforcement, and allow them to proceed on the murder case unhindered. Our primary task is to determine if the victim has a child, as Shane apparently believed, and if that child is in fact missing, and, if so, to recover the boy alive. Anything else is secondary, including, at the moment, the safe return of Randall Shane—and that's the way he'd want it, I'm sure. Clear? Good. We'll reconvene at 7:00 a.m. for the morning brief. Jack, given the early kickoff tomorrow morning, you may want to spend the night at the residence."

"Only if there's a chocolate mint under my pillow."

"Always. Further thoughts, anyone?"

Jack impishly raises his hand. "Comment on 'Ironic,' the so-called pop song by Alanis What's-her-face. A traffic jam when you're already late is not ironic, it's maddening or unfortunate. Red Sox beating Baltimore seventeen to ten and Don Orsillo announcing, 'This is a real pitcher's battle.' That's irony. Case closed."

Naomi rolls her eyes.

Chapter Six

Why Murder Is like Real Estate

An invitation to meet a source at a certain upscale lounge on Boylston Street means dressing for the occasion. In this case, for Jack Delancey, that means slightly down. He has changed into an off-the-rack JoS. A. Bank blue blazer, one that dry-cleans easily, and a pair of light, cotton twill dress slacks with knife-sharp creases. Top-Sider shoes, ever so slightly scuffed, because the outfit is already kind of boaty, so why not go all the way?

Upon entering the retail area of the cigar store, Jack is waved past the bar and through into the lounge. Not a large venue by any means, but nicely furnished, and one of the few places in the city where a man—or a woman, for that matter—can legally enjoy an alcoholic beverage and a tobacco product at the same time, in a nonfurtive manner. The source awaits him, puffing on a fat Padron Maduro, a snifter of port at his side. He doesn't bother to rise. "Hey, Jacko. Very sporty."

Jack adjusts his slacks and takes a seat in a very comfortable leather chair, not far from the fireplace, directly opposite the source. "Captain Tolliver, my pleasure."

Glenn Tolliver, a captain of detectives with the Massachusetts State Police, chuckles. "If we're going to be formal, guess I'll have to address you as Special Asshole in Charge."

"Special Asshole, Retired. Or resigned. I'm too young to retire, right?"

"You smokin' tonight, kid?"

"That's a Padron 1926 you got there? What is it, thirty-five bucks?"

"A little more. Live a little—I already started your tab. The way I figure, if I'm going for the most expensive drink in the joint, I might as well have the most expensive cigar. Especially if my hotshot pal from the private sector is paying."

"So, how is the port?"

"Excellent. Dow's 30 Year, Tawny. Maybe when I'm retired or resigned, or whatever it is you are, I'll be able to afford a place like this. You think your boss would hire me?"

"Wouldn't count on it."

"Not as long as she has you, is that it?"

"Something like that."

Jack decides what the hell, he should be able to expense this somehow, so he orders what Tolliver is having. Soon enough they're puffing like a couple of locomotives, snug in the luxuriant stink of fine tobacco, and Jack thinks, not for the first time, that sometimes in life you get what you pay for. Which in this case includes a high-ranking detective in the state police. No one has dared call him Piggy (on account of his slightly upturned nose) since his days as a linebacker for Boston College. In his mid-forties now, and somewhat florid of face, Tolliver still has the military bearing of a uniform trooper, and the cool, calculating eyes of a man who has observed the worst of human behavior, from careless murder to child abuse. As is so often the case, his response has been to develop a sense of humor so deep and dark and apparently careless that it can frighten civilians.

"Ah," says Tolliver, exuding a plume of smoke from the pricey cigar. "Thank God the man got murdered on the left side of the river. If it was Boston we couldn't touch it. Murder is like real estate: location, location, location."

"I'm sure the good professor was happy to oblige."

"Poor bastard. All those brains and they end up all over the floor."

"You put eyes on the scene?"

"Always, Jack. I need to see it for myself. What better way to work up an appetite? So what's your interest in the croak?"

"Croak? Is that new?"

"Word up, dude," Tolliver says, affecting a much younger voice. "Got it off a paramedic who looks to be about twelve years old. He says, and I quote, 'Excuse me, sir, but when can we move the croak?'"

"Kids these days."

"Yeah. So? Your interest?"

"The big guy."

Tolliver sits up a little straighter. "No shit? Randall goddamn Shane. I should have known. You probably knew him since the Academy, eh?"

"Exactly that long. How'd you get onto him so quick?"

"Wait, hold on now, you wouldn't be harboring a fugitive, would you? Doing a favor for an old friend?"

"No, I would not."

"Swear on your little black book?"

"My little black book went away when I married Eileen, but yes, I swear."

"Because I couldn't help you there. Other than to suggest you counsel the suspect to surrender himself post-haste."

"Posthaste?"

"I have an education. Nuns gave their lives, and their rulers."

Jack purses his lips, thinking over his next move. "Okay, here it is. I'll tell you everything I know about where Shane might be if you'll share why you want him for this."

The state police detective sits back, smoking luxuriantly and thinking it over, or pretending to. All part of the tease because they both knew they were going to share before entering the premises, or the meet would not have taken place, certainly not on Jack's dime.

"It was all very convenient," Tolliver begins. "The tip came down from on high."

"How high?"

"Not God himself, but close. A heads-up to be on the lookout for this former federal agent who had been observed entering and exiting the home of the victim."

"The professor was under surveillance? Why?"

"I believe the term 'national security' may have been uttered. No details, of course. Other than that if we do pick him up we're supposed to turn him over to the feds immediately."

"What agency?"

"The notification came through Homeland. Which as you know doesn't necessarily mean it originated there. Homeland can be a communication conduit for almost any other government agency, even those it doesn't actively manage, like FBI and CIA."

"And this tipster specified a local motel where Shane might be conveniently located?"

Tolliver is decidedly not amused. "Tell me that wasn't you torching the vehicle."

"It wasn't me," Jack says, pleased that he can be honest, at least in a technical sense. "Glenn, you should know I did have contact with your suspect later on in the day, before he was apprehended."

"Apprehended? Like hell. I'd know if we had him in custody."

"Not by you. Apprehended by others. Guys in black ski masks, very professional."

The captain of detectives looks startled, then quickly regains some of his humor, shaking his head ruefully. "What do you know, they got there first. I can tell this is going to be a good one. What's your interest? I mean besides the fact that you and the suspect were Academy sweethearts."

"Mostly that. You know about his wife and kid?"

"I read the file, Jack."

"Well, some of us keep an eye on Shane, help out when we can. He's one of the good guys."

"Yeah? If he's so good what does that make the victim? One of the bad guys? And if we didn't put your pal in cuffs, exactly who did?"

Jack, who has learned to balance his boss's orders with the practicalities of maintaining access to various law enforcement agencies, decides to tell the captain of detectives what happened, mostly. He does so succinctly and without elaboration, as if writing a police report. By the time he gets to the end, Tolliver is openly gaping.

"Holy shit, a black helicopter? For real?"

"Figure of speech. No idea what color the thing actually was. But I swear you could barely hear it. Some kind of stealth version."

"Still, I thought that was an urban legend."

"Apparently not."

"And they never showed a warrant?"

"Never said a word. Slam, bam, not even a 'thank you, ma'am.'"

"Your boss must be freaked."

"Naomi doesn't freak."

Tolliver shrugs, as if he doesn't quite believe it. "So I heard. Good for her. Must be kind of weird, working for a female, huh?"

"Not weird at all."

"No?"

Jack shakes his head, enough already.

Tolliver sighs. "Hey, one of these days maybe you'll wangle me an invitation. I'd love to see the inside of that place."

Jack changes the subject. "Long way around, Shane was not the shooter. That's a definite. He's that rarest of things, an innocent man."

Tolliver snorts. "Nobody is innocent in this world, least of all Randall Shane. We have a garment with blood on it. A shirt, extra large, 17-inch neck, 37-inch sleeves. The shirt would fit your average gorilla. It has discernible splatter on the right sleeve, indicative of proximity to a gunshot. It will take a while, lab work being what it is, but I'll bet you a bottle of this port that the blood belongs to the vic and the garment links to Mr. Shane."

"No bet. You're probably correct about the matchups but there's an explanation: the shirt was deliberately used in the crime, donned by the real shooter and then planted. And if Shane never got back into his motel room, how did it get there?"

"Working on that. It's not only the garment, which you already knew about from the detectives on scene, and don't think I didn't know that. There's something else. Something way better."

"Oh?" says the former FBI agent, the little hairs stirring on the back of his well-barbered neck.

"We have the murder weapon, Jack. Registered to your pal, and his prints are all over it."

"What? Where?"

"Located behind a Dumpster on the same block. Like he tried to chuck it away and threw it a little too far."

"Shit," says Jack.

"Very deep shit," the detective agrees, puffing happily on his forty-dollar cigar.

Chapter Seven

She Needs the Knowing

Maybe it was all that talk about Randall Shane's sleep disorder, or the slice of strawberry rhubarb pie and the glass of ice-cold milk I quaffed an hour before bed (it can be dangerously tempting, having a superb chef living under the same roof), or the thought of a child so missing that people doubt he even exists, but for whatever reason, I can't sleep a wink. Staring at the ceiling won't work. Counting sheep, or anything, puts me in mind of bookkeeping, a wakeful activity. My mind is bright and will not shadow—lie awake long enough and I'll start obsessing on my fake husband, and that leads to the money he swindled, the house we lost, hurtful things my sister said and so on, into an endless loop.

Times like this, the only thing that helps is to get up, don a robe and soft slippers and pad through the residence taking deep, restful breaths. The central lighting system has switched to the sleep mode, meaning the equivalent of night-lights at ankle height, providing soft illumination. Passing the room Jack Delancey uses when he's spending the night in town, I detect the dirty-sock scent of the cigar smoke he carried home on his clothing, and smile to myself. Boys will be boys. Doubtless

Jack was out with his cop buddies, sampling various bad-for-his-health potions. Did he learn anything interesting or useful? If so, he'll make it known in the morning meet, which is something to look forward to.

Farther down the hall there are lights on under Teddy's door, and the faint electric-train hum of the fans that cool his computers. He'll be deep into the hunt. Ignoring the impulse to drop in, see how it's going—our barefoot boy doesn't need the distraction—I head on down the long hallway, over intervals of thick Persian carpets and cool hardwood flooring and take the back stairs, descending to the ground floor.

Despite the fact that we'd been invaded by armed thugs a little more than fifteen hours ago, I feel safer in the residence than anywhere else; safe because I know it intimately, the specific physicality of the place, and because my posse is within shouting distance. Naomi and Jack and, just lately, young Teddy, and even Mrs. Beasley. No, especially Mrs. Beasley, who I'm confident would defend me with her life, as I would her. Maybe this is what marines feel like, at night in their foxholes, surrounded by mortal danger but in the company of true, take-a-bullet buddies.

This wing of the residence has unusually high ceilings. On account of a very unusual architectural feature, a fifteenth-century Japanese Zen sand garden courtesy of the Boston Museum of Fine Arts. The original that was for many decades located in the Asian Gallery, not to be confused with the modern, picnic-friendly version located outside in the museum courtyard. According to Jack, who was already here when I came on board, the exact reproduction of the ancient garden was a gift of the Benefactor, who had loved it as a child. That's his theory—when asked, Naomi manages to be quite vague on how the garden happened to move from the museum to the residence. Vague or not, she frequently seeks a kind of meditation there, although she refuses to use the word.

Relaxing, she calls it. Thinking.

And there she is in her favorite silk kimono, sitting on a stone bench in the lotus position, scratching in the recently raked sand with a long stick. Nocturnal lights of the city shaft through the skylights, softening the shadows. Already I'm feeling a little more relaxed, knowing that boss lady is adhering to routine, finding a pattern.

"Welcome," she says, not the least surprised to see me wandering the residence at this time of night. "Be seated."

"Ah," I sigh, and park my butt on the unforgiving stone. "Have you ever considered cushions?"

"It's more comfortable cross-legged."

"Sorry, I don't pretzel."

"You need to learn to relax, my dear."

"I need to know if there's a missing kid. If there isn't, I can relax. If there is, I relax by getting to work. Either way, I need the knowing."

Naomi takes a long, slow inhale, as if savoring the slightly minty air, then exhales slowly, deliberately. "Me, too," she says. "We'll know more tomorrow but for now I'm thinking, yes, there is a missing child, based on nothing more than gut instinct."

"How so?"

"I've been going over all the stuff Teddy found on Randall Shane. Shane doesn't seem to be the type who is easily fooled. Quite the opposite. Plus he's always been discerning, not to say cold-blooded, about the cases he agrees to work. If he's not convinced a child is alive, he won't proceed. Really, it's the only way to fly. Otherwise you get sucked into the vortex of desperate parents who cling to hope, despite all evidence to the contrary."

The way she says it makes me think, for a moment, that she's been there, in the vortex. Then in the darkness she smiles and the certainty dissipates. She's merely speaking from professional experience. Nobody is as cool and calculated about accepting cases as Naomi Nantz, who I have seen turn down weeping mothers camped out on the doorstep, begging for help. Generally speaking, a case must first be brought to Dane Porter, where it gets rigorously vetted as to merit and the possibility of success. Often there's nothing to be done, or we can't improve on what's already being accomplished through normal law enforcement channels. But every now and then, a glimmer of hope shines through, and that seems to be happening now, based on nothing more than experience and judgment of character.

"I want in on this," I say. "I want to help."

"You're always helpful, Alice. That's why I hired you."

"I mean out in the field."

Her left eyebrow arches slightly. "What did you have in mind?"

"Let me chat with the neighbors. If the professor ever had a kid around, somebody must have noticed. Jack has more than enough ground to cover—this is something I can handle. Just chatting."

Naomi draws a few more lines with her funny little rake. Looking up to meet my eyes she finally says, "Why not? You don't look like a typical cop or an investigator and that may prove useful. Just be careful."

"I'm always careful."

"Except when you aren't," she says with a smile.

There's no reason at all that our brief conversation

should help ease me into sleep, but for some reason it does. That and the sense, mostly unspoken, that if a child is missing, we'll work the case until the child is found, or the sun goes cold, whichever comes first.

Chapter Eight

The Bad Boys Club

Taylor Gatling, Jr., the young founder and CEO of Gatling Security Group, likes to think that no matter how rich he gets, how much wealth and power he accumulates, a man should still empty his own spittoon. Unpleasant as it might be—and the thing has a vile smell, no question—it's not a job to be delegated. Even if the man happens to have thousands of employees depending on his every whim, some of whom would no doubt consider it an honor to flush away the boss's effluents, and scour the antique brass receptacle, and return it with a snappy salute and a brisk "Yes, sir! No problem, sir!"

Nope. He'll handle the spittoon himself, thank you very much. A leader has to take responsibility for certain unpleasant tasks, something his own father never quite learned. And in this case it means he gets to spend a few moments by himself, out on his boathouse deck in New Castle, New Hampshire, overlooking the deep and roiled waters of the Piscataqua River, racing in the moonlight like a band of undulating mercury. Across the broad tidal river, shadowed and stark on its own few acres of island, rises the concrete carcass of the old Portsmouth Naval Prison, now abandoned, a fairy-tale castle with towers and turrets. Beyond that, the spiky tree line of the farther shore, interrupted by the occasional and very tasteful colonial mansions peeking out at the water from behind ancient guardians of spruce and fir. Elegant yachts moored in the cove, masts tick-tocking as hulls absorb the swell. Gatling smiles to himself when he recalls the real estate agent who handled the sale standing in this very spot and saying, "You can't buy a view like this." Pure salesman's babble, and nonsense, because of course that's exactly what Gatling was doing, he was buying the view. At the time the original century-old boathouse was falling into the mud, and would take half a million or so to restore to the current state of comfortably rustic, his own personal and very unofficial bad boys club. A luxury shack, lovingly restored, where he and his buds gather late into the night, playing poker, drinking and jubilantly spitting dip into their personally inscribed spittoons.

From inside comes a roar of laughter. A filthy joke has been told and celebrated. Gatling upends the spittoon, dumping the noxious contents into the tidal currents that curl around the deck pilings. No doubt in violation of some law of the current nanny state. No spitting in the river. Lift the seat before peeing. Women allowed everywhere. Not here, though. No wives, no girlfriends. Y chromosomes required, no exceptions.

When he steps into the card room, all eyes meet his. Taylor A. Gatling is the alpha wolf in this particular setting, well aware of his status. Thirty-eight years of age and just recently edged over into the billionaire level. Fit and trim, focused and self-contained, confident of his rarely expressed but deeply felt opinions. This is his place, his party, and the endless ribbing and mutual insults are all part of the camaraderie. The world being what it is, he keeps a security detail outside on the grounds, but here in the boathouse he's just one of the boys, and he's careful never to play at being the owner, or to show his cards unless called.

"You in?" asks one of his boys, dealing smartly, snapping the cards.

"Next game. I need a refill."

He puts down the spittoon to mark his seat—that's become the tradition—and heads over to the bar. Nothing fancy about it. Just a thick mahogany plank, three feet wide—hewn from a single tree, of course—a few wooden stools, a standard bar cooler for beer, a shelf of liquor displayed against a mirrored backing. Mostly high-end vodkas and some ridiculously overpriced bottles, a few oddly shaped, of single malt Scotch. Gatling pours two fingers of Macallan 18 into a fat-bottomed glass, and is about to return to the table—Jake the Snake is calling five card, jacks or better—when Lee Shipley sidles up the bar, puts a hand on his arm, briefly.

Lee, a retired New Castle cop old enough to be his father, keeps his raspy voice low and says, "Something you should know."

Gatling sips from the glass. "Lay it on me, Chief," he says, ready to make a joke of it, knowing the old man's penchant for one-liners.

Lee glances at the table, where the first round of betting is under way—cash is the rule, no effing chips—and says, "I got a call from a brother officer, an old pal of mine who's still on the job in Cambridge, Taxachusetts, and you'll never guess who's just been named in a murder inquiry."

"No idea," Gatling responds, playing along. "Mother Teresa? Martha Stewart?"

"This is serious, Taylor," Lee says. "Randall Shane. They expect to have him in custody any moment."

Taylor looks blank. "Sorry, Chief, I don't get it."

"Shane. That FBI jerk who testified against your dad."

"That was twenty years ago. Lots of witnesses testified against him."

"Yeah, but this guy Shane, he was the one got your father convicted. That's what your dad believed. Told me so himself."

"Yeah? Well, he never told me. If you recall, we weren't exactly on speaking terms at the time. I was eighteen that summer—I'd just enlisted with the Marine Corps so I could get away from all that crap."

Lee looks at him, can't quite meet his eyes. They both know how it ended for Gatling's father.

"Just thought you'd want to know."

"Thanks, Lee. Best forgotten, though. Water under the bridge, or over the dam, or wherever it's supposed to go."

"Sorry," the old man says, shrinking a little, now embarrassed.

"Hey. No need to be sorry. I appreciate your concern. You were his good and loyal friend when times got tough, and I'll never forget that. Get yourself a glass, we'll have a little toast."

Lee Shipley, relieved, pours a splash from the same bottle, raises his glass.

"To the old man," Taylor says. "May he rest in peace."

"Amen to that."

They sit down to play poker, and not another word is said about his late father. But inside, behind his bad boy smile, Gatling is very pleased by the news. Randall Shane, the so-called hero, is down for a count of murder in the first degree, a charge long overdue.

Good.

Chapter Nine

What the Cat Lady Said

There's nothing very grand about the neighborhood where Professor Keener lived and died. The modest two-story house is one of a hundred similar wood-framed dwellings situated along this particular stretch of Putnam Avenue, some with actual white picket fences, in the area dubbed "Cambridgeport" because the Charles River winds around it like a dirty shawl. Keener's place, built narrow and deep to fit the lot, appears to date from the 1940s, but it could easily be considerably older, having been renovated a few times along the way. Asphalt shingle siding removed, clapboards repaired and painted. Inside, carpets and linoleum have been taken up to expose the original hard-pine floors, a few interior walls taken down to open up the downstairs—I can see that much by peering through the windows from the narrow, slightly sagging front porch.

The front door has been sealed with yellow crime tape, but it doesn't matter. It's not like I'd attempt a break-in in broad daylight, or at any time, for that matter. The place has been thoroughly searched by professionals, and if there's any evidence that Professor Keener had a son, surely it exists in the minds of neighbors, colleagues, friends. Memories can't be so easily erased. Anyhow, that was my argument to boss lady, who normally doesn't approve of me playing investigator, as she calls it. The homes on this block are close together, barely room to park a vehicle between them, and my plan is to prowl around the porch playing looky-loo until someone in the neighborhood responds, if only to tell me to mind my own business.

As it happens the watchful neighbor is a retired school bus driver, Toni Jo Nadeau, recently widowed, and she couldn't be nicer. Pleasantly pear-shaped in velour loungewear, big hair and with the keen eyes of a nosey parker—in other words, exactly the person I was hoping to find.

"Excuse me," she begins, having come out to her own little porch, right next door. "Are you looking for the professor?"

"Oh dear," I say, clutching my handbag, acting a bit frazzled, which isn't difficult. "No, no, I know he's gone. Murdered, I should say, but that's such an ugly word. Awful! No, I'm looking for his son? His five-year-old boy?"

Mrs. Nadeau gives me the once-over, decides I'm okay and introduces herself, including the part about her late husband. Then she glances up and down the street, as if to check if we're being observed. "You mean the Chinese kid? Come around the back," she says, gesturing down the narrow driveway. "My cats own the front rooms, we can talk in the kitchen."

Unlike some of the other homes in the neighborhood, Toni Jo's house has not been upgraded in the last few decades, and the kitchen still has the feel—and smell—of a place where cooking happens. Most recently, roast lamb with a few cloves of fresh garlic, if my nose hasn't failed me. She urges me to have a seat at her little counter, offers coffee, which I decline, having already topped up on caffeine, courtesy of Mrs. Beasley. "I'm good, thank you. Alice Crane," I say, offering my hand. "I work in the physics department. As a secretary slash office manager, I wouldn't know an electron if it bit me on the ankle! This is so nice of you. I'm at my wit's end. Did you say Chinese boy? I've been so worried."

"Oh yeah?" she says cautiously, attempting to suss me out.

"Couldn't sleep a wink last night, worrying about that poor little guy."

"Wait," she says, her eyes hooding slightly. "You know the kid?"

"No, no," I say, shaking my head and keeping up the frazzled bit. "Never met him myself, and nobody in the department seems to know where he is, or who has legal custody. But everybody says Joe had a little boy, so he must be somewhere, mustn't he?"

"Everybody, huh?"

"You know how it is. People talk."

"And they say the kid is Professor Keener's son, do they?"

It's easy enough to look befuddled. "Do I have it wrong? Oh dear, maybe I'm worried about nothing. But you said—what was it you said?"

"Haven't yet," she says, going all cagey. "Joe, is that what his friends called him? Really? He was always Professor Keener to me. Very formal man, very private about himself. First time I went over there and introduced myself he looked at the ground and said, 'Professor Keener,' and that's how it stayed. It fit him, too. He was the perfect neighbor, really. Anyhow, he used to have a little kid that came around on a regular basis, but that stopped a couple of years ago. Not every day, but like on weekends. A toddler, couldn't have been more than three years old, the last time I noticed. Played in the backyard a few times, but mostly they kept him inside."

"They?" I ask, genuinely surprised.

"The Chinese lady I assumed to be his wife. Or ex-wife, or whatever. She was always here with the boy and she was obviously his mother. She's a real beauty, an exotic type, wears those formal Chinese dresses, doesn't speak a word of English. At least not to me."

"But you haven't seen her or the boy for the last two years?"

"Something like that. At first I thought maybe she was just a friend of his. They didn't look like a couple, if you know what I mean. Not even a divorced couple. But one day one of my ninjas got out."

"Excuse me?"

"My kitty cats. Ninjas, I call 'em. I'm owned by four cats, shelter cats, and they like to hide under the furniture, whack your ankles as you go by. Anyhow, Jeepers got out and bolted over to Professor Keener's yard, and the little boy was sitting in the sandbox, playing with a scoop, and wouldn't you know, Jeepers was interested in the sandbox, or that's what I thought. I go running out, afraid the kid might get scratched, but the cat was sitting there, perfectly well behaved, letting the little boy pet her. Very cute, I wish I'd had my camera. The professor came out at the same time, and I retrieved Jeepers and he retrieved the boy, and we had ourselves a little conversation. Which is all you ever got with the professor. I said, what an adorable child, I can see he takes after his father, and he smiled and said, 'He's my keyboard kid,' and that was all. Not another word. I mean, what does that mean, 'keyboard kid'? I asked, but the conversation was obviously over. He never even told me the boy's name."

"But you took him to mean the boy was his son."

"Absolutely. You could tell, the way he was holding him, the pride in his eyes. He actually looked me in the eye that one time, just for a second, and I could tell how much he loved the boy. And close-up like that you could see the resemblance, I wasn't kidding about that."

"You haven't seen the child in at least two years. Did you ever ask Professor Keener where his son was? Why he didn't come around anymore? What happened to the boy's mother? Anything like that?"

Mrs. Nadeau shakes her head, gives me a flinty, dismissive look, almost scornful. "Who are you really?" she wants to know. "If you worked with Professor Keener, you'd know what he was like. You'd know not to ask him personal questions like that. What are you, some kind of reporter?"

Boss lady always says that when you're engaged on a case, it's best to season your prevarication with just enough truth to make it edible—and be ready to alter the recipe on the fly. "Not a reporter, no, absolutely not," I say, backpedaling in place. "And to be totally truthful with you—I'm so sorry I fibbed—I never actually worked in the physics department and I never met Professor Keener personally. But before he died, before he got killed, Keener hired a friend of mine to help him find his missing five-year-old son. It was my friend—he's a former FBI agent who specializes in child recovery—it was my friend who found the body, okay? And my friend who is now a suspect in the murder."

To my surprise, Toni Jo Nadeau grins at me. "This is a much better story, sugar," she says, eyes bright with interest. "Some of it might even be true."

"Please don't tell the police. They'll think I'm meddling."

"Describe this 'friend' of yours and I'll think about it."

"You want to know what he looks like?"

She shakes her head. "I know what he looks like. I want to know if you know what he looks like."

"You know… Oh, I get it. You happened to notice when he visited Professor Keener, is that it?"

"I'm waiting, sugar."

"Okay, what he looks like. Here goes. Well, for starters, he's a hunk, big and lean and tall. Way over six foot—I mean, I barely come up to his shoulders, you know? Soulful eyes. And a cute little salt-and-pepper chin beard."

Mrs. Nadeau nods along with the description. "You had me at *hunk,* sugar. That's our boy. I saw him ringing the bell over there last week and my first thought, I wish he was ringing the bell over here, you know what I mean? No offense, but your man is *tasty.*"

As you may have noticed, I'm rarely at a loss for words, but that pretty much stops my tongue. Mrs. Nadeau notices my discomfort and reaches out to pat my hand. "Wispy little thing like you, I'm guessing he really is just a friend. Don't look so worried, these things take time."

Wispy? I'm wearing what I call my librarian glasses, Target clothing and a cloth handbag, going for the non-threatening mousy look. But wispy? Really?

"Man like that, he'd want a woman with some meat on her bones," Mrs. Nadeau says. "Somebody with a little bounce in her jounce. But he may come around. You just hang in there."

When my power of speech finally resumes, I say,

"Yesterday morning, when it happened, did you notice anything wrong?"

Mrs. Nadeau explains that because of her allergies—she's allergic to cats, why is that no surprise?—she takes an antihistamine before bed and sleeps, in her words, like a dead dodo bird. Therefore she has no awareness of what happened in the early hours, or who might have murdered Joseph Keener.

"The sirens woke me. That's the first I knew something was wrong. The cops wouldn't tell me what happened, but when I saw that body bag coming out I knew it was bad. The worst. The poor, poor man. I wonder who'll get the house."

On my way out the narrow driveway, I stop to take a gander at the dead man's backyard. And there, partially obscured by fallen leaves, is a child's sandbox, covered with a plastic turtle lid. Looks like it hasn't been used in a while, but that fits with what the cat lady said, and as far as I'm concerned proves beyond doubt that a child once played here.

A little boy, missing.

Chapter Ten

Promises to Keep

Kidder loops the big brass padlock over his index finger and shows it to the woman he thinks of as New Mommy.

"You'll be safe," he says in his teasing, wheedling way. "It's a finished basement with a kitchenette, full bath, a nice pool table and a big-screen TV. Plenty of room for the kid's keyboard. It's not like you'll be locked up in a dungeon."

"The basement is fine, but why do we have to be locked in?" she says. Seated on a divan, the little brat clinging to her side.

"Because your boyfriend said so, that's why."

"He's not my boyfriend."

"Whatever you say."

"Shane saved my life once. I owe him."

"That's sweet. Down you go."

The boy has tucked his head into her hip, averting his face. She strokes his hair, tries to calm him, but the kid picks up on her nervous tension and avoids making eye contact with Kidder. Nothing new there, the brat has never liked him.

"I need to speak to Shane," the woman pleads. "I want Shane to tell me why we have to be locked into the basement whenever you go out. It's not like I'm going to run away."

"I told you, it's for your own protection. You and the kid. I'm a bodyguard, I'm guarding, and that's really all you need to know. Those were his instructions and I intend to follow them to the letter."

"This isn't right," she mutters.

Kidder squats so that he's at eye level. His predatory grin has all the warmth and welcome of a chilled ice pick. "This is not a topic for discussion," he says softly. "The word comes down from the big guy, we obey. End of story."

"But why—"

Kidder puts a finger on her mouth, feels her trembling inside. "Sssh," he says. "You're going to play in the basement for a while, isn't that right? You and the kid will be nice and cozy, safe as churches. I'll be back this evening, we'll have pizza, maybe watch a movie."

The touch of his fingertip is like a button shutting off her resistance. Less than a minute later he snaps the padlock on the hardened steel door of the secure room in the cottage basement, heads for his vehicle and is soon exiting the gated estate. A few miles west of the rocky coastline, this scenic road will intersect a major highway. Until then he makes sure to keep just below the speed limit. It would be very awkward if one of the local cops pulls him over, wants to see what he has defrosting in the trunk.

Yikes.

Kidder feels content with his purpose—this new, last-minute assignment is going to be fun. Challenging but fun. He glances at Google Maps in his lap and thinks happy thoughts.

Chapter Eleven

Where It Gets Complicated

I return to the residence walking on air.

Alice Crane, Super Investigator, able to successfully interrogate reluctant neighbors, discover leaf-obscured sandboxes and enter tall buildings in a single bound. Okay, the neighbor wasn't exactly reluctant, but still, it was my idea and I came away with an eyewitness account that proves beyond doubt, to me at least, that Joseph Keener was the father of a small child. Considering the circumstance, I shouldn't feel this happy—a kid is missing, what is there to be happy about?—but the success of the mission makes me want to punch the air and shout *yes!* just like they do in the movies, only Mrs. Beasley might see me and throw a stale muffin at my head. Not that her baked items ever last long enough to go stale, but you get the idea.

Be cool, girl. Like it's all in a day's work.

Right, right, let me give it a try. Trying, trying. Nope, never happen. I'll never be cool. Not unless cool involves shouting, "I did it! I did it!" while bounding up the stairs to the command center.

Only to find the big room hushed and empty.

For one horrible moment I imagine that the mysterious assault team returned in my absence, abducting everyone but me. And then light footsteps come padding along the hallway carpet and boss lady pokes her head inside the door.

"You screamed?" she says, and beckons me to follow.

She and Teddy have been hunkered down at his main computer terminal, all agog over some new spy program developed by our young software genius.

"It's so simple that it's almost beautiful," boss lady enthuses, acting very much like a proud mother. "And it's functioning perfectly."

"Simple also means limited," he reminds her. "We can look but not touch."

"It's a kind of invisible, undetectable window into their system," Naomi explains, attempting to share. "Planted by Jack's operative at Keener's company, QuantaGate."

"More like a reflection of a window," Teddy corrects. He manages to look embarrassed and pleased at the same time. Then, as if to deflect attention away from his faux-hawked self, he goes, "Alice? Um, what happened out there?"

"Oh, nothing much. Just proved that the dead professor had a kid, that's all. With a mysterious Chinese lady."

That finally gets their attention.

"Details," boss lady demands.

"I should save it for the next case briefing."

"Don't be cute," she says, giving me The Squint. The Squint means we've had our fun but joke-time is over, wisecracks are no longer appreciated. It's boss lady turning off the friendly switch and getting serious and making you serious, too. And so I give her the play-by-play, including the demon cats and the sandbox, and Professor Keener calling the child his "keyboard kid."

"Odd that he would call him that," she says. "I wonder what it means, exactly. It must mean something."

Riffing, I say, "Maybe if you're a weird genius that's a term of endearment. Anyhow, the point is, whatever their names are, the mother and child used to visit frequently, but the visits stopped two years ago. Haven't been seen since, at least by the neighbor. They stopped coming around. Does that mean the mother broke up with the professor, possibly returned to China?"

"I suppose anything is possible at this point. Whoever this woman is, Keener kept her off the grid. Randall Shane never mentioned anything about the mother being Chinese."

"He didn't have time to mention much of anything before the windows got kicked in."

"Good point. Give Jack and Dane a call, let them know about the boy."

"Will do."

Boss lady nods, frowning to herself. "I'd love to know what the 'keyboard kid' reference means. We'll try Googling the phrase, but off the top of your head, what first comes to mind when you hear the word *keyboard?*"

I shrug. "Computers, I guess. And pianos."

"Pianos?"

"Pianos have keyboards."

"Right! Of course they do. Hmm. Interesting."

Without formally ending the conversation—a habit she has when distracted—Naomi wanders away, looking even more thoughtful than usual, which is sort of like saying a saint looks even more religious when the halo blinks on.

Chapter Twelve

Waves of Water, Waves of Light

The good ship *Lady Luck* currently resides at an up-scale marina in Quincy, just south of the city, in sight of the skyscrapers in the financial district, which seems fitting. Speaking of skyscrapers, Jonny Bing's hundred-and-ninety-foot yacht looms over every other boat in the marina, many of them quite sizable, but nothing much compared to four stories of *Lady Luck,* gleaming like a huge pile of freshly laundered cash.

Jack Delancey positions his spotless vehicle in the far reaches of the marina parking lot, where it's less likely to get dinged. He's just back from Concord, New Hampshire, three and a half hours turnaround, a waste of time, most of it spent behind the wheel, and he's more than ready to stretch his legs on this last little task before reporting back to Naomi. He happily saunters past a waterfront condo development, which includes a few trendy restaurants and at least one destination bar that's been cited numerous times for an infestation of noisy, wine-quaffing yuppies. The rent-a-cop at the gate picks up on Jack's cop vibe and waves him through with a lazy salute that makes the former FBI agent grin to himself. Beyond the breakwater the harbor sparkles under a clear sky, although the view is more than a little restricted by the sheer bulk of *Lady Luck*.

He proceeds along a system of floating docks. Thirty yards from the enormous yacht, Jack pauses to flip open his cell. By previous arrangement he identifies himself and announces his proximity. Less than a minute later a little Asian dude wearing a faded pink guayabera, baggy shorts and a jaunty gold-braided captain's hat comes out to what Jack assumes is the bridge and waves him aboard. A red-carpeted gangway delivers him to one of the lower decks, where he waits for further guidance. Almost immediately the little dude with the spiffy captain's hat leans over a rail of an upper deck and asks, in a distinctive Boston accent, "You wearing deck shoes, Mr. Delancey?"

Jack shakes his head, sticks out a perfectly polished leather shoe. "Morellis."

"Ten and a half?"

"Eleven."

"Wait there."

Minutes pass. The little dude returns with a pair of brand-new Sperry Top-Siders, still in the box. He comes down a curving, mahogany-railed stairway, hands the box to Jack. "Keep 'em," he says. "We've got plenty."

"You're Jonny Bing."

"The one and only," the little dude says, pleased to be recognized.

Jack unlaces his Italian handmades, slips on the Top-Siders. "Thanks for seeing me on short notice. It's much appreciated."

"Any friend of Dane's. Although I do prefer friends of the female persuasion, whatever their sexual orientation. Just so you know."

Jack follows Bing up the staircase to the second deck,

then in through the open doors of a palatial salon, furnished with several leather thrones. The salon, obviously where Bing does his entertaining, is designed to make jaws drop and offshore bank accounts wither. It spans the width of the vessel, and could have been furnished by Michael Jackson, back in the day, were it not for the distinct lack of chimpanzees. Lushly draped polarized windows reveal a spectacular view of the harbor. Must be ten varieties of exotic blond hardwoods at play in the trim, all curving and varnished. The inlaid teak deck beneath his Top-Siders feels as solid and unmoving as gold bullion.

Jack whistles in appreciation, which pleases Jonny Bing.

"Hundred million," he says, waving Jack to one of the lushly upholstered leather thrones. "Not that you asked. But people want to know."

"I did wonder. Thanks for sharing."

Bing takes off his captain's hat, revealing a thatch of thick, glossy black hair, cut fashionably short on the sides, and with what looks suspiciously like an emo bang over his left eye. Add that to his diminutive size and the slightness of his build, and the second-generation Chinese-American billionaire looks like an eager teenager, but Jack happens to know that he's in his late thirties. Bing's slightly mischievous expression is more welcoming than might be expected, considering the high-altitude circles where he flies, or, more accurately, cruises. Jack has met his share of the super wealthy, and usually finds them guarded with strangers, or at least more outwardly canny. Jonny Bing looks like a boy who has just come down to Christmas, found everything he ever dreamed of under the tree and is willing to share his new toys with anyone who comes in the door. Or hatch, or whatever it is. Notwithstanding the fact that he's a native of Gloucester, Jack's experience with boats is somewhat limited—an endless summer when he was sixteen, toiling on his uncle Leo's leaky, smelly scallop dragger as penance for various infractions, and the occasional striper fishing with a Marblehead cop-buddy who married money, and therefore can afford a nice thirty-foot center cockpit with twin outboards. The striper boat, which is Jack's idea of rich, would fit comfortably in the far corner of the *Lucky Lady*'s main salon, with plenty of room left over for a bowling alley.

"Sorry about the lack of fawning servants," says Jonny Bing, lounging back in his throne, which threatens to engulf him. "In ten days *Lady* heads for Bermuda, so the crew is on furlough through the weekend. We have the place to ourselves. There's a full bar, or I could manage a juice or a coffee or whatever. Sparkling water?"

"I'm good," Jack says. "This chair is so comfortable I may never get up. What kind of leather is this?"

"Sick, eh? It's made from the skin of young virgins."

"Excuse me?"

"Kidskin. Young goats," Bing adds impishly.

"Ah," Jack says, a little relieved in spite of himself, visions of billionaire psychopaths receding into bad movie land. "Obviously you heard about Professor Keener."

For the first time Jonny Bing breaks eye contact. He sighs and drums his fingers on the arm of his chair. "I couldn't believe it. Who'd want to kill poor Joe? It doesn't make any sense. You know how they always say 'he didn't have an enemy in the world.' Well, Joe really didn't."

"He had at least one," Jack points out.

Bing shudders. "I keep thinking it was a mistake.

Like they went to the wrong address, or mistook him for someone else."

"I suppose mistaken identity remains a possibility, but it doesn't look to go that way," Jack says. "More like a professional hit."

"That's insane."

"I think Dane mentioned we're looking for background on Joseph Keener. Your name came up."

"Whatever you need."

"It's usually best to start at the beginning. How did you happen to invest in Professor Keener's company?"

Bing touches his slender fingertips together as if making a steeple. "How it usually happens. He was brought to my attention by one of my researchers."

Jack has his reporter's notebook open on one knee, ballpoint pen in hand. "In what context?" he asks.

Bing seems amused by the question. "You know how it works in the game of venture capitalism, Mr. Delancey? No? Why should you, you're a man of action, am I right? Not a banker. So I could bullshit you about computer modeling and try to make it sound all scientific, but the truth is, what I do is gamble on brilliant people. And to do that I have to know about them. As you may be aware, my investments are in emerging technology. That's my area of expertise. I made my first three hundred million betting on video streaming software while I was still at the B School. I heard about a couple of BU geeks who had an interesting idea and I backed them with money from my parents' restaurant, and we all got very, very rich. But you can't rely on the grapevine to bring you opportunity. You have to be tuned in. You have to find the next new thing and make your own luck, which, believe me, is not so easy. What happened in this case, Joe published a paper in a scientific journal that caused something of a stir, and we decided to meet with him and see if he had any ideas for practical applications. He supplies the ideas, we provide finance and structure for the business model. I'm an entrepreneur, not a physicist, and I do not pretend to understand Joe's theories about gated photons, but I understood immediately that he was a genius."

"How so?"

Bing smiles, as if at a pleasant recollection. "You and I look out this window and see a beautiful scene. Joe looks out and sees how light works, on the very smallest level. What happens when an individual photon, the tiniest component in a beam of light, is either absorbed or reflected. Joe saw and understood the energy within waves: waves of water, waves of light. At first he didn't even want to talk with us, and swore he had no interest in founding a private research lab, but my instincts told me otherwise, and so I persisted, and finally he began to talk about light, and that's when I knew. That's why I succeed where others fail, Mr. Delancey, because I am tenacious by nature. I fasten my teeth on the ankles of genius and I won't let go."

Jack looks up from his notebook. "Strange way to put it, Mr. Bing."

"Call me Jonny. No, not strange at all. I know exactly who I am, okay? I'm a little bulldog, I don't give up. I keep fighting. And believe me, Joseph Keener was worth fighting for. And not just because of the financial opportunity. His ideas, the particular way he thought about things, it's a privilege to know a person like that, because there are only a handful alive in the world at any one time."

"So what was he like on a personal level?"

Bing chuckles, sounding surprisingly girlish. "Joe

didn't really have a personal level, not one he could share. Do you know what Asperger's is, Mr. Delancey?"

"Not really. I've heard the term. Something to do with autism."

"That's right, and at the moment it's a very trendy diagnosis. There's been a lot of nonsense talked about Asperger's syndrome, mostly by pop shrinks who should know better. They'd like us to think that every creative and difficult person suffered from a mild form of autism, from Leonardo to Einstein. It's become the excuse for behaving like a selfish asshole. Sorry, my Asperger's made me do it! Asperger's means I can be rude and it's not my fault! But I think Joe really did have some form of the disorder. He struggled mightily to deal with us mere humans, if you know what I mean."

"Don't think I do," Jacks says. "What was he like? Personally, I mean."

"Difficult to describe. It's as if Joe wanted to connect with people but didn't quite know how. Early on I mentioned his shyness and told him that it wouldn't be a problem, he didn't have to meet or talk with anyone who made him uncomfortable, and he told me the most remarkable thing. He said he wasn't really shy, but that he had learned to mimic shyness because it's more socially acceptable than explaining that he prefers to be alone because the only place he ever felt comfortable was inside his own head."

"That may be helpful," Jack says, making a note. "Did he ever mention growing up in foster care?"

"Mention it?" Bing shrugs. "Not directly. I know his parents died when he was an infant, and that he was raised by a succession of foster parents. I asked him what was that like once, he said it was adequate."

"Adequate? A strange way to put it."

"That was Joe. He once told me his real father was the public library. That's where he discovered who he was, by looking in books and finding math and physics and so on."

"What was the connection to Caltech, do you know? How he happened to go there at such a young age? To the other end of the country?"

Bing smiles. "Again, it was light. He read an article by someone who taught at Caltech and decided he had to go there. Distance from home didn't matter, since he didn't think of himself as having a home in the usual sense. I believe his high school principal made a few calls. Everybody knew he was special, you knew it the moment you met him. Different, but special. I can't really explain it, but he was."

"You're doing fine, Mr. Bing. I'm getting the picture. The victim—excuse me, Joseph Keener—was brilliant but socially inept."

Jack has been waiting to drop a particular bomb ever since he heard from Alice, earlier in the day. Good stuff, and he happily decides to make use of it. "How did he happen to meet that Chinese girlfriend of his, do you know?"

Bing appears stunned by the question, maybe even a little hurt. As if he'd been under the impression that he and Jack were becoming quite chummy, and a question like that was simply out of bounds.

"Chinese girlfriend?" Bing says. "No, I don't think so. I seriously doubt that. Joe didn't have a girlfriend that I know of. Chinese or any other kind. No, no, no."

"I thought maybe you put them together."

Bing puts a small hand to his heart. "Me? Why would you think that?"

"You know lots of beautiful women, Mr. Bing. Maybe

Joe was at one of your, um, gatherings, and you introduced him to a lady, something like that."

"Because you think he had a Chinese girlfriend, I had to be involved? I'm insulted."

"No insult intended. I mean, where else would Keener have had the opportunity to cross paths with such an exotic beauty? I'm sure it was quite innocent. A social occasion, two people meet who happen to have you in common. No big deal. Not insult worthy."

Bing keeps shaking his head, disturbing the emo bang, and looks, for a brief moment, something like his age. "No, no, no. Never happened."

"So you wouldn't know about the baby they had? A five-year-old?"

"Definitely, I am *now* insulted." Bing studies his small hands, examining his beautifully buffed nails. He seems to have recovered his aplomb. "Someone has given you bad information, Mr. Delancey. That is the only explanation. As far as I know, Joe Keener never had an actual relationship with a woman, or with anybody, really. Not that kind of relationship."

"It doesn't take a relationship to father a child," Jack points out.

Jonny Bing laughs, a little too sharply. "Believe me, I know that! But seriously, someone has been pulling your leg. Not Joe. No way."

"Okay," says Jack, letting it go for the time being. "What about enemies, threats, anything of that nature? Something connected with QuantaGate, perhaps?"

Bing thinks about it. "I'm the prime investor, but that doesn't mean I have anything to do with the day-to-day operations. Quite the opposite. Still, I would know if there was anything to be concerned about. Corporate espionage is always a worry, but those types steal information—trade secrets and so on—they don't kill."

"But there is something worth stealing?"

"Absolutely," Bing says, folding his spindly little arms.

"So what exactly do they make at QuantaGate?" Jack asks, pressing.

Another big, boyish grin as Bing raises his eyes, looks directly at Jack. "I could tell you, but then I'd have to kill you—sorry, bad joke under the circumstances. The truth is, I don't know or understand the technical specifics, but it's public knowledge that the company has an exploratory contract with the Defense Department to develop a new way for computers to communicate over long distances. Joe had a theory about that, which he believed had practical applications. That was the basis for the company, taking one of his ideas and finding a way to make it work."

"And did he? Make it work?"

Jonny Bing smoothes the thatch of hair away from his eyes, grimacing slightly. "No, not yet. There are many difficulties, which is to be expected with a breakthrough technology. To my surprise, the DOD has shown remarkable patience and has continued to fund the project. They seem to understand that they're dealing with the future, and that it will take a while to get there."

"And now that Professor Keener is gone?"

The smaller man shrugs. "The project continues as long as there is funding. We will continue to work on developing practical applications to Joe's theories. Beyond that, I have no way of knowing. Time will tell."

"Who gets his share of the company?"

Bing winces, looking slightly embarrassed. "I was looking into that just before you arrived. The answer is, I don't know, not yet. Voting control of the shares, which are privately held, reverts to the partners. That's me, mostly. But any income derived will go to his estate."

"So you won't benefit financially?"

A somber expression adds years to his youthful appearance, making him look closer to forty than thirty. "I don't benefit at all, Mr. Delancey. No, no, no. Joe dying is absolutely the worst thing that could happen. If faith in QuantaGate collapses the whole investment is in jeopardy." Bing sighs, fishes a vibrating cell phone out of one of the guayabera's many pockets, checks the screen. "Sorry, it's been really cool talking with an action dude like you, but I have calls to catch up on. Can you find your way out?"

"No problem." Jack stands up, shoots his cuffs. "Just one thing. You mentioned a concern about corporate espionage. Who handles security for QuantaGate?"

"The usual rent-a-cops, I suppose," Bing says vaguely, as if he couldn't care less. "Sorry, but that kind of day-to-day really isn't my thing. I'm a big picture guy."

"I can see that," Jack says affably, offering his hand.

"Tell Dane to have her people call my people. Joke, joke. She has my number."

"Thanks again for your time," Jack says. "And have a blast in Bermuda."

Kidder observes the marina from his vehicle, from a carefully chosen location not covered by any of the security cameras he's been able to identify. Most of the cameras are along the shoreline, focused on the floating dock area, which makes sense, and presents a mild level of difficulty. All part of the game. As is the constant awareness that he has an item in the trunk that will be defrosting in the heat, and that must be delivered before it goes bad.

Tick tock.

Watching through his pair of small Nikon binoculars, Kidder sees the lean, athletic man in the sharp suit exiting the big yacht, striding purposefully toward the security gate, obviously leaving the area. This is good. Every inch of the guy says "senior investigator," and Kidder doesn't need the complication of dealing with a professional, not when he has to find a way around the security cameras.

Using the Nikons, he follows the sharp dresser to the back of the marina parking lot, and manages to pick up the plate number on the gleaming Lincoln Town Car as it makes the turn. What is the guy, a glorified chauffeur? Would any self-respecting investigator have an uncool ride like that? Maybe he's misread Mr. Sharp, maybe he's an empty suit, but that can all be resolved later, when he runs the plate.

For now, keep to the task at hand. Kidder glasses the big yacht, notes again that it's tied to the farthest of the floating piers, just inside the breakwater. Kidder grunts, having arrived at a solution. There's more than one way to skin a cat—not that he's ever skinned one, he sort of likes cats, cats are killers—and more than one way to board a fat-cat yacht.

One if by land, he thinks, grinning to himself, two if by sea.

Chapter Thirteen

Life Is Short But She's Not

Dane Porter perches at a sidewalk table in downtown D.C., seething. Her arms are firmly crossed, her brow furrowed. She has never been so humiliated. First she's refused entrance to the FBI by a pudgy female with a smug attitude, and then she's ordered to cool her heels—and heels is where the trouble began—at a Five Guys hamburger joint.

As if. A French fry hasn't passed her lips in two birthdays, at least, which is part of how she maintains her lithe and youthful figure and a body mass index of nineteen. She's in the open air, but every time the restaurant doors open she can feel deep-fried calories exuding through the atmosphere.

Twenty minutes, the voice on the cell had promised, and sure enough in twenty minutes exactly Assistant Director of Counterterrorism Monica Bevins comes striding up the sidewalk, all six foot plus of her, looking in every way formidable. Smart, no-nonsense hairdo, power pantsuit, black executive handbag on a long strap slung from her wide athletic shoulders. Ready to leap tall bureaucracies in a single bound, save the planet, no problem that can't be solved.

"Attorney Porter?"

Dane stands, formally shakes the big lady's hand, figuring that's what you do with high-ranking feds, you tug the forelock and curtsy, or whatever.

Bevins towers over her.

"Let's go inside, shall we?"

Dane opens her mouth to demur—she loathes the smell of frying cow—but AD Bevins is already moving through the door. A force-of-nature type, obviously, and used to assuming full command of any given situation. Bevins marches to a recently vacated table in the back of the place, sweeps away the peanut shells, slips into a seat, points Dane to a chair.

"You hungry? You want something?"

"I'm good, you?"

"I'd love a dog and fries but I'm dieting."

"Oh?"

"I'm always dieting. Dieting sucks. You wouldn't know because you've never weighed more than what, a hundred and five?"

Dane wants to tell the big lady that she, too, has to watch her weight, but knows from past experience that, given the exquisite petiteness of her figure, nobody wants to hear it. "So what are we doing here?" Dane asks. "I offered to take you to lunch at Café Milano. They have lovely salads."

"Ambient noise," the big woman intones, lowering her voice. "Lots of ambient at Five Guys."

"You think we might get bugged?"

Bevins smiles and shrugs. "Better safe than sorry. Considering who may be involved."

"There's a 'who'?" Dane says, bright with excitement. "What have you learned?"

"First, tell me what happened at the checkpoint. All

I heard, Naomi Nantz's personal attorney failed to pass security."

"My heels," Dane says, showing off her Pampili strap-ons. "This horrible woman made me take them off so she could measure. Said the maximum heel length allowed is three-and-a-half inches and mine were five, and I'd have to leave them with her if I wanted to enter the building. I said I wasn't going to walk the halls of Justice in my bare feet and that was that."

AD Bevins smiles, her eyes twinkling.

"Glad to amuse you," Dane says tartly. "These heels cleared Homeland Security at Logan Airport. That should be good enough."

"Logan will never be good enough," Bevins responds darkly. "Flight 11? Mohamed Atta? Ancient history, but it still rankles." The big woman grimaces and leans forward, her face inches from Dane's, as she begins to speak very quietly, almost a murmur that very nearly blends into the bright background noise of the restaurant. Her breath is mouthwash-minty. "You first. I understand you bring news of my friend Randall Shane. What's the latest?"

Keeping her voice equally low, Dane says, "In the last hour or so we confirmed that his client, Joseph Keener, did indeed have a child, possibly out of wedlock. All evidence of the child had been erased from the crime scene. Well, almost all evidence: one of our investigators found a sandbox under some leaves in the backyard, and a neighbor who will swear to the little boy's existence, and to the fact that the mother is Chinese, possibly a Chinese national. It's clear that the victim was secretive about the child, for reasons yet to be determined."

"I never doubted it," Bevins says.

"That the kid was real?"

The big woman nods. "Shane wouldn't make that kind of mistake. He can be fooled—we all can, depending on circumstance—but not like that. Not Randall Shane."

"What's your take on the case against him? All the physical evidence indicates he killed the professor."

"Crap. His own gun? A bloody shirt? Shane does the deed, then keeps blood evidence? No way."

"So you believe he's been set up?"

Bevins nods, keeping direct eye contact with Dane. "No doubt. There are national security implications I can't discuss with you, and which I'm not fully briefed on myself, but you can take it to the bank. Shane is being framed."

"By who?"

Bevins looks grim. "Unknown to me at present."

"Why? What possible motive?"

"Also unknown."

"Come on, who took him? You must have some idea. Some theory."

"Lots of ideas, no evidence. But I've been making noise, letting it be known that one of the FBI's own has been detained, and that if he's harmed we'll be all over it."

Dane sits back. The place is packed, quite noisy, and nobody obvious is listening in to the conversation. "Can we speak normally for a bit? I can call you Monica?"

"Not if you worked for me, but you don't. Monica is fine for civilians. As to the conversation, proceed. I'll stop you if we need to go SV."

"SV?"

"Sotto voce. With a hushed quality."

"Got it. Is that FBI lingo now?"

Monica shakes her head, shows the hint of a smile. "Just me."

"Interesting," Dane says, filing it away under Personal Eccentricities. Because she works for Naomi Nantz the file has numerous entries, starting with the boss. "So. You and Shane go way back."

Bevins nods, her eyes large. "All the way to boot camp at Quantico. I came in straight out of law school, he'd been on the FBI civilian side for a couple years as a technical expert, then decided to apply for Special Agent. We're both big, so we got lumped together, sort of. I fell in love with him in about twenty minutes."

Dane is startled by the confession. "Seriously?"

Bevins shrugs. "He was married, so I kept it to myself. He figured it out, of course. So he played it like we were going to be best friends. And you know what? That's how it worked out in the long run. I got over the crush after a while, but never the friendship. Randall Shane is the bravest, truest, most decent human being I've ever known. Point one. You're aware of his personal tragedy? Wife and daughter? Ever since, he's devoted his life to rescuing children. Most of his cases are pro bono. Long as he's got enough to put gas in that big fat car of his, he's good to go. Therefore incorruptible as to financial temptation. Point two, to my certain knowledge he's a red-blooded, salute-the-flag, die-for-your-country patriot who would never do anything to threaten the security of the good old U.S.A. Caveat: unless a child's life is in danger, then it might get complicated."

"So you believe there might be national security implications?"

Bevins ever so casually checks the burger crowd to see if anybody is paying particular attention. Satisfied, she puts her elbows on the table, goes into sotto voce mode.

"Genius physicist working on a top-secret project,

who just so happens to have a secret Chinese mistress and a missing child? *Of course* there are national security implications. Not that any agency has admitted to involvement. And believe me, I've been asking. Like I said, making noise to let them know we know. Kicked in a few doors, metaphorically speaking. Folks look blank, shake their heads. Never heard of Shane, no business of snatching him in plain sight, cross their hearts and hope to die."

"Somebody made it happen. From all descriptions, this was a professional, military kind of outfit, precision-executing a mission."

Bevins nods in recognition. "Covert special ops. Which leaves us with at least a couple of possibilities. One of our agencies dispatched an elite unit to seize and detain a U.S. citizen on U.S. soil and has somehow managed not to share that fact with any of the other interested national security agencies, mine included. Or some evildoer has it in for Shane and sent mercenaries to snatch him."

"Evildoer?"

"That's how we talk in the FBI. Saves a lot of explaining. 'Evildoer' covers terrorist, dictator, gang boss, Wall Street banker, the Yankees, take your pick of the loathsome."

Dane looks startled. "The Yankees?"

"I'm from Jamaica Plain. My dad was a Boston cop."

"No kidding? I should have known that."

"You can't know everything."

"Anything I found on Google, it alluded to you growing up on Long Island."

Bevins reveals a sly smile. "Evildoers might want to target family. Search engines can provide a useful smoke screen. We call it 'identity diversion.' Simple but effective."

Dane nods thoughtfully. "You're FBI from Boston and Shane's your BFF, so you must know Jack Delancey."

After a slight hesitation, Bevins says, "That's an affirmative."

"You could be telling this to him."

"You're the better choice."

"You and Jack don't get along?"

Bevins shrugs. "We never saw eye to eye, and that's his problem. Me being tall."

"What?" Dane does a double take. "Your height? Seriously?"

"He calls me 'The 50 Foot Woman,' as in *Attack of The 50 Foot Woman,* some cheesy horror flick he finds amusing. As I'm sure you've noticed, Jack loves women. What you may not have noticed, he only loves 'em if they're five foot ten or less. Turns out, he can't handle a female boss who's taller than he is. Admitted as much. I'm one of the reasons he resigned. The other, of course, is that a higher salary means he can buy more suits. And wives."

"I'll give him your love."

"Do that. Really, it's not a problem. We get along fine just as long as we don't have to speak, or see each other."

The shiny-top table starts to vibrate delicately. Bevins retrieves a cell phone from her briefcase, flips it open, checks the display. "Sorry, gotta go. You'll keep me informed?"

Dane stands, takes a deep breath. "Monica? One more question. Do you think Shane is still alive?"

The big woman blinks, holding herself still. "Absolutely. I'd bet everything that he's been taken alive for interrogation purposes. Whoever it is behind this, they think he knows something."

"What? What could he know?"

Bevins hoists the handbag strap to her shoulder. "If I knew *that,* we wouldn't be having this conversation. It wouldn't be you, it would be Shane, and he'd be buying bacon cheese dogs for two and insisting I eat with him, because life is short but we're not."

Chapter Fourteen

The Invisible Man Revealed

The first time I saw Naomi destroy one of her beautiful watercolors, I screamed for her to stop. She gave me a look as flat as Death Valley and kept slowly and methodically shredding the damp paper.

"Get used to it," she said.

Three years, close to a thousand attempts at perfection, and I'm still not used to it.

Here's the deal. Almost every day at 3:00 p.m., boss lady goes to the ground-floor solarium, which has the requisite northern lighting, and arranges a still life on a small table kept there for that purpose. Could be cut flowers, or an antique cream pitcher, or a found object, or all three. When she has the arrangement just so, she tapes a heavy, pre-cut sheet of Arches watercolor paper on to a small, horizontally-tilted drawing table. She selects her brushes and colors. She takes a deep breath and does some sort of Zen thing that involves closing her eyes and holding her hands out, palms up. Then she sets a timer for thirty minutes and gets to work. First a quick pencil sketch. That never takes more than a minute or two. Then she wets her brushes and begins. Sometimes the mistake happens right away, in the first pass of the brush. More often the timer will ding and she'll step back, look at the still-life arrangement, glance at her painted version—almost always lovely, in my opinion—and then calmly peel it away from the drawing board, tear it into strips and feed the pieces into a paper shredder.

Zzzt, zzzt, zzzt. It's gotten to be a sound that makes my teeth hurt.

Today is no different, except that the arrangement involves a folding carpenter's ruler, a combination square and a brass bevel, donated to the cause by Danny Bechst, who once told me, in confidence, that Naomi was like van Gogh, except better looking and with two ears. Apparently van Gogh wrecked a lot of his paintings, too. A fact you wouldn't expect the average carpenter to know, but in Boston there are no average carpenters. Most of them seem to have Ph.D.'s. Anyhow, Danny isn't as appalled by the daily destruction as I am. Says he understands a quest for perfection and that one of these days when the bell dings, voilà, a flawless masterpiece.

As for Naomi, you'd think that failing on a daily basis would bother her, but she insists that the process is relaxing. Indeed, she always appears to be calm as she methodically destroys her creation. Maybe driving me crazy makes her feel serene. All part of the unwritten job description.

Today the shredder sounds about twenty minutes into the process, cuing me to enter the studio with the latest update on the investigation. Naomi, breaking down the still life, looks up, raises an eyebrow.

"Dane called," I tell her. "Shuttle delayed out of Reagan National, but they should be wheels down at Logan by five. She has some interesting tidbits about possible evildoers, but nothing solid."

"Evildoers?"

"Dane does enjoy the evocative phrase."

"Worth the trip, just to show the flag."

"Jack's day has been more productive. He interviewed Jonny Bing, the venture capitalist, and formed, he says, 'an opinion.' Declined to specify what opinion, exactly. Before that he made a quick run up to New Hampshire to talk to the foster care folks about Joseph Keener's childhood. Said he uncovered some 'facts of interest.' He'll fill us in tonight."

"Our first formal case dinner," Naomi says. "I'm looking forward to it. Beasley always outdoes herself."

"Speaking of which, Jack is relaying a request from the operative who infiltrated QuantaGate. The Invisible Man? His name is Milton Bean and he wants to make his report in person this evening."

"Oh? Why?"

"Apparently, while some men dream of virgins awaiting them in heaven, or winning the Powerball, Milton Bean dreams of having dinner with Naomi Nantz."

"Ah."

"Decision, please, so I can inform Beasley if necessary."

"He's freelanced for us, what, four times?"

"If you know, and you always do, why do you ask?"

As usual Naomi ignores my wisecracks. "Issue him an invitation. I'm curious to see what the Invisible Man looks like."

I bow and scrape.

Chapter Fifteen

Mrs. Beasley Presents

Yves Cuilleron Condrieu, Les Chaillets 2000
Fresh Beet Carpaccio with Shivered Scallions
Shrimp & Shiitake Sausage
Broiled Swordfish with Potato Dauphin Puree
Honeyed Heart of Endive Salad
Vanilla Ice Cream with Ginger Sauce

Teddy, having scanned a folded menu card, sidles up to me and whispers, "'Beet' carpaccio? 'Shivered' scallions? Are those typos or what?"

I smile and shake my head. "It's Beasley having fun. But I'm impressed that you even know that carpaccio is usually beef."

"I know a lot of weird stuff."

"Indeed. And very useful it proves to be, too."

This will be our first formal evening meal of the case, therefore a "working dinner" and as is Naomi's habit—she and our supremely gifted chef always consult over the selections—the food will be light but interesting. Hence the playful but undoubtedly delicious opening course; shivered scallions indeed.

Case dinners are usually seated at 7:00 p.m., to allow

plenty of time for informed discussion between courses, and this evening's meal is no exception. The formal dining room is exactly large enough to accommodate a table for eight, a couple of narrow but highly functional sideboards and a pair of simple but elegant Waterford crystal chandeliers gifted to the residence by a satisfied client. There are three high-set windows that have a view of the sky in the winter months, or a heavily leafed beech tree in season, but which ensure street-view privacy when guests are seated at the table. Near the sideboards, an ancient but still functional dumbwaiter brings goodies up from Mrs. Beasley's kitchen. On the northern wall hang stunning reproductions of Naomi's three favorite Sargent watercolors. Stunning not just because of their subject matter—sunlight on dappled walls—but because they look good and true enough to be the originals, although Naomi swears they're not, the Benefactor's generosity notwithstanding.

First to arrive is Jack Delancey, accompanied by his special guest, the operative he sometimes refers to as the Invisible Man. Otherwise known as Mr. Milton Bean. Not invisible this evening, but carefully presented in Brooks Brothers gray slacks and a blue blazer with four brass buttons on each sleeve. Purchased for the occasion under Jack's expert tutelage, if I'm not mistaken. Like bringing a date home to Mother, they both want to make a good impression.

Last in house, our land shark lawyer Dane Porter, who, from the slightly damp look of her scruffed pixie hairdo, barely had time to shower and change after her much delayed flight from Washington.

When we're all assembled, Naomi appears, regal in a dark crimson silk blouse and ankle-length black silk skirt. Leading us into the formal dining room, where two bottles of the excellent condrieu have already been de-canted, she pours generously. When we all have glasses in hand, she proposes a toast:

"To the son of Joseph Keener. May he be recovered alive and well."

We sip dutifully—oh my God, the wine is fabulous—but boss lady isn't done raising her glass.

"To Randall Shane," she intones, with a glance at Jack. "May his innocence be proved, if true, and may he be returned to his exemplary life."

Another careful sip. Mustn't rush a condrieu of this quality. Speaking as one who, prior to my association with Naomi Nantz, thought Trader Joe's wine selection was the height of sophistication, I don't have anything against Charles Shaw, but really, you can't keep a girl swilling Two Buck Chuck once she's tasted the best of Paree. Or Sonoma Valley, for that matter. In matters of the vine I remain a neophyte, easily dazzled, but can't help noticing that the Invisible Man's eyes have gotten very round and large.

"Wow," he says.

"Mr. Bean, welcome."

The bland gentleman dips his unremarkable head. "Honored, ma'am."

"'Ma'am' is the queen of England. My name is Naomi, and you're welcome to use it."

"Sorry. Didn't mean to offend. The wine is... I've never had anything quite like it. Amazingly, uh, amaz-ing."

"Great vineyard, great vintage, perfect temperature," Naomi purrs. "Now, as to our protocol for case dinners. You're among trusted colleagues who will be sharing privileged information and you are expected to partici-pate, withholding not even the smallest detail. That's how we do it around here. So please keep that in mind as you enjoy our hospitality. I will call upon you in turn."

A small rodent might assume an expression something like Mr. Bean's, having discovered his cheese-seeking paw firmly pinned in a trap. He shoots Jack a look that says "help me, please" and is studiously ignored. Having begged for an invitation, the no-longer-invisible man is on his own and will have to suffer the consequences.

"Alice? You go first. Bring us up to speed on Professor Keener's neighborhood."

My description of the encounter with Toni Jo Nadeau concludes as the first course is being served. Paper-thin golden beets garnished with capers, minced chives and the mouth-intriguing "shivered" scallions. Which according to Beasley are briefly soaked in ice-cold seawater before being tossed into hot olive oil. Imagine if popcorn was tiny little onions, only way, way better.

"Keyboard kid?" Jack says, probing the details of my report. "That was the phrase?"

"That's how Mrs. Nadeau remembers it."

"And the mother impressed her as being native-born Chinese?"

"Mrs. Nadeau said she spoke very little English, wore what she described as 'those formal Chinese dresses.' The silk kind with embroidered patterns. Quite old-fashioned, really. Most of the Chinese-American women I see around town wear designer jeans."

"The supposition being, someone from Hong Kong or mainland China."

"That was her impression, yes."

Jack puts down his salad fork, rubs his hand on his jaw. "I don't get it. The guy has a baby out of wedlock, so what? Why the big secret? In this day and age? Unless it has to do with the mother."

"Go on," Naomi says.

"I'm just riffing here, but what if the big secret is that she was already married to someone else? The professor has a torrid affair with a married woman, she gets pregnant and lets her husband think the kid is his. Along those lines. Wouldn't be the first time it's happened."

"Or the ten millionth," Dane adds knowingly.

Naomi says, "It's a theory, based entirely on supposition, but interesting nonetheless. Are you thinking this could be the spouse of a colleague? A visiting professor?"

"That, or maybe a diplomat's wife…" Jack says. "Stationed at the Boston consulate maybe? That might explain the traditional dress."

Naomi shakes her head. "There are Chinese consulates in New York, Washington, Chicago, Los Angeles, San Francisco and Houston, but not Boston."

Jack grins. "Off the top of your head?"

"Just something I know."

"Okay, so maybe she takes the Amtrak up from New York. Maybe not. I'm not married to the idea she's a diplomat's wife—pun *intended,* by the way—but my gut tells me the mother is key, and could be connected to someone very powerful and/or dangerous. Hence the need for secrecy, and possibly kidnapping. And maybe hence the need to murder."

"One of the tongs?" Teddy suggests, his voice barely audible.

"Strictly speaking, tongs are American, not Chinese," Naomi says. "But I take your point. What if the mystery woman is the gun moll of a gang leader? How would that play out?"

"I never said 'gun moll,' whatever that is," Teddy objects. "And what do you mean tongs are not Chinese?"

Naomi lapses into her dinner lecture mode. "Not, technically, any more than Italian-American crime syndicates are the same as the Italian Mafia. Tongs are a distinctly Western version of the Tiandihui, the original secret criminal societies in China, today known as triads. First established in San Francisco in the nineteenth century, when many Chinese arrived to labor on the railroads, and began to organize themselves for protection. Still very powerful, but quite staid and old-fashioned as modern gangs go. The tong presence here in Boston has a hand in gambling, extortion and loan shark rackets, but only rarely resorts to murder. The Hong Kong–based triads tend to be more deadly than the American tongs, and from what I hear the local Vietnamese gangs, if not more powerful, are certainly younger, more violent and much more dangerous."

"So maybe she's Vietnamese," Teddy insists, a little louder and a lot more stubborn. "Why not? The neighbor is probably not being specific, saying 'Chinese.'"

Naomi looks pleased. This is the kind of give-and-take that she encourages, and which Teddy hasn't much engaged in until very recently. "Well argued. Regardless of ethnicity or country of origin, the notion of a criminal or gang connection has to be taken into account," Naomi assures him. "Jack?"

"I'll ask around."

"Excellent. Tell us about Mr. Bing."

"Quite the character," Jack says. "I rather like him. Not at all what I expected."

Jack would be a great storyteller if he didn't keep reverting to cop speak. Even with the stilted phrases, he paints an intriguing picture of the young venture capitalist luxuriating in splendid isolation on his enormous yacht, explaining his decision to invest in Joseph Keener as a business opportunity, and as a friend of sorts, in hopes that the victim's understanding of light might one day prove to be immensely profitable.

"My impression is he's telling the truth, mostly. In the sense that he genuinely liked and admired the professor, and has some interesting insights into what made him tick. But he's lying about not knowing about the Chinese girlfriend, and the fact they had a kid."

"Your gut?"

Jack nods.

"Good enough. So why is Mr. Bing lying? What's his motive?"

"If I had to guess, he may think he's protecting Keener's reputation, or the boy, or both. I'm going to give him a day to think about it, then go back at him."

While we digest Jack's presentation, Beasley serves the second course, a sliced grilled sausage stuffed with shrimp and mushrooms and various secret ingredients that can't be pried out of her with any sort of bribe, or even the threat of waterboarding. The merest hint of cardamom, obviously, and at least one of us (me) detects black truffle lurking among the shiitake, but beyond that the chef's unsmiling lips are sealed.

"Teddy? Your turn. Please bring us all up to date."

"Um, there's not really a lot to report yet. With Mr. Bean's help—he placed a memory stick into one of their computers, uploading this really cool program—ah, we established mirrored access to the QuantaGate office computer system. We'll just have to wait until something interesting pops."

Naomi favors him with an indulgent smile. "Explain mirrored access, for those who might not be familiar."

Teddy shrugs, as if it's no big deal. "Means we're limited to what people are actively keyboarding in real time.

We can't explore the system or access files—that would set off alarm bells—all we can do is follow keystrokes and mouse clicks from stations in the network, but at least we get all of them. That means, during normal work hours, anywhere between sixteen and twenty keyboards clacking away. A lot more data than can be followed by any single observer. So we're feeding all the entries into a developing database, subdivided into categories of interest. Payroll, accounts receivable, inter-staff memos, gossip threads. Like that."

"And any category or search term we care to add in the future?"

"Right, sure. No problem."

"Dane? What's our legal exposure on this?"

Our legal eagle rolls her eyes. "Seriously?"

"Confined to prosecutable infractions."

"Specifically exposure under the U.S. Criminal Code 1030, 'Fraud and Related Activity in Connection with Computers'?"

"If you say so."

Dane looks thoughtful, pursing her pretty, plumped lips like a small, dazzling tropical fish. Say a well-coiffed piranha. "I'd say, very serious exposure. Under subhead 5A, the language concerns harm done by unauthorized access of protected computer. So the key to staying out of jail is to do no harm. On the other hand, subhead 2 makes it illegal to obtain protected information from any department or agency of the United States. A zealous prosecutor might well argue that a private company with a contract from the Department of Defense falls under that umbrella. Basically, criminal liability depends on what you do with information obtained. Pass it on to a foreign agent, you'd be facing charges of espionage and/or treason for sure."

Naomi nods and turns her head. "Teddy? Do you intend to pass information to a foreign agent?"

"No freakin' way! Plus, what we're looking at in the cyber mirror doesn't include whatever system they have in the actual lab. We're culling data from cubicle workers, not scientists. It's strictly look, don't touch."

Dane remains mildly skeptical. "Then I suppose cogent arguments could be made in favor of the defendant, should an arrest occur. My humble opinion? If the worst happens, felony conviction remains a real possibility."

Teddy sits up straight, adding about three inches in height. "You mean I might be a defendant?"

"Always possible, given what we do and who we do it to," Naomi makes clear.

"Cool."

"No, not cool. Unless by cool you mean you'll take every precaution to make sure you won't get caught."

"Absolutely, that's what I mean."

"This isn't a cybercafé. There will soon be powerful forces arrayed against us, if they're not already in place."

"I get it," Teddy says, somewhat petulant.

Before he can be further cautioned, the swordfish swims onto our plates, and for a good ten minutes nobody says a word. A few moans of pleasure, but no actual words.

Our first-time guest Milton Bean, gingerly forking slices mouthward, continues to look pleasantly, not to say orgasmically, dumbfounded. Orgasmic in the foodie sense, of course. Dumbfounded in the oh-my-God-never-have-I-tasted-anything-as-divine-as-this sense. Not that he's forgotten the price that must be paid for his presence at this table, and which Naomi is now poised to extract.

"I see you're enjoying our little meal," she observes.

"Take my word, it only gets better. Mrs. Beasley's home-made ice cream with ginger sauce has been known to make fully grown humans weep with pleasure."

"I, um, can't wait," he says. Shrinking a little, aware what comes next.

Boss lady favors our guest with one of her cool, controlling smiles. "Mr. Bean, you have done exemplary work for us in the past, as a freelance operative, and given what you have been able to accomplish with so little muss and fuss, I certainly want the relationship to continue. However, we need to be assured that your particular talents will not put us in legal jeopardy. Your sponsor, Mr. Delancey, would have us believe you somehow melt through security by way of human camouflage. Or by borrowing Harry Potter's cloak of invisibility. Jack has read all the Potter books, by the way, because at heart he's deeply romantic. Whereas I saw part of one movie and found it tedious, undoubtedly because I don't believe in magic, and don't want to, not even a little bit. To the contrary I believe in data, in facts on the ground and in the scientific method. Which made me wonder how you do it, how you manage to evade security wherever you happen to be assigned, even on very short notice. There being no satisfactory explanation, I have concluded that you are not, in fact, evading security."

Milton flinches, ever so slightly.

"It seems very likely that you have in your possession valid identification that allows unfettered access to a variety of venues," she continues, not simply a statement but a pronouncement of fact. "The possibilities are actually quite limited. You could be with the state police, FBI or IRS, any of which could get you through security in most places, but none of those agencies have you on any database we can find. So by a process of elimination, if you are not a card-carrying member of a government law enforcement agency, you must be affiliated with one of the major auditing firms. How am I doing, Mr. Bean?"

The Invisible Man couldn't be more stunned if boss lady had firmly tapped him on the temple with a large rubber mallet. "How did you figure that out?" he finally manages to ask.

Naomi allows herself a small sniff of satisfaction. "Sheer surmise. No other explanation suffices. Publicly traded corporations are required to submit to unscheduled spot checks from auditing firms. That's especially true of any company with Department of Defense contracts. Ergo."

"Ergo?"

"Therefore, hence, it follows," she says, defining the word with a thin, prim smile. "Fret not, Mr. Bean, your secret is safe with us, just as our secrets will be safe with you."

Naomi doesn't need to add any threatening qualifiers, like "on pain of death" or "on pain of never again being invited to share Mrs. Beasley's cooking." The Invisible Man, with a dip of his head, surrenders to her powers of deduction. Far from the first, unlikely to be the last.

"You got me," he says, with a sigh that could be relief.

"Details, please."

"Three years ago I was a forensic CPA with—" and he names one of the major national auditing firms, here redacted. "Your basic Mr. Bland with a calculator, making sure it all added up. That was my life. Checking the numbers, following the money. It was a career I chose, because it fit me. Milton Bean, CPA. Then in the course of my work I stumbled on this, um, let's call it an elaborate scheme to divert revenue from one financial entity to another, and then another, round the world, for the pur-

poses of avoiding taxes and as well as cheating the share-
holders. I'd call it a musical-chairs variation on a Ponzi
scheme, but virtually undetectable unless you happened
to get lucky, which I did. In more ways than one. Much
to my surprise, and very much to my boss's surprise, I
ended up as a whistle-blower, of a sort."

"Meaning you didn't blow it very loud."

Milton Bean smiles, betraying, for the first time in our
presence, a slight glow of personal pride. "As whistle-
blowers go, I was very discreet. A tiny little tweet, you
might say. There were several large financial corporations involved—of the too-big-to-fail variety—as well
as long-standing complicity from my own firm at the
very highest levels. Also, the likely failure of several
highly leveraged institutions, and many innocent victims, if I testified. So we all came to a reasonable ac-
commodation. The corporations agreed to make good
on the taxes they had been avoiding, plus pay very substantial fines, and I received a generous cash settlement
and also got to keep my job, with all the usual benefits.
Except I draw no salary and never have to show up for
work."

"You liked being undercover," Naomi says, nodding
to herself. "Blowing that very discreet whistle."

He grins. "It's way more fun than being an accountant."

At a certain angle, in a certain light, he really does
bear the smallest possible resemblance to Brad Pitt, if
Brad Pitt was a certified public accountant with a receding hairline and forgettable eyes.

"All my life people tended not to notice me, and I pretended not to be bothered by not being noticed. Milton
Milquetoast, the man who blends into the background.

Now I get to use that personal camouflage to my advantage. Playing to my strength, you might say."

"I do say," Naomi says, impressed. "Bravo, sir! Well told! Now that your special talent has been sorted—the details of which will not leave this room, rest assured—please report on your visit to QuantaGate."

According to Milton, the employees of the small research and development firm are in a deep state of shock and disbelief, stunned by the sudden death of their legendary founder. Not that anyone on the staff pretends actually to have known Professor Keener other than in passing. According to office chatter, Keener was formally polite but remained very much aloof, spending most of his time in his personal lab. More than one QG employee described him as "impossible to know."

"It's as if they all labored in the shadows of his genius, attempting to develop functional equivalents of his theoretical constructs. Which I gather has something to do with a new form of communication between high-speed computers," Milton adds.

"Functional equivalents? Theoretical constructs?" Naomi asks, probing. "Did they use those terms, exactly?"

He nods. "More than once. Understand, as an auditor I was not permitted access to the secure labs and workshops. My movements were restricted to the general office area and the cafeteria. The support staff."

"Who restricted your movements?"

"Security."

"Wackenhut or Gama Guards?" Naomi asks, naming two of the biggest private security providers.

"Gama Guards," Milton says. "Your basic corporate rent-a-cops, in uniform. Cordial but firm—mere accountants are not allowed into the labs. That requires another level of clearance, plus fingerprint and iris recognition. There's not that many lab employees—less than thirty, according to the payroll—so presumably they all know each other. No way I could have gotten back there unobserved."

"Understood. Jack, do you have any contacts with Gama Guards?"

"One or two. Cops who went private."

"Be nice to check out the lab, or at the very least chat with someone who works in the secure area."

"I'll make some calls," Jack says, making a note of it.

"Okay," Naomi says. "This is all good. We're making progress of a sort." She turns to our guest. "I'm sure you're eagerly awaiting the dessert course, Mr. Bean. That will follow my brief summation, and it is our habit to enjoy the final course in silence, understood?"

He licks his lips and nods. "Perfectly," he says, posture attentive.

"First, let me state the obvious," says Naomi, forming a steeple with her elegant fingers. "Two missing persons are the object of our collective concern, three if you count the mother, whose identity and location remain unknown to us. Our primary focus will be upon finding and recovering Joey, the so-called 'keyboard kid,' but it is beginning to look as if we'll have to find Randall Shane first, before we can develop a productive line of inquiry on the child. As to possible motives for Professor Keener's murder, indications are that he was suspected of espionage. That the mother of the missing boy might be a Chinese national could be crucial. Bear in mind that the Chinese government, working with various Chinese universities not unlike our own MIT, has launched hundreds of cyber attacks in the U.S., including one that triggered a blackout in a major Florida power grid. These assaults are intended to steal our military and industrial secrets, probe our defenses and evaluate how to shut us down if we ever became involved in an active, forces-on-the-ground war with China. Therefore a great deal of emphasis has recently been put on developing new ways to communicate—methods that cannot be compromised or hacked—and we know that Professor Keener has been involved in developing just such a system. That much is public knowledge, and mentioned prominently in the prospectus for QuantaGate.

"Which brings us to the question of who. Who ordered Professor Keener's execution? Keener may have been killed by someone on our side—it could even be that Randall Shane is guilty—or at the behest of a foreign power, to ensure his silence. Or it may have been personal, or somehow tong related, or both. We are not yet able to rule out any of these possibilities, but I'm confident we'll do so over the next few days."

Jack then does the unthinkable. Something remarkable, in fact. Rather vehemently, he interrupts Naomi in the middle of her summation to argue a point. "No way did Shane do it."

Naomi gives him a cool look. "We won't argue the point at this time," she says. "Unlike you, I'm keeping an open mind on the subject."

Jack opens his mouth to reply, thinks better of it and makes a sign that boss lady should continue.

"Okay," she says. "As to who seized the suspect— and he does remain a suspect, however much we all may want him to be proved innocent—possible candidates include Central Intelligence Agency, National Security Agency and Defense Intelligence Agency, all of which have assumed extraordinary powers under the Patriot Act. It's rare that a U.S. citizen be detained under the

Patriot Act, but it does happen—and quite possibly more frequently than we know, since the secret court orders are sealed.

"We should bear in mind that there are sixteen named U.S. intelligence agencies, and an unknown number that operate beyond public scrutiny. Plus agencies from any number of foreign governments. Any might be culpable. Or none. A grim reminder that we are in murky, dangerous waters. To my regret, I cannot guarantee the personal safety of anyone associated with our enterprise. Given the obvious danger, if any of you want to resign from this particular case, you have only to ask. No opprobrium attached."

I break the resultant silence—and the tension—by cracking wise. "Opprobrium?" I say. "Is that a fancy perfume?"

Boss lady ignores me. "Are we all in agreement? We do our best to locate and recover the missing child. If in agreement, please say so. Jack?"

"Yes, agreed."

"Dane?"

"Against my better judgment, yes."

"Teddy?"

"Way yes."

"Mr. Bean?"

"Honored to be included. Yes."

Saving me for last. "Alice?"

"Where you go, I go. Hell, yes."

"Good. Settled. And now for the dessert course."

In communal silence we savor Beasley's homemade vanilla ice cream with ginger sauce. Hot and cold, sweet and tangy, all in one bite. Imagine the best ice cream you ever had as a child, on an occasion when taste was exalted and joy was pure. Say your tenth birthday.

This is way, way better.

Chapter Sixteen

Baked Alaska

Three steps from the dining room, with the pleasant buzz of ginger still humming in his mouth, Jack Delancey reaches for the cell phone vibrating in his right trouser pocket. An incoming call from Glenn Tolliver, of the Massachusetts State Police. Funny, he was just thinking that the perfect finish to the meal might be a leisurely stroll along Comm Ave while puffing on a short La Gloria. Maybe if Piggy is in town, the better option would be Cigar Masters, with a nice port or cognac.

Jack flips open the phone, effectively wrecking his plans.

"One question," Tolliver says brusquely, sirens in the background. "Did you happen to drop by Jonny Bing's boat today? Or his ship or yacht or whatever it is?"

"I did."

"Good answer. Get down here."

"The marina? What happened?"

"That's what you're going to explain. Pronto, if not sooner."

"Twenty minutes."

Some idiot tipped over a box truck on the Southeast Expressway, scattering a few tons of watermelons, so it's more like forty minutes before Jack eases his boaty Lincoln Town Car into the Quincy Bay Marina visitor's parking lot. Hard to find a space, what with all the fire trucks and patrol cars. The last flush of late June twilight lingers, so all the flashing lights make for a festive sunset. If he didn't know better he'd think a traveling carnival had set up along the waterfront, complete with glittering arcs of spray from the fireboats out in the harbor.

The object of all this attention is the *Lady Luck*. To all outward appearances Bing's massive yacht is unharmed, but Jack has a pretty good idea this is about more than a false alarm. He finds Glenn Tolliver in uniform, confabbing with plainclothes detectives, state and local. Tolliver catches sight of him and dismisses his troops.

"Hey," says Jack, trying to sound casual. Captain Tolliver in full regalia is an imposing sight. "What's with the bag?"

"Never mind my uniform. I want to know everything you know."

"That'll take a lifetime."

"Can the wiseass."

"Fine. No problem. Is Bing alive or dead?"

"I'm asking the questions. Over there," he says, jutting his massive chin at a white canvas crime scene tent that's been staked into the asphalt a few feet from the dock system.

Jack follows him to the tent and sits, as indicated, in one of several folding chairs situated near a portable table equipped with a couple of big coffee urns. Tolliver grabs himself a cup, doesn't bother offering. Not that Jack, spoiled by the good stuff, has any interest in gray, parboiled caffeine.

Tolliver takes a seat, heaves a sigh. "What a mess,"

he says. "I was speaking at a graduation ceremony. Supposed to."

"Your daughter."

"My daughter, yeah. Made it through eighth grade. With honors, actually. My ex was there, of course. And I get the call ten minutes before I'm due at the microphone, prepared to drone on about how the future has yet to be made, and how they'll be making it. Her generation."

"I thought she was in, like, first grade."

"She was, seven years ago. Time flies, Jack. They say life is like a roll of toilet paper—the closer you get to the end, the faster it rolls."

"That's a lovely image, Glenn. What happened to Bing?"

The big trooper's smile is thin enough to have been cut with a scalpel. "You first. Your visit with Jonny Bing. Word for word, or as close as you can get."

"No problem," says Jack, and begins his recitation.

Fifteen minutes later, Tolliver heaves another sigh. "That's it?"

"My best recollection."

"Ace interrogator like you, there's still no clear indication as to who might have killed Professor Keener, or why? Assuming, for the sake of argument, it wasn't your pal Shane."

"It wasn't, and no. Bing seems genuinely puzzled. Convincing on the subject of how the sudden death of his partner might wreck the company and ruin his investment. If he's lying, he's damn good at it. Which he might be, for all I know."

Tolliver studies the back of his meaty hand. "Maybe."

"My gut says the only thing he was holding back concerns Keener's missing kid."

"Holding back what?"

Jack shrugs. "Claimed he never heard of Keener having a child, in or out of wedlock. But he knows something. I'm going to have another go at him."

"No," Tolliver says. "You're not."

"I'm not?"

"Not unless you can commune with the dead."

The news doesn't exactly shock Jack, given the general mood, not to mention the overwhelming response from law enforcement. "Well, that sucks," he says, lightly drumming his well-manicured fingers on the tabletop. "How'd it go down?"

"You know I can't share details of an ongoing investigation."

"Walk me through it, maybe something will pop. Something he said that I couldn't recall at first. I'll share."

Tolliver favors him with a sour look. "You neglected to tell me something, in your exhaustive recollection of the interview?"

"I'm just saying."

The big man considers. "Walk with me," he says.

Lady Luck has had a bath, mostly seawater from the fireboats. Jack can smell the tang of salt, and under that a lingering odor of gasoline and smoke, and something worse than smoke. He's not keen about getting the drips on his shoes—fine leather doesn't like salt—but knows better than to complain as Tolliver stomps through the slop in his highly polished knee-high dress boots, heading along a companionway. They haven't bothered with crime scene tape because the entire yacht is a crime scene.

As the big state cop leads the way, he says, "Surveillance cameras show you boarding this tub at 10:20 a.m., exiting by the same route at 11:10 a.m. Sound about right?"

"Yup."

"Silly question, but was Bing alive when you left him?"

"Not a silly question, and yes, he was. Alive and more or less relaxed. Certainly unaware that something bad was about to happen."

"No security on board, you said. Or staff."

"Yeah, and I thought that was a little odd. But then Jonny Bing is—I mean *was*—more than a little odd. Wealthy enough to be eccentric, I guess. He apologized for the lack of fawning servants—his words—and said the crew had a few days off because the boat would soon be leaving for Bermuda. So, far as I could tell, he was alone. But then he could have had a dozen blondes stashed in his master bedroom, for all I know."

Tolliver glances back. "Or a dozen disco boys."

Jack hazards a raised eyebrow. "Is that the word on Bing?"

"Word is Jonny wasn't particular as to gender. But you got the blond part right, apparently. And it was only one. Maybe he was cutting down."

"So it was a lover's tiff?"

"Nah," Tolliver says, gesturing for Jack to step ahead of him. "Go through that door or hatch or whatever they call it, then turn left."

"Door, I think," says Jack, lifting his cuffs as he steps into about an inch of standing water flecked with suds of chemical foam.

Unlike Jack and Tolliver, the on-site crime team members are wearing white rubber boots and white disposable overalls. They have digital cameras set up on tripods, laser measuring devices, a chemical sniffer, all the toys.

The objects of forensic interest lie on a partially melted bed—a giant round mattress, like something out of an old Hugh Hefner fantasy—set up on a hardwood pedestal. Behind the thronelike bed, the curving wall is mirrored. Narrow, vertical mirrors joined together like some giant diamond. More like cubic zirconia. Because to Jack the whole setup looks cheesy, very unlike the elegant salon where Bing had made him welcome, or the rest of the luxuriously appointed yacht. Maybe the sleaze of the playboy bedroom made it appealing, a retro thing. Different strokes.

Jonny Bing, still recognizable even in sudden, violent death, lies on his side among the pink satin sheets. Pink from the blood that was washed away before it had time to soak in. In the strobe flash of the cameras, the glittery wetness makes him seem almost alive. Almost. Bing's left eye looks wrong.

"Shot to the head took him down," Tolliver explains. "We think small caliber because there's no apparent exit wound. Same with the shot to the heart—no exit. So, a classic double tap. Same deal with the boyfriend, except he got it in the forehead instead of the eye. Small entry wound, no apparent exit. Bullet bounces around, it's like an instant Cuisinart for the brain." The trooper gives Jack a look, almost friendly, like the old days when they were professional colleagues of a sort. "Tell that to Naomi Nantz the next time she dices up sweetmeats, what a bullet does when it rattles around inside a skull."

"She'll appreciate that," Jack says, smiling but not feeling it. Feeling instead the slosh of contaminated water soaking into his Italian leather shoes.

"The precision of this, both vics hit exactly the same way, makes me favor the lone gunman theory."

"Looks that way," Jack agrees.

The second victim, assumed to be the sexual partner because, like Bing, he's naked, tangled in satin sheets, is a Caucasian youth with shoulder-length bleached-blond hair. In life the victim had been lithe and athletic, at least a foot taller than his partner. On the floor a few yards from the giant bed is the real puzzle. Lying on its side like a partially charred log is the fully clothed body of an Asian male. Thirtysomething, is Jack's guess, but he could be off ten years in either direction, on account of the fire damage, or whatever made the man's flesh start to slough off.

"You'll notice the human barbecue has a gun in its hand." The big trooper crouches, pointing. "See the fingers? They look broken to me. We'll know for sure after the autopsy, but the M.E., who hates getting his feet wet just like you, he concurs: fingers busted. Like somebody put the gun in his hand, had to force it."

"Made this guy fire the weapon?"

Tolliver stands up, snorts. "Are you serious? A double, double tap? No extra shots fired? Whoever did this is a genuine marksman, a skilled assassin. Not some frozen corpse with a busted hand."

Jack's eyes are watering from the smell. "Frozen? What are you talking about?"

"This guy here. He's charred on the outside, frozen underneath. M.E. tried for a liver temp, said it was like bumping up against a stone. Pretty neat trick, eh? We're calling him Baked Alaska."

Jack takes a step back, letting his eyes drift over the scene, putting it all together. "Okay. Bing and his buddy are shot in bed. The shooter then drags in a frozen corpse, plants the gun, douses the place with gasoline? That's your theory of the crime? The assassin was creating a particular scenario, or attempting to?"

Tolliver nods approvingly. "Pretty quick for a retired dude. Yeah, and I'll bet my next pulled-pork sandwich that Mr. Baked Alaska will turn out to be connected to one of the local Asian gangs."

"So it's supposed to look like a gang hit that went wrong somehow?"

"Yeah. Might have worked, too, but the genius who set this up didn't know about the fire suppression system on board. He got ignition but no liftoff."

"Surveillance?"

"No cameras in the bedroom, which is a surprise. Wouldn't have surprised me if that little horn-dog Jonny Bing wanted to keep mementos of his conquests, but apparently not. There is a pretty elaborate surveillance system in place elsewhere, covering the hallways, engine room, bridge, decks and so on. The bad boy who did this was smart enough to figure that out, and yanked the hard drive. I'm assuming he got to the surveillance DVR after he killed the victims, but before he attempted to torch the place. So he had a plan. Messed up with the fire part, but he got away undetected. Which is a genuine mystery. And you know how I hate mysteries."

Jack frowns. "Wait. You clocked me on the marina surveillance but not the shooter?"

"Not so far. We're assuming the shooter approached from the water, using the ship as a screen from the marina surveillance cameras, which cover the floating dock system, but obviously can't see through the ship. We're checking any and all surveillance systems all along the bay, from Boston Harbor to Hull, but that will take a while."

Jack has had enough of the smell. He carefully wades out to the companionway, trying to keep his trouser cuffs dry, and failing. "This sucks," he mutters.

"What's the big deal?" Tolliver responds impatiently. "Take your fancy threads to the dry cleaner. Bill it as an expense."

"No, it's not that," Jack says. "I'm just thinking, if I hadn't dropped in on Jonny Bing, he'd probably still be alive."

The big trooper shrugs. "Maybe. Or maybe he was already scheduled for demolition."

"Yeah."

"I'd be curious to know what your boss thinks."

"Me, too," says Jack.

Chapter Seventeen

In the Name of Shane

Kidder has to force himself to drive just below the speed limit. What he wants to do is put the pedal to the metal, open the windows and dry the goo out of his hair. He'd attempted to rinse away the gunk with seawater, once he'd managed to get clear of the marina, but it still feels like he's been basted with a sticky white sauce that makes his skin itch. Some kind of foamy stuff jetting from a system of tiny nozzles he'd never even noticed, and certainly hadn't been notified about.

When it happened he'd been madder than a wet hen—more like psychotic rooster pumped for a cockfight—and his heart had been pounding because he knew the sudden discharge of foam would be triggering a remote fire alarm. So he'd been fleeing the scene from the moment the crap drenched him, and a good thing, too. The local fire trucks were at the marina in less than ten minutes, way ahead of the slow-moving fire tugs, and if the freakin' outboard hadn't started on the first try he'd have been nabbed for sure. But it had started—hurray Yamaha!—and he had managed to ease away from the marina and put a half mile or so between himself and *Lady Luck* before the flashing lights and sirens arrived.

Flooded with the adrenaline thrill of a narrow escape, and of having freshly killed, he eventually worked his way down the busy coastline of Quincy Bay, to the place on shore where he'd left his vehicle, and made his getaway.

Luck: you had to have it in this business. No matter what your skill level—and his own was high—you still needed luck, he knew that in his bones, and so far his luck was holding.

Rather than risk heading north through the city, getting stuck in Boston traffic while under possible pursuit, he'd opted to head west onto good old 128, loop all the way around and back up to the north. Cost him an extra hour of discomfort, longing for a hot soapy shower, while forcing himself to leave it on cruise control, keep to the right-hand lane like a good little citizen.

Finally, back to base without further incident. That's how he'd report it. Target terminated. Keep it simple. The gooksicle had been his own idea and it hadn't worked out, but so what? It would definitely add to the confusion, and that was a good thing. Nothing to apologize for, no excuses that needed making.

The man who calls himself Kidder punches in the code, causing the paneled door of the cedar-shingled garage to lift. Once inside, garage door sealed, he slips out of the vehicle, strips off his soggy clothing and pads barefoot to the shower located in the first-floor exercise room. Six, count 'em, six showerheads, steaming and clean. He luxuriates in the stinging warmth, cleansing away the loathsome goo, using plenty of soap and body lotion. The place may be referred to as a guest cottage, but it has all the amenities. An excellent, if rather small, gym furnished with top-flight equipment, a nicely appointed entertainment center—love that Bose!—a superb kitchen, a casual-at-first-glance-but-really-formal dining room and three upstairs guest suites, each with a distant view of the sea.

Oh yeah, and the basement safe room, disguised for the pleasure of the guests as a "rumpus room," complete with a top-grade billiard table, every kind of game controller, plus bath, bar, kitchenette—even spare beds concealed in the puffy sofas. Very handy and, indeed, the reason why this particular residence had been selected for the operation. Simple enough to swap around the dead-bolt system, clip the phone and alarm lines and make the safe room into a very well-appointed cage. Whenever Kidder has to leave the premises, whether on a particular assignment or just to stretch his legs, he simply puts New Mommy and the Chinese brat into the basement and locks the impregnable door "for their own protection."

As he dries himself, puffing his skin to a healthy pink, he thinks about the present situation, anticipating the inevitability of change. So far the female, who can sometimes be troublesome or mouthy, has acquiesced in the name of Shane, whom she appears to worship on some level that Kidder doesn't get. The big guy was about as infallible as your average pope, from what Kidder can gather, but so far invoking his name has worked, kept her in line, as well as deeply in the dark. Eventually she'll rebel, they always do, and when that happens he'll require further instruction.

Kidder has the answer, when it comes to that.

Chapter Eighteen

Gaba-dabba-doo

Just so you know, Naomi Nantz has a thing about leaving the residence. She's not exactly agoraphobic, so far as I can tell. It's not like she goes all wobbly when she steps out the door, or has a panic attack, nothing like that. But she does so reluctantly, and only for a purpose—a dentist or doctor appointment, for example—and sometimes a few weeks will go by without her leaving these familiar confines at all. If she feels the need for sunshine and fresh air she goes to the solarium and opens a window, or joins me up on the roof deck for a view of the Charles and a little breeze in her face. Rarely does she hit the street while on a case. That's what investigators and operatives are for, to do the legwork, to go out in the world and bring back information she can gnaw on, like a really intelligent bulldog with an interesting bone. A beautiful bulldog with eyes that can bore through the human heart, with all its deviance and deception, seeking the truth.

On the morning after Jonny Bing's murder we're in the breakfast nook, me and Naomi and Jack and Teddy. Naomi in one of her quiet, thinking modes, processing information based on the meager evidence. Most of us—

me, for sure—are more than a little flummoxed by the rapid turn of events. A famous kid finder suspected in the murder of a genius professor with a missing child, a billionaire financier and his bedmate executed, a semi-frozen body left at the scene, what does it all mean? Jack brooding because boss lady is keeping an open mind on the possibility that Shane might be guilty, for reasons yet to be determined. Meanwhile, Mrs. Beasley is fussing over us to relieve the tension. Sensing the gloomy mood, she's trying to tempt us with a rather amazing variation on sourdough French toast, which involves a cast-iron fry pan that she calls a "spider," and a butane torch. Naomi has nodded her approval—she's reading her newspapers, maintaining silence—and Jack and I are on second helpings, but Teddy Boyle has thus far declined, much to Beasley's consternation.

"But you love my sourdough bread," she says, shaking her silver-haired head in consternation. "You love maple syrup—you put syrup on Cheerios! So what's the problem?"

Teddy shrugs and smiles his beatific little grin. Today his hair is newly tinged with a disturbing shade of pink, and he's swapped out his nostril ring for a small gold stud.

"It's nothing personal," he explains to Beasley. "I'm not eating animals today."

"French toast is not an animal."

"Eggs and milk," Teddy points out. "Product of animals, and therefore animal in nature."

Beasley takes her hands out of her apron pockets, looking stunned. "You've gone vegan?"

"Just for today. Cleansing."

"You're cleansing." She considers that, makes some sort of calculation and nods to herself. "Fine. As it so happens, I know a special variation that will work with French toast. No eggs, no milk. No animal product of any kind. Give me ten minutes."

"Wow," Teddy says. "Thanks. I'll have two slices, please."

Nine minutes later Beasley beams as the rail-thin boy scoffs up her syrup-soaked slices in less time than it takes for Naomi to put down her newspaper and say, "No eggs? No milk? How is that possible?"

The question is purely rhetorical, since Beasley will not discuss her trade secrets while a meal is being consumed, if ever. Also, at precisely that moment a small wall-mounted bulb begins to flash, indicating an incoming call on boss lady's private, ultra-secure landline. The one with the number restricted to a chosen few. She takes the call in an alcove off the kitchen—a pantry, really— and returns to us with a gleam in her eyes, and the trace of a smile on her lips.

"Randall Shane," she says. "Dropped off at Mass General E.R. within the last fifteen minutes."

And so it is that Naomi Nantz takes leave of the residence, not at a walk but at a full run. On a good day the hospital is a brisk twenty-minute saunter from the residence, but time is of the essence, so we race to Commonwealth Avenue, cross the mall at a run and hail a taxi going east. Basically we hijacked the Haitian driver, who mistakenly thought he was off duty and idling at the curb, sipping a Starbucks. Naomi, accepting no excuses, declares an emergency and directs him up Storrow Drive to Embankment Road, and around the loop to the Fruit Street entrance. Four minutes, door-to-door, and the shaken driver—instructions having been crisply issued directly into his right ear—accepts a hundred-dollar bill and flees the scene, looking shell-shocked by the experience. The sirens behind us could be from an approaching ambulance, but are more likely the local cops, having been alerted to a yellow taxi briefly hitting ninety in the Back Bay neighborhood.

We're about to enter the E.R. when Jack Delancey screeches to a halt in his big Lincoln, activates his blinking parking lights and joins us.

"Told you I could beat a damn taxicab," he says, straightening his tie as we step through the sliding door.

"But you didn't."

"Close enough," he says. "Who was that on the phone? Who gave you the heads-up?"

"Doesn't matter," Naomi says, avoiding his gaze as she quickens her pace. "We haven't much time. The police will figure it out soon enough."

"The Benefactor," Jack confides to me. "Mr. Big, whoever he is. That's my guess."

Naomi Nantz in full order-issuing mode is a thing to behold. Just as the taxi driver found himself obeying her commands to dart through city traffic, the duty nurse, a hardened soul who looks like she herself could direct battalions without flinching, is soon escorting us to a curtained cubicle, where an E.R. doc is attempting to assess the condition of the huge slab of a man more or less unconscious on the gurney, eyelids fluttering.

So far as I can tell Shane is wearing the same clothes he had on when they kicked in the windows and took him down. His shirt has been opened for examination, revealing his enormous chest and diaphragm. There are no obvious bruises, but who knows what they've done to him inside? His complexion is a sickening shade of gray and his eyes have sunk so deeply into his skull that he looks to have aged a decade, at least. Wherever he's been, whatever has been done to him, it's taken a terrible toll.

"Bastards," Jack growls, his voice catching.

The startled doctor, a blonde, cherub-cheeked female who at first glance appears to be about twelve years old, wants to know what connection we have to the patient.

"Are you the ones who dumped this man at the curb with a note pinned to his shirt?"

Naomi soon sets her straight, without sharing any of the more interesting details. "The patient is our associate. We have reason to believe he was abducted for purposes of interrogation."

"Interrogation?" the young doc shoots back. "More like tortured, from the look of him."

"The note pinned to his shirt," Naomi says. "What did it say?"

At first the young doctor seems determined not to share information but, under Naomi's persuasive gaze, soon changes her mind. "Just three words, one of them nonsense. The first two were 'Randall Shane,' I'm assuming that's his name. I put him into our database, but he's never been admitted here."

"The third word?"

The doc shrugs. "'Gaba,' whatever that means."

"Gaba," I say. "Like baby talk?"

"No," says Naomi, remaining focused on the doctor. "As a matter of fact, 'gaba' explains it. Gamma-aminobutyric acid. If the word had been 'GABA analogue' or 'GABAergic' you'd have understood immediately, as you were intended to."

The young E.R. doc has turned crimson. "Of course! He's been drugged with some sort of barbiturate, or benzodiazepine."

"Possibly both," Naomi suggests. "He was taken down with a very powerful tranquilizer dart, just for starters."

The doc's jaw drops. "What! What the hell is going on here? Who is this guy?"

Before anyone can form a reply, Shane's head lolls to one side and his sunken eyelids open. Instantly, Jack is there, crouching beside the gurney. "Randall? Can you talk? We don't have much time, old friend. Cops are on the way."

Shane gives him a loopy grin and says, "Bah-doo." Working his lips, struggling to form a word.

Jack looks up. "Whatever they drugged him with, it's starting to wear off."

"Anything you can give him?" Naomi asks the doc. "To bring him around quicker?"

The E.R. doc looks deeply offended by the suggestion. "No way. Not without a full assessment. This man needs to be admitted and monitored."

"He may know the location of a missing child," Naomi says, pressing. "A five-year-old boy."

The doc remains adamant. "I can't treat him until I know what he's been drugged with."

"We've established that," Naomi reminds her patiently. "One of the GABAergics."

The doctor shakes her head, crosses her arms defensively. "Because 'gaba' was scrawled on a piece of paper? Not good enough. We need to determine the specific drug. Child or no child, I will not put this patient's life at risk because you want to chat."

"Fine," says Naomi, turning her attention to the man on the gurney. "Mr. Shane? The clock is ticking. Very soon you'll be taken into custody. Do you know where the boy is? Or who took him?"

Still unable to raise his head, or keep his eyes focused,

the big guy is obviously concentrating, devoting all of his energy to the task of making his mouth and tongue function. "Joey," he manages to say. "Joey Keener. Five years old."

"Joey, yes," says Naomi. "Is he alive?"

Shane manages to nod. "Yes," he says. "Alive."

"Where is he? Can you guess? Anything, Shane. Give us something to work with."

He desperately tries to form another word, and then his eyes lose focus and he lapses back into semiconsciousness, totally spent.

Ten seconds later the cops arrive.

Part 2.
Realm of the Righteous

Chapter Nineteen

A Little Kitten Made of Music

More than anything, Joey wants to escape. Not only from the finished basement where he and New Mommy have been banished, and which is like a real house except without windows, but from the inside of his own head. It hurts to think about Mi Ma, his real mommy, because worrying about her puts a painful lump in his throat, makes it hard to breathe. In his short life Joey has often been moved from place to place, had to get used to new rooms and even new caregivers, but in all that time his real mommy was always there. They had never been separated for more than a day or so, and then she would come rushing back and sweep him into her arms, and it was almost worth it, her being away, because it's so wonderful when she comes back. It feels like music bubbling up from everywhere, not just from the keyboard into his earphones, but from the walls and the air and from somewhere deep inside. That's what being happy feels like, and he longs for it. At such times, when she has had to be away, Mi Ma sings for him, whole songs almost perfectly in key—bad notes make him grimace, even when he's trying to be polite—but his mother has a very good voice, almost as true in timbre as the notes emitting from his keyboard, the measured chords and octaves that flow from his small fingertips.

Sometimes the music comes through his fingers in a kind of tickle, like he's touching something soft and alive, a little kitten made of music, and he just keeps stroking the keys without having to think about it. What Mi Ma calls "Joey music," because it belongs to him. Other times, like today, he looks at notes on paper and the music enters through his eyes and comes out through his hands, again without him having to think about it very much, but the experience is very different. As if he's tuning to a different channel inside his head, the channel where Mozart is always playing. Joey loves the way the numbers and key signatures of the early Mozart sonatas flow so perfectly, bringing themselves to life, each note exactly the right note, all bubbling up into a stream of living music. Sonata no. 1 in C Major, Sonata no. 2 in F Major and then of course the Third Sonata in B-flat Major. Perfect. It could be no other way, and the rightness of it calms him.

When it comes to reading words on a page, Joey's skills are rudimentary at best. In that respect he's a typical five-year-old. He knows the alphabet but has trouble sounding out the words, which don't always make sense. Sometimes two words together sound unpleasantly dissonant and he hates to look at them. Not like when he reads musical notation, which always makes sense, and which he doesn't have to think about or struggle over. He can hear the music when he sees the notes, and it is a simple matter to press the correct keys in the correct order to let the music out. Except of course when his fingers make a mistake. Which is why he can sometimes lose himself in playing the same piece over and over, until his fingers learn how to do it on their own, because he hates to make unpleasant sounds happen.

Joey escapes into the soothing repetition. It takes him to a place where nothing exists but the music and his hands and the notes resonating in his earphones. Tuning out the world around him, easing his anxiety. Letting him forget, for a while, how much he misses his real mommy and how much the big man scares him, and how more than anything he wants to go home so Mi Ma can sing to him.

He escapes so completely into the music that he never notices New Mommy searching along the walls of the basement, looking for a way out, should an escape become necessary, one eye on the padlocked door, fearful that Kidder may return.

Chapter Twenty

Black Hole

The fear is deep, abiding and specific. He fears that part of his brain has been removed, or in some other way destroyed. That's the only rational explanation for the huge hole in his memory, and the cool black nothingness from which he has finally emerged, alive but damaged. It's not like the memories are buried somewhere deep inside his mind, submerged by trauma. They're simply gone. Removed.

Memories of something bad, he concludes, something terrible, because his left wrist is chained to the hospital bed and there's a uniformed cop guarding the door, and because the woman attending him seems fearful, as if he might lunge at her, take a bite.

"Mr. Shane? Randall Shane? I'm Dr. Gallagher. You've been admitted to Massachusetts General Hospital. I'm sorry about the handcuffs, but they insisted."

"Killer," he says, the word rumbling from the hollow in his throat.

"Excuse me?" the pretty doctor says, flinching.

He rattles the cuff. "Who did I kill?"

"I, um, don't know anything about your legal situation, Mr. Shane. All I know is, you're under my care, and will remain here until I'm satisfied it's medically safe for you to be released. You've been rather badly beaten. It wasn't obvious when you were first admitted, but your body is massed with bruises. Most of the fingers on your right hand were dislocated, and the ligaments have been badly strained."

Shane glances at his right hand. Noticing the elaborate splint must trigger something, because now it hurts like hell.

"The physical bruising is actually the least of it," the pretty young doctor continues. "Bruises heal. My real concern is neurological damage from the drugs. We know you were given a massive dose of benzodiazepine, enough to black out an elephant, frankly. You must have been on a drip for hours, or possibly even days. And there's evidence of other psychotropic drugs, of a type we've not been able to identity. We do know they were quite powerful, because there's been evidence of dementia."

"I'm demented," he says, not the least surprised.

"You seem to be coming out of it, slowly," she assures him. "It will be some time before we can assess whether there's been any long-term damage."

Shane looks at her, carefully forming his words before letting them go. "They removed part of my brain," he says, confiding.

She smiles. "So you've been saying ever since you regained consciousness. Let me assure you once again: there's absolutely no evidence of surgery. None. No such surgery took place. The MRI revealed perfectly normal brain mass. No lesions, no sign of intrusion. Whatever loss you're feeling, Mr. Shane, is a result of the drugs that were administered."

"Drill," he insists, the memory bursting. "They drilled a hole in my head."

The sound of the drill bit vibrating through his skull, rattling his eyes in their sockets. Screeching as it hits bone.

But the pretty doctor says, "No. No. Nothing like that happened. Perhaps it was suggested to you, when you were under the influence of the benzodiazepine. Maybe they used the sound of a drill to frighten you. But I assure you, no holes have been drilled in your skull. You're perfectly intact. The only damage that concerns me is from the drugs themselves, and there's simply no way of knowing about long-term neurological effects— you might well make a complete recovery. Although it's doubtful you'll regain the short-term memory of whatever transpired. You've lost a few days, Mr. Shane. They're gone. You'll just have to accept that."

"Bastards."

"Whoever did this to you, yes."

"Sleepy."

"You've been given a mild sedative. Nothing like the powerful hypnotics you were given, but it will help with the anxiety."

"No," he says, struggling to rise. "The boy! The boy!"

He sleeps.

"Hey, Shane. That's what they call you right? Just plain Shane? I'm your attorney. And don't you worry, we're going to get 'em."

"What?" he asks, mouth dry.

Strange, but he doesn't remember waking up. Another young woman. Pixie with big eyes. Not like the doctor, who has freckles, chubby cheeks and seems to be afraid of him. This one isn't afraid.

"The bad guys," the pixie says. "Identity as yet unknown. We'll find 'em, though. Naomi Nantz is on the case, and she always gets her man, ha-ha. Seriously, she does. So, do you remember anything at all?"

"Nothing there to remember. Black hole. Who you?"

"Sorry. Dane Porter. I'm the only one allowed to talk with you, other than your physician."

"Lawyer."

"Correct. I'm representing you. This murder beef is bull, we know that much. A bad frame job, way over the top. I've been on the horn with Tommy Costello, he's the Middlesex D.A., about what kind of guy you are, a genuine hero, and how there's no way you shot your client, not a possibility, did not happen. He'll come around. Leave that to me. Until then, the important thing is to find the kid, right? The little boy? Your client's missing child? Joey? That's the boy's name, correct?"

Shane feels as if a small, dim light has been turned on, in the darkness inside his head. "Little Joey, yes. Call his father, please. Very important." He searches, is astonished to find the name. "Joseph Keener," he exclaims. "Professor, MIT."

The pixie winces. "Sorry. Professor Keener was killed in his home. You found the body. I'm sorry, I assumed you remembered that much."

"I found the body?"

"Uh-huh. Called 911 to report it, then arranged to meet your buddy Jack Delancey. He brought you to see Naomi Nantz. But before you had a chance to tell us much about the case, a team of badass cowboys kicked in the windows, put you down, took you away."

"Cowboys?"

"Figure of speech. More like a covert special-ops

team. They had you for three days. You were tortured, drugged, then dumped at this hospital."

"Wrecked my brain. Stole my memories."

"Yeah, that really sucks, I'm sure," she says kindly. "We're hoping you get it back. The memories. Not the torture memories, it might best if you forgot that part entirely. But anything you know about the boy. Where he might be. Who might be holding him. And for that matter what happened to his mother."

"Here," Shane says instantly, the word firing like a bullet from a waking synapse in his brain. "Joey is here."

"Oh my God," the pixie says. "You remembered something! The boy is here? Where, exactly? Do you know?"

Shane shakes his head, trying to clear away the tendrils of emptiness. "Bridge," he says suddenly. "Crossing Harvard Bridge. Video."

The pixie looms closer, her eyes as large as moons. "Let me get this: you saw a video recording of Joey Keener crossing Harvard Bridge?"

"Yes."

"By himself?"

"Can't remember. No, somebody else was there."

"His mother?"

"Can't remember. No, not his mother."

"Where did you see this video? Was it part of a ransom demand?"

Shane grits his teeth, concentrates. Nothing. Wherever it came from, the memory has retreated.

"Gone," he says, and collapses back on his pillow.

Somebody groans in pain. Can't be the pretty pixie, voice too deep. Then the darkness reaches up, pulls him down.

He doesn't fight it.

Chapter Twenty-One

8-Ballers

"That's huge," Naomi says. "Harvard Bridge. That puts Joey right in the middle of the MIT campus, not far from the professor's residence."

"Maybe he was going the other way," Teddy points out. "From Cambridge to Boston. Like running away."

"A possibility," boss lady concedes. "Jack? Any thoughts?"

"Shane might well be referring to a video ransom note, as Dane suggests. Sent to the father, I'm assuming. We've got your son, close enough for you to reach out and touch. Here's proof, now pay up or else. Or give us the secret, or whatever they're after. Whoever *they* are."

"There were no cameras or computers found at the residence," Naomi points out. "No DVDs. Not even a cell phone. Nothing to store a video file."

"We already knew the place was wiped clean," Jack responds, his arms folded.

We're in the command center, convening. More like kibitzing, firing out ideas, hoping something will stick. Everybody is pumped. Hope is alive, feeding us energy.

"Teddy? Find out if there are traffic cams on Harvard

Bridge. If so, we need access to any recordings within, say, a two-week time frame."

Naomi leans back from her desk. Her eyes have that faraway look that means she's processing information. We all wait. Thirty seconds pass. A very long half minute. I'm studying my nails—what to do about the cuticles?—when she snaps back, totally in the moment, and goes, "What about Shane? He started out as a computer geek, right? Therefore he would have had a laptop, at the very least. Was it recovered at his motel room by the state police?"

"If so, they're not sharing," Jack says thoughtfully. "But you're right, he'd have had a laptop. Absolutely."

"So that's another question that needs answering: where is Shane's laptop?"

"Wait," says Jack, sitting up even straighter. "Damn! He has an iPhone. That's how he called me. Not on the professor's landline, because his name popped up like it always does, and when I met him in Kendall Square he had the iPhone in his hand, slipped it into his pocket."

Naomi considers, then pronounces, "Forget the phone. His assailants will have seized that, and accessed whatever it may or may not contain. But the laptop is interesting. Obviously he didn't have it with him when he came to us. That leaves three possibilities. One: he left it in his motel room, and it has been seized and taken into evidence by law enforcement. Two: he secreted it somewhere in his vehicle, which has been impounded and, we assume, thoroughly searched by Cambridge felony detectives. Three: he hid it elsewhere."

Jack is already shaking his head. "No way he left it in his ride. He knew the car would be impounded at the scene. He assumed the vehicle was compromised because his gun had been taken. That's why he abandoned the car and proceeded on foot to Kendall Square to meet me."

"He told you that, specifically?"

"Didn't have to. That's what I would have done. The missing gun told him everything. From that moment, Shane knew he was in the middle of a frame. He couldn't risk driving the car—for all he knew, it had already been tagged with a GPS tracker."

"Again, he discussed this with you?"

"No discussion required. It's an understood thing."

"So you and Shane have, what, a psychic connection?"

Another man might have been insulted by the caustic comment, but Jack, knowing boss lady's methods, shrugs it off. "We received the same training. To a certain extent, in operative terms, we think alike."

"Operative terms."

"Correct."

"Acknowledged," she says, satisfied. "Good point. Find out if the Cambridge cops found a tracking device in his car."

"Done," says Jack. He opens his cell and steps out of the room.

Naomi swivels in her chair. "Teddy? Any joy on the traffic cams?"

Teddy looks up from the screen, grimaces. "Nope. None on Harvard Bridge. There may be MIT security cameras somewhere in the area, farther up Mass Ave. If so, they won't be advertised. I'm looking."

The swiveling chair turns in my direction. "Alice? Are you up for another visit across the river?"

Silly question.

The Massachusetts Institute of Technology spans a mile or so of Cambridge frontage on the Charles River, facing Boston and the world. *Love that dirty water,* as they used to sing. And still do in certain Boston bars at closing time. Or so I've heard. I'm not a closing-time kind of girl, for the most part. Not surprisingly my ex-husband, the con man, he knew all the words to "Dirty Water" so he could croon along with the inebriated locals, even though his knowledge of the city, as I now understand, came mostly from old reruns of *Cheers*.

Enough about my ex. He can't even really be my ex if he was still married to the last three wives he bamboozled, right? They didn't call him Wedding Willy for nothing. Okay, so I'll shut up about Mr. Adorable, whatever his real name is. May he rot in hell, or Toronto, or wherever they've got him under lock and key.

I'm over him. Totally.

It being a fair kind of late-spring day—blue skies, warm breezes wafting the perfume of steaming asphalt— I retrieve my bike from the garage, don the dorky helmet and pedal across the river on my new Trek Soho, the urban model with the cool carbon belt instead of a chain. Knowing full well that to impress a typical MIT undergraduate I'd have to be riding a unicycle on top of a skateboard while juggling spheres of plutonium. No, not common old plutonium, that's so yesterday—make it antimatter. Anything less and a fully adult female becomes invisible to college kids, assuming she's more or less fully clothed and hasn't had humungous breast implants recently. Not that it matters—I'm not here for the undergrads, and a little invisibility might be useful, even if it doesn't exactly keep the ego properly inflated.

The quarry, courtesy of a boss lady brain fart—excuse me, sudden inspiration—is the faculty lounge in the Department of Physics. Not as easy as it sounds, because it turns out the physics department is spread all over the campus, and the physics professors, all hundred and twenty of them, find all sorts of places to consort with each other. Like extremely intelligent cockroaches, as one undergraduate blogger put it. Charming thought. I envision a bunch of geeky dudes with unbrushed mandibles, chittering away as they consume, cups and all, Styrofoam containers of heavily sugared coffee. The same blogger (he calls himself "Gregor," by the way, and yes, I got it) refers to the physics faculty as "8-Ballers" because the courses all begin with that number. 8.01 being the introductory course, 8.04 being Quantum Physics and so on.

8-Ballers. Sounds sort of cute. In contrast to the hollow-eyed summer-semester students who stumble around campus fueled by energy drinks, swelling their talented brains with ever more information. None of those spotted in the halls of physics actually have white tape wrapped around the stems of their glasses, clichéd geek style, but pocket protectors are much in evidence—almost, it seems, as an act of defiance, or even a badge of honor. A fair description of the average complexion would have to include the word *pasty,* and that applies to the dark-skinned students as well as the light. Every last one of them looks like she or he could use a day at the beach. I never do find a faculty lounge—so much for boss lady's big idea—but instead eventually stumble upon a cubicle corral of administrative assistants, one of whom instantly bursts into tears when I ask if any of them knew Professor Keener.

"Oh my God, it's so, so sad," she says, sniffing. "Are you a friend?"

"Yes," I tell her, and then amend, "Well, not exactly, but I have good intentions."

The weeper, a slightly heavy woman of forty or so,

wears large thick-lensed glasses that magnify her watery blue eyes, distorting what would otherwise be an attractive, lightly freckled face. The fact that she's weeping makes me like her instantly—she's the first to exhibit an openly emotional reaction to the professor's violent death. Without saying another word—her cubicle mates are eyeballing the stranger who started the waterworks—she gets up from her desk and indicates that I should follow out into a foyer area that serves as a waiting room. No windows, pale walls, the only decoration a series of neatly framed black-and-white high-speed photographs of a bullet piercing a textbook, finally emerging with a little puff of exploded paper. Is shooting books an MIT thing? Somehow that seems unlikely. Whatever, it's not the mystery I'm here to solve.

The weeper plops heavily onto a couch, opens her purse and removes a tissue, using it to wipe her delicate, upturned nose. She sniffs, takes a deep breath and then in a surprisingly strong voice demands, "What do you mean, 'good intentions'?"

The couch being the only seat in the little room, I perch on the opposite end, so as not to crowd her. "We're trying to locate his little boy. He's missing."

"Joey," she says, almost defiantly. "His name is Joey."

"So you know about him?" I say, dumbfounded.

"Who are you, exactly?" she wants to know, suddenly guarded.

"My name is Alice Crane. I work for a private investigator."

"So you're like a detective?"

I shake my head ruefully. "More like a secretary running an errand. My boss wants to know if Professor Keener's colleagues are aware that he has a child. Our impression was that he'd been keeping it a secret, for reasons yet to be determined. But the fact that you know about Joey, that pretty much changes everything. I can't wait to tell boss lady she's wrong."

The guarded look has turned suspicious. "Maybe you better show me some ID."

I open my wallet, hand her my driver's license.

"This could be fake."

"Could be, but it's not. We have reason to believe Joey is missing. Would you know anything about that?"

"You think I'd kidnap a little boy?"

"No, of course not. By the way, you know my name is Alice," I say. "What's yours?"

She thinks about not telling me, decides against it. "Clare," she says, as if daring me to contradict her.

"You seem to be angry, Clare. I'm sorry if I made you feel that way. I'm just trying to help my boss find a missing child."

"Not angry," she says, dropping her voice to barely a whisper. "Afraid."

"Afraid of me?" I say, incredulous.

"Maybe. If you're one of them."

"I'm sorry," I say. "One of *who?*"

"One of Professor Keener's enemies."

Clare crosses her plump little arms, looking brave and afraid and defiant, all at once. And then she tells me, bit by bit, the most amazing tale.

"A few months after founding QuantaGate, Joseph met a beautiful Chinese woman at a party hosted by Jonny Bing, on his big yacht. He didn't want to go—Joseph wasn't exactly a party animal—but Bing insisted he make an appearance, it was important to the company. Anyhow, she was there at the party. Ming-Mei. I don't know if that's a stage name or what, but she claimed to be a singer and actress in Hong Kong. Didn't speak

English, so Jonny Bing acted as translator. Very attractive, obviously. Ming-Mei, I mean. After a few days she returned to Hong Kong, and then a week or so later, with the help of an English-speaking friend, she contacted Joseph by email. Result, she returns to Boston—I happened to know that Joseph paid for her ticket—and he leased her an apartment in Chinatown. He thought she'd be more comfortable around Cantonese speakers, although he insisted that she take English lessons, with an eye toward applying for citizenship. I know this because Joseph asked me to find her a tutor."

"So it was a romantic involvement."

Clare shrugged. "I'm not sure Joseph really understood romance, but for sure he was under her spell. A real manipulator, that one."

"So you got to know her?"

She shakes her head. "Only from what Joseph told me. He wanted to marry Ming-Mei, and help her establish a career in America, but she claimed to already be married to a man who had abandoned her and that she had some difficulty obtaining a divorce. Joseph believed her, but I didn't. You understand about him, right? His problem?"

"There was some allusion to Asperger's syndrome."

"Yeah, well, the poor man could have been a poster boy for high-achieving autistics. He knew everything there is to know about quantum physics, but nothing about people in general, and certainly less than nothing about women. My opinion, in her real life Ming-Mei might have been an escort or prostitute. But that's just a guess, from the way she acted. At the very least she's a gold digger. She very conveniently got pregnant within a few months of arriving in Boston."

"How did Professor Keener react to that?"

"Hard to tell—you'd have to have known him to know

how hard—but I think he was pleased in that he assumed it meant Ming-Mei would marry him. Oddly enough—although not odd for Joseph—he didn't assume they would actually live together when married. At one point he was shopping for another home in his neighborhood, a house that would be for Ming-Mei and the baby. He was quite specific about the impossibility of sharing a house with anyone, even the mother of his child."

"Because of his Asperger's."

Clare shrugs. "Or his shyness, or his being a genius, or whatever. Despite what was obvious to me and to most people who knew him, Joseph didn't believe he had Asperger's. He always said it was just that he preferred to be alone most of the time."

"The baby, Clare. Where was he born?"

She shrugs. "The Cambridge Birthing Center. And no, Joseph didn't attend. I could have told her that—he found the whole idea of the actual birth process very icky."

Keener hadn't attended the birth of his son. Assuming Ming-Mei hadn't wanted to name him as the father for some reason, that would explain why his name was never associated with the boy in the official birth records.

"So did he buy her that house nearby?"

"Not then, no. A month or so after the baby was born she returned to Hong Kong so that relatives could help her care for the infant. At least that was her story. And the odd thing is, Joseph wasn't as upset as you might expect. He was freaked out whenever baby Joey cried or soiled his diaper, and seemed to be satisfied with video versions."

"The video version?" I say, thinking of what Shane had mentioned.

"Clips attached to his email. Typical new-mother stuff. The baby eating, the baby cooing and so on."

"Which he shared with you."

Clare's look tells me I'll never understand her relationship to the professor and I should probably quit trying. "He'd put them up on his computer screen and then leave his office while I watched. Which was typical of Joseph. He wanted to share but he didn't want to be there when it happened."

"If he did have something like Asperger's, he might well have found loud noises intolerable," I point out. "A baby's cry can be very loud. Very...disturbing."

Clare concedes the point. Joseph did indeed find the baby's crying quite difficult to handle, and he remained content with being a video dad for the first year or so.

"He never visited Hong Kong?"

She shakes her head. "Not then, no. And when Joey was a year old Ming-Mei came back and set up house in an Arlington condo. I helped Joseph pick it out—you won't be surprised to hear he couldn't stand dealing with the real estate people. He gave her that condo, too. He insisted that the title be in her name."

"You really don't like her," I say.

"That phony bitch?" Clare crosses her plump, freckled arms. "Why would I?"

Chapter Twenty-Two

Do Tell

All of which I repeat to Naomi. "My opinion, she loved the guy," I add.

Naomi leans back in her seat at the command center, tents her fingers. "Nothing about the man sounds particularly lovable."

"Since when has that stopped anyone of the female persuasion? Or the male, for that matter? Okay, think of her as an office wife. There's no doubt Professor Keener relied on Clare, and unless she's an amazing liar, he confided in her. Told her things he apparently told no one else."

"Clare Jeanne O'Malley," Naomi says, sounding skeptical. "Teddy's running a background as we speak."

"I'll bet you a box of sugar donuts she comes up clean."

"I don't eat sugar donuts," she says with a shudder.

"No, but I do."

"So, what happened next, did they ever move in together?"

"Well, according to Clare, things are peachy for a couple of years. The professor has his house in Cambridge. Ming-Mei and the baby have their place in Arlington. Clare has the impression he rarely if ever visited them there, that by arrangement they visited him. This was apparently at Ming-Mei's insistence. She ran the show. The professor danced to her tune, according to Clare, who thought at the time that Ming-Mei was trying to get him used to having people in his house. Sort of preparing the ground so she could eventually move in, or persuade him to buy a much bigger and grander house where they'd all live together. Which he was resisting. Professor Keener liked things just the way they were. He may have danced to the lady's tune, but he was also very stubborn. Liked things distant but close. Again, Clare's impression, and her words, 'distant but close.' Recall she never actually met Ming-Mei, and got this in bits and pieces from a man who wasn't exactly a great communicator. So her version is very one-sided."

"Understood."

"My impression: some of his strangeness rubbed off on her. Clare, I mean. Anyhow, she convinced herself, Clare again, that the hot romance aspect had cooled once Ming-Mei was pregnant, and over the years the relationship evolved into something else entirely. Keener still wanted to marry her, but only to legitimize the boy. Maybe that was Clare's wishful thinking, maybe not. But she was very definite about what happened next.

"When Joey was about three, Ming-Mei insisted, out of the blue, that she and the boy needed to visit her family in Hong Kong, right away. This was fine with the professor—naturally he financed the trip, had Clare arrange for last-minute first-class tickets. She distinctly recalls the airline, Cathay Pacific, and the price, a little over fourteen thousand, round-trip. Clare was outraged on his behalf—what was wrong with business class, why did she have to fly first?—but the professor didn't bat an eye. So off they go to Hong Kong, mother and son, but the thing is, they never return. The ticket is open—one reason it was so pricey—and the visit, which was supposed to be for a few weeks, stretched into months. The professor started getting antsy—there had been no emailed video clips to amuse him during this interval—and six months into the separation, he flew to Hong Kong intending, or so he told Clare, to persuade Ming-Mei to return.

"The visit did not go well. Clare doesn't know the details—he clammed up even more than usual—but when he got back he was so upset that he canceled his lectures and refused to leave his house for a couple of weeks—Clare had to have his work messengered back and forth. Keener had returned a changed man, more difficult than ever, and started spending more and more time at his lab at QuantaGate. As a consequence, Clare saw less and less of him, and can only guess at what was really going on. Nothing good, was her conclusion. She surmised the breakup had been final—maybe there was another man, maybe not, Clare couldn't tell—and Ming-Mei was making it difficult for him to see Joey, or even to communicate with the boy. Then, about a year after Ming-Mei returned to Hong Kong, one of her relatives—Clare thinks it was an aunt—called the professor with devastating news. Joey had been kidnapped. Snatched from an upscale mall while Ming-Mei shopped, gone in an instant when she looked away. The aunt and everybody else in the family—and the local police, too, apparently—assumed the boy had been stolen by one of the mainland gangs that procure replacement kids for parents who lost children in the earthquake."

"So the boy has been missing for more than a year."

"Apparently, yes. Immediately on hearing the news

Professor Keener took a leave of absence, went to Hong Kong and from there to the mainland to search for the boy. He was gone for two months—took medical leave with MIT's permission—and returned broken inside. Clare described him as 'hollowed out.' The experience would have been difficult for a normal person—for him having to deal with strangers was torture. He had bribed police in Hong Kong, hired private investigators in Beijing, pleaded with government officials, all to no avail. He came back to Cambridge convinced he would never see Joey again. Clare tried to get through to him, suggested grief counseling and so on, but he refused help and threw himself into his work. Clare says he began spending about eighty percent of his time at Quanta-Gate, often sleeping over in his lab. And showing up on campus only when it was absolutely necessary."

"You don't recover from a thing like that."

"Right," I agree. "But there's a strange kind of twist. For the first time, the professor alluded to his distrust of Ming-Mei. Apparently he suspected that she may have been involved in the kidnapping of her own child. Clare never liked the woman, but she was dismissive of the idea—the woman she'd seen in all those video clips had clearly loved the boy. She said the professor never could figure people out, that he had no ability to read faces. He was 'easy to fool and got people wrong,' that's how she put it. Plus, he'd become increasingly paranoid. Clare got the impression that he believed he was being spied on."

"Oh? Now, that's interesting," Naomi says. "Spied on by who?"

"Clare didn't know, and she thinks he didn't know, not really, although he complained about his own security guards poking around. That's how she put it, 'poking around.'"

"At the university? No, unlikely," she says, correcting herself. "At his company."

"Correct. QuantaGate."

"Fascinating."

"Thought you'd like it. But there's more. Another twist. Ten days before he was killed, Keener took Clare aside. Everything had changed yet again, his whole demeanor. He had suddenly become convinced that he'd been 'wrong about everything.' Clare's words. She'd never seen him so agitated or excited. And the weird thing was, he was happy. No, happy is wrong—her impression was that he was 'filled with hope,' which isn't the same thing as happy, necessarily. I asked, did he tell her why he was suddenly hopeful, and she said no, not exactly, but her gut told her it had something to do with Joey—what else could it be? He did tell her that 'someone was going to help,' and that it would 'soon be over.' Clare had no idea who or what he was referring to, but I'm assuming that the 'someone' was Randall Shane."

Naomi nods. "Makes sense. That's about when Shane came into the picture."

"That was their final conversation, and his last visit to his campus office. Clare texted him various messages about physics department business, but he never responded. He was either in the lab at QuantaGate, or home."

"We can't know his location for a certainty, and we shouldn't presume."

"True. We have nine days unaccounted for. For all we know he could have been in Paris or London or Hong Kong. But somehow I doubt it. He was waiting for his son to be returned."

"When Shane recovers, we'll have a much better idea of the timeline."

"*If* he recovers."

"Yes. If."

Silence, while we think about that and what it might mean, both for Randall Shane and the missing boy.

"One thing that bothers me," I say. "Why would anybody shoot a textbook and put pictures of it on the wall, in a place of learning?"

Naomi smiles. Understanding that this is my gift, a chance to dazzle and impress me with her amazing mind and memory. She doesn't fail.

"Harold Edgerton, the inventor of the stroboscopic flashbulb," she says, not missing a beat. "Born 1903, died 1990. Famous for his amazing stop-action photographs, taken in his lab at MIT. A droplet of milk that looks like a miniature crown, captured in a microsecond. A bullet exploding through an apple, that's his most famous shot. Doc Edgerton loved his bullets, loved to stop them in time."

"Too bad he isn't still around," I say, musing. "We could use a guy who can stop bullets."

Chapter Twenty-Three

Rumors of Interest

Dane Porter has excellent thumbs, and if there is ever to be a contest for dexterous and speedy texting, she feels confident that she'd win. Her client, Randall Shane, is conked out for the moment, and in any event isn't likely to complain if she parks her butt on the windowsill of his private—and very secure—room and brings her Black-Berry up to date. Legal matters, social engagements and enough gossip to fuel a reality show, if only they knew. Which they probably do, given that her list of correspondents includes a number of media-savvy individuals otherwise known as celebrities.

She's bouncing flirts off an old girlfriend when a tall, broad-shouldered woman ducks in, having flashed an ID at the police officer stationed just outside the door.

"Monica?"

The assistant director ignores her greeting, heads straight for the patient. Right, Dane thinks, old pals, possibly lovers. Bevins touches Randall Shane's hand, cupping it gently in both her own, but the big guy remains unconscious, submerged in deep sleep.

Dane remains perched on the windowsill, not wanting to intrude, but not wanting to disturb the moment by leaving, either. And when the attending physician enters to offer a consult, and Dane makes her move to exit, Bevins locks eyes with her, indicates that she should stay.

Three minutes later, the doctor having slipped away, Monica Bevins picks up a chair in one hand, quietly positions it next to the windowsill and sinks her long and large frame onto the seat with a sigh.

"I was hoping you'd be here," the big woman says, her voice barely above a whisper. "We need to talk."

Dane is a bit surprised by the opening gambit, but then she gets it. "Assistant Director Bevins, you know I can't disclose anything the suspect may have said to me in confidence. Lawyer/client privilege."

If it's possible to snort quietly, that's what the FBI agent does. "Lawyers," she says, wrinkling her nose. "I'm here as a friend, you idiot. Not to build a case against a man I love like a brother. Give me a freakin' break."

"Sorry. My mistake."

Bevins sighs, glances at the man in the bed, her eyes moist. "My God, look at him," she says. "I bet he hasn't slept that good, or that deeply, since the accident. You know about that, of course."

"His wife and daughter. Yes."

Bevins nods. "The doc says what he's doing, he's catching up. That whatever was done to him, it involved keeping him awake in a heavily drugged state for days. That, combined with his existing sleep disorder, may have deeply affected his memory."

Dane checks to make sure the police officer remains on the far side of the open door, unable to overhear their whispered conversation. That was part of the deal, along with the handcuff to the bed rail, that the door would have to remain open, to prevent what the custody detec-

tives called "any funny stuff." There's the usual ambient
noise of a hospital, plus the urban symphony of perpetual
construction—jackhammers rattling in the distance—
and the hiss and moan of traffic on Storrow Drive. Dane
concludes that as long as they keep it low, there's no way
they can be overheard.

"He remembers that Joey is alive," Dane confides.
"The professor's missing son."

Bevins instantly perks up. "Location?"

"Unknown. But Joey was spotted in the vicinity." She
explains that in a moment of apparent lucidity, Shane
recalled having seen a video of Joey taken on a bridge
crossing the Charles River.

"A ransom clip?"

"Possibly. He didn't say. That was earlier today, we're
trying to run it down."

"And you've shared this information with who?"

Dane shrugs. "With my boss."

"Not with the authorities?"

Dane gives her a level look. "It was the 'authorities'
who did this to him. Look, he's been interrogated for
seventy-two hours straight and then discarded. The 'authorities,' which happen to include you, have already
been alerted to the possibility of a kidnapped child. We
informed the Boston cops, the Cambridge cops and the
local field office of the FBI, as I'm sure you know. The
reaction? Professor Keener didn't have a child, so how
could a kid that doesn't exist be missing or abducted?"

Bevins's smile is grim, acknowledging the truth of
what Dane is saying.

"Mostly I didn't want a goon squad of macho detectives in here interrogating him yet again. The poor guy
already thinks somebody removed part of his brain."

Bevins winces. "Dr. Gallagher mentioned that that will pass."

"Let's hope she's right. Meantime, Naomi Nantz is on the case. No small thing."

"And you think having your boss in the hunt, that's better than any of these 'authorities' you so clearly mistrust?"

"Absolutely. The local cops have already decided he's a stone killer and your FBI colleagues in the Boston office have yet to respond to our inquiries. We don't expect them to. The Bureau never shares, not with civilians."

Bevins glances at the open doorway again, her eyes calculating. "I'm about to share, but it can't have come from me, do you understand? At this point I can't be seen conferring with a private investigator. Which is why I was hoping to catch you here at the hospital. I'm logged as visiting a sick friend, period."

"Understood."

The agent takes a breath, hesitates.

"Naomi is famous for her discretion," Dane assures her. "You must know that."

"Yeah," Bevins says. "But what about you?"

"I'd pretend to be insulted but, really, what's the point?"

"Okay, fine. If you work for Nantz you must be okay. Here's the deal. When I spoke to you in Washington, I was under the impression that the Bureau never had Professor Keener on its radar, and that we certainly had nothing to do with Shane's rendition, if that's what it was. The latter is still true, but I was mistaken about Keener. He's been a subject of interest."

Instantly, Dane focuses. "In what way a subject of interest?"

"An anonymous memo came through Homeland, alerting the Bureau to the fact that Keener, whose company is apparently involved in top-secret research, had made at least two unexplained visits to China. The inference being, he might be passing information to Chinese intelligence agents."

"And was he?"

Bevins shrugs her wide shoulders. "I have no way of knowing. The Bureau did due diligence, concluded the subject had no contact with foreign agents. He'd been seen conversing with quite a number of Chinese people—not exactly surprising if you're visiting China—but none were identified as agents of the Chinese government. Therefore no evidence that he was passing secrets, either in China or here in the U.S., and therefore no further action was warranted. That information was bounced back to Homeland, as required, and there it stayed, with access restricted to the highest levels."

"So the professor was no longer under surveillance?"

"Not by the Bureau, no. It's still within FBI purview to take the lead in espionage cases, but in the real world, post-911, and with the exception of the odd batch of Russians infiltrating the suburbs, the emphasis has been on counterterrorism, not spy catching. We're focused on the guy with the bomb strapped to his underwear, not the scientist with the laptop full of data. That's just how it is."

"So the Bureau isn't interested, but others might be. Are you saying Professor Keener was under investigation by another agency? Can you be more specific?"

Bevins shakes her head. "Sorry, no. Can't, because I don't know for sure. Just a rumor of interest, you might call it. Persistent questions about Keener's connections to China—it was known that he had a Chinese girlfriend—

but no actual evidence to warrant FBI involvement. Somebody in the community didn't trust him, that's for sure."

"This 'rumor of interest,' did it mention the boy?"

Monica Bevins looks down, studying her large but somehow elegantly shaped hands. Elegant but for the fact that some of her nails are chewed to the quick. "There was a mention, yes, in the context of family vulnerabilities. It was noted that agents of the People's Liberation Army are known to intimidate their targets by making threats, usually very vague, about the well-being of family members who still reside in China."

"That's it? No mention that Joey Keener was actually missing?"

Bevins shakes her head. "The circulated memo was a simple series of questions, the point of which was to stimulate an active response from interested agencies. Why had Professor Keener frequently emailed an address in Hong Kong? Why did he go there? What was he doing in mainland China? Who did he meet there? Was the mother of his illegitimate child an agent of the PLA? Was the child being used as leverage? Like that."

"And you have no idea who circulated this memo?"

"I can guess, but sharing the specific source would be a felony, and I can't go there, not even for Naomi Nantz."

"Not even for Randall Shane?"

Bevins's cold glare makes Dane feel like she's been drenched by a bucket of ice water. "The Bureau looks out for its own," the big woman says, hotly. "We're now fully involved. There's an FBI alert out for the missing child, as of this morning. That's all you need to know."

Before the young lawyer can apologize—testing and probing, that's her job, nothing personal—the patient groans from his hospital bed. They both turn to see Shane attempting to sit up.

"Monica!" he cries in a ragged whisper.

A moment later the two old friends are embracing, faces wet with tears, and this time Dane Porter follows her best instincts and steps out of the room for a few minutes. Texting quietly as she goes.

Chapter Twenty-Four

The Bogie Man Says Boo

He always carries his own bag. No cart, no caddy, and the best part, today he's playing alone. Not quite a scratch golfer, but close, and perfectly capable of birdieing this, the seventeenth hole. Salt water on two sides, as blue as the sky above. Seagulls wheel like silent drones in the high summer air. Unarmed, he hopes, chuckling to himself. On this course, with so many ducks and seabirds in the general vicinity, members wear hats to avoid the splat.

Taylor Gatling, Jr., finds himself in an excellent mood, savoring life. It helps that he owns the course, and that he's arranged to have this part of it to himself. Nobody ahead, nobody behind. Could a man ask for more?

Oh yes, a chilled martini back at the clubhouse. That will make it a perfect day for bananafish, as his dad used to say, in reference to some silly story Taylor never bothered to read. Taylor has never cared for fiction. Why bother, when reality is so much more interesting?

With no other players pressing he can take his own sweet time, savoring the moment, imagining his triumph. Two hundred and fifteen yards to the pin, no problem, sir, consider it done. He selects his club, extracts it from the bag. An easy three-wood will impart the necessary backspin, placing the ball tight on the green.

Taylor can feel the birdie, has it firmly in his mind. He's in the act of bending down to place the ball on the tee when he detects the putt-putt of an approaching tractor mower, and curses softly. He waits, assuming that the groundskeeper, upon seeing the owner himself poised to drive, will turn around and leave the area.

The tractor keeps coming, chugging up the slope. Oddly enough, the blades in the rig are not engaged. The damned fool isn't even mowing. Taylor focuses on remaining calm. The man must be a simpleton, don't let him ruin the moment. The tractor approaches a long bunker, one the machine can't possibly traverse, but instead of swinging around to leave, the groundskeeper sets the brake and climbs down from the little green bucket seat and strides up toward the tee.

Taylor can't quite make out the man's face—the sun is behind him—but he recognizes the type of wide straw hat often worn by those who maintain the fairways and greens. And then, jarringly, he suddenly recognizes the jaunty stride of a man who is most certainly not one of the groundskeepers.

"Hey, boss, how they hanging?"

"What the hell are you doing here? I told you never to—"

"Yeah, yeah," says the man who insists on calling himself Kidder. "Never speak to you in public. Well, this isn't public, is it? This is a private course and you own it. Plus there's nobody here but us chickens. Or ducks or seagulls or whatever."

"Son of a bitch," Taylor says, scanning the area to make damn sure they're alone. "Are you out of your mind? What do you want?"

"I tried you at, what do you call it, your bad little boys club? Nobody home. And you won't give me a cell phone number, which is just a tiny bit insulting."

"You were at the boathouse?" Taylor hisses, throttling his three-wood. "Were you seen?"

"I'm sure your security cameras clocked me, but you can erase that, right? The point is, we need to have a conversation, so I made it happen."

"This is beyond the pale!"

Kidder chuckles. "Really? *Beyond the pale?* I always wondered what that means. I mean, what is the pale, exactly, and how do you get beyond it? I'll bet that's one of the things your father used to say."

"Leave my father out of this!"

"Hey, no problem." Kidder zips his lips. "Total silence in the father department. I could care less about fathers, if you want to know the truth. My concern is mother and child."

"You're never to contact me. We communicate through an intermediary, that was the arrangement."

"Yeah, well, there's always an exception, and this is it. The situation is getting to be a problem and needs to be resolved. Permanently, would be my preference."

Taylor walks in a tight circle, tapping the ground with the heel of his club. "Not yet," he says, jaw clenching. "Absolutely not. Direct order."

"I don't get it," Kidder says, as if bemused. "The operation is over. Time to tidy up."

"What makes you think it's over?"

"Looks over to me. The evildoers are dead, if not quite buried, and the target is in custody, with enough evidence to plant his bony ass in jail for life. Done and dusted. Over."

"It's not your call, damn it! And for your information the operation is not over. Not quite."

"No? That's fine. I'm always up for more. So what happens next? Give me a clue."

"You'll know when you get your orders."

Kidder is amused. "My orders? We're no longer in the field, Captain. I'm an independent contractor."

Taylor glares.

Kidder remains affable. "Okay, fine. I'll maintain status quo, await instruction. But I know what you're thinking, Cap. I always knew what you were thinking back in the day, and I do now."

"What am I thinking?"

"You're thinking I need my ticket punched, once this is all over. Tie up the last of the loose ends. Bury me in a foxhole and move on."

"You're wrong. I'd never—"

"Yeah, you would," Kidder interrupts. "I get it, a man in your position. So much to lose. Thing is, I've taken precautions. If I go down, you'll be right behind me. That's a certainty, Cap. I'll be saving you a place in hell."

"What have you done?" Taylor hisses, struggling to keep his voice down.

"Taken precautions. So put it out of your mind. And do please let me know what happens next. Provide me with a contact number. And soon, or I'll have to go all rogue, and you always hated that."

Taylor waits until the smart-mouthed bastard is over the hill and gone, and then he takes a deep breath and swings at the little white ball.

And misses.

In his mind his dead father laughs and says, *strike one, my son.*

Chapter Twenty-Five

Nine Little Words

I'm updating the case notes into my personal shorthand when a blinking light on my desk indicates an incoming call on the secure line.

I lift the handset and announce, "Alice Crane, Secretary of Ambivalence."

"Hey, Alice."

"Hey, Dane. 'Sup?"

"Nothing earthshaking," she says, way too casually. "Listen, I just remembered I left my lipstick in that little bathroom down the hall from Naomi's office? Could you check when you get the chance? Pale Peach."

"Not a problem. Later, alligator."

I grab my purse, give a shout-out to boss lady, letting her know there's an errand needs running, and leave the residence. The call for lipstick is a coded signal that Dane needs my ears to her lips, with no chance the conversation will be overheard, electronically or otherwise. Plus we never say "office," always "command center" or "command," so misuse of a common word underlines the importance of a request. She's staked out in Randall Shane's room at the hospital and won't be letting him out of her sight until the indictment comes down, so that means hoofing it to Mass General and hearing whatever it is that's too important to wait for the evening briefing.

With all the talk of spies and secret security agencies, and what I know firsthand about hovering helicopters, you might say my sense of awareness has been heightened. Or I'm getting to be as paranoid as the late professor. Whatever, I hit the street with eyes peeled, after deciding to proceed on foot rather than bike or taxi. Figuring as a pedestrian I've got a better chance of spotting a tail, and a brisk walk will do me good.

All is serene for several blocks. Considering Back Bay is in the heart of the city, it's amazing how lush and varied the urban vegetation gets this time of year. There are places where the canopy of white ash trees almost entirely spans the narrower streets, and many of the tulip trees and dogwoods are still in full bloom. I'm striding east on Beacon, in the vicinity of Fisher College, when I finally spot her. A young, professional-looking female quickly exiting a black SUV half a block ahead of me, on the opposite side of the street. What gives her away is a telling glance—she's checking my precise location before pretending to wander along Beacon, as if looking for a particularly hard-to-find address.

My guru and mentor in the art of spotting tails is Jack Delancey, so I know enough to drop my purse—oops, how clumsy!—and get a slant on the block behind me. A young, casually dressed male wearing sunglasses and a Bluetooth ear set studiously ignores me and walks right on by without offering to help with the spilled purse. So there are at least two tails and probably a third somewhere, waiting to be dropped off by the roving SUV, as well as another vehicle running backup, assuming this is a standard tail job with a full crew.

Useful to know that I'm under surveillance—that

probably means all of us are, which means a big operation, lots of manpower—but there's not a lot I can do
about it right at the moment, not without getting silly,
not to mention sweaty. Besides, if they're any good at all
they'll have already guessed that I'm heading to the hospital. Plus the trick with the purse will have confirmed
my awareness of being followed.

They know that I know that they know.

Having established the mutual awareness, I give a
friendly wave to the young lady dropped off by the SUV
and carry on, speed-walking up Beacon. Take a left for
six short blocks on Charles Street, and thence—as boss
lady might say—into Mass General, and up to the secure
floor where Randall Shane is being treated.

I'm not cleared to enter his room—that privilege has
now been restricted to his attorney, no casual visitors
allowed—so Dane meets me at the end of the hallway,
near the nurses' station, where I make a show of handing over a tube of my own lipstick.

"What, no Pale Peach?" she says with a grin.

"Just so you know, I was tailed from the residence. A
team effort."

Dane seems not the least surprised. She links her arm
in mine and says, "I think we need a trip to the ladies'."
Steering me farther on down the hallway, until we're
out of sight of the uniformed officer stationed outside of
Shane's room.

To my surprise, Dane walks us past the public rest-
room, and into a small utility closet, shutting the door
and blocking it with her hip. Obviously a location she'd
scouted for just this eventuality as a place unlikely to be
bugged. The utility closet—a small room, really—reeks
of Pine-Sol, with a distinct and recent whiff of illicit
cigarette smoke. Custodians sneaking a puff, or maybe

nurses. Or doctors, for that matter. Whoever, it won't be long before some needy nicotine addict tries the door.

"Shortly after his giant girlfriend left, the big guy beckoned me."

"Beckoned?" I say.

"With the hand that isn't cuffed," she says. "Wanted me to bend down so he could whisper in my ear."

"That's great," I say. "What did he tell you?"

Dane, eyes lively with conspiratorial glee, puts her lips to my ear, quite literally, and imparts, in nine succinct words, an extremely important piece of new information.

Back at the residence, I confer with boss lady, who seems to be slightly peeved that I didn't mention the particulars of my errand before leaving.

"It's not the being followed, that's to be expected," she says, giving me the cold eye of her disapproval. "It's that you could have been snatched from the street upon your return and interrogated, or worse."

"I took a taxi back."

Boss lady is not impressed. "These people smashed their way into this residence and dragged our client out in a net. You think they wouldn't stop a taxicab?"

I shrug and say, "Trust me, this isn't the same crowd. If a special-ops team had me under surveillance, I doubt I'd have spotted them. This was more like the FBI we all know and love. Could even be a local police operation, but I seriously doubt the locals have the resources to dispatch an entire surveillance team whenever one of us leaves the residence. Hence my vote for our pals at the Bureau."

Naomi shakes her head. "Maybe, maybe not, but from

now on no one leaves without letting me know where they're going and why."

"Fine, but tell me again why we can't be bugged? Why you're so sure they're not listening to us right now?"

She rolls her eyes but indulges me. "Intruders could well have placed bugs in the residence, but it doesn't matter because there's no way any bug can transmit from this location. When the building was gutted and renovated it was made secure against electronic surveillance of all types. There's no radio frequency or variable signal that can penetrate, meaning any and all bugs are inoperable or will fail to transmit. That's why cell phones have to be routed through the roof antenna. The same signal interference system is used in the shielded areas of U.S. embassies deemed vulnerable to espionage. London, Moscow, Beijing, Baghdad. So we're good. Speak freely."

"I'm sure you're right," I say, grabbing a pencil and a steno pad. "But I prefer to write this down."

"If you must," she concedes with a sigh.

Kendall Square. Behind Dumpster. Shane's laptop. Jack will know.

Naomi's big brown eyes are suddenly all aglow. This is potentially our biggest break in the case thus far, assuming that the hidden laptop can be recovered. When she gets like this, stoked by her keen intelligence with positive energy, I sometimes get the impression that she'd like to give me a hug, share the glow, but she never does. Touchy-feely is not part of her outward nature, or if it is she manages to keep it firmly under control.

"Okay, we'll play it your way, on the off chance," she says, feeding the piece of paper into the shredder. Then she leans out the command center doorway and calls out, loud enough to be heard at the FBI field office at One Center Plaza, with or without bugs. "Teddy! Stop whatever it is you're doing! Alice wants to take you shopping!"

Chapter Twenty-Six

Soon to Be Swooshed

When it comes to shedding tails, Teddy Boyle is a mere tadpole, but surprisingly enthusiastic at being given the opportunity.

"This is sort of what Matt Damon does," he confides as we head out on foot.

"Matt Damon has stunt doubles," I remind him. "He's not *really* driving cars a hundred miles an hour on a wrong-way street."

"Cool," Teddy says. "But you should know I don't have a driver's license."

"You won't need one. We won't be wrecking Lamborghinis or jumping from rooftop to rooftop. All we're going to do is go into the Nike outlet and shop."

"That's it?" he says, sounding disappointed.

"The cool thing about this, you get to buy something, for real. I'm thinking, at the very least, a hoodie and kicks."

"I hate the swoosh," he says scornfully.

"Think of it as taking one for Team Nantz."

So far, the black SUV is hanging back, but I have to assume they've got someone cruising the blocks ahead of us as we approach Newbury Street, which is to Boston what Rodeo Drive is to Beverly Hills, except with way less celebrities and movie stars. Way less, but not none—I once spotted the aforementioned Mr. Damon coming out of Daisy Buchanan's, all on his own, no entourage. Take my word for it, he's even better looking in person.

"I think I see 'em!" Teddy hisses.

"Pay no attention. We're almost there."

I'm not old enough to be Teddy's mother, but big sister fits comfortably, and that's the role I assume upon entering Niketown, on the corner of Newbury and Exeter streets. Handing over my own credit card, an act of faith I'm reasonably sure the young hacker won't abuse. And if he does I'll cancel his ass so fast he'll be gulping like a guppy. Actually, he's quite attentive when I explain the drill.

"'Kay, first I pick out shoes, then we go upstairs and find a hoodie," he says, repeating the instructions. "Try it on, pay for everything and then leave with the hood up."

"You got it."

"And somewhere along the way, you'll, like, vanish or something."

"Or something."

"It's way too warm for a hoodie."

"Look around, it's never too warm for a hoodie. Guys your age wear them down to breakfast while Mom pours the cheery little O's. Inside, outside, the hood is always up."

"Guys like that are morons."

"No argument. But the peepers will think you're attempting to disguise yourself. They'll pay attention."

"Peepers? Is that even a word?"

"Try to stay focused. This is very important."

No fool, Teddy, when it comes right down to it, he selects a pricey pair of the Zoom Kobes and a green cotton hoodie, one of the retro styles—or as I like to think, *timeless*—and hands the charge card to a teenage clerk who, from the look in her doelike eyes, finds my little brother totally fascinating, from the tip-top of his gelled hair spikes to his soon-to-be zooming feet. Her glance at me is dismissive—clearly a late-twenties female lacking in neck tattoos is no competition. On the positive side she's more than willing to clip away the tags so he can wear the product out of the store.

Bambi hands bashful Teddy a bag for the shoes and does everything but roll over with her paws in the air.

When he rejoins me I point out, "All you have to do is whistle."

"Huh?" he responds, genuinely puzzled. Brilliant as he may be in all things internet, when it comes to girls he's as pathetically impaired as any teenage male.

"Never mind. We're going to make one last circuit of this floor, over by that double rack of T-shirts, and then you're going to put up the hood and head downstairs like you're in a hurry. Show your receipt if you have to, but when you get out the door, go very quickly up Exeter Street and turn left on Boylston. Look around as if you might be followed, because you will be. Don't worry about the peepers, even if you do spot them. They'll hang back. Go one block west to the corner of Dartmouth Street and go down into the T-stop. Take the green line to Park Street, exit onto the Common. Find a bench, sit down and pretend to be waiting for someone important. Give it ten minutes or so, then get all agitated when they don't show and make your way back to the residence."

"I could try to lose them in the Public Garden, easy."

"I don't want you to lose them. Ready?"

"'Kay, sure."

He whips up the hood, hurries down the crowded stairway. Meanwhile, I step around the T-shirt display, scoot through a couple of racks in the busiest part of the store and take the staff stairway to the ground floor. Removing a plastic security card from my purse, I disarm the alarm for the door that exits onto the brick alley behind the store (what can I say, once upon a time we did a huge favor for a Nike exec). Crossing the alley I gain access to the Exeter Street parking garage through an unmarked door and meet Jack Delancey on the second floor of the garage.

"Your chariot awaits," he says with a grin, opening the passenger door to the generic sedan he's just rented.

Swoosh, we're out of there, undetected.

Chapter Twenty-Seven

Think Like Shane

Before leaving the garage, Jack takes off his tie and blazer, carefully folds both items, places them on the passenger seat, then dons wraparound sunglasses and a Red Sox cap. He suggests that I slump down in the backseat until we've cleared the area. A rental car is being utilized for a couple of reasons. First, the working assumption that Jack's regular ride has been compromised, planted with bugs and/or a tracking device. And more generally because even if that's not the case, his Town Car has no doubt been visually identified as to make and plate, and would pop on any surveillance team watch list.

"How did you ditch them?" I ask, chin on the floor mat. "The old car wash trick?"

He laughs. "Works every time."

Jack has an associate—actually an old high school crony—who owns a chain of car washes. All he has to do, show up at one of the venues, swap out drivers while the suds are flying, and Jack's car drives off in one direction and Jack in another. Simple but effective—and it helps that the same crony also has a car rental franchise, and will rent for cash, making it that much harder to trace.

Jack says, "So what exactly did Shane say?"

"According to Dane, he said, 'Kendall Square. Behind Dumpster. My laptop. Jack will know.'"

"He said I'd know, huh?"

"Does it ring a bell?"

"I recall the Dumpster. It was in the vicinity when I picked him up in Kendall Square. But if he left his laptop behind the Dumpster, somebody will have found it by now. Has to be hidden somehow."

I can't help saying, "Well, duh."

"I'm thinking out loud, Alice," he snaps. "Give me a break."

"Sorry. Can I sit up now?"

"Yeah. And fasten your seat belt, please."

We've made it to Storrow Drive. Jack Delancey has the skills of a NASCAR driver, and is putting them to good use on the curving, lane-switching highway that hugs the Charles River. If there's anybody attempting to follow us, they have my sympathy. Vroom, vroom, then we're somehow off Storrow and crossing the river into Cambridge before my brain can quite catch up with Jack's expert maneuvering.

"Whoa doggies," I say, sighing with relief as we finally begin to reenter earth orbit.

"Whoa doggies? Who are you, Annie Oakley?"

"Maybe. Is she a babe?"

"Sort of. Annie Oakley was a famous sharpshooter in a Wild West show. Shot a cigarette out of her husband's mouth."

"Great idea," I say. "Wish I'd thought of it."

"Yeah, well," says Jack, who's been hitched and unhitched so many times that he knows his way to the barn, so to speak.

He swings onto Cardinal Medeiros Avenue, keeping

slightly below the limit, and slows further as we enter Kendall Square. Not a lot going on here. Harvard Square, Central Square, those are the action areas in the People's Republic of Cambridge. Kendall is a sleepy backwater, quiet and somehow dignified, despite being only a few blocks from the MIT campus. Jack pulls around, just off the square, and parks a few yards from where the train tracks cross Binney Street.

"There," he says, indicating a battered green Dumpster behind a plumbing supply warehouse. "Are you clear?"

I'm scanning the area. We seem to be the only living beings on this particular block. "Looks clear, but I don't have your eyes."

"Give yourself credit, kid. You spotted the first tail."

"Lucky."

He shakes his handsome head. "Luck wasn't involved. Your gut told you to look for them. What's your gut say now?"

"Time to make the donuts," I say, opening the door.

Jack looks over the top of the rental at me. "I heard about that. Save one for me."

We cross the deserted street to the Dumpster. Have a peek over the rusty edge. Emptied recently.

"Okay, here I am," Jack says. "Waiting for me."

He means he's putting himself in Shane's place, hiding behind the Dumpster until his good friend Jack Delancey arrives like the cavalry and they proceed with the fun and games of blowing up an innocent vehicle in the vicinity of Shane's motel room.

He crouches, reaches out and sifts a few bits of gravel, eyes surveying the limited landscape. The Dumpster, a chain-link fence, the tracks, a nearby warehouse. I back away, not wanting to disturb his line of sight. He puts his cheek to the ground, eyeballing the underside of the Dumpster. Dismisses that particular possibility, and stands up, dusting his knees. Question: How can a guy crouch in the gravel and still look so immaculate?

Jack nods to himself and begins to probe along the fence, where pieces of weather-beaten cardboard have escaped from the Dumpster and been blown into the chain links, stirred by the slow passage of trains, or gusts of wind. At a place where the chain has been partially separated from the galvanized fence pole, he slips through to the other side. Walking slowly, looking down, nudging aside thick hunks of rain-soaked cardboard.

A hundred feet or so from the road, in an area alongside the tracks where the tufts of grass are knee-high, he looks back at me and flashes a beautiful white smile that makes him look about twelve years old.

I'm thinking, go, Jack, do it, think like Shane, but he doesn't need any encouragement from me. He circles around like a dog preparing to lie down. Then he bends gracefully at the waist, hooks his right hand in something and stands up, showing me the find.

A laptop carrier, clotted with tufts of dirt and bits of grass.

If the boy wonder was any more amped his fauxhawk would explode. He's had quite a day so far, leading tails around the city, and now back home at his bench, doing his thing with the recovered laptop.

"This could be the mother lode," Teddy says, lifting the lid of Randall Shane's small 13-inch MacBook Pro. "Let's see if she boots."

We're gathered in the command center—everybody but Dane, still holding vigil at the hospital—more or less standing over Teddy's narrow shoulders, watching with keen anticipation as he presses the power button.

There's a low-key *dong* and the screen illuminates, soon followed by the gray Apple logo in the center.

"System loading," Teddy says, hushed.

Twenty-eight seconds later—by his count—he's trolling for downloaded video files.

"I'll start with the most recent," he says, selecting from a pop-up menu. "This was attached to an email that originated from jvkeener@mit.edu.org. I'm assuming that's the professor."

"Bingo," says Naomi, almost before the video-player image has a chance to form on the screen.

A little boy on Harvard Bridge, looking into the camera with what could be fear or nervous anticipation, hard to say. A little boy, possibly Eurasian, maybe five years old, with a mop of thick dark brown hair in a bowl cut, straight across his forehead. Intelligent, wary eyes glancing upward and to the side. The camera zooms back to reveal a skinny Caucasian woman holding the child's hand. She has a similar, wary look when her eyes flick nervously at the camera. She says something but we can't hear it, and then the clip ends abruptly.

Teddy runs it again—the whole clip lasts a mere seven seconds—and I start to take in some of the details. For instance the child and the woman are close to the bridge rail, facing south, with the Cambridge shore behind them.

"Sound?"

"There's an open audio track," Teddy says, tapping a finger on the screen, indicating a graphic. "No volume. My guess, this was recorded with a cell phone. I'll run lip recognition software, see if we can figure out what she's saying."

"She's saying, 'where do we go?'" I tell him.

Teddy reruns that segment several times, and we study her moving lips.

"Alice is right, it fits," Naomi says, nodding.

"'Where do we go?'" Jack says, musing. "Like she has no real idea what's going on, or what's supposed to happen next, or why they're in that particular location."

"Who's shooting this, do you think?" Naomi asks.

"Not Shane," says Jack. "She's frightened, or at the very least uneasy. So is the boy. Kids don't respond to Shane with fear. Quite the opposite."

"The woman isn't his mother, obviously," Naomi says. "Is she in league with the kidnapper?"

Jack shrugs. "Run it again, please."

We see it all again. Close-up on little Joey, then a shaky pullback revealing a slender, nervous-looking woman clinging to the boy's hand.

"He's not afraid of her," Naomi says. "He's not trying to get away. See how he leans in her direction? She's his caregiver."

"Like a nanny?"

Boss lady shrugs. "Like someone who knows how to make a child trust her."

"This is real," I say. "She's worried for the boy's safety."

"Maybe."

"If she's in league with the kidnappers, why show her face? Why not keep it close on the boy?"

Naomi, looking thoughtful, gives me a nod of approval. "Good point. This was done with a purpose. Teddy? Check Shane's search history, his email. Who, if anybody, did he search for or contact after downloading this video?"

"On it."

"I suggest we back away, give the young man some breathing room," Naomi says. "There will be much to download and ponder. Iced tea on the rooftop deck, I think."

She buzzes Beasley.

"Can I smoke a cigar?" Jack asks, straightening his blazer. "In celebration?"

"If you have one for me," Naomi says, not missing a beat.

"Are you kidding?" Jack says, taken aback.

"Yes, I'm kidding. But permission to wreck your lungs is granted."

"I never inhale."

"That's what they all say," Naomi says, leading the way to the roof.

Chapter Twenty-Eight

Two if by Drone

Taylor Gatling, Jr., steps from his office to the second-floor balcony overlooking the airfield, lifting the binoculars to his eyes. Thinking, not for the first time, that to call this an airfield isn't to do it justice.

The former Pease Air Force Base in Newington, New Hampshire. Miles upon miles of wide concrete runways built heavy enough and long enough to accommodate squadrons of B-52 bombers. Now reconfigured into a civilian trade port, but back in the day this was a fully manned SAC base. Strategic Air Command, charged with keeping a third of the fleet in the air at all times, armed with nuclear weapons, just in case the Russians decided to go for the final option, a first strike. The golden age of atomic bombs and mutually assured destruction, long before Gatling was born. Method of delivery, the magnificent B-52 Stratofortress, with a wingspan of nearly two hundred feet and an enormous tail section towering more than forty feet above the tarmac. Loaded weight of a hundred and thirty tons, which explains the overbuilt runways, since one of the heavy beasts was landing every fifteen minutes, like clockwork. More like deathwork, really. That was the point. Making sure the

194 *Chris Jordan*

Russians understood that a first strike would leave hundreds of the enormous bombers still airborne, capable of destroying at least three thousand targets in the old Soviet Union. A million megatons of atomic madness delivered right to your door, Mr. Khrushchev, turning Mother Russia to glowing dust. Your call.

Glory days. Back when not even U.S. presidents dared mess with General Curtis "Bombs Away" LeMay, who personally selected the enemy targets and didn't bother to share the list with the Pentagon, for security reasons laid out by the general himself. There was no second-guessing in LeMay's Air Force, just a perpetual readiness to unleash Hell. And it worked. The Russians never dared to pull the trigger and the old Soviet Union eventually collapsed under the weight of all that armament. All because one righteous man was willing to take a stand.

Something to keep in mind when the going gets tough, as it surely will in the next few days and weeks. The reckless insubordinate Kidder being just one of the many problems to be solved.

"Sir? Bird One on vector, sir."

Below the balcony one of the young technicians calls up, notifying him that the drone aircraft is about to be recovered. Taylor sweeps the binoculars to the southwest and is pleased to pick up the glint of wings just above the tree line. The new Predator RQ-Mini isn't easy to see, for obvious reasons. The Mini has a wingspan of only twelve feet, and is transparent to radar. Virtually undetectable once airborne, unless you know exactly where to look. The little craft is limited to low altitude and has a fairly short range, but is capable of making the fifty-mile trip to the designated target, in this case downtown Boston, and hovering at low altitude for up to three hours before returning to base. Armed not with weapons but with state-of-the-art hi-res video cameras and signal detection receivers. A million bucks per unit, not including the remote-control console, and well worth the cost, although this particular bird hasn't delivered, for reasons yet to be determined, although he has strong suspicions in that regard.

Gatling joins the tech on the tarmac, awaiting recovery.

"Bird One is down," the tech announces. "Bird Two in place over the target, circling at seven hundred feet."

"Any joy?"

"Like before. Nice pictures, no signal."

No signal meaning the drones have been unable to recover data from the bugs the recovery team left in place. There's only one possible explanation. Gatling waits until the little unmanned aircraft—there are model airplanes bigger—taxis into the open hangar under remote control. Then he heads for the control room, housed in an unassuming one-story cinder-block building that was once a bunk room for bomber crews, and therefore christened the Bunker.

The Bunker is his own dedicated unit, off-line and off the books. Here in the States, GSG has recently acquired a long-established company that supplies uniformed security guards, patrolling office buildings, investigating employee theft and so on. But the bulk of GSG's business—the big revenue generator—remains overseas, employing ex-military in a number of venues. Armed security details for civilian contractors, plus load and flight crews for the full-size missile-firing Predators deployed over countries identified as terrorist hot spots. That particular subsidiary, tasked with operating unmanned aerial vehicles, is funded by an open-end, no-bid contract worth hundreds of millions per annum. All of which has made it possible for him to run his own security operations here at home, in his own stomping ground, as it were, without regard to budget. An operation that includes not only reconnaissance UAVs and the tech crews required to run them, but a stealth helicopter and a superbly trained special-ops team available on a moment's notice.

In Gatling's mind he's continuing in the patriotic tradition of General Curtis LeMay, who for a crucial time in American history had the entire Strategic Air Command under his unquestioned leadership, answerable to himself alone. Like his hero, Taylor Gatling, Jr., is prepared to cut through the bullshit and accept the responsibility of making difficult decisions for the protection of the homeland. He may not have access to thousands of nuclear warheads, but in his own small way he's making a difference, standing guard against those who want to destroy America. In particular, unreliable characters like the late Joseph Keener, who openly consorted with the enemy, and who, if he wasn't actively passing secrets to the enemy, certainly had the capacity to do so. The FBI, in Gatling's opinion a bunch of useless, vacillating, butt-covering 'crats, had declined to keep the professor under close surveillance. So Gatling had made the call, and even though the unexpected had happened and the crap had hit the fan, he didn't regret the original decision. Plus, how could he resist the opportunity to put a personal enemy's reputation in the shredder?

Things hadn't gone according to plan; it happens, and when it does a righteous leader makes adjustments. That's what he's doing now, making adjustments.

In the Bunker, Gatling makes straight for the team controlling the Minis. A couple of New Hampshire kids, fraternal twins, who'd started out as gamers and progressed to joysticking—or "sticking"—unmanned aerial vehicles. Known in the Bunker as B1 and B2, the brothers affect swamp-water Yankee accents—"ayuh, bubba" their equivalent of "hey, bro"—but they're bright and capable and love what they're doing. Gatling likes hanging out at their consoles because their enthusiasm is infectious, and because they defer to him as something of a legend, a local boy who made spectacularly good and who has all the toys to prove it.

The brothers look up from the glow of their LCDs, shaking heads in tandem. B1, aka Bart, has the active bird, with images split on screen. B2, or Bert, has control of the Mini that has just landed, and is going through the remote checklist as the plane is refueled.

"Sorry, boss. We tweaked the receiver to high-gain but the birds are still deaf."

The phrase "birds are still deaf" pronounced without recourse to the letter *r*. Gatling grins like a sympathetic older sibling, slaps them both on the back. "Not to worry, boys. You've established that the building has state-of-the-art shielding, just as I suspected. So now we know."

"That sucks," says B2. "But look here, boss, what we got on viz. Intruders."

Introodahs.

"Damn," says Gatling, watching the LCD as a black SUV circles the block, dropping off operatives, picking them up. "When was this?"

"Within the hour. Plus we picked up a scrambled broadcast from a white van parked on the same block. Some kind of walkie-talkie bullshit on an FBI frequency."

Gatling's expression darkens as he turns serious, and none-too-pleased. "For future reference, I need to know this in real time. Pull the bird pronto. Get it out of there."

"Boss, there's no way that—"

"Now."

At the tone of his voice, brooking no argument, the twins seem to shrink into their swivel chairs. "You got it," says Bart softly, working the joystick. "Bird Two disengaging target area."

"Vector eleven degrees until clear of Logan airspace," says Bert, flipping though the checklist. "Maintain seven hundred feet."

"Vector eleven, maintaining seven hundred."

"Cleared target area. Going to auto."

"Standby for next waypoint."

"Standing by."

The brothers push back from their consoles, letting the Mini fly itself to the next waypoint. Obvious, from their tense postures, that they're awaiting further instruction, expecting to be reprimanded.

Gatling takes a deep breath, calming himself. "I thought I had made it clear at the beginning of the operation, but let me explain again. It is absolutely essential that any and all surveillance of this particular target go undetected. No one can know we're there. No one can suspect. And now that you've detected an FBI operation in progress—congrats on that, by the way, job well done—our invisibility is even more critical. If I can spot a Mini a thousand yards away, coming in for a landing, then a Bureau agent might do so as well, even if the odds are against it. For the time being we will stand down. All recon flights suspended. Understood?"

"Yes, sir," they say in tandem.

Without another word—how could these morons have failed to understand?—Gatling exits the Bunker and trudges back to his office, all lightness gone from his step. Talk about a mood crash. He'd anticipated the FBI or some other Homeland agency would investigate the mysterious death of Professor Keener—that was a given, from the moment it happened—but running a full-scale surveillance on the private investigator Naomi Nantz? That made him extremely uneasy. What did they hope to find? His great disdain for bureaucrats—that's why they call it the Bureau—doesn't blind him to the fact that if enough monkeys type on enough keyboards, eventually a plausible story will emerge.

It's essential that whatever scenario the Bureau comes up with, that it not include Gatling Security Group in any meaningful way. Which means that finding a solution for the Kidder problem is all the more crucial.

On the way into his office Gatling briskly instructs his secretary to hold all calls. He locks the door, reclines on his ten-thousand-dollar leather couch and for the next hour or so thinks seriously about murder.

Chapter Twenty-Nine

Enemies in High Places

As I organize my notes for this narrative, it becomes clear that this was the day when the case finally began to break wide open. Day Four. The day we went up to the roof deck for iced tea while Teddy examined Shane's laptop, and Jack Delancey smoked his smelly but interesting cigar, and Naomi and I stared out at the river, wondering aloud why the FBI had us under surveillance.

"Shane's old boss visits him in the hospital, chats with Dane, next thing we're being followed," I say, making my point. "Can't be a coincidence."

"She was never Shane's boss," Naomi says, taking a sip of her tea. "They were colleagues. Friends. In Dane's opinion she's sincerely concerned for his well-being."

"Still, she's a big mucky-muck. Director of Counterterrorism."

"Assistant director. There's only one director of the FBI. The subordinates are designated as deputy director, associate deputy director and, down the line, a number of assistant directors. AD Monica Bevins reports to the associate deputy director, who reports directly to the director."

I stare at her. "So you know the whole organizational

chart? You do. You have it in your head, from the big boss at the top to the part-time custodian at the bottom."

She shrugs, admitting as much.

Typical.

I say, "My point is, whatever her title, she has the power to make things happen, and what happens when she gets here to visit her sick friend? She puts us under surveillance. Why? Are we suspects in the murder or the kidnapping?"

"No. But we're representing the only suspect. Maybe we know things."

"So they know about the missing laptop?"

"Possibly. Although, if so, I'd have suspected a wide-spread search of the area, or even a search of these premises, based on the fact that this was Shane's last stop before he was abducted. And yet none of that happened."

"It still could."

"Possibly."

"But you have another theory."

Again with the shrug. "There's also the possibility that we're in the middle of a turf war," she says.

Jack, releasing a perfect O of white smoke, chimes in. "That fits.... That's what I'm thinking, now that I've had time to, you know, actually think about it. Monica knows we were hit by some other agency. Maybe she knows who it is, maybe she doesn't. But she wants to find out. So she puts eyes on us."

"You know the woman," Naomi says. "You worked for her, albeit briefly. In your estimation is that how she'd react?"

He shrugs. "All bureaucrats want more information. She has the authority to order surveillance, therefore she did."

Naomi leans back, fingertips brushing the glass of tea.

"So in your opinion the FBI has two objectives. One, to keep an eye on us. Two, to see who else is keeping an eye on us."

"Exactly," he says. "Hey, did you see that?"

Pointing skyward with his cigar, eyes squinting, a puzzled look on his face.

"What?"

"Like an eagle, circling."

"An eagle?" I say. "You mean over the harbor?"

"The harbor's too far away—my eyes aren't that good. No, straight overhead. Whatever it was, it had a big wingspan."

We all study the sky. Other than a TV news chopper in the vicinity of Bunker Hill, and a plane climbing out of Logan, there doesn't seem to be much in the way of birds at the moment.

"Maybe it was an osprey."

"I know what an osprey looks like. We've got tons of ospreys in Gloucester. No, this was much bigger."

"And you're convinced it was an eagle."

"Hell, no. Just that it was bigger than an ordinary bird."

Naomi looks thoughtful. But then, that's her default expression. Sensing that she has an idea or opinion, we wait for it.

"Let's go back inside," Naomi suggests, picking up her glass. As we enter the stairwell she says, "So tell me, Jack, is the FBI in the habit of employing surveillance drones, do you know?"

Back in the command center, Teddy looks like he's given birth. Okay, I'm exaggerating just a teensy bit, but he does look quite pleased with himself.

"Kathleen Mancero," he announces before we've had

a chance to settle. "Born Kathleen O'Hara. Divorced but kept her married name. Driver's license has her current residence as Olathe, Kansas."

Our young computer whiz is no longer working directly from Shane's laptop, having transferred the contents to his own workstation. Identifying the woman in the emailed video attachment turns out to have been straightforward and relatively simple, as such things go. She popped almost immediately in the facial recognition software because she had once been a suspect in the disappearance of her own daughter, a seven-year-old girl.

Young Teddy has done an amazing job of organizing available data into a concise narrative, exactly as Naomi has taught him.

"It all started five years ago in Kansas City, Missouri," he begins, laying out the story. "Her husband was a big-time car dealer—Hummers—who dumped her for a newer model. His secretary, so no imagination there. A nasty custody battle ensues. The husband tried to make it look like his soon-to-be ex-wife was involved in kiddy porn—selling images of her own daughter over the internet—and when little Stacy goes missing, it's assumed that Mrs. Mancero has kidnapped her own daughter to sell her to the highest bidder."

"Damn," says Jack. "That's the connection. Shane."

"Right, right," says Teddy.

"Yeah, I remember this one," Jack goes on. "Not the details, but I remember Shane going to KC to help some poor woman who he said was being framed. As I recall, there wasn't a happy ending."

Teddy's gel-stiffened hairdo bobs in agreement. "Yup, you're right. According to media accounts, former FBI Special Agent Randall Shane established that it was in fact the husband who had traded images of his own daughter online. The husband, Gerald 'The Hummer Man' Mancero, was eventually arrested on pedophile charges and the wife was proved innocent. Shane managed to prove that the images of the daughter were downloaded by one Jason Hargrove, who was a crony of the husband's. Hargrove, scion of a wealthy family in the chemical business, confessed to kidnapping and killing seven-year-old Stacy Mancero, and disposing of her body in such a way that not much of anything was ever recovered. Dissolved the remains in a vat of acid, courtesy of the family business."

"What a nightmare," says Jack. "And it didn't end there. The husband shot the guy, right? The killer? As he was being transferred for arraignment? And then, let me see, was in turn shot dead by courtroom officers. They called it 'The Kansas City Bloodbath.'"

Watching Naomi, I get the distinct impression that she had the whole awful case in mind as soon as Teddy spoke the woman's name, but hadn't said so because she wanted to let him make a full presentation of the facts. Now that he has, she's free to comment.

"There's no doubt in your mind that Kathleen Mancero is the woman in the video clip?" she asks.

In answer, Teddy puts the image of her driver's license up on the screen next to a still from the video and lets the pictures speak for themselves. Same eyes, same facial structure. Clearly both images are of the same woman.

"What happened next?" Naomi says, prompting him.

"After the shoot-out Mrs. Mancero had a serious breakdown. She became delusional, kept seeing her daughter in the faces of unrelated children—rushing up to families in malls, and so on—and was several times taken into protective custody. Eventually she voluntarily checked into a psychiatric hospital and was treated for six months. According to a follow-up story in the *Kansas City Star,* which ran a year ago, she was finally able to accept the fact that her daughter was dead, even though there was never a body to recover or bury. She also continued to have contact with Shane."

"What kind of contact?"

"Emails. Information she forwarded about other missing children. Mostly stuff she pulled off various websites. There are, like, a zillion sites about missing kids. From the tone of the emails, Mrs. Mancero sounds obsessed with the idea that she can do something for other missing children. My sense is, she wanted to help Shane somehow, as she had attempted to do, and failed, in her own daughter's case."

"How sad," says Naomi, maintaining an expression of studied indifference. "Did he encourage her?"

Teddy shakes his head. "Just the opposite. He was really nice about it, but it's clear that Shane wanted her to stop looking into what he called 'the abyss.'"

"The abyss?"

"He doesn't explain it. It's like part of a continuing discussion. Something they talked about when she was in the psychiatric hospital."

"He visited her there?"

Teddy shrugs. "Don't think so. My impression is, he spoke to her by phone."

"Had they communicated recently?"

"The last exchange of emails was two months ago. She forwarded yet another missing-child story, taken from one of the websites, and he politely but firmly declined to get involved."

"And the video clip that Professor Keener forwarded to Shane? What's the date stamp?"

"The day Keener was killed. It logs as being downloaded into Shane's email server at 5:12 a.m., at about the same time the professor called him. Which makes sense, assuming he was calling Shane's attention to the clip. Maybe he just got it and wanted to share."

Jack says, "So the first Shane knows of the Mancero involvement is the video clip. And the world blows to hell before he can do anything about it. That explains a lot, actually."

Naomi leaves her empty glass on a table by the door, for eventual collection by Mrs. Beasley. She takes her seat behind her desk, catty-corner to where Teddy has been working, and leans back in her chair with her slender arms folded, as if in a posture of defense. "This is a particularly awful example of the dark side experienced by anyone who investigates missing children. By that I mean what Shane referred to as 'the abyss.' When things go wrong they stay wrong forever and the survivors are sometimes dragged over the edge, into a cycle of grief and despair that's very difficult to escape. Clearly that's what happened to Kathleen Mancero. Just as clearly, she would never have willingly participated in the abduction of someone else's child. There must be another explanation. Theories, anyone?"

I resist raising my hands, which isn't strictly required during informal discussions. "Maybe she came across something about Keener's case, forwarded it to Shane and somehow got involved? Trying to help?"

"Any evidence of that on the laptop?" Naomi asks Teddy.

Giving me a "sorry" look, he shakes his head. "There's a bit of emailing between Shane and the professor, but it all seems to have occurred after Keener first contacted him by phone. There's no mention of Mrs. Mancero. And for that matter no real specifics about the professor's case. Mostly Shane's notification of when he'll arrive, where he'll be staying."

Jack, sprawled in one of the narrow chairs, says, "Randall would never discuss the specifics of a case by email. No way. And he would have been particularly cautious, knowing there were national security implications."

"And how would he have known that?" Naomi asks.

"Experience and instinct," Jack says, sounding slightly defensive of his old friend. "Genius scientist with a top-secret project and a missing kid? Stands to reason he'd be monitored by the kinds of people who read emails and tap phones."

After a pause she nods and says, "Agreed."

"Yeah, sure, okay," I say, jumping back into the discussion. "An experienced guy like Randall Shane wouldn't have discussed specifics in his email or texts or whatever. But what about poor Mrs. Mancero? Would she have been so careful? Maybe someone flagged her emails to Shane, did a little background research and decided she could be exploited."

"Good point," says Jack.

Naomi purses her lips, gives it some thought. "That theory has considerable merit," she decides. "Teddy, we need deeper background on what Kathleen Mancero has been up to recently. See what you can find in Olathe. It's an upscale suburb of Kansas City, surely her neighbors would know her story. There may be those willing to share."

"Or gossip," I add.

"You know I hate that word."

"Just because you hate it doesn't mean it can't be useful." I happen to glance across the desk to where our resident hacker is hunched over his keyboard. "Teddy? You're blushing."

"I, um, already contacted a few of her neighbors on Facebook," he admits. "As if I was, um, trying to reconnect with my cousin, Kathleen."

If he's been expecting disapproval, he's wrong.

"Excellent ploy!" Naomi leans forward, elbows precisely planted on a foam mat situated on the glass surface of her desk. "What did they say?"

He shrugs. "Not much, really. Expressions of sympathy, but I got the impression Mrs. Mancero made people uncomfortable just by being there. She left Olathe about a month ago, supposedly to care for a sick relative, and it's like nobody is exactly eager to have her back." Teddy appears flustered, as well as embarrassed. "I don't get it. It's like she has an infectious disease or something."

"In a way she does," Naomi says. "She's a reminder that bad things, unimaginable things, can happen to ordinary people. Sometimes, in some cases, a kind of shunning occurs, intentional or otherwise. In this instance the victim may have made it worse by being so openly disturbed, by showing and sharing her pain. It's similar to social reactions experienced by individuals with terminal disease. Healthy people don't want to be reminded that death is always around the corner, and find ways to avoid meaningful contact. An ugly and often cruel reaction but, alas, very human."

"Same thing happens on a football field when a player get injured," says Jack. "Nobody wants to look at the injured guy, or talk to him, like it might be catching."

Naomi, who normally loathes sports analogies, does not object. She's more interested in the timing. "For purposes of this investigation let's work from the assumption that Kathleen Mancero was somehow drawn into this case by subterfuge. Her connection to Shane is clear, and very public. There are two possible explanations. Either Randall Shane is himself involved in the kidnapping of Joey Keener and involved Mrs. Mancero as an accomplice, or he has very powerful enemies who went to great lengths to link him to this case. Any thoughts?"

"No way Shane is a kidnapper or a killer. Cross it off the list," Jack says adamantly.

"I tend to agree," Naomi says. "Shane as villain has always been a low probability. At this point we'll proceed on the theory that Shane has a powerful enemy, one willing and able to frame him as a kidnapper/killer. Our task is to identify this enemy and that will lead us to the boy, if he still lives. Are we in agreement?"

We all agree.

Naomi says, "Teddy, Jack, we need to go deeper into Shane's past. A client who holds him responsible for a child's death, or his failure to solve a case. Someone in a high government position who feels threatened by him. A friend who believes himself or herself betrayed. Someone who hates him enough to take great risks. Someone with power enough to do the types of things we've been witness to of late."

Teddy hunches over his keyboard, fingers flying.

Jack closes his notebook, and prepares to leave the command center, cell in hand. He pauses, gives boss lady a sideways look. "On the subject of enemies in high places, have we been swept recently?" he asks, holding up his phone.

Naomi cocks an eyebrow. "This morning, as a matter of fact. Just as a precaution."

"And?"

"As expected, your pals in the helicopter left a few presents behind. Also as expected, none of the devices were able to broadcast. Bear in mind that cell phone calls originating outside of the residence have no such expectation of privacy."

"Big bro could be listening."

"Always best to proceed under that assumption."

Which makes me feel all warm and virtuous for having taken such precautions in the last few hours while out in the field, acting like a real investigator. Shaking tails, locating lost laptops, helping to break the case wide open. Until, moments later, I realize that unlike Teddy and Jack, I haven't been given an assignment.

"Hey," I say. "What about me?"

"Case notes," boss lady says, without hesitation. "Bring the timeline up to date. It's crucial that at this juncture we remain organized and coherent in our purpose."

"So you want me to be a secretary," I say, not sure whether to be indignant, insulted or disappointed, or a combination of all three.

"Recording secretary and chief factotum," Naomi says with the hint of a smile. "None better. Now get to work."

Chapter Thirty

Avoiding the Abyss

The Murder of Joseph Vincent Keener, Ph.D.
Investigation Timeline, updated:

DAY ONE
5:15 AM (approx.) Distress call
5:30 AM (approx.) Shane arrives Keener residence
5:35 AM (approx.) State police alerted
5:42 AM (exact) 911
5:57 AM (exact) Shane calls Jack
7:00 AM (approx.) Rendezvous warehouse
8:25 AM (approx.) Rendezvous Nantz residence
8:55 AM (exact) Smash & grab
9:10 AM (approx.) INVESTIGATION BEGINS
Staff: Naomi, Alice, Teddy
Operatives: Jack, Dane, Milton

DAY TWO
9:05 AM (exact) Milton enters QuantaGate
9:26 AM (exact) Teddy monitors QG interoffice
system
10:05 AM (approx.) Alice confirms existence of
missing child

10:20 AM (approx.) Jack interviews Jonny Bing
11:55 AM (exact) Dane confers with Monica Bevins,
FBI
7:00 PM (approx.) Milton reports
9:40 PM (approx.) Jack interviewed re Jonny Bing
murder

DAY THREE
8:46 AM (exact) Randall Shane admitted to Mass
General
9:27 AM (exact) Shane reveals name of missing child
1:10 PM (approx.) Shane reports seeing video of
boy on bridge
2:40 PM (approx.) Alice interviews Clare O'Malley
at MIT, establishes backstory re mother & child

DAY FOUR
9:05 AM (approx.) FBI AD Monica Bevins visits
Shane at MGH
12:10 PM (approx.) Shane tells Dane missing laptop
location
12:45 PM (approx.) Alice reports to MGH, confers
with Dane (see above)
1:40 PM (approx.) Alice & Teddy shake tail, assumed to be FBI
2:16 PM (exact) Jack recovers missing laptop
3:50 PM (approx.) Teddy ID's mystery woman,
Kathleen Mancero
4:15 PM (approx.) Operatives given assignments
4:16 PM (exact) Alice miffed, compiles boring
timeline

Okay, maybe not so boring. And laid out like that, hour
for hour, it does give me a much clearer picture of what

has transpired since the case first began, and where the ongoing investigation has taken us. At a glance, the most important break in the case by far is the identification of Kathleen Mancero. As Naomi was quick to point out, that's a game changer. Establishing a connection between Randall Shane and a woman involved in an abduction means one of two things. Either the legendary kid finder is up to his neck in a murder/kidnapping—guilty as sin itself—or he's an innocent victim with a very powerful enemy who wants to destroy everything he stands for.

"We don't know if this enemy is also responsible for Professor Keener's murder, or if he simply seized on the opportunity to do Shane further harm," Naomi says as she looks over the updated timeline. "We don't know if those who interrogated Shane were involved in the assassination, or if they were simply doing what covert agencies do, investigating a possible security breach. Much is yet to be determined."

"Or she," I say, just to be snippy.

"Excuse me?"

"You said 'he.' 'He' framed Shane. Why couldn't it be a she? Hell hath no fury like, that sort of thing."

Boss lady nods agreeably. "I stand corrected. He or she. Either is plausible, assuming that whoever has done this has attained a position of power, enabling them to orchestrate or take advantage. Mrs. Mancero doesn't seem to have that much power at first glance." Naomi pauses, gives me a thoughtful look. "It might be useful if you make a list of what we know and what we don't."

I'm still in a mood, and therefore resist. *"We can't know what we don't know.* Quoting the great philosopher Donald Rumsfeld."

"Not even slightly true," Naomi says, amused. "I've just pointed out a couple of things we don't know. There are many more, and they're all pertinent to the case and may help clear the way to a solution. Right and left columns, please."

"You're serious."

This warrants a stern look. "When am I not?"

True enough. Fully aware there is merit to her suggestion, I begin to lay out the knowns and unknowns.

KNOWN
- MIT Professor Joseph Keener founds QuantaGate, top-secret research facility, with financial backing of investor J. Bing
- Keener meets Chinese female, Ming-Mei (stage name?)
- Keener brings Ming-Mei to Boston
- Keener and Ming-Mei have baby, born in Cambridge
- Ming-Mei returns to Hong Kong with boy, Joey
- Ming-Mei reports Joey abducted from Hong Kong mall
- Keener goes to Hong Kong & China, searching for missing son; no result
- 18 months later, Keener contacts Randall Shane
- Keener receives video of Joey in custody of K. Mancero
- K. Mancero known to Shane from previous case
- Keener executed with Shane's gun
- Blood evidence planted, Shane's motel
- State police alerted via Homeland
- Shane abducted by covert ops, for purposes of enhanced interrogation
- J. Bing killed shortly after interview with Jack

UNKNOWN
- Did Prof. Keener pass secrets to foreign agents?

- Ming-Mei's real name
- Ming-Mei's relationships (if any) in Hong Kong
- Who abducted Joey in Hong Kong
- Why Joey was abducted
- Where Joey's been held for the last 18 months
- Who brought Joey back to U.S.
- How K. Mancero got involved
- Present location of Joey
- Who killed Professor Keener
- Who framed Shane for the murder
- Why Shane is being framed
- What covert agency grabbed Shane
- Who killed J. Bing
- Why J. Bing killed

Very discouraging. Listed like this it makes it look like we don't know much of anything worth knowing, but that can't be true, can it? Surely it matters that we've identified the mystery woman, that we're virtually certain Randall Shane has been framed by powerful enemies, that the boy is alive, that...wait, hold on.

Going back to the boy, five-year-old Joey, my pencil hesitates over his name like a nervous dowsing rod. Alive? Do we know that? We know he was alive when the video was shot, but that was before the professor was executed in his own home. At which point everything changed, did it not? With the father dead, is there any reason to keep the boy alive? Whatever leverage the child may have represented, surely that no longer applies. Would he not be expendable?

Taking my shorthand pad, I quick-walk back to the command center, drop it on Naomi's desk. Busy at the phone, she barely gives me a glance.

"Alive or dead, your call."

She looks up, cups her hand to the phone. "Alice?"

"Joey Keener, age five. Which column? Alive or dead?"

Naomi hangs up with a crisp "I'll get back to you." She glances at the shorthand notebook, which I'm ninety percent sure she can't decipher, and leans back in her seat, signaling me to continue.

I say, "Whoever took the boy had a reason. To pry secrets out of his father, to make him cooperate, whatever. Didn't that reason end when Keener died?"

"Quite possibly, but we knew that. We've known it all along. Nothing has changed." Naomi's expression remains maddeningly neutral, as if the subject under discussion is purely theoretical. "Not an hour ago, when we were discussing recent developments I said, 'if he still lives,' in reference to the boy. Odds for his survival can't be calculated. He is either in one state or the other, alive or dead, and speculation on our part will have no effect on his survival. True, we have not yet established a scenario in which it makes logical sense for the abductors to keep the boy alive. Also true, we do not know the precise motivations for kidnapping the child in the first place, therefore our predictive results may be flawed. And the third truth, the one I suggest you cling to, is that Randall Shane believes the boy is alive. Those were among his very first words, upon regaining consciousness."

"But the poor man had been *drugged out of his mind*," I say, voice rising. "He'd been beaten by experts. He thinks they *bored into his skull* with a power drill and *cut out part of his brain!*"

"Nevertheless," Naomi says, exuding patience, "everything we've learned about Randall Shane indicates that saving children is at the core of what keeps him alive. Even damaged, having survived the cruelest form of torture, he believes at the very center of his being that the boy survives. Further, we have established that he refuses to accept truly hopeless cases because he understands that peering into the abyss of endless grief is, for him, particularly dangerous. Therefore his certainty about the child is based on something solid, something real, some knowledge he has about the case that we've not yet been able to discern, and which he has not yet been able to communicate."

"But you just said—"

"I know what I said," she says, cutting me off. "And I know what Shane said. Forget the odds. Forget logic. This isn't a quantum calculation. This is human hope, a form of energy that doesn't conform to rules, or laws of nature."

"So you're saying, assume the boy is alive and go from there."

She nods. "Trust Shane. Avoid the abyss."

Chapter Thirty-One

Sneakers Make the Man

Dane finally shows up just before dinner, looking all flushed and claiming she can't stay for the meal (main course: broiled filet of wahoo) much to her regret. Not that she actually seems to be experiencing regret. Quite the opposite. It seems there's this newbie attorney who just started working for the Middlesex District Attorney's Office, and she and Dane think they have a lot in common, a possibility that simply has to be explored over an intimate dinner at Aujourd'hui, scheduled to begin in less than an hour, and Dane still needs to shower and change.

"We're not even a little bit interested in your social life," Naomi says, speaking for herself alone. "If you've left Shane unattended and are deigning to make a pit stop here, you must have something to relate. Please do so."

You've probably guessed as much, but Naomi hates last-minute dinner cancellations. She's also not keen on Dane's self-acknowledged promiscuity, although she's never said so, not in so many words. But it's out there, her disapproval, and remains an interesting point of contention between two extremely willful and confident people.

Hands on her petite hips, Dane gives Naomi a look. "My, my," she says. "I'll bet your ancestors came over on the *Mayflower*. Being such Puritans."

"I think you mean Pilgrims."

"I know what I said. Puritans, the stuffy, stuck-up, disapproving kind who probably had sex fully clothed, if at all."

"So you're here to discuss sex?" Naomi says, ignoring the taunt.

"I came to discuss the arrangement I just finalized with Tommy Costello. You know, the D.A. who has been threatening to have Randall Shane thrown in a cell with actual criminals?"

"Fine," says Naomi with a small smile. "You're forgiven for skipping dinner, okay? Please give us the details. Alice will take notes."

Dane plops into one of the little decorative chairs that line the hallway—chairs much too narrow for the average human derriere—and gives us the gist of it.

"It's a big profile case, founder of QuantaGate murdered in his own home, so naturally Tommy wants to make the most of it. In case you didn't know, he's planning a run for governor. Anyhow, we've been fencing over this—he's all parry and no thrust, is Tommy Boy— and he finally came around to seeing it my way. Our way. That there's a possibility it will all blow up in his face— the whole covert security angle, Shane being framed and so on—and that he therefore needs to be careful, which means not sticking Randall Shane, a certified hero, into the Middlesex County holding cells without bail. How would it look, if he eventually is proven innocent, if the man who saved untold numbers of children gets stuck with a shiv by some low-life child molester, which they happen to have a surfeit of at the moment, at the Middlesex, awaiting trial? Disaster, right? So he signed off, did Tommy. Randall Shane remains under the care of his doctors, in a very comfy room at MG—we agreed on the little suite with the fireplace, the one reserved for VIPs—and we'll agree to post a bond in case he attempts to escape. In addition Shane will have access to his full legal team, which means anyone I care to designate, including investigators, which means everybody. So how's that for a good deal? Deserving of a night on the town to celebrate or what?"

"Well done," Naomi says. "What kind of bond?"

"Nothing special." Dane pauses. "A million bucks."

"The fee on a million-dollar bond is a hundred grand, nonrefundable. You agreed to that?"

A firm headshake. "No, I did not. This isn't a bail bond because he isn't being bailed, and therefore the normal fees do not apply. This is a kind of surety bond."

"What kind, specifically?"

"The kind between three parties—Shane, us and the County of Middlesex. We're the surety party and therefore no bondsman is involved. It only kicks in if Shane escapes custody."

"You're telling me that as the surety party we'd be responsible for the entire bond. One million dollars."

Dane shrugs. "That was the deal. I took it. Is there a problem?"

"You might have called," Naomi points out, with all the warmth of an iceberg eyeing up a passing cruise ship.

"It just happened within the last fifteen minutes!" Dane says, clearly exasperated. "I repeat, is there a problem? Because I already signed off, and if we need to rescind I'll have to call Tommy, like, right now."

"You signed in your capacity as legal representative of the corporate entity that funds this enterprise?"

Dane nods. "Yup, I did."

"That should be okay," Naomi says, relenting. "You'll regret missing the wahoo."

Dane pops up from the chair, grinning. "I have no intention of missing the 'wahoo!' part. It'll just come later, after dessert, and maybe a little cognac. If I get lucky, that—"

"Your business," Naomi interjects, primly.

Flashing me a conspiratorial grin, Dane makes a dash for the door.

Elena Walch "Beyond The Clouds" (Alto Adige, Italy)
Fresh Goat Cheese, Merriman Farms
Satsuma Plum Compote
New Peas & New Potatoes
Broiled Wahoo Filet with Wasabi Sauce
Strawberry Surprise
Château Climens Barsac

At the appointed hour, 7:00 p.m. precisely, having donned a lovely pair of silver wire earrings, Naomi reappears, accompanied by this evening's guest, a slight, distracted-looking young man with myopic, bespectacled eyes, distinctly watery with either a lack of sleep or from the effects of allergies, or both. The guest has long shoulder-length hair, and is dressed perfunctorily in an ill-fitting suit that could have come from the back rack of the local Goodwill and probably did, quite recently. Clean enough—the suit—but a little long in the leg, so that the trouser cuffs bunch over what are obviously a pair of worn but comfortable sneakers.

Sneakers! At one of Mrs. Beasley's formal dinners. The very idea makes me giddy.

"Allow me to present Sherman Elliot," Naomi says, leading him to his seat at the table. "Mr. Elliot is, or was, one of Professor Keener's graduate students."

She looks around the table, as if to discourage any possible comment or reaction to the guest's lack of sartorial elegance. It should be noted that for the first month or so in residence, Teddy exhibited a similar resistance to donning proper dinner attire, refusing to knot his tie and so on, and once appeared in shorts and sandals. Only once. Any sort of hairstyle is deemed acceptable at the Nantz table, as are facial tattoos and piercings, but house rules require jacket and tie for males, evening dress for females and what Naomi calls "dress-up shoes" for both genders. My guess is, she somehow wrestled Elliot into a hastily obtained suit, but failed to persuade him to relinquish the sneakers.

When we're all seated, and the first wine course has been poured, boss lady makes an announcement. "Alice has your reports, and the events of the day have been duly noted. We won't be discussing any specifics of the case over dinner, in deference to our special guest."

We mutter assent. Obviously we don't share the details of any case with any guest not specifically employed—and therefore vetted—by Naomi Nantz. This young gentleman has not only not been vetted, he apparently has an aversion to showers and shampoo, if the dandruff dust on his narrow shoulders is any indication.

All such derogatory and no doubt unfair thoughts vanish as soon as the kid opens his mouth. A character reevaluation is in order: Sherman has the deep, resonant voice of an old-time radio broadcaster, and that kind of confidence in his speaking ability.

"Allow me to apologize," he begins. "I've spent the last four days sleeping on a friend's couch in a damp basement. With a large German shepherd named Adolph. I left my own apartment without a change of clothes, or my own phone, and the term 'sleep' is an exaggeration because I haven't really slept, not since Professor Keener died. *Was killed* is the more accurate term, I suppose, because I wouldn't have had to run away if he'd just, you know, died of natural causes."

Sherman pauses to take a sip of his wine. Unlike his voice, his smile is shy, unassuming.

"No doubt you'll think I'm being paranoid—I think that myself, when I'm not being afraid—but Professor Keener warned me about them, the men who were out to get him, and once I saw them, I knew he was speaking the truth."

"And what men would those be?" Naomi asks, by way of prompting him.

"The men who came through the lab the morning he was killed."

"The lab at QuantaGate?" Jack asks.

"No, at MIT. Keener's teaching lab. Where he keeps the electron gun."

"Electron gun? Is that a weapon?"

Sherman smiles a little sadly. "I wish. No, Professor Keener used it in his lectures. There's nothing special about an electron gun, anyone can buy one. Any school, I mean, they're pretty expensive. The lab is where we keep all of the toys. The electron gun, a couple of lasers and the single-photon generators. It's all gone. They took everything. He told me they'd be coming but I didn't believe him."

"Who came, Sherman, can you give us a description?"

He shrugs. "Dudes in uniform. Security guards from his company, they showed up after hours, when nobody was around but me. They marched into the lab and took everything there. Papers, files, personal computers. Seized for evidence, they said. They packed everything in boxes and took it away. And then one of them, this dude who acted like it was all very amusing, he comes up to me in the lab and he says they'll be wanting to ask me a few questions, and that I'd better tell the truth or I'd end up in Gitmo, and nobody would ever know I was there. And I said I thought Gitmo was closed and he just laughed. That's what really scared me, the way he laughed."

"A security detail from QuantaGate," Naomi tells us. "I checked with the university and also with QuantaGate. Gama Guards security detail was dispatched to seize all computers and equipment associated with Keener's research. Evidence was sealed and placed in the secure labs at QuantaGate, where it remains. Nobody is disputing Mr. Elliot's version of events, except for the part about threatening him with rendition, which they say must have been a misunderstanding."

"Not the FBI," Jack says. "This was initiated by the company itself?"

Naomi nods. "Apparently by instruction of the Department of Defense. That's yet to be confirmed, but it sounds right. They'd have been concerned the professor might have brought sensitive materials from the company lab to the university, and wanted to round it all up and keep it in one place, under lock and key."

"Standard procedure, more or less," Jack says. "Except I would have expected the FBI to be tasked, not corporate rent-a-cops."

Sherman pipes up in his resonant voice. "That's who he was afraid of, the professor. He said his own company was spying on him, that they didn't believe him."

"This is the interesting part," says Naomi. "Go ahead. Tell us what he said."

"They didn't believe him about the research. That he'd got it wrong. It was never going to work, you see, because there's no practical application for the theory, that's what he discovered. Not now and maybe not ever."

Jack puts down his glass of wine, a look of surprise passing over his handsome face. "You're saying that whatever QuantaGate is trying to make for the Defense Department, it isn't working?"

Sherman Elliot nods eagerly. "Exactly," he says. "Professor Keener managed to pull off an experimental version in the lab, using paired photons over a long distance, but when it comes to a full stream of gated photons, which is what you need for real communication, there's just no way. The method has an inherent flaw that simply can't be overcome, without changing the laws of physics, and no one can do that, not even Joseph Keener."

Jack puts up a hand, as if stopping traffic. "Hold on there, son. If you're about to divulge secret information, we'd rather you didn't. We're not in the spy business here."

Young Sherman smiles for the first time in our company, and it's a rather splendid smile. Handsome, almost. "No worries, mate. Isn't that what the Aussies say? Look, I'm a grad student at a university lab. I never worked for QuantaGate, I don't have security clearance and everything I'm telling you has already been published. It's out there. Except the part about it not working. Is that a top secret, if something doesn't work?"

"Actually, it might be," Jack says. "You already know about this part, right, Naomi?"

"I do," she says. "The information is not confined to Mr. Elliot. It's been a matter of open speculation on various scientific forums, dating back several months. Go ahead, Mr. Elliot, explain. As if you're teaching not-very-bright students."

"Really? Okay. Let me see. You guys know about binary computer language, right? Ones and zeros? When you boil it down to the basics, that's how all software is written, in a string of ones and zeros. Dots and dashes is another way to think about it. No matter how complicated the message, it can be translated into dots and dashes, like in Morse code. Anyhow, the professor had this idea for a practical application, using quantum dots, a particular type of photon. That probably sounds complicated, but really it isn't, not in concept. The laws of quantum physics predict that two photons that have interacted together are somehow bonded forever, by a phenomenon known as 'entanglement.' That means that if you observe one of the paired photons, the other photon will collapse into the same state as the first, no matter how far away it is."

"Totally lost," Jack says. "What's a photon again? Is it like a little flashlight?"

Sherman begins to giggle. A deep giggle, but a giggle just the same. "Sure, why not?" he says. "Like a very small flashlight. The smallest flashlight that can possibly exist. A single quantum of light. Look, you don't have to understand that part, all you have to know is that Keener's Theorem predicts a way to use a stream of entangled photons to communicate over a long distance, without resorting to fiber optic cables, or satellites, or radio waves. According to the theorem, if you typed a message into a quantum computer here in this room, the identical message would appear in an identical quantum computer, a 'paired' computer, on the other side of the world. Or the other side of the universe, for that matter.

In real time. There would be no possible way to intercept the message. No need for encoded messages or firewalls. Perfect, instantaneous communication that can never be hacked."

"But the theory is wrong."

"No, no, the theorem still has an elegant solution," Elliot insists, using his expressive hands as if shaping calculations in the air. "In theory, it should be possible. But Keener's idea about how to generate a functioning stream of entangled photons—the actual machinery of it—*that* turns out to be totally wrong. They haven't been able to make it work in the real world, and he finally figured out why, and the reason is such, without getting into the math, that it will never work."

"So the company, QuantaGate, it's a bust?"

Sherman nods happily. "That's about the size of it, yes."

"What's the word on campus? Do they expect the company to actually go bankrupt?"

"Oh no. Not with that huge DOD contract. We all expect they'll keep milking that for years. Especially now that Professor Keener isn't there to stop them."

Chapter Thirty-Two

Say a Little Prayer

She waits until Joey is sound asleep before making her move. The boy had been awake for hours past his bedtime, fretting about his mother, who he calls Mi Ma. He's a smart kid—some sort of musical genius or prodigy—and he knows that something is terribly wrong, how could he not? Spirited away from his piano class and put in the care of strangers, flown halfway around the world and lately locked in what amounts to a luxuriously appointed dungeon for days at a time. What is he supposed to think? He keeps asking why he can't talk to Mi Ma on the phone and there's no good answer, beyond "your mommy is too sick to talk but she'll be better soon." No surprise, the poor kid has begun to worry that Mi Ma is dead and that no one will tell him the truth.

Joey isn't the only one who knows something is wrong. When Kathleen agreed to help, alerted by a text message from Randall Shane, she was informed that the boy's mother had to be taken into protective custody— some sort of gang problem, apparently, or maybe the mother had been undercover, it was never made clear— and Shane needed someone he could trust to look after her five-year-old son. The strong implication was that

Joey was also in danger and that the only recourse was to lie low for a few weeks while Shane straightened things out.

In the beginning it had all been very exciting. Prior to this, Randall Shane had refused her offers of assistance and eventually convinced her that focusing on missing children wasn't the best thing for her particular situation. She hated the whole concept of getting on with her life, which is what everyone kept urging her to do, it sounded so pathetic and cheesy, but that's what she was doing, like someone slowly awakening from an endless nightmare. Accepting the awful reality that she was alive in the world and her daughter wasn't, and that would never change. Then, out of the blue, an urgent text to her cell, begging for her help. Sent under duress, obviously, because he was in pursuit of some bad guys. Not that he had called them bad guys—in the message he'd referred to them as "foreign agents," which Kathleen can only imagine are some sort of spies or terrorists. Whatever, she quickly visualized them as the kind of evil, lying monsters who pretend to be good—who pretend to love you—all the while putting a mother in danger and threatening her child. The instruction had been simple: get herself to the Aircenter in Olathe at precisely 11:00 p.m. A man called Kidder would meet her there—he would know what she looked like—and she was to follow his instructions.

It was all very exciting.

Kidder, who seemed to know a lot about Randall Shane, was quite charming at first, and pretended to listen to her opinions of child rearing as they sped through a moonlit sky in a private jet with leather seats and a sleek hardwood interior that she and Kidder had all to themselves. First stop, Seattle, which she recognized from the Space Needle—Kidder wouldn't say where they were, said it was on a need-to-know basis and she didn't need to know. Then another long flight over open water, the Pacific, obviously, heading for a destination he at first refused to divulge but finally admitted was Hong Kong. Hong Kong! Not that she saw any of it beyond the small windows of the little jet—she was not allowed to leave the confines of the aircraft when, after many hours, it landed on a remote island runway to refuel. Just as well, she'd thought at the time. Considering that she didn't even have a passport. Not that there had been anything like customs. No officials at all while they waited on the tarmac. The pilot and copilot had actually refueled the plane themselves, which Kathleen thought was odd, but they were of necessity all keeping a super low profile, so maybe that's how it was done. Finally they arrived in Hong Kong in broad daylight—she could see the glittering city and the surrounding hills as they came in to land. Again they refueled and in less than an hour a shiny black SUV had appeared on the runway, and a small frightened boy was whisked into the plane and Kathleen had her hands full comforting Joey as they took off and returned to Seattle, and then eventually to the East Coast, where a very similar black SUV had met them at a private airport of some sort and then delivered them here, to the guesthouse of a remote oceanfront estate. Really to the dungeon, because that's where Kidder has been keeping them.

There was a time when she accepted Kidder's lies as part of the deal. It made sense that she would not be informed of everything that was going on, whatever dangers lurked or threatened. Her task was simply to care for Joey, to protect him with something like a mother's love, while Shane did whatever he had to do to protect Joey's real mother. It had even made sense that Shane would not be able to communicate during this dangerous time, that it was simply too risky. Texts, emails, phone calls, they could all be intercepted, used to locate those in hiding. So she had gone along, let Kidder run things the way he saw fit. After all, Shane had tasked him to be the bodyguard. So when he said he was locking them in the safe room—the entire finished basement had been fitted out as a safe room—for their own protection, who was she to argue? It was scary, but surely Shane and Kidder knew what they were doing.

Lately she's come to doubt not only Kidder, but the whole purpose of the mission. Kidder lies about everything, even when the lie serves no purpose that she can see, and he has a creepy quality that extends much deeper than his routine lewdness. There's something about him that scares the hell out of her, that makes her flesh crawl. Would Randall Shane, a real gentleman, the kindest and most decent human being she'd ever met, would he really employ a man like Kidder? Or was the whole thing some sort of con, initiated by a text message that she now realizes could have originated from anywhere, and which had caused her to react immediately, obeying the request without question.

There's only one way to find out what's really going on, and if, as she fears, she and Joey are in danger, not from some nameless "foreign agents," but from Kidder himself. Somehow she has to contact Randall Shane, or at the very least see if she can find out what he's involved in. There are no phones in what she has come to think of as the dungeon. Plenty of jacks but no phones. Supposedly to prevent any calls being traced back to the source. The cable connection is dead, too, meaning that she hasn't even seen the news in almost two weeks.

Because, Kidder has explained, having the cable turned on would indicate that the guesthouse is occupied, and might therefore draw attention to them. Asked if she could possibly have a radio to listen to, Kidder hadn't even bothered to make up an excuse, he'd simply refused.

That's when she knew she had to come up with an escape plan. With Kidder gone for hours at a time, leaving them locked in the so-called safe room, she's had plenty of time to explore. So far she's found a couple of what she hopes will be useful items. The first, a small adjustable wrench in the drawer of a bedside table. The second, and this isn't so much of a find as a discovery, she managed to trace the cable back to the connection box where it enters the basement.

The coaxial cable has been disconnected at the connection box, not turned off. Another Kidder lie. Which she already knew because she had heard, faintly but distinctly, a live TV broadcast coming out of his room one night. The son of a bitch was listening to Leno, laughing along like some laugh-track moron, that's what inspired her to check out the cable in the first place.

It had been simple enough to test. Using the little wrench, she reattached the cable connection, turned on one of the TVs with the sound already down and there it was, broadcast television, in HD no less. Because she never knew when Kidder was going to return she quickly turned the TV off and disconnected the cable and reattached it only late at night, when she barricaded herself in the bedroom she shared with Joey. Figuring if Kidder broke the door down she'd still have time to turn the TV off and pretend like she was scared of the foreign agents and that's why she'd blocked the door.

For two nights running she's been switching between CNN and a local news station out of Boston, reading the closed-captioned crawl with the sound down. Nothing so far. Lots of news about celebrities and politics, but no mention of anything that gave a clue about what Shane might be up to. Not yet.

It feels just a bit like praying at an altar, but instead of lighting candles she's illuminated by the silent TV screen. Bathed in light and waiting for the word. Waiting for something, some indication from the world outside.

Please, God, give me a sign.

Late that night her prayers are answered and it changes everything, everything.

Chapter Thirty-Three

The Smell Test

It is almost impossible to accurately describe Mrs. Beasley's Strawberry Surprise, other than to say that it involves a pastry crust that probably has a stick of butter in each serving, and that the element of surprise is not simply an intriguing name for the dish, but key to the taste experience. Sherman Elliot, departing from his normal diet of microwaved man food, was reduced to moans of pleasure and rolling his eyes at each bite, and then gasping like a boated fish after the last crumb vanished into his yearning mouth.

Speaking of fish, the grilled wahoo was—and this was no surprise—*wahoo!* worthy. So, an exemplary dining experience, and one that a half-starved grad student will no doubt never forget. It turns out that prior to inviting Elliot to join us, Naomi had arranged for him to make a voluntary statement to the FBI, and encouraged him to go back to his apartment and resume his life.

"Everything you have to say on the subject has been entered into official record, which means there would be no point in anyone, certainly not a bullying rent-a-cop, dragging you off for further questioning," Naomi says, escorting him to the door. "It will be clear to anyone who cares to check that you never worked for QuantaGate and never knew the details of whatever device they've been attempting to perfect. Your part in this affair is over. Go back to your life, Mr. Elliot. Live long and prosper."

He appears shocked at her turn of phrase. "You're a fan?" he asks.

"Always had a thing for Vulcans."

She offers her hand. He takes it, bowing slightly, as if auditioning for a part he never expected to play. "What can I say but 'wow.' And thank you."

After the door is shut and firmly locked behind him, I go, "Really? You're a *Star Trek* fan? Since when?"

"I enjoyed the most recent movie, the one where they're all quite young. Before Captain Kirk wore a girdle."

"And you came across Sherman Elliot how?"

She shrugs. "By posting a query on the grad student forum. Mr. Elliot was one of a dozen who responded, and seemed to have formed the most interesting impressions of the last days of Joseph Keener."

"So you never left the residence, or your desk, for that matter."

"No need," she says. "Teddy was a big help, of course, pointing me in the right direction. By the way, Elliot wasn't the only grad student who thinks that Professor Keener failed in his quest to design a functioning quantum computer. The belief is widely held in the physics department, and these are not people afraid of expressing opinions, to say the least. So I don't think Mr. Elliot was ever really in danger from our friends in the stealth helicopters."

Jack Delancey has just returned from the washroom. He's fastidious about his white smile, and usually carries a little traveler's toothbrush in the inside breast pocket of his suit jacket. His grin is freshly scrubbed. "That was interesting," he says. "Security cops threatening students with rendition. Makes you wonder."

"Indeed," says Naomi. "Much to discuss. Anyone interested in joining me for a small brandy in the library?"

When we're all seated and sipping from the tiny crystal glasses—she's not kidding about the "small" part—Naomi leans back in her leather armchair and kicks off her heels. "I trust no one is offended? Good. These have been killing me all evening."

Teddy looks as if he'd like to join her in the shoeless department but, at a glance from Jack, thinks better. A woman in sheer stockings is one thing, a man in socks quite another. Addressing herself to Jack, Naomi says, "If my recollection is correct, you have an acquaintance employed by Gama Guards. Anything of interest there?"

Jack, looking wry and thoughtful, eases back in his own chair. "I didn't think so. Like Wackenhut, they supply security guards to corporations. Basic rent-a-cops. My acquaintance retired from the sheriff's department, went into middle management at Gama Guards, recruiting retired law enforcement officers much like himself. No chance of advancement—that goes to the younger career guys—but he's happy enough, collects his paycheck, takes all his vacation days."

"Nothing out of the ordinary."

"Not in my old pal's department. But in light of what the kid said, we need to dig deeper. It doesn't surprise me that the professor would have been paranoid about his own guards checking up on him—that's part of their job, after all—but when it comes to seizing sensitive materials and documents during a felony investigation, that should have been the FBI, or at the very least the state police. Not private-sector goofballs who get off on threatening students. This doesn't pass the smell test."

"Teddy?" Naomi says.

"Deep background on Gama Guards," our young hacker says, standing up, his brandy untouched. "I'll get right on it."

Jack watches him go, waits until he's clear of the room and then says, "The kid gets better every day. I had my doubts when you first brought him aboard, but no longer. If we could fix that ridiculous hairdo he'd be perfect."

"I rather like the 'hawk," Naomi says plainly. "Back to the matter at hand. In light of what Mr. Elliot had to say, I can think of at least three possible variations that need to be explored. One: Keener failed, and someone who wished to keep that failure a secret arranged to have him silenced. Two: Keener was lying to his grad students as a kind of smoke screen, hoping that the message of his failure would be picked up by the kidnappers, who would then have no reason to keep holding his son as leverage for his cooperation. Three: some variation on the above, which involves Keener going to extraordinary lengths to recover Joey, and engaging in actions that have not yet come to light, but which marked him for execution."

"You mean he tried to double-cross someone?"

"Or some government," she suggests.

I say, "Everything we know about this guy suggests he was a bad judge of people. Couldn't read them. And nothing suggests he was good at lying. Maybe that got him in trouble. Either someone believed him about his project being a failure, and killed him, or someone didn't believe him, and killed him."

"Or we're missing something huge that's staring us right in the face," Jack says. He starts to add something and then stops, a dark expression passing like a cloud across his handsome features.

He means Shane.

What if we've got it all wrong?

Kathleen Mancero lies awake on the twin-size bed, a yard or so from the bed where Joey sleeps soundly, his breathing as easy and regular as clockwork. After hours of playing almost frantically on his keyboard, head bobbing inside the headphones, he finally crawled up on the bed, allowed her to read him a story and then promptly fell deeply asleep. Joey may be a musical prodigy—he won't let her hear what he's playing as he thumps the keys, so it's hard to know for sure, not that she's any judge of classical music, anyhow—but in all other respects he's a typical little boy, and shares with most children that amazing ability to sleep soundly when all around them the world is falling apart. How she envies that gift, to sleep in the face of adversity, to escape from the constant fear.

Kathleen may never sleep again, her mind electric with what she finally learned from the silent TV, courtesy of a closed-captioned local news broadcast.

Randall Shane has been hospitalized in Boston and is under arrest for the murder of Joey's father, who had hired him to find his missing son. Until that moment she hadn't even known Joey's last name, but the breaking-news description of the dead professor confirms all her worst fears.

She's been used, tricked into thinking that she was helping Shane, when in fact she's been assisting the kidnappers. She has no idea what's really going on—there are suggestions in the news blogs that Professor Keener had been suspected of espionage—but one thing she does know for sure. Kidder terrifies her. Not because she cares so much about her own life—everything has been such a struggle since her daughter was taken that death is no longer something to be feared—but because she's convinced that Joey is in terrible danger. Not from the "foreign agents" Kidder so knowingly alludes to, but from Kidder himself. There's a palpable darkness about him, a vibe of pure evil. He's planning to kill them both. She can feel it in her bones, in every beat of her heart.

She has to find a way to save Joey, even if it kills her.

Chapter Thirty-Four

The Pretty Cool Connection

It's probably just my imagination, but I swear when Teddy Boyle is excited his hair stands up straighter and brightens in color, like a pheasant showing off his tail feathers. Mrs. Beasley notices and announces he's to have only decaffeinated coffee this morning so he won't be, as she puts it, "overstimulated."

Too late for that. He's found us in the breakfast nook, where Naomi is absorbing her newspapers and I'm trying and failing to balance the column of knowns with the columns of unknowns. It seems like the more we discover the less we know for certain, and the trend is discouraging. Jack, irritatingly dapper at this hour, carefully sips Mrs. Beasley's French press coffee while going over the notes in his lined reporter's notebook. Now and then he consults his silenced BlackBerry, scrolling for clues apparently. I wish he'd find one, we could all use a good clue. And Dane, well, Dane has yet to call in, presumably because she had a late night with her new friend in the D.A.'s office.

"Interesting fact about Gama Guards," our young hacker announces, dropping into the booth. "They were acquired last year by another company, Gatling Security Group. GSG. That's who really employs the guards at QuantaGate."

"GSG," Naomi says, musing. "Rings a bell."

"Sounds familiar to me, too," says Jack, keenly interested.

"Dazzle us with details," Naomi says.

Teddy is eager to comply. "They're hot-wired to the Pentagon, supplying private contractors to Iraq, Afghanistan, Pakistan, just about anywhere the U.S. military has been deployed. Among many other activities, GSG contractors oversee interrogations for the CIA. And get this: GSG has been implicated in one of the torture scandals. At the behest of the CIA they kidnapped suspects, transported them to remote locations and used what they called 'enhanced interrogation techniques' to extract information. Sound familiar?"

It's clear that Teddy hasn't slept, and also clear that for him pulling an all-nighter has been somehow invigorating. His eyes are red-rimmed but full of excitement and maybe a little righteous indignation, which becomes clear as he shares what he has discovered about the company that supplies security guards to QuantaGate.

"Begin at the beginning," Naomi says, very firmly. "Deep background first. Lay the foundation and go from there."

"Okay, sure, you're right," Teddy says, taking a deep breath to steady himself. "The beginning isn't that long ago, for such a big company. Gatling Security Group was founded by Taylor Gatling, Jr., a young Delta Force officer, the day he resigned from the military. I can't get to the specifics, because the records are buried deep in the Pentagon, but it looks like the deal was in place before he resigned. He had it wired. That is, he had a contract ready to fulfill the minute he took off the uniform. Started out fairly modest, supplying a dozen or so civilian contractors to work with the CIA as scouts, identifying terrorist targets in Afghanistan, out in the remote tribal areas. Dangerous work, and they did it very well. Within a few months GSG had more than fifty people on the payroll, with an open-ended, no-bid contract. By the end of the first year it was over five hundred. Today there are GSG crews in Afghanistan who detain and interrogate suspects, supposedly under CIA supervision. There are GSG crews who load missiles into Predator drones, crews who pilot the drones by remote control, crews of mechanics who keep the drones fueled and ready to fly. They currently bill nearly half a billion per annum, and that's only the contracts that come under the sunshine laws. Covert operations are under the general operating budget of the CIA, or whatever agency is sponsoring a particular operation, and those we don't know about. We do know the company is privately held, with controlling ownership in the hands of Taylor Gatling, Jr., and a substantial minority share held by a private hedge fund controlled by recently retired generals. The company currently employs more than three thousand people worldwide, including Gama Guards. Not bad for a Delta Force captain with good connections. The guy put the pedal to the metal and went from zero to a billion in seven years. It's all very cozy, although—and this is what knocks me out—not even slightly illegal."

"Were you able to ascertain specifics on the torture allegations?" Jack asks, looking up from his notebook.

"Just what was mentioned by reporters who covered the Congressional investigations. Most of the details are redacted. But whatever support the GSG crews provided, apparently it didn't involve waterboarding. They were adamant about that. When someone asked about chemi-

cal interrogations—administering powerful drugs to suspects—the committee went into closed session. Nothing
on the record, not that I can get a hold of."

Naomi's eyes are almost as bright as Teddy's. "Chemical interrogation," she says. "That's what happened to
Shane."

The young hacker appears to be full to bursting. "And
I saved the best for last. You'll never guess where Gatling
Security Group world headquarters is located."

I get the distinct impression that Naomi does, in fact,
know the location, that the interesting factoid has already
surfaced in her remarkable mind, but she's circumspect
enough to let him complete the thought.

"Pease International Tradeport in Newington, New
Hampshire," he says, triumphant. "Less than fifty miles
from here by air. A former military base with a massive
runway. You could land a 747 there, no problem."

"Or a stealth helicopter," Naomi adds.

"Exactly," says Teddy. "Pretty cool, huh?"

Chapter Thirty-Five

Mr. Invisible and the Hands of Iron

Jack Delancey, bird-watcher.

He's costumed appropriately, in a floppy hat, khaki walking pants, waterproof hiking boots and a shirt with way too many pockets. Binoculars of course. That's what makes the disguise so useful, the ability to wander around with a pair of powerful lenses, supposedly looking for an eagle nesting area. Part of the nature trail, conveniently marked on a handout map, that parallels the vast concrete runway area at the Tradeport. So he's got a great excuse to be clocking the old airbase where, it is said, eagles do actually soar, rising on currents of hot air over the runways. This despite a steady stream of civilian aircraft still using the facility, as well as a National Guard refueling unit. Maybe the eagles are smart enough to get out of the way, or maybe that's why they are, as the saying goes, rare birds.

No eagles today, but plenty of turkey vultures, spinning up like paper kites. A kettle, that's what one of the real bird-watchers told him, stopping to chat. Vultures swirling on updrafts are called a kettle. Interesting fact. Not that Jack has any intention of taking up the hobby. His idea of strolling in the woods involves a blonde, not a bird. Or a brunette. Or for that matter, a redhead. He's not fussy, which is one reason he's had four wives. Although as far as he's concerned Eileen will be the last because his roving days are over, hand to his heart, this time he means it, amen.

Tromping though the underbrush he finds a suitable area, one that affords a view of the Gatling Security Group "world headquarters," which sounds a little too grand to be taken seriously. They'll know more about that when Milton reports at end of day. He should be in there by now, flashing his CPA credentials and then melting into the office background, as he does so well. Jack's mission is to ascertain if the company happens to have a stealth helicopter hidden away in one of those big old hangars. Because the coincidence of GSG providing security guards for QuantaGate and also being expert in the fine art of spiriting suspects away for interrogations is just too much. The working theory is that upon learning of Keener's murder, a covert agency—Defense Intelligence, perhaps—tasked GSG with securing sensitive documents and interrogating the chief suspect, namely Shane. Unless, of course, the civilian firm had also been involved in framing Randall Shane for the crime, which raises a whole lot of other interesting possibilities. Like, for instance, the possibility that they may have information about Joey Keener. All of which is speculation at the moment. They have suspicions but no proof, which is why Milty's in there and Jack is out here, tromping through the pucker-brush with a pair of binoculars welded to his eye sockets.

The hangars are huge, built for repairing giant bombers, which begs the question of why GSG acquired the buildings in the first place. Must be a bitch to heat in the winter. But then, this isn't winter, that's for sure, and even from his hidden spot under the trees Jack can feel the heat radiating from the miles of runways. So maybe it's a moot point. He can't get any closer without showing himself and he's not ready to do that, not yet, so this vantage will have to do. The enormous shed doors are partway open, leaving most of the vast interior in shadow. Even with the binocs, he can't see very far inside. There are a couple of vehicles in the shade, transport vans, probably, and a private jet. A couple of guys in overalls are polishing the jet, taking their own sweet time, but if there's a helicopter hiding in the shadows, Jack can't make it out. Which doesn't mean it's not there.

Set back from the hangar is a long bunkerlike structure bristling with antennae, looks like it might date from the 1950s, a couple of smaller warehouse structures and, behind that, a new two-story office building emblazoned with the company logo. *GSG—For A Safer World.* That's where the office staff will be located, hunched over terminals and counting all that Pentagon-funded money. With any luck, Milton has already claimed one of those terminals and has begun his "audit."

Jack wishes him luck. Better luck than he's having out here in mosquitoville, staring at shadows.

The company prefers to keep its employees fully caffeinated. True, there's a decaf option, but mostly the requests are for high-octane, as prepared by a tag team of young gals from the cafeteria staff, who act as baristas during the midmorning break. Unlike Starbucks, there are no fancy macchiatos or mochas on menu, but steamed lattes are available, cheerfully dispensed, and there's a fresh BestWhip dispenser for those who want to top off their espressos. All in all, a vast improvement on the usual corporate swill, and Milton is happily sipping his latte and milling around with a dozen or so of the office staff, most of whom happen to be female. Despite the novelty of barista-brewed coffee, GSG is in many ways a very traditional setup. A throwback, really, in which the mostly male bosses have glass-fronted offices on a mezzanine, overlooking the mostly female staff assigned to workstations on the main floor. The formal breaks are staggered so that no more than a quarter of the staffers are absent from their workstations at any one time.

As a visiting auditor Milton will be able to roam, but has so far been concentrating on receivables, where time cards and per-diem expenses are processed. Mostly paperless PDF files sent from BlackBerries half a world away, and which are then sorted, assembled, reprocessed and forwarded to the Pentagon under the provisions of The Contract. That's how staff refer to it, with capital letters, and with the reverence of patriots quoting from the Constitution. The Contract states this, The Contract states that. Not surprising, since an understanding of the minutiae of the contract enables the company to make a guaranteed profit on every aspect of the business, and thus keep generous salaries and benefits flowing to all of the employees.

The second most common phrase uttered by staffers is "Taylor wants," and although Milton has yet to see the big boss, he has already formed a pretty good picture of the man, who is held in very high regard by his staff. Something of a local legend, apparently. Star running back of the high school football team, awarded the Bronze Star for his military service and now founder of one of the biggest employers in the area, although most of the actual employees, and by far the most highly paid, are "day" contractors assigned to posts in Afghanistan.

"Over there," says one of his coffee mates, under her breath. "That's him."

Taylor Gatling, Jr., is in the house. Nodding and giving little celebrity waves as he makes his way quickly over the main floor and lightly ascends the steps to the mezzanine. A fit-looking man in his mid-thirties, with a military-style haircut, casually dressed in short sleeves and slacks, designer sunglasses hanging from a shirt pocket. Ready to take on the world, no doubt about it, that much is obvious from a glance.

"What a cutie," says one of the bookkeepers, and is quickly shushed, although the shushing is accompanied by knowing smiles. "Hey, it's not like he's married," she adds, and then drops it upon being gently elbowed.

A few minutes later Milton is back at his workstation, sifting through on-screen files, when a supervisor taps him on the shoulder. "Mr. Bean? Could you follow me, please?"

Milton stands, aware that his cloak of invisibility is fraying—every eye on the main floor has him in focus—and nods meekly. "Of course, is there some problem?"

"No problem at all," he is assured. "Strictly routine. We'll have you back at work in a jiffy."

He follows the supervisor up to the mezzanine, where he's led into one of the glass-fronted offices. Hip perched on a desk, Taylor Gatling, Jr., greets him with a cool smile. "Milton Bean? Nice to meet you."

He holds out a hand. Milton shakes. Thinking, it's okay to be nervous, I'm a nervous little guy who dislikes being singled out, that's my cover and also who I am.

"Have a seat, Mr. Bean, this won't take but a moment," he says, using a remote to adjust the window shades for privacy.

There are two other men in the room, both of whom

share the boss's level of fitness, as well as the military haircuts. Casually dressed but nothing remotely casual about them. Security, Milton guesses. Definitely ex-military. Neither of them says a word.

"So, Milton, it's my understanding that you're a spot auditor. May I ask who you're working for?"

"My CPA firm," Milton says, naming the firm that once employed him and still keeps his ID current. "I'm a forensic accountant."

"Yeah, we get that, but who hired your firm? DOD? IRS? They both have the right to run audits at any time, without advance notification. Which is it?"

"Can't say, because I don't know."

"I'm thinking IRS. Maybe that ID of yours is a cover and you really work directly for the Infernal Revenue. Is that it?"

"No, sir. It's a spot audit, that's all. We, um, do it all the time. I suggest you call my supervisor." Milton takes a business card from his wallet, places it on the desk.

Taylor Gatling, Jr., doesn't touch the card. He seems faintly amused by the ploy. "No doubt if we call that number, your place of employment will be confirmed. My concern isn't the validity of your ID, Mr. Bean. It is, frankly, you."

"Excuse me?"

"As you may have noticed, we have a state-of-the-art security system. When you presented your ID this morning your name and identification number ran through the system. Your name popped and the system notified us that a few days ago you were busily auditing accounts at QuantaGate, in Waltham, Massachusetts. Correct?"

"That's correct, yes."

"It can't be a coincidence, Mr. Bean."

Milton allows himself a shrug, as if his motives are

questioned every day, part of the job. He's ready with a plausible fallback position. "There was a question about the time cards for the security guards. Whether or not Gama Guards may have billed for more personnel than were actually on the premises over the last two quarters. GSG owns Gama Guards, so here I am."

"Ah," Taylor says, arms folded comfortably across his chest. "So you're investigating possible fraud, is that it? Billing for no-show workers?"

"Just checking the books."

"Because, funny thing, Gama Guards is located in Delaware. You want to hire Gama Guards security guards, you call the office in Wilmington. It all goes through Wilmington. All billing, all time cards, all paychecks, all ledgers, all books. Everything. Somebody made a mistake. You're in the wrong office in the wrong state, Mr. Bean."

Milton does his best to look dumbfounded, which isn't all that difficult. "There's obviously been a mistake," he says, as obsequiously as possible. "All I can do is apologize. It's company policy that forensic accountants leave the target premises upon request, pending legal resolution. I'll get my things and leave immediately."

As Milton attempts to rise, the two subordinates force him back down in the chair, not a word spoken, and hold him there with grips of iron. Without him quite knowing how they did it, they have moved behind him, cutting off any possible angle of escape.

Taylor gives him a grim, self-satisfied smile. "We have a few more questions," he says.

It happens so fast that Milton doesn't have time to draw a breath. One moment he's projecting confusion and nervous subservience—he's just a little man sent out on a job without adequate information, an office mouse—the next he's blind, a black sack covering his head and a powerful hand clamped over his mouth.

As they lift him into the air, his legs kick futilely.

Chapter Thirty-Six

Sleeping Giants

It's the fireplace that fools him. When Randall Shane first awakens his eyes focus on the bouquet of flowers that have been placed in the hearth—bright yellow blossoms. Mums, perhaps?—and for a while, for entire thrilling moments of anticipation, he thinks he's in a room at the Woodstock Inn, in Vermont. Jean must be in the shower, he can hear something like water drumming, and it comes back to him, what happened last night. It's Jean's twenty-fifth birthday, that's why they've gone to the extravagance of a weekend in Woodstock, and after they finished making love, or paused, really, Jean had plumped the pillows and sat with her knees drawn up to her chin and announced that she was pregnant. A secret she'd been keeping for a whole twenty-four hours, waiting until this special moment to share it with him. *It's a girl,* had been his instantaneous response, and when Jean asked how he could possibly know, he'd said he just did, and if he's right can they please call her Amy, and Jean said whoa there, big boy, you're jumping the gun.

His mind begins to clear. One of the happiest moments of his life drains away and he's left with the awful knowledge that this isn't the Woodstock Inn and Jean isn't showering in the bathroom because she's dead and gone, as is the precious child whose existence was revealed to him that night. He falls for miles, plummeting through memories that haven't the strength to buoy him up, or soften the landing, and the pain of recollection is so overwhelming that he whimpers like a child fighting off a nightmare.

"Mr. Shane? Are you awake?"

He blinks away the tears, focuses on the young woman in the white jacket.

"I'm Dr. Gallagher. You're being treated at Mass General, in Boston."

"I know who you are," he says, taking a deep breath. "Thank you, you've been very kind."

"Oh?" The doctor looks surprised, but not displeased. "Do you recall our last conversation?"

He grimaces, probing his memory. "You explained about the handcuffs. They were bruising my wrist and you'd asked the sheriff's department to have them removed and wanted to know if I was okay with a GPS ankle monitor instead. I said I was."

The young doctor pulls a chair close to the bed and takes a seat, putting them at eye level. "Well, now, this is real progress," she says. "Do you know that's the first time you've awakened without asking who I am and where you are?"

"Really?"

"Tell me what happened to your brain."

"My brain? My brain is very tired."

"Yes, but what happened to make you so tired, Mr. Shane? Can you recall?"

He thinks for a moment, and the answer comes without having to search for it. "I was interrogated by professionals. Beaten and then heavily drugged. No, that's not quite right. I was drugged, beaten, then drugged again. The drugged parts are all in a fog. Hallucinatory. I do recall a bright, blinding light and being threatened with a drill bit. No doubt I told them whatever they wanted to know."

"Remarkable," says the doctor.

"What?"

"The capacity of the mind to heal itself. We'd been thinking it might be months, if ever, but it appears that you're already well on your way to recovery."

"I feel awful."

"The beating alone would likely leave you feeling physically depressed. And however much your mental state may be improving, it will be some weeks before you're healed. Which means you will stay in my custody for the time being."

"In your custody and under arrest for murder," he says. "I didn't do it, by the way."

"Glad to hear it," she says. "I don't know much about murderers, Mr. Shane, but you certainly don't seem like the sort of man who would kill someone in cold blood."

"Not in cold blood," he says, but then thinks again of his wife and daughter. "Not on purpose."

If he hadn't fallen asleep in the car they'd still be alive, of that he's convinced. Over the years he's learned to live with the knowledge, but the truth of it hasn't changed.

"Confinement is confinement," the doctor says. "We'll just have to make do until this sorts itself out. That's what your attorney promises, that she'll eventually per-suade them to drop the charges. Despite the guards at the door and the device on your ankle, I hope you'll find your stay here tolerable. This just so happens to be one of the nicest rooms in the hospital, reserved for foreign dignitaries. It helps to be friends with Naomi Nantz, obviously."

Shane smiles, although it makes his jaw ache to do so. "I met her once, very briefly."

"Then you must have made quite an impression. Her people pulled a lot of very powerful strings and made sure you have everything you need. TV, books, phone, access to your legal team. Now that your mind is back we can get on with your physical therapy. Shall we say tomorrow?"

"Tomorrow is good. Why am I so sleepy? I never sleep."

"Nature's way of healing," the doctor says.

She's about to add something but is stopped by his gentle snore.

Chapter Thirty-Seven

Truth & Consequences

When the black hood is pulled from his head, Milton finds himself blinded by a powerful light. His hands are bound behind him, held by what feels like plastic straps. Slowly his eyes adjust. He's inside what could be a metal shed—he can't actually see beyond the shadow edge, outside the bright circle of light—but he can hear the faint metallic creaking of metal siding as it flexes in the wind. He's been seated, hard enough to jar his bones, on a short three-legged stool, the kind used for milking cows. He assumes the short stool is to emphasize his insignificance. If so, it's working—he's never felt so small and powerless in his life. He can just make out the figure of a man looming behind the light source.

Milton has seen this kind of thing often enough in movies, as suspects are interrogated, but the actual experience is quite different. The fact that he knows these are psychological tools intended to frighten him into submission does not lessen the effect. He's terrified. Adrenaline has so flooded his system that he's shaking and can't stop.

"When you got up this morning, I'll bet you didn't expect this to happen," says a man from behind the light.

Taylor Gatling, Jr., he recognizes the voice.

Finding that he can't speak, Milton shakes his head, agreeing.

"You should have. This is what happens to spies, Mr. Bean. You have been detained under authority of the Patriot Act, and if you wish to survive the experience you must cooperate. Answer truthfully and you will be released from custody. Attempt to hide, prevaricate or deceive us in any way, and you will be detained for an indefinite period. Stubborn cases languish for years. Nod if you understand."

Milton nods.

"Good. I'm turning you over to the professionals. Make them happy."

The figure recedes into the shadows. Another voice begins:

"Milton Franklin Bean, you are in violation of U.S. Code titles one and ten, in contravention of security act H.R. 2975, as amended to the Foreign Intelligence Surveillance Act of 1978 and the Electronics Privacy Act of 1986. Habeas corpus no longer applies. As such you have no right of representation, no right of notification, no right to seek relief from detention. Although perfectly legal, as set out by the above amendments to U.S. Code, this is not a legal proceeding. There will be no judge, no jury of your peers. You stand accused and will remain in custody until you have satisfied this authority that you are not a clear and present danger to this nation."

Milton, whose heart rate has slowed somewhat, manages to summon enough spit to ask, "What authority?"

The stool is kicked out from under him. Unable to balance the fall because his hands are bound, he lands heavily on his side with an *oof!* that empties his lungs.

"By *that* authority," says the voice, with a drill sergeant's barking cadence. "The authority to kick your sorry ass from here to Timbuktu, if that's what it takes. The authority to drop you into a hole so deep you won't hit bottom until your hundredth birthday. The authority to make you wish you'd never been born. Okay, get him back on the stool before he wets his pants. We'll put you in Depends if that happens, Milton, that's how we do it when suspects have leaky bladders, so I advise you to hold your water."

"Okay," says Milton, breathing heavily as they set him back on the stool. "Anything you say."

"Answer me: true or false, you entered this premises under false pretenses."

"True."

"True or false, you're employed by the IRS."

"What? No. Even if I was, what's that got to do with national security?"

Instantly the stool disappears. This time he falls backward. When they put him back on the stool his head is ringing from where it thumped the concrete.

"True or false. Those are the only acceptable answers. One or the other. I repeat, true or false, you are employed by the IRS."

"False."

"True or false, you are employed by the Defense Intelligence Agency."

"False."

"True or false, you are employed by Naomi Nantz, a private investigator."

He hesitates. This time he lands on his face, skidding on the point of his chin. Might have chipped a tooth, hard to say.

"T-t-true," he says, checking the tooth with the tip of his tongue. Chipped, definitely.

Somebody laughs, and he hears hands slap together, as if in congratulations.

"Very good, Mr. Bean. That's the correct answer. Someone fitting your description was recorded entering the Nantz residence a few days ago. The description being 'average man with indistinguishable features,' which certainly fits. Oddly enough, we didn't get a hit on our facial recognition software. It's like you blur, or something generic. So by admitting you're employed by Naomi Nantz you've confirmed a favorite theory, which makes us very happy. For that you'll be rewarded with a drink of water."

A bucket of icy cold water is thrown in his face.

"Hoo-ha!" someone hoots, as hands slap again.

He crouches on the little stool, shivering. Milton is not one of those who never imagined himself being brave while undergoing torture. The scary thing is, they haven't really got to the torture part yet. Not the part where they break his fingers or tenderize every muscle and ligament in his body, as they obviously did to Randall Shane. Never mind what they did to his brain.

Milton concentrates on not crapping his pants, and vows to answer every question truthfully, or to supply whatever answers they so desire, truthful or not, to do whatever it takes to avoid being physically damaged or mentally impaired.

"Concentrate, Mr. Bean. Can you do that? Can you focus?"

"Yes."

"Good. True or false, you recently entered Quanta-Gate under false pretenses."

"True."

"True or false, you were spying for Naomi Nantz."

"True."

"This is good, Mr. Bean, we're getting into the rhythm here. You're adapting to a new reality, and understand that you are powerless to resist. True or false?"

"True."

The stool vanishes again and he lands on his tailbone.

"Never anticipate, Mr. Bean. Never assume. Punishment can happen at any time, for any infraction, or for no infraction. Punishment can come because we feel like it, and because it is our task to grind you up and spit you out. You're the dog shit sticking to my shoe and I'm going to wipe you off. You are a stool sample and need to be flushed. True or false?"

"True," he says, expecting the worst.

The stool stays.

"True or false, the day you entered QuantaGate you gained access to secure files."

"False!"

"No need to raise your voice, Mr. Bean."

"I checked out the system. No way I could get into the secure files without setting off alarms. Even trying would have set off alarms, shut down the system."

"This is good, very good. You have begun to elaborate. What else, Mr. Bean?"

Before he can answer, the stool vanishes again. Landing straight down on his tailbone again, registering like an electric shock from his butt to the base of his skull.

They pick him up, put him back on the stool.

"True or false, you tampered with the software at QuantaGate."

"True."

"You installed spy software at a top-secret research facility."

"Yes, I did. True."

"Therefore you are a spy, a traitor, and you have committed treason against your country."

"No. False. We're looking for the boy, that's all. We don't c-c-care about secrets."

"You don't ca-ca-care?"

Milton shakes his head so vehemently he makes himself dizzy.

"We care," the man says, moving closer.

"We're looking for the boy, that's all," says Milton, begging. "A little boy."

"What little boy?" the man asks, as if genuinely surprised. "What are you talking about?"

"Professor Keener's boy. His son, J-J-Joey."

Behind the light, voices mumble and mutter, as if conferring. Milton waits, infinitely more miserable and afraid than he's ever been in his life. Far worse than his worst nightmare. His willingness, his eagerness to cooperate hurts worst of all. He's not a man and never was; he's something to be scraped from a shoe.

The murmuring stops. A different voice, a new voice, says, "True or false, Naomi Nantz is acting on behalf of agents of the Chinese government."

"F-f-false."

Times passes as he shivers on the little stool. The voices return to the murmur level. He doesn't even bother trying to listen to the words being spoken, because that might result in punishment.

Somewhere in the distance, a wheel begins to squeak, at first faintly and then louder, so loud he can't ignore it. The mad wheel of a grocery cart, spinning as it tracks sideways down the aisle. Coming to get him. Louder, closer, screaming inside his mind like a rat trying to claw its way out of his skull.

A gurney appears in the circle of light. A narrow,

thinly padded gurney equipped with sturdy Velcro straps, the better to hold a struggling body.

"No," Milton whispers.

"Strap him down," a voice commands. "We're going chemical. I don't believe anything the little turd blossom says, do you?"

Milton writhes as they lift him from the stool and dump him on the gurney. "No!" he screams. "Please, no!"

A gunshot echoes inside the warehouse, loud enough to hurt Milton's ears. He hears the insane whine of a bullet ricocheting from the concrete floor and connecting with something metallic.

"Nobody move," says a new voice, a familiar voice. "The weapon in my hand is a Glock Super Ten. There are fifteen rounds left in the magazine and I'm prepared to shoot all three of you dead and take the consequences. Now get him off the gurney before my finger slips."

Jack Delancey.

Milton wets his pants in gratitude.

Chapter Thirty-Eight

Back to the Shed, with Cookies

The first battle report comes in from a Kmart in Seabrook, New Hampshire. Jack has detoured off the highway ten miles south of Pease Tradeport because Milton Bean needs a change of clothing and insists that only Kmart will do.

"He's obviously suffering from post-traumatic stress," Jack says, keeping it breezy on the unsecured cell phone connection. "The poor guy got fired, I guess he can't handle it."

"Fired?"

"Yeah, from his job," Jack says.

"What?"

"Don't be stupid, Alice. The job, okay?"

He hangs up.

Weird. Jack has never called me stupid, and would not do so simply because I asked a question. So it has to be code for something. Milton got fired? Not by us, surely. Therefore by Gatling Security Group? The time is all wrong, though. It's midafternoon and if GSG had refused him entry we'd have heard the bad news well before noon.

I locate boss lady on the ground floor of the residence, in the Zen sand garden. As always the place is cool and peaceful, exuding something of the fifteenth century, from which it dates. The natural lighting is indirect and soothing. Naomi is seated on a stone bench in the lotus position, palms open, eyes closed. The very thought makes my hips hurt, but she claims to find it relaxing. Opens her mind, allows that amazing brain to make random connections that have so often proved useful in our investigations.

Much as I hate to disturb her when she's doing the Zen thing, or wrecking watercolors in the studio—which appears to be another, very different form of brain exercise—this is in my judgment a call she needs to know about. As it happens, she agrees, unfolding herself from the lotus without complaint and walking me out of the garden as I recount, pretty much word for word, the strange message from Jack Delancey.

"Jack at Kmart?" she says. "How odd. In a pinch he might deign to shop at Macy's. But never Kmart. Something went wrong, obviously."

"What do we do about it? Jack turned his phone off, it goes directly to voice mail."

We've reached the command center. Naomi goes to her desk, takes a seat and leans back in her ergonomic chair. "We wait," she says. "Pardon me, but I want to finish my train of thought."

She closes her eyes and begins to breathe deeply and slowly.

I've been dismissed, obviously. Not being a Zen master, or any sort of genius, I'm left with nothing to do but pace and fret, worrying about our boys and what might have befallen them, out there in the big bad world.

An hour later they come in through the garage, both of them as giddy as children. Jack in filthy, torn clothing, his face scratched, and Milton wearing new duds from Kmart.

"We had to run through the woods," Jack tells us unnecessarily. "We ran through the brambles where a rabbit couldn't go."

"Ran through the bushes," Milton insists, piping up. "That's where a rabbit couldn't go. Not the brambles and not the briars. Bushes."

"We're arguing about a song," Jack explains, clapping Milton on the back. "Johnny Horton, 'The Battle of New Orleans.' We ran so fast the hounds couldn't catch us."

"'Down the Mississippi to the Gulf of Mexico,'" Milton sings.

"Down the highway to Seabrook is more like it. That's where I made damn sure they didn't have a tail on us."

"I need to use the bathroom," Milton says, quite suddenly in a sober voice. "Can I use the bathroom?"

"Of course. Down the hall, second door on the right."

Jack waits until Milton has left the room. The smile drops from his face. "We're bonding," he explains. "Milton was being tortured, I rescued him, we escaped through the woods. I've been cheering him up. Letting him know it's okay to pee your pants when you're being threatened with brain death. He was really embarrassed, which is silly, don't you think?"

"Very silly," says Naomi. "Jack, listen to me carefully. Go to your room, shower and change and then report to the library for debriefing."

At first the suggestion startles or rankles, but then he seems to settle back into the more familiar, coplike Jack. "Okay. Sure. Makes sense."

He trudges away, suddenly exhausted.

"Adrenaline and shock," Naomi offers by way of explanation. "They've been through something awful."

"Jack did mention torture."

"He did, didn't he? Mrs. Beasley? A pitcher of iced tea, if you please. And sugar cookies. They'll need energy."

I head upstairs and prepare to receive the conquering heroes.

Sugar cookies. The obvious remedy for shock and torture, why didn't I think of that?

Milton settles gingerly into a Windsor-style chair in the library, wincing. I pop up, offer the man a cushion, which he accepts gratefully.

"I'll be fine," he assures us. "Just bruising, nothing broken."

"You were kicked?" Naomi asks.

"Not directly. It was more like—"

"Let him tell it from the beginning," Jack suggests.

"Absolutely," Naomi says. "Take your time, Mr. Bean."

Milton's eyes are so deep, they appear to have been pushed back into his head by heavy thumbs, but according to his account it's exhaustion that has so altered his appearance, not physical torture. He tells us he was summoned from his workstation to an office where company owner Taylor Gatling briefly questioned him. And then a black hood was whipped over his head and he was lifted into the air and carried from the building.

"I presume down a back stairway. I'm quite sure I wasn't taken out through the main door."

"Hooding the face is psychological torture 101," Naomi says. "Accomplishes two things: makes the suspect disoriented and instills fear."

"It worked beautifully," Milton says. "I was scared to death."

"What was the nature of the interrogation?" Naomi says. "What kind of questions did they ask?"

"At first, when Mr. Gatling was present, they wanted to know if I was working for the Department of Defense or for the IRS. If you're a Pentagon contractor, the contract often stipulates that the DOD can run a spot audit at any time, without giving notice."

"Hmm," says Naomi. "I find the fear of an IRS audit more telling. They must have something to hide."

"You mean besides torturing accountants or kid finders?" I say.

"Yes, besides that," Naomi says, not flinching. "Something financial."

"They knew I had entered under false pretenses. I could have been arrested and prosecuted," Milton says. "They went another route, one that could put them in legal jeopardy."

"Will you be suing?" Naomi says. "Reporting this to the authorities and pushing for an arrest? Unlawful detention comes to mind, for starters. You certainly have cause."

"Do I have to make up my mind on that right away?" Milton asks. "I'd rather wait until we've got Joey safe and sound."

Naomi nods agreeably, and it's obvious that's the direction she'd prefer to go. "Just so you know the option remains open. Difficult as it might be to sustain in court, without corroboration."

"I don't know about that," Jack snaps. "I'm the star witness. I saw three men carry a struggling, hooded figure out the back door of GSG world headquarters and hustle him into a nearby shed. I don't care if Milton was trespassing, technically, or even if he was, technically, committing a felony by misrepresenting himself, that doesn't excuse an unlawful detention."

"We don't know that the detention was unlawful, under the Patriot Act," Naomi reminds him. "For all we know it might have been authorized by the Pentagon. But let's put that argument aside for now. I'm more interested in exactly what form the questions took, once they had Mr. Bean in the shed." She looks around, puzzled. "Where's Dane? She should be here."

"At the hospital," I tell her. "Shane is having a lucid period and nobody knows how long it will last, so she decided he was top priority."

Naomi nods quickly. "Quite right. Mr. Bean? Back to the shed. If you will excuse the turn of phrase."

"They put me on a low stool and kept kicking it out from under me. That's how I got bruised. Doesn't sound so awful, me telling about it. More like a prank than torture. I guess you had to be there."

"Who ran the interrogation? Was it Taylor Gatling himself?"

Milton shakes his head. "In his words he 'turned me over to the professionals.' I assume he left the building. He wasn't there when the cavalry arrived, was he, Jack?"

"No, he was not."

Milton describes, in a fairly dispassionate tone considering what he's been through, being questioned by interrogators who remained behind a very bright light. Having satisfied themselves that he wasn't working for either the DOD or the IRS, they soon established that he worked for Naomi Nantz.

"I'm not making excuses for myself, because by then I was ready to tell them anything they wanted to know. But they already knew about my arrangement here. They have this place under surveillance and they had an image of me entering the residence."

"This is important," Naomi says, pushing aside her glass of iced tea. "Exactly how was the question phrased?"

"In the form of true or false. 'True or false, you were spying for Naomi Nantz.'"

Naomi turns to Jack. "You realize what this means? If they have us under surveillance that means they've already established our connection to Randall Shane, and undoubtedly had him under surveillance, leading, eventually, to us. That makes it approximately certain that Gatling's organization abducted Randall Shane in the first place, which is why our investigation has attracted their interest. They have confirmed our hypothesis."

Jack says, "It was confirmed for me the moment we made the connection between Gatling and the security guards."

"I have a slightly higher standard," Naomi says loftily, "but as usual your investigative instincts are well focused."

Jack rolls his eyes and leans back with his arms folded across his chest. Hair still damp from the shower, but dressed, as we've all come to expect, immaculately.

"Oh!" says Milton, raising his hand like a kid in class. "Oh! I just remembered. They know about the program, Teddy. The one you had me install."

Teddy looks crestfallen, and then a little scared.

Naomi reacts sharply. "They knew, or you revealed?"

"No, no. They knew all about it. They accused me of installing spy software. Said I was guilty of treason and could disappear down a black hole for the rest of my life. That's when I told them about Joey. That we weren't trying to steal secrets, we only wanted to find the missing child. I was eager to tell them. I told them everything I knew. Everything."

"Milt, you didn't do anything wrong," Jack assures him. He again reaches out to pat the smaller man on the back, which is in itself unusual, because Jack's not a back slapper, and from what I've observed, despite having mostly male friends, he goes out of his way to avoid physical contact with other men. On the other hand Milton looks way more than crestfallen and embarrassed. It's as if something essential in him has been destroyed. Now that the adrenaline has had a chance to abate, it's obvious that he's been crushed by his recent experience.

I push the plate of Mrs. Beasley's cookies closer to him, without any real hope that they will have their intended medicinal effect.

Naomi says, "Mr. Bean, I want to make one thing abundantly clear. My questions are intended to reveal what may be crucial clues as to what, exactly, has been GSG's involvement in the case of Professor Keener. In no way are you to be held responsible for anything that may have been revealed under duress. Your task, penetrating through company security, is by its very nature dangerous. You were in peril from the moment you agreed to enter QuantaGate. You knew the danger and yet you persisted, which demonstrates great courage on your part. Particularly after we all learned what had been done to Randall Shane. Clearly, these were professional interrogators using proven techniques. In my book you were a hero the minute you entered the door. Do you understand what I'm saying, Mr. Bean?"

"Sure. You're trying to make me feel better. I appreciate it."

"I hope you come to accept that it is *we* who appreciate *you*. Now I'm afraid we have to get back to this business, however painful it may be to relive the experience, because a little boy is still out there and I'm very much afraid that our time may be slipping away. So, how exactly did they react when you mentioned Joey?"

"They were surprised."

"Surprised?"

"Or they did a really good job of acting surprised. I remember being surprised myself, because I assumed that if they had been investigating Professor Keener they had to know about his son."

"Think back, Mr. Bean. Was the boy's existence a surprise to them, or was it our involvement in his recovery?"

Milton puts a hand to his forehead, closes his eyes. "I don't know. That's my honest reaction. All I know is, once I mentioned Joey they stopped asking questions for a little while and conferred among themselves. Something had changed and the next question they asked was about you."

"About me?"

"'True or false, Naomi Nantz is acting on behalf of agents of the Chinese government.' I said 'false,' and their reaction was to wheel out the gurney and tell me they were 'going chemical,' because they didn't believe a thing I'd told them. That's when Jack broke me out of there. He's the real hero."

And with that, Milton Bean nibbles at his sugar cookie, stares at the floor and begins weeping silently.

Chapter Thirty-Nine

Anything Is Possible

We find Randall Shane sitting up in a comfortable armchair, looking perky and alert. His eyes are clear. He's clean-shaven, which makes him look younger and thinner, although the thinness may be the result of actual weight loss. He's been given a VIP room, obviously, complete with a small fireplace and a lovely view of the Charles, but the food still comes from the hospital kitchens and according to his doctor he hasn't developed much of an appetite.

"If you can persuade him to eat, that would be great," Dr. Gallagher had told us over the phone. "He's a big guy, he needs his calories, especially when the body is healing."

As a consequence Naomi arrives bearing a Tupperware container from Mrs. Beasley's kitchen.

"We heard you lost your appetite" are her first words to the patient.

He shrugs. "Not a big deal. I have weight to spare."

"Not that much, from the look of you," Naomi says, popping the container into a small microwave. "First you'll do me the favor of trying Mrs. Beasley's macaroni and cheese, and then we'll sweep the room for bugs and have a conversation."

"I'm really not hungry."

"That's why I brought this particular dish. It has been known to stimulate an interest in food."

Naomi carefully dishes a portion into a white crockery bowl, supplies it with a fork and hands it to the reluctant patient. Shane places it on the table beside him but makes no move to eat. Naomi, persisting, removes a small shaker of salt from her purse. "Sea salt," she announces briskly. "It makes a difference. I checked your chart, you have no prohibition against salt."

"Really, Miss Nantz," he says, looking annoyed.

"Call me Naomi or Nantz, but never Miss Nantz."

"Okay, Nantz. Thanks for the food. Maybe I'll try it later."

"By then it will be cold and it won't reheat well for a second time. Let me describe the contents, which are exceedingly simple but nevertheless not like any similar dish you may have had in the past. Certainly not like whatever glop the hospital, or indeed most restaurants, calls macaroni and cheese."

"Look, I appreciate everything you've done, really I do, but—"

"No buts. Allow me to finish," Naomi says, overriding his protest. "Mrs. Beasley first makes fresh pasta according to her own recipe, in this case rotini in shape, and boils it to a precise state of al dente. The steaming pasta is then transferred to a casserole pan. Over the pasta she grates a precise quantity of truly exceptional aged cheddar, sharp but not too sharp. On the top, a crust of toasted bread crumbs moistened with drawn butter. The dish is then baked for thirty minutes at three hundred and fifty degrees so that the cheese melts and achieves a kind of

magical balance with the pasta. As a last touch the casserole is taken from the oven and the bread-crumb crust
is browned with a hand torch and lightly sprinkled with
select parmigiano. The result is simple, nutritious, delicious and easy to digest. I dare you to take one bite and
prove me wrong."

Shane grimaces. "You don't give up, do you, Nantz?"

"Never. Be glad of it."

He sighs and reluctantly lifts a small forkful to his
mouth. His pale blue eyes brighten. Without saying another word he adds a few shakes of sea salt and empties
the bowl in about three minutes. He then heaves a sigh
and says, "Oh my God. Who is Mrs. Beasley?"

"A woman of many mysteries. Shall I dish out another
portion?"

"No, I'm good. You're right, it was delicious. Familiar
but at the same time not like anything I've ever tasted
before. Wait, wait. Changed my mind. Yes, please," he
says, handing her the bowl.

In the end he empties the Tupperware. I'm not one of
those women who derive any particular satisfaction from
watching a man eat, but there's something about Randall
Shane that makes me want to pay attention to whatever
he happens to be doing at the moment. Not my type, not
my type at all, but still. *Interesting* is how I'd put it. Like
watching a pacing tiger is interesting. Makes you feel
sorry for the cage, if he ever wants to escape.

When he's done Shane pushes himself back in the
armchair and flexes the ankle that has the plastic mon-
itoring device attached. "We need to talk about Kathy
Mancero," he says.

Naomi stops him. "Not quite yet. Sweep first."

She steps out of the room and returns with Dane Porter and a gentleman, a consulting expert who shall not

be named or described in this narrative, per his explicit request. Suffice to say that he's the same gentleman who designed and implemented the electronic-surveillance shielding system at the residence, and checking a hospital room for bugs is something he could do in his sleep. The process takes about fifteen minutes, wanding his detector over every square inch of the room, and in the end he pronounces the place bug free.

"Excellent," Naomi replies.

"That being said," the expert continues, "my concern is the windows. Glass transmits sound vibrations, which can be detected from a considerable distance by a laser microphone. Before leaving I'm going to place a small, battery-operated device on the windowsill that generates random masking vibrations, but even so I suggest you keep the conversation as quiet as possible and be sure to face the wall, not the windows. Any questions?"

Shane has several, all geeky technical stuff—he knows a lot about bugs and bug prevention—but in the interests of not boring the reader, I will refrain from mentioning anything that involves interferometers, beam splitters or microprocessors. With the geeky stuff concluded and our consulting expert having taken his leave, the conversation resumes at just above a whisper. The three of us, me, Naomi and Dane, as close to the big guy as we can get without sitting in his lap.

"Kathleen Mancero," he begins. "You looked her up, right?"

"We have everything available from published sources. What can you add?"

"Only that her involvement is my fault. I want that to be on the record. Whatever Kathy's done, it's because I was never quite able to say no to her. Not absolutely. She desperately wanted a mission, much like the one I've made for myself, and for similar reasons. They took advantage of that. If she's helping them with Joey Keener, it has to be because she thinks she's helping me. That's the only explanation."

"We assumed as much."

"You did?" He looks much relieved. "Well, good then."

"I notice, Mr. Shane, that you're still referring to the kidnappers as 'they.'"

"Just Shane, please, no mister. I say 'they' because I don't know who 'they' are."

"Because you can't remember?"

"Because I never knew. Professor Keener believed that his son had been taken into custody by agents of the Chinese government, in an attempt to persuade him to share secrets. That was my assumption, too, until I saw the video of Kathy and the boy. That changed everything. If the Chinese were involved they'd have used one of their own, not gone prospecting for a nanny in Kansas. So it has to be domestic. One of our own spy agencies."

Naomi nods in agreement. "Did he share?"

"Keener? You mean was he complicit in an act of treason? No, I don't think so. He said not, and in my judgment he lacked the ability to lie convincingly. Then again, I've been wrong about so much, maybe I was wrong about that, too."

"Possibly," Naomi says. "That has yet to be determined. Tell me what you recall of your interrogation."

He grimaces. "Not much is clear. I was with you, in your office. There's a lot of noise and then something hits me and I pass out. When I come to I'm strapped to a gurney. Someone asks me about Joseph Keener and I tell them everything I know, but that isn't enough. They beat me, they drug me some more and then it all gets very vague and blurry."

"Could you identify any of your interrogators?"

He shakes his head. "Never saw them."

Naomi sits up straight, takes a breath. "We have news to impart. As yet we have no line on who has Joey, precisely, or what they hope to gain by holding him after his father's death, but we do know who abducted you."

Naomi delivers a succinct description of the events of the day, in particular the threat to "go chemical" on Milton Bean, and the convenience of a nearby airfield with professional interrogators on-site. Midway through the account something relaxes in Shane's expression, and when Naomi concludes, he says, "Taylor Gatling, I'll be damned. Haven't heard the name in twenty years, but that explains it."

"How so?"

"Keener told me he was under surveillance by his own security guards, but I never made the connection between Gama Guards and Taylor Gatling, Jr. Now it all makes sense. Or some of it does."

"Gatling is previously known to you?"

Shane shakes his head. "His father was. I had no idea his son owned a security firm. This all happened so long ago, he must have been a kid at the time. I have no recollection of him at the trial."

"Trial?"

"The father, Taylor Gatling, Sr., was an embezzler. A very bold and clever one, too. Owned a chain of automotive dealerships, had his face all over the local television stations promoting sales. *Get the Taylor-made deal on the car of your dreams!*—that was his pitch. Very successful, but it wasn't quite enough to sustain his lifestyle, or his many mistresses, and Gatling came up with an elaborate scheme to defraud the finance company that floorplanned his cars. I won't go into the details, which involved a confederate at the Department of Motor Vehicles, but basically he sold cars while pretending to still have them on one of his many lots. Because it was interstate fraud, the Bureau got involved. I was a newbie with a computer background and they decided to put me undercover as a car salesman, where I might get a chance to examine the paperwork, find out how he was doing it. Which was kind of a joke, me as a car salesman, since I never managed to sell a car. Not one! But I did collect VIN numbers, and figured out who was assisting at the DMV—one of his girlfriends—and we were able to put it all together and prove the fraud."

"So you sent Taylor Gatling's father to prison."

"I wish that was all it amounted to. Despite being a con man, or maybe because of it, Taylor was one of the most charming guys I ever met. You couldn't help but like him. But he was guilty as sin, there was no way around it, and he was eventually sentenced to five years in a federal lockup. Where he could have practiced his tennis with the rest of the embezzlers and tax cheats. Except that on the day that he was supposed to surrender to the federal marshals he shot himself."

Naomi shakes her head. "How come we didn't run into that when we researched Taylor Gatling, Jr.?"

Shane shrugs. "Just a guess, but if he's been as successful as you suggest, he's probably had as much of it scrubbed as possible. That takes a lot of money and a lot of effort, siccing lawyers on search engines and archives, but it can be done. Plus you were researching the son, not the father."

"Plus once we found Gatling Security Group, that's

what we researched, not so much the owner," I chime in, defending Teddy.

"It's been less than twelve hours, for cryin' out loud," says Dane. "Look at it that way, the kid found a lot. He was the one who made the connection, started the ball rolling."

Naomi is having none of it, and waves me off. "Thank you, Alice, thank you, Dane, but there's really no excuse. I don't blame Teddy, I blame myself."

She turns back to Shane, who looks puzzled at our exchange. "So let me get this right," she says. "Taylor Gatling, Jr., blames you for his father's suicide and is taking his revenge? After all those years?"

"Looks that way. Unless someone is framing him by framing me."

Naomi sighs. "The very thought of that makes my head hurt."

"Wheels within wheels, Nantz." Shane grins, as if enlivened by the idea. "Gatling and company have been working on behalf of the so-called intelligence community. Anything is possible."

Chapter Forty

Walk This Way

"Who scratched your face?" Tolliver wants to know. "Your wife or your girlfriend?"

"Not funny, Glenn."

"Or maybe it was a threesome. Hey, come to think of it my wife might go for a threesome as long as I wasn't invited."

Jack stands up, as if to go.

"C'mon, Jack. You want a beer?"

"Hey, sure. One beer can't hurt."

The state police captain has something he wants to impart, supposedly, which is why Jack has agreed to meet his old friend at The Diamondback on Boylston, up the stairs to the rooftop café so Glenn can have a smoke if he wants. The D-back being approximately the least coplike bar in this part of Boston, which means they're unlikely to be overheard by colleagues. Plus Piggy likes the nachos, and the rules of the arrangement mean that Jack will be picking up the tab.

The rush of rescuing Milton, guns blazing, has gone away, leaving Jack cranky and not in the mood for macho camaraderie, but things are breaking so fast that he can't risk putting Tolliver off until tomorrow. As his friend returns from the bar with a couple of drafts, Jack tries to put on his game face, get into the swing of things.

"Happy hour," he says, forcing a grin. "Look at these kids. I'm old enough to be their father."

"Yeah? Be glad you're not," Tolliver says, eyes roving over some of the fair young items who've come up to the roof to suck on their long white cigarettes. All bright and giggly in short skirts and makeup, primping and priming for a night at the clubs.

"Nachos on the way," Jack says.

"Good. Great. Seriously, kid, you look like you've been running with the wolves."

Jack shrugs. "Things are happening."

"You're not in violation of any statutes, though, right?"

"Not in the Commonwealth of Massachusetts, no."

Tolliver gives him a look. "I never know when you're kidding."

"I'm always kidding, Glenn. Cheers."

They tap glasses, drink.

"Mr. Baked Alaska, the frozen croak at the Bing murder?" Tolliver says, sucking air through the gap in his teeth. "We made the ID. His prints were in the system."

"Oh yeah?"

"No surprise, a low-level gangbanger out of Chinatown, goes by the name of Micky Lee. Muscle for a protection racket. Look familiar at all?"

Tolliver hands over a small mug shot. Jack studies and returns it. "No," he says. "Any connection to Jonny Bing?"

"Not that we can find, no. Bing moved in more rarified circles. He might have known the banger's boss, but probably not the banger."

"You think Bing was involved with a protection racket?" says Jack, surprised.

"No, no, I'm just saying. It's a fairly small circle, the rich, connected Chinese in Boston. Bing knew 'em all, at least socially. Liked to show off, throw shindigs on his fancy boat, appear at all the local Chinese charity dinners. So he could have crossed paths with this particular guy's boss. We're looking into it."

"Good to hear. Whoever killed the little dude, it wasn't Randall Shane."

"No? Why not?"

Jack lifts an eyebrow, wondering how much the trooper already knows. "Because when Bing was getting whacked Shane was being tortured by the bad guys."

"Oh yeah? What bad guys?"

"Yet to be determined. All we have are theories at the moment."

"Which you can't discuss."

Jack shrugs, finishes his beer.

Tolliver scoots his chair closer. "Here's my theory. Shane knows we have him dead to rights, so he tries to put the frame on Jonny Bing somehow, only it all goes wrong when the boat doesn't burn."

"It was more like a ship."

"Whatever. Just because that dyke lawyer of yours has Tommy Costello all hot and bothered, and persuades him to treat the suspect like royalty and not even take him into proper custody or bring him to court for arraignment, that doesn't mean he isn't guilty of doing that weirdo professor, even if he didn't do Bing."

"*Dyke* is an ugly word," Jack says, dander up.

"Hey, they use it, why can't I?"

"The way you say it."

Tolliver looks ever so slightly abashed. "Okay, lesbian

or gay or whatever. I'm sorry, no offense intended. I get it, Jack, she's a friend of yours, but it really takes the cake, our suspect getting a deluxe room with a view instead of a holding cell at the Middlesex Courthouse. All because the D.A. has political ambitions and he's afraid Naomi Nantz will embarrass him somehow."

"The D.A. gets it that Shane was most likely framed. The gun, the bloody shirt? You said so yourself, it's way too perfect."

"Yeah, I did. But once an arrest is made it should follow the rules."

"A suspect confined to a hospital bed is hardly against the rules, Glenn. Half the Mafia dons spent years in hospitals, in their silk pajamas, awaiting trial. If you'd seen the guy, okay? They beat the crap out of him, shot him full of some kind of designer truth serum. For a while he thought they drilled a hole in his head, scrambled his brains. He needs to be under a doctor's care. That would be true even if he was guilty, *and he's not.*"

"That's the point," the trooper says, truculent. "We never saw him. Cut off at the pass by lawyers. They all stick together no matter what side they're on."

"Okay, we can agree on something."

Tolliver clinks his glass to Jack's and makes a toast. "Dead lawyers."

"Dead lawyers."

They drain their glasses.

Kidder leaves his rental at a metered space on Newbury Street, feeds his quarters in the slot like a good doobie and places the receipt on the dash, as instructed. Sometimes it makes sense to play by the rules. Son of Sam got caught because he failed to pay the meter. Save a dime and spend the rest of your life in a concrete pod?

Dumb ass. Not that Kidder is really afraid of the local flatfoots, who arrested that moron Shane, exactly as intended, on evidence so planted it practically sprouted.

Randall Shane being a moron in Kidder's opinion because he could have made millions but didn't. What's wrong with a little reward for your efforts, all the years spent learning your craft? Which is why Kidder left the military and went mercenary, because that's where the money was—the *private* sector—and because he was sick of higher-ranking officers treating him like a three-year-old. He still had his bosses—lately just the one—but no one can assign him to the burn detail, where drums of human waste get drenched in diesel fuel and then torched. A stench he can never quite erase from his mind.

First stop, a Starbucks. Love that Mocha Frappuccino, dude. Kidder hums to himself as he stands in line. For some reason Aerosmith's "Walk This Way" is sticking in his brain this evening. A song so freaking ancient that he was barely born when it first came out. Still, when in Rome, or in this case Bean Town.

"Here you are, sir."

Lost in thought, Kidder looks up to see a chickee holding out the tall plastic cup. Trying out a tentative smile.

"Beautiful," Kidder says, taking the glass. "You know what they say?"

"What's that?"

"You ain't seen nothing 'til you're down on a muffin," Kidder intones, staring into her little brown eyes as his mouth finds the straw.

Back on the street he strolls, enjoying the season. Five in the evening with hours left of daylight. Oodles of time to kill.

Kidder laughs.

On the sidewalk a young couple, arm in arm, register a brutal-looking, steel-built man chuckling to himself, and instinctively move away. He gives them a wink— Son of Sam never had such style!—and takes the vacated space with a jaunty sense of entitlement.

"Gimme a kiss," he says to the shying-away couple. "Like this!"

He heads north on Exeter Street, bringing himself one block closer to the Naomi Nantz residence. Thinking it's about time he checked it out with his own eyes, instead of relying on images taken by a circling drone.

Street level is always best. You never know when you might want to make a personal visit, arriving unannounced, in the dark of night, with a properly silenced weapon. And before that can happen, he'll have to find a way in.

Chapter Forty-One

Facts as We Know Them

When the door chime sounds at nine-fifteen I'm in the library, updating the timeline. So far as I'm aware we're not expecting guests at this hour. Boss lady had declared a pizza night, releasing Mrs. Beasley from her duties. We, that is all those currently in the residence, happily chowed down on slices from Regina's, picked up curbside by yours truly, and then called it a day. Milton, understandably uneasy about returning to his home, has been offered a guest room, for which he seemed pleased and grateful. Dane has returned to her own residence, located a few blocks away, and promises to be available at a moment's notice. Jack called from some bar, sounding more stressed than he usually lets on, and announced he would be returning to Gloucester for the night and would report first thing in the morning. Apparently his thrilling escape from the woods of New Hampshire left him in need of quality time with his current spouse, although he didn't say so, not in those words. Teddy, dismayed by his failure to discover the now-obvious connection between Randall Shane and Taylor Gatling, Jr., retreated to his bat cave (others might call it a bedroom, but bat cave is more illustrative, believe me) where he's currently sucking down energy drinks and playing the latest version of "God of War," which is his form of sulking. No doubt he'll slay a few thousand adversaries before daylight and return to the real world renewed if not exactly refreshed.

Boss lady, believe it or not, is watching a baseball game. When I left her she had the sound down and was staring rather listlessly at the screen—the Sox struggling in Toronto—obviously lost in her own thoughts.

"I'm missing something," she said, and refused to elaborate.

Which is why I'd returned to the timeline and my notes, looking to find something that had been over-looked, something that might be useful. No matter how I fiddle and push, and even including the rather tumul-tuous revelations of the past twenty-four hours, there are still way more unknowns than knowns. By far the most important being the location of Kathleen Mancero and Joey Keener.

Responding to the door chime happens to be one of my many duties. In this particular instance whoever is pushing the button won't stop, so I'm more than ready to read whoever it is the riot act.

The security camera reveals a tall, middle-aged female with the build of a college linebacker. Unknown to me. For all I know she could be lost, or selling something, or intend-ing to murder us all. So I press the intercom and request that she state her name clearly and into the microphone.

"Mon-i-ca Bevins. *B-e-v-i-n-s,*" she says, spelling it out. "*F-B-I.* Clear enough? Now open the damn door!"

She really gets pissed when I make her show ID, but it can't be helped, those are the house rules.

We convene in the library. We being me, Teddy, Naomi and Dane. Our intrepid attorney having arrived in less than five minutes, so she obviously wasn't fibbing about being at home for the evening. Milton Bean, sound asleep in a guest room, has not been awakened, by instructions of the boss. This could be a need-to-know kind of deal and she'll make that determination when the facts are in place.

Although neither as tall nor as large of frame as Randall Shane, Monica Bevins is nevertheless imposing in a similar manner, and it doesn't help that she seems to be in foul temper. She strides around the room as if looking for something to hit, which may explain why Teddy cringes slightly whenever she veers in range.

"First, I want your assurance that what I have to say will not be taped or in any way recorded," she demands.

"You have it," Naomi responds instantly.

"If anybody gets wind of this, I'm finished. Ruined. I'd be prosecuted for sure."

One of boss lady's best traits is that the more difficult the situation, the more calm she exudes. Maybe it's a Zen thing, but wherever she gets it from, it works. Faced with Naomi's utter calm, Bevins's rage slowly subsides and she eventually begins to circle one of the larger armchairs and finally perches like some great bird of prey, ready to plummet from on high if a target presents itself.

She says, in a calmer tone, "The only reason we can do this at all is because I happen to know this place, this building, is secure from wiretapping. Because you *are* under surveillance, you know that, right?"

"By your minions and others," Naomi says. "Therefore it will already be known that you came to this door and entered this residence."

"I'm aware of that," Bevins snaps.

"Perhaps you are here to demand answers. In which case your presence is justified."

Bevins shakes her head. "An assistant director doesn't do fieldwork, or conduct interviews out of office, or take statements that can't be confirmed by another agent. We most certainly do not confide details of an ongoing investigation to a private investigator."

Naomi cocks her head. "Ah, so that's the dilemma. You need a reason to be here."

Bevins, looking miserable, nods.

"Perhaps I refused your request for an interview, but agreed to make a statement to you alone, under my own terms," Naomi suggests, adding, "I do have that sort of reputation."

Bevins remains skeptical. "What would be the nature of your statement? What can I take back that would hold up?"

Naomi shrugs. "How about this: we know who abducted Randall Shane and why."

Bevins appears to be shocked. Some of her poised-to-leap strength seems to weaken. "You do?"

"Certainly. The operation to detain and interrogate Randall Shane was ordered if not directly supervised by Taylor Gatling, Jr., under the aegis of his company, Gatling Security Group, and with, we must assume, the direction and approval of his bosses at the Pentagon or Homeland. The specific agency has not yet been determined by us, but we assume that whoever it is acts under authority of the Patriot Act. Had you waited until tomorrow, this would have been duly reported by Attorney Porter, either to you or to the Agent In Charge."

Bevins looks thoughtful. "I am the AIC of this particular case," she points out.

"Which case? The frame Randall Shane case? The missing-child case?"

"The Joseph Keener case. Because of national security, his murder takes precedence over the missing child."

"Ah," says Naomi.

"It wasn't up to me."

"No, of course it wasn't," Naomi says.

"I'm a cog in a very large machine," Bevins says. "Although that could change tomorrow. Would you really have reported your suspicions about GSG involvement?"

Very carefully Naomi says, "I would never lie about a thing like that. Moreover, I want the FBI involved in the hunt for Joey Keener."

"So that's my excuse for being here?"

"Sounds legitimate to me," says Naomi. "Surely you can make it sound convincing."

"Maybe I can at that." The big woman clears her throat. "Can I ask you a favor? Could I get a glass of water?"

Naomi doesn't have to ask. I leap to my feet and return in flash time with water, ice and glasses for everyone. Teddy had mouthed the words *Red Bull* as I left the room, but I pretended not to notice, since he's already shivering from the effects of too much caffeine.

After drinking deeply, Bevins carefully cradles the empty water glass in both hands, as if absorbing the coolness. Apparently resolved to continue, despite whatever legal, moral or personal jeopardy may be involved.

"Just as well you made the Gatling connection," she begins. "I won't have to explain that part. You're familiar with what his company does in the war zone?"

"In general," Naomi says. "As a private contractor, GSG provides security, interrogation and forward reconnaissance, including target identification. Also heavy involvement in Predator drones, the arming, flight and maintenance thereof. Young Mr. Gatling seems to have a hand in every aspect of the war on terror."

Bevins nods slowly. "That he does. And that's where the problem lies. He's become, shall we say, just a bit too enthusiastic."

"By enthusiasm, you mean torture."

Bevins looks surprised. "No, that's not what I meant. Okay, yes, you're right, his crews have been accused of taking it too far, the so-called chemical interrogations, but that's not what I came to tell you about. You already know that part."

"There's another part?"

"Oh yes," Bevins says. "The part where Taylor Gatling goes rogue. The part where he plays God. The part where his powerful friends, many of whom have become rich with his help, have conspired to assist him in his mission, or at least to cover for him when the crap hits the fan."

That has us all sitting up straight, paying attention.

"What I'm about to tell you is classified. The mere fact that I'm sharing it with you is a crime."

"Only if someone in this room testified to such," Naomi says. "I assure you, that's not going to happen."

"Okay," Bevins says. "Here goes. You're aware that Gatling's interrogation units were accused of injecting suspects with so-called 'truth serum' drugs, correct? That was in the public record. That's when the so-called Intelligence Committee went into executive session, to hear the rest of the testimony. The minutes of that meeting have been heavily redacted, but I was able to look at the original testimony. GSG actions go way beyond chemical interrogations. On more than one occasion his civilian crews have targeted suspected terrorists without authorization. They have launched Predator missiles, Hellfire missiles and taken out targets *on their own.* This is clear from the testimony. For months Gatling had been complaining to his Pentagon superiors that the CIA, which has the authority to order assassination strikes, had frequently refused to do so because they didn't trust some of the targets identified by Gatling's men. Thought they were being overenthusiastic, IDing every tribal leader with a beard as al Qaeda. Gatling disagreed, vehemently. He's one of the righteous, a true patriot, and they're a bunch of CIA wimps afraid to pull the trigger, defend their own country, even if it does mean the occasional wedding party gets blown to smithereens, or a school is mistakenly targeted, both of which happened. You get the picture? Taylor Gatling is running his own private war. He has the men, he has the ability to deliver death from the air and he has used it. This is well-known within the Pentagon, but if you think that means Gatling is about to be prosecuted or his contracts canceled, you would be wrong."

"Because of the retired generals, the ones who invested in Gatling Security Group."

"Exactly, and a number of lower-ranking officers, all of whom covet high-paying jobs with GSG when they retire or resign. Which means they're willing to provide cover by retroactively approving Gatling's targets. Covering both his ass and theirs. Pretending it was all a mistake, the authorization got lost in the paperwork. The Intelligence Sub-Committee has so far done nothing about it, and if we're waiting for them to grow balls, we could be waiting forever. It's far easier, and less dangerous politically, to look the other way."

"It has ever been thus," Naomi points out. "But what has this to do with Professor Keener?"

Bevins gives boss lady a steely look, as if daring her to make the connection. "Nothing, directly. But something else came up before the committee, in secret testimony. Something very instructive, if you know enough to pay attention. There was a question about GSG's involvement in unauthorized domestic surveillance."

"QuantaGate."

"Yes. QuantaGate, and specifically Professor Keener. That push to have the FBI investigate Keener? It came from Gatling himself. And when the Bureau reported finding no evidence of espionage, Mr. Gatling apparently decided to take matters into his own hands. He had become convinced that Keener was, indeed, passing secrets to the Chinese, and initiated what he called 'countermeasures.' He claims, and the committee apparently believes him, that the so-called countermeasures were nothing more than surveillance, as authorized by the Patriot Act."

"But you don't believe that."

"Someone targeted Keener for assassination. It could have been Gatling."

"And he framed Shane at the same time, as revenge for testifying against his father?"

Bevins shrugs her agreement. "Two birds with one stone."

"This all makes sense," Naomi says. "It fits the facts as we know them. But one thing I don't understand, one thing that haunts me: If Gatling knew he was going to have Keener taken out, to prevent him passing secrets, why kidnap the boy at all? Why take Joey Keener?"

Bevins has a strange look on her face. The same look people get just before they're going to be sick. "I was hoping you knew," she says.

As near as he can determine, the security system at the Nantz residence is state-of-the-art. There are no cheesy stickers guaranteeing quick response, because pros know that the logos are a dead giveaway as to what kind of system is in place, and therefore how to defeat it. The installation has been subtle, but Kidder knows what to look for. Every window, door and lock has been equipped with pressure-sensitive alarm devices. There are at least a dozen mini surveillance cameras mounted on various corners, and those are only the ones he can see. No doubt they'd been installed by professionals and cover every conceivable angle. Bust out a single pane, an alarm starts blaring, either at a security service, or the local cops, or both. Plus you'll be starring on the video cameras. Hi there, world, this is me on my way to prison.

Too bad Nantz hasn't contracted with Gama Guards. The very thought makes him want to giggle. That would be too easy, and not all that much fun. Bottom line, it doesn't matter what kind of system she has, or how foolproof they think it is, there's one surefire, never-fail way around it.

All he has to do is determine who the first responders are.

Kidder finds a nice, comfortable spot behind a Dumpster in the so-called public alley. He's good at waiting. Back in the day when he'd been in the military, an elite warrior trained to kill with his bare hands, he'd once had to hold position for fifteen hours until the target, a terrified gray-haired hajji with a comically hooked nose and a rap star's gold tooth, finally crawled out of the wreckage of what had been his home. Thought he'd made it, too, until he felt the cold muzzle against the base of his skull. Kidder put him down like Old Yeller—his own personal joke, because of the tooth. Of course he kept the tooth as a souvenir, who wouldn't? Had it drilled and put on a matching gold chain which he wears around his neck as a reminder of the fun times over there in the sandbox.

Old Yeller, yuk, yuk.

With infinite patience Kidder begins to assemble his custom-made weapon. The twelve-inch rifled barrel from where it has been strapped to his leg. The plastic hand-stock from his right trouser pocket. The spring-loaded trigger mechanism from his left trouser pocket. And from beneath the carefully buttoned flap of his shirt pocket, a single fifty-caliber, five-hundred-and-seventy grain, center-fire, round-tipped, soft-nose bullet.

Just the one bullet. Because all he needs is one shot.

Chapter Forty-Two

Elephants Not in the Room

I'm dreaming about prison when the alarm begins to whoop. In my dream the prison cells are a kind of concrete maze, with some cells branching off into dead ends, others leading to the next cell and the next. There are no prisoners, none that I can find. The prison/maze seems to be empty. Except I keep hearing something on the other side of the concrete walls, just around the next corner. Something furtive but alive. Something, or someone, that I have to find, and which keeps me hunting from cell to cell, heart pounding.

Whoop whoop whoop.

The alarm isn't particularly loud, but is accompanied by flashing lights throughout the residence. And if that isn't enough to wake me, Teddy pounds on my door. "Alice! Get up! Someone's trying to break in!"

The nightmare about the prison hasn't cleared from my mind, and at first I think that it's *me* that's trying to break in. Finally I surface enough to get what's going on, hurry into a bathrobe and find Teddy prancing around outside the door like his feet are on fire.

"Come on," he says, grabbing my arm. "We have to get to the safe room!"

That's the drill. If the security alarm goes off, indicating a possible break-in, we're all supposed to pile into the safe room—a windowless vault not far from the library—and wait until the first responders from Beacon Hill Security clear the premises. Mrs. Beasley, clad in a very handsome pair of men's pajamas, has beat us to the safe room and sits there with her arms crossed, looking somewhere between bored and resolute. Naomi, fully, if hastily, dressed, arrives a moment later with Milton Bean in tow. Mr. Bean has wrapped himself in a sheet and looks like he escaped from a toga party, and isn't sure if he should be amused or terrified.

"What's going on?" he wants to know.

"Probably just a false alarm, but we need to take precautions."

Naomi helps Teddy secure the door to the safe room. The vault is appointed like a small airport executive lounge, with low-level lighting, comfortable seating, a small refrigerator stocked with food and beverages and a video console wirelessly connected to all the security cameras in and around the residence. We watch as first one Beacon Hill Security patrol car rolls up in the public alley, then another, and finally a Boston Police patrol car arrives street-side. The Boston cops will secure the exterior of the building, which means they'll walk the perimeter and check for signs of break-in. The Beacon Hill Security guards will, by previous arrangement, enter the residence and conduct a room-by-room search.

Fifteen minutes after the alarm first sounds, the Beacon Hill boss punches into the safe-room intercom, enters the code and informs us that the premises are clear and the situation is, his word, "contained." And so we emerge unscathed if bleary-eyed to the news that a bullet has been fired through the third-floor window of

Jack's bedroom. That's what triggered the alarm. No one has actually attempted to enter the premises.

"That glass is supposed to be bullet-resistant," Naomi says, shocked by the news.

"Under normal circumstances it would be," the security chief tells her.

"What's that supposed to mean?"

"Whoever did this was firing something like an elephant gun. We found a large hunk of lead in the bedroom ceiling. Had to be a fifty caliber, and to get through the glass—it punched a hole as big as a grapefruit. The angle indicates it was fired from ground level, from the vicinity of the alley."

"An elephant gun, you say?"

He shrugs. "Something powerful enough to stop an elephant. Your window barriers will stop penetration from small-arms fire, up to and including an Uzi on full auto. So this had to have been a high-powered rifle with special ammunition. We're going to turn the slug over to the police, see what they make of it. With your permission."

Naomi nods her permission and turns to me. "My God, what if Jack had been there?"

"Saved by his wife, you might say. I'll be sure to tell him that."

"This is serious."

"I am serious. Jack should know that in his case there's an advantage to staying married." When she frowns her disapproval at my jocularity, I add, "Come on, this was a drive-by shooting, not a serious assassination attempt."

"With an elephant gun."

"Don't get hung up on the size of the gun. Whoever did this obviously knew they needed a powerful weapon to make a statement. Had they wanted to kill one of us, they'd have fired into a room that was occupied. The lights never came on in Jack's room because he never came back from happy hour with his state cop buddy. It can't be a coincidence that the shot was fired into an unoccupied room. And into the ceiling at that."

Naomi stares at me, her brain buzzing through the possibilities, and in the end she agrees with my assessment. "The odds favor your theory," she admits. "This was likely a warning shot, intended to discourage our investigation."

"No chance of that."

"None whatsoever," Naomi says, resolute. "As a precaution I'll keep the Beacon Hill security guards stationed outside the residence, at least for now."

"So we can all go back to bed?"

"That's advisable. We're all going to need as much rest as we can get. That goes for you, young man," she says to Teddy, who has lingered nearby, awaiting instructions. "By my estimation you haven't had a full sleep cycle in at least three days. I want your mind clear for the next assignment, which is going to be difficult."

"What's the next assignment?" he asks instantly, beating me to it.

"I'll know more tomorrow," Naomi says enigmatically, and marches off to her room, as if on a mission.

Teddy waits until she's gone before touching me on the arm to get my attention. "She'll know more tomorrow?" he asks, puzzled. "What's she going to do?"

I think about it. "My guess? She's going to call the Benefactor."

Our young computer genius says not a word to that, but looks like he's seen a ghost.

Part 3.
Joey

Chapter Forty-Three

Under a Veil of Leaves

Over the course of the next forty-eight hours absolutely nothing of interest happens. Okay, the Red Sox did somehow manage to win, barely, all three of their away games at Toronto. And a city councilman from Dorchester was found gamboling in the duck pond at the Public Garden, having declared his intention to interfere with the swans. He was stark naked. Lucky for the big birds he was too drunk to accomplish his task. Or maybe lucky for him, considering how aggressively swans tend to respond when under attack from naked councilmen. In Revere, a group of rowdy teens was arrested for underage drinking at the beach, and in Lexington a possibly rabid fox terrorized a neighborhood before lying down to take a nap on someone's porch and being identified as a perfectly healthy Pomeranian called, appropriately enough, Barker. The dog was taken into custody without incident and returned to its owner.

Okay, so I take it back about nothing of interest happening. I'm learning to be more specific: nothing of interest happened concerning our current case, at least nothing we knew about. We being everyone but Naomi, who spent hours on her secure line, waving me away whenever I happened to approach in a vain attempt to eavesdrop. Whatever she's up to, she won't discuss it, although my bets are all placed on our mysterious Benefactor, who, as we know from previous cases, has influence in very high places. Jack occupies himself with legwork, following up on the late Jonny Bing's possible connection to the frozen corpse found at the foot of his bed in the vain hope that it might somehow, improbably, lead to Joey Keener. Teddy continues to plumb the depths of the World Wide Web, hoping to uncover something that will prove Taylor Gatling's complicity in the murder of Professor Keener or the abduction of his missing son. Dane has been spending most of her time at the hospital, where Randall Shane continues to improve both physically and mentally, to the point that she's worried the politically ambitious Middlesex County District Attorney will change his mind and put Shane behind bars while he awaits trial. Everything Shane has recalled in the past couple of days confirms what we already know, which is gratifying but essentially useless.

We still don't know what we don't know, and it's making me as crazy as that overactive Pomeranian snapping at ankles in historic, upscale Lexington, birthplace of American liberty and Rachel Dratch. Our only suspect, Pentagon darling Taylor Gatling, has a motive for silencing the professor, who he suspected of treason, and for framing Randall Shane, revenge served cold, but what possible reason would he have for stealing and keeping Joey Keener? Teddy, whose eyes are beginning to rotate in his head like the cherries on a slot machine, has been unable to find any link with Keener and Gatling, other than the obvious connection having to do with Gama Guards contracting to provide security for QuantaGate. Despite the coincidence of both victim and suspect being from New Hampshire, the two men seem to have had nothing in common. Gatling was raised in the southern part of the state, on the seacoast, to a moneyed-at-the-time family, and Keener bounced around foster homes in the north. Moreover, Keener being ten years older than Gatling, he was already out of state as a Caltech undergrad when Gatling was pulling pigtails in elementary school. Their one undeniable connection is that both profited from Pentagon contracts, but the same could be said of thousands if not tens of thousands of individuals.

In the late afternoon of the second day of nothing, Jack finds me on the roof, where I've been watching the dinky sailboats to-ing and fro-ing on the Charles.

"Those are dinghies, not dinkies, and they're tacking, not to-ing."

"I say they're to-ing and fro-ing. Tacking is something upholsterers do."

Jack laughs, shaking his handsome head. As usual he looks like he just stepped out of the pages of *GQ*, sporting a pair of Armani sunglasses that perfectly complement his gorgeous summer-weight suit. The dark glasses fail to hide his frustration because with Jack it's all in the lips, that's where he expresses himself, from cynical sneers to pensive, pouting moues. "Teddy's been asking me about the Benefactor," he says.

"What did you tell him?"

"Identity unknown to me. And that if he tried to dig something up, and somehow managed to establish a possible connection between Naomi and a wealthy and influential individual who might be financing this enterprise, he would be fired so quick his Mohawk would smolder from the friction."

"Fauxhawk. And did you really?"

"I didn't actually mention his hairdo. But I did remind him that when he came aboard as a full-time employee he signed a document pledging to respect her privacy."

"There's nothing there for him to find," I suggest.

"How can you be so sure?"

"Because if it was there to be found, someone would have found it by now and used it against her. There have been many enemies, many opportunities."

"Yeah," he says. "There have at that."

"Pledging not to look doesn't mean we can't speculate. So far I've narrowed it down to a former spouse or lover, or a Saudi prince who owes her big-time. Or it could as easily be the Wizard of Oz."

"You think she has family?"

"Everyone has a family, even if they're all deceased."

"Or it's all Naomi and there's no Benefactor. That's just an excuse to tell us we can't use the jet or whatever."

"You think she's been talking to herself for the last two days?"

He shrugs. "I guess not. Sounds stupid when you put it like that."

I look up at the sky, endless blue but for a few wispy clouds out over the harbor. "Is that an eagle?"

Jack studies where I'm pointing. "Turkey vulture," he says. "Sometimes mistakenly referred to as a buzzard."

"But definitely not a drone."

"Definitely not," he says.

"I keep thinking of Predator drones equipped with Hellfire missiles."

Jack takes off his sunglasses, looks me in the eye. "Put it out of your mind, kid. They'd never dare do that on U.S. soil. This is Boston, not Afghanistan."

"You're sure?"

"Pretty sure. I'll be downstairs if you need me."

"Thanks."

Can't say why, exactly, but I sort of like it when he calls me "kid."

The result of Naomi's secret machinations arrives in the evening, shortly after dinner (Mrs. Beasley's special variation on chicken tikka) when we've been instructed to take our coffee and lemon cookies into the library and wait quietly like good little employees. The excellent coffee is quaffed, the cookies devoured to the last crumb. Many minutes pass uneventfully. There is much twiddling of thumbs, and some interesting speculation about swans and inebriated councilmen, and the nerve of a certain very private investigator who refuses to drop even the smallest hint about what is supposed to transpire on this fine, early-summer evening

Teddy, haunting the street-side window, finally announces, "It's a limo."

We all crowd to the windows. The streetlights are on but the twilight has lingered and the only impediments to sight are the fully leaved tree branches that obscure the hood of what is unmistakably an airport limousine. A driver, in full chauffeur livery, gets out and pops the trunk. He deposits several pieces of matching luggage on the curb and then, adjusting his cap, opens the passenger door with something like a bow.

A petite woman slowly climbs out and stands teetering for a moment, as if struggling with her balance. The driver rushes to offer his big, strong arm. She takes it.

"Wow," says Teddy.

"Double that," says Jack.

The woman, slender and young and elegantly attired, is Asian. Chinese, in all probability. And beautiful, breathtakingly. I know because the males in the room are taking deep breaths, and Dane Porter gives forth with a little sigh of contented surprise, and because even a female of the heterosexual persuasion feels her heart do a little jump, confronted by such a vision of perfection.

She looks up, our mystery woman, and then vanishes from sight, passing under a veil of leaves on her way to the front door, tall heels clicking.

"Amazing," says Jack in a soft, admiring voice. "How did she do it?"

He means Naomi, and because we've been firmly instructed to remain in the library, we'll just have to wait for the answer to come up the stairs and find us.

Chapter Forty-Four

True Confessions

"My name is Michelle Chen, also known as Ming-Mei, and I have come for my son, Joey."

I can't speak for the others, but our mystery guest's mastery of English shocks me almost as much as her ethereal, porcelain beauty. Clearly both the cat lady and Clare had got that part wrong, because while Ming-Mei's very slight accent suggests that she's foreign born, it also becomes abundantly clear as the evening progresses that she's been speaking English for many years, if not for most of her life. This is no traditional Mandarin doll, and her perfectly tailored Western-style suit is linen, not silk.

"Miss Chen is eager to assist us in our efforts," Naomi says carefully. "She has had a very long flight and must be exhausted, but I'm hoping she can give us some background before the jet lag kicks in."

"No jet lag," says Ming-Mei with a resolute shake of her head. "I slept on the plane. The Gulfstream was most comfortable. Tell me where my son is. Find him, then I will sleep."

"As we discussed by phone, Miss Chen, we're working on that."

Ming-Mei turns to boss lady with something like fire

in her big, gorgeous eyes. "You know who took him, right? Who keeps him?"

Naomi, who has yet to take a seat, nods her agreement and explains to those of us who are still a bit stunned by our guest's arrival: "I shared the video clip with Miss Chen. She did not recognize Kathleen Mancero, but the Harvard Bridge area is very familiar to her."

Ming-Mei says, "Joey and me, we walked along the river when he was an infant. He was in a sling, you know, that carries in front? And when he heard the water he would become very excited. It pleased him to listen to the river, even as a tiny baby. To him it was music. This woman who has him, does she know about the music? Does she know he will starve without his music?"

At this point Ming-Mei, who has been holding herself very erect, collapses into a puddle of tears, and begins to cry in that way that can make it hard to breathe, so strong are the convulsions of grief.

Jack, ever gallant, leaps up to console our beautiful young guest, but Naomi quickly dismisses the notion, as if she already knows what Ming-Mei will tolerate and what she won't. Physical comforting from a male stranger is apparently out, and the most Jack is allowed to do is provide her with a clean white handkerchief. Ming-Mei covers her face with it, tips her head back, and gradually her chest stops heaving. She sighs deeply, removes the tear-soaked handkerchief and with a much less imperious voice says, "Twenty hours on the plane, I don't cry, not once. Now I can't stop. Because all the time I'm thinking, wouldn't it be a nice surprise if Joey is waiting for me? In my dream you found him while I was en route. That was my hope."

"I'm so sorry, Miss Chen. Had such a happy event occurred, you would have been informed immediately."

"I know," she says, weeping freely. "But still I hope."

"Take your time, Miss Chen. If you'll allow me, I'd like to give my people a more informed introduction. As far as they're concerned, you've dropped out of the clear blue sky."

This elicits a faint smile. "Oh, but I did."

"I suppose you did at that," Naomi says. She tilts her head slightly, in that certain way that signals she expects us to pay close attention. "I was able to locate Miss Chen with the help of an intermediary. This person, who shall remain nameless, contacted a certain staffer in the U.S. Embassy in Hong Kong, who in turn put me in touch with a local investigator familiar with the entertainment industry. As it turns out, the singer Ming-Mei is well-known on the club circuit. She was contacted through yet another intermediary. Miss Chen's performance contract happens to be owned by one of the most powerful triads, so getting through to her was a delicate matter. As you may or may not know, the ancient triad societies of Hong Kong have gained power under the new regime by establishing relationships of mutual benefit with certain high-ranking Communist party members. This particular triad is heavily invested in the entertainment industry, and protects those investments with the usual strong-arm tactics, up to and including murder. Which meant that contacting Miss Chen presented certain difficulties."

Ming-Mei says, "She means my old boyfriend, Sammy Lee. He's a four eight nine, okay? Triads have numeric codes. That way names are not used, for protection in case of arrest. Four eight nine is the dragon head. He's the big boss. You must do what the dragon head wants, no question. When I went with Sammy the first time, I was seventeen years old and more than anything I want to be a big Cantonese pop star like Gillian Chung, and sing songs on TV and be a movie star." Ming-Mei laughs ruefully. "I was a very stupid girl."

"You had ambition," Naomi points out.

"Oh yes, ambition. But no brains. I thought, just let me succeed, let me have a hit song, I can separate myself from Sammy Lee, no problem. But that is impossible. It doesn't work that way. Once a dragon has you in his claws, he holds on tight."

"Tell us about Professor Keener," Naomi suggests. "How it all started."

Ming-Mei's small, perfect chin thrusts out. "Four eight nine will kill me if he finds out, but I don't care. He won't help me find Joey, and you will, is that not so?"

Naomi says, very carefully, "If Joey can be found, we'll find him."

Ming-Mei registers the chilling subtext, but it does not deter her from continuing.

"Okay," she says, hands folded primly in her lap. "Three years go by. I don't have a hit song yet, I'm not a movie star, but I sing in Sammy Lee's clubs five nights a week and he pays for acting lessons and provides me with a flash apartment and spending money, even a car and driver. The driver is there to keep an eye on me, of course. He's a forty-nine, a triad soldier, and everything I do or say, he reports to the dragon head. It makes me feel very important because, like I say, I'm a stupid girl with only one thing on her mind, becoming famous like Gillian Chung. I have a good voice. Not good enough to sing opera, but good enough for Cantonese pop, which is more about the look of the singer, okay? And even more about the producer, what song they choose, the beat, how they arrange the sound. Without a good producer, there is no chance of success, and Sammy, he keeps promising he will find me a top-cat producer. That's what he calls them, 'top cats.' But it's all a lie because by then I am too old for Sammy Lee, he wants only girls seventeen and younger. When he stops coming to my apartment for sex I don't complain. Why should I? He's disgusting. But then when I try to find a producer on my own, Sammy sends his four two six, his enforcer, to make sure the producers all know who owns me. He threatens to take away my apartment and make me a prostitute if I don't stay in his clubs and obey. The dragon head owns many prostitutes, so this is no idle threat. I want to run away but I don't know where to go and I have no money. Stupid girl, what was I thinking?

"Then one day everything changes. The dragon head comes to my apartment, but this time not to threaten. Suddenly he's acting very nice, very gentlemanly, and this is because he wants a big favor. He has important friends in government, and these friends are looking for a girl like me, he says. No, not to be a whore, he says, not like that. More in the line of acting, okay? All I have to do, be beautiful and pretend I have no English. The no English part is important, they stress that. Plus, if I do what they want, if I 'play the game,' someday I will have a real record producer. Of course I know the dragon head is lying, but what can I do? They fly me to the U.S.A., to Boston, and one of the government people, a woman, she makes sure I'm dressed in traditional clothing, which I have never worn, and sends me to a party on a big boat in Boston Harbor. Lots of people, some of them very rich, but many just young and beautiful. I'd be lying if I said this wasn't exciting. The colonel, she tells me I'm part of something very secret and very important to all Chinese people. And all I have to do is make eyes at this *sai yan,* this important Western man who will be there. Just look. No talk, no touching, no sex."

"Joseph Keener?"

"Yes," she says with a sad nod. "That was the first time I met poor Joe. Right away I knew something was strange about him. Most men—all my life it's the same—they want to touch me, if only to shake my hand. Not Joe. He's very shy. Not just shy, but different from other men. He never wanted to be touched, even when later on we had sex. I know that sounds impossible, but believe me, it is not. But that is much later. The first night all I do is look at the man and make my eyes do this."

Ming-Mei poses with her eyes downcast, and slowly looks up through her thick eyelashes, making eye contact.

Jack sighs and says, "He didn't stand a chance."

If Teddy's jaw drops any farther it will be unhinged. Men.

"The one who hosted the party, this was Jonny Bing?" Naomi asks.

She nods. "He was very nice to me. I went there excited, but afraid, you know? I have never been to the U.S.A., I'm being watched by the triad people and Chinese government spies and I don't know what they really want. But Jonny told me not to worry, he would do everything, all I had to do was be beautiful and be quiet. Can you do that? he asks, and I say, yes, no problem, I can do that. At the party nothing really happens. I make sure the *sai yan* sees me, and knows that I see him, and that's it. That night, after the party, Jonny tells me they will take care of everything."

"Excuse me for interrupting," Naomi says. "But who is 'they'?"

"Jonny and the government woman. I won't tell you

her name—I'm sure it wasn't her real name in any case. Later I learn she's a colonel in the Chinese military, the People's Liberation Army, and a spy, but at the time all I know is dragon head wants me to do what she says. I have no choice. What happens next, they put me in a small apartment in Chinatown and tell me to wait. The PLA colonel stays with me, to make sure I don't leave Chinatown. Those are the orders. Mostly we sit all day in the apartment and watch American television, which I like very much. It's almost like me and the spy woman are becoming friends. Two weeks later she has me dress up in traditional clothes and pack up all my things and takes me to the airport. Naturally I assume I'm being returned to Hong Kong. But no, that is not the plan. The PLA colonel says to me, so you want to be a pop star? You want to sing and act like Gillian Chung? Now is your chance. This is your scenario: you have been emailing the *sai yan* professor for the last two weeks, with the help of a friend who speaks English, and your relationship has progressed. He wants to see you again and has sent you a ticket. You have just arrived in Boston and in five minutes he will come through that door to greet you. Are you ready for the rest of your life? Then she laughs, very cruel. 'Are you ready for the rest of your life,' that comes from a game show we've been watching together.

"My only real instruction is that I am to speak only a few words of English. I ask her why no English, wouldn't it be easier for me to talk to the *sai yan* in his own language? She doesn't really explain this part to me, but I figure it out after a while. Speaking only Chinese makes me appear more exotic to him, and allows him to make up his own mind about who I am. It relieves him of having to make conversation, which he is very bad at. Also the colonel will be able to control what I say, because she will act as my interpreter—it's really she who has been emailing him all along, pretending to be me. Or this exotic, traditional version of me.

"It all goes according to the script. Joe arrives at the airport, accompanied by his good friend Jonny Bing. Everybody is very formal. We do a lot of bowing, which I think is very funny but I don't dare laugh because everyone else is being so serious. We all go to a teahouse in Chinatown and have a traditional tea, and the arrangement is worked out through my 'interpreter.' Joe agrees to lease me an apartment—the same place I have been staying all along!—and will pay for a tutor to teach me English—that would be the PLA colonel, of course. Even on that first meeting there is talk of an eventual marriage, but right away the colonel tells him I'm married to a very bad man who has abandoned me, and divorce is difficult. This is something they had already discussed in the emails, and he accepts it. It isn't until we're finally back at the apartment that the colonel tells me what she really wants."

"A baby."

"Yes," says Ming-Mei. "I haven't even kissed this strange man, and already they are talking about when I have the baby."

"They?"

"She and Jonny. This has been their plan all along. So of course I respond with a temper tantrum. How dare they! I am not a whore paid to have babies! And so on and so forth. They played it like on American TV. Good cop and bad cop. She was the bad cop. Fail to cooperate and I would be sent to a 'reeducation camp' in one of the northern provinces. And Jonny would be sweet and understanding and explain that everything would be okay, and that having a baby didn't mean I couldn't be a big star like Gillian Chung."

"So you agreed to the plan."

"Yes, to my shame, I did."

"And eventually you got pregnant."

She nods.

"Did Professor Keener ever discuss his company with you? What he was working on at QuantaGate?"

"No, never."

"So you don't know what he was developing."

She shrugs. "Something to do with computers, that's all. Please understand, everything changed when I got pregnant. The stupid girl who wants to be like Gillian Chung? She grew up. All she could think about was the baby, the baby. So that's what we talked about, Joe and me. By then I had 'learned' enough English to have a real conversation. In a strange way, I began to like him. I say strange, because he was like no man I had ever met before. I understood that he was a great genius in his work, but at home, in his personal life, he was more like a child. In social matters he was very unsure of himself. He knew he didn't really understand other people, or how they think, but there was nothing he could do about that." She pauses, once again with her eyes downcast and her hands folded palm up in her lap. "The thing I am most ashamed of is not seducing poor Joe, because that's what I did, I seduced him in every way a man can be seduced. No, it was making him think he could trust me, and knowing that when I lied he would believe me. I lied to him about everything. This was shameful. Because even if they didn't tell me why they wanted me to have Joe's baby, I understood that it had to do with tricking him, using him."

"He would be compromised."

"Yes."

"Because he would want to protect you and the baby."

"Yes."

"And is that what happened?"

"More or less. The strategy was to keep him off balance. While I was pregnant I stayed here in Boston and saw him every few days. He went with me to the birthing center the day Joey was born, although he could not make himself witness the delivery. After a few days he held the baby, briefly, but I could tell he really didn't like it."

"He didn't like Joey?" Naomi says, surprised.

"No, no. He loved Joey in his way, of this I am sure. It was the holding part he didn't enjoy. He kept saying, 'I'm afraid I'll break him.' He was frightened. I was frightened, too, but not about holding Joey. I loved that part right from the start. It was being a mother that scared me. I had no idea what to do, not at first."

"It's our understanding that soon after giving birth you returned to Hong Kong."

"Yes, true. When Joey was about a month old I went home."

"This was your idea?"

"I made no objection—I wanted to go home, to resume my old life—but no, it was not my idea. They arranged it. I was to tell him I wanted to show the baby to my relatives and then I would simply keep making excuses and never get around to coming back to the U.S.A. Their intention was that Joe would want to visit me and the baby in Hong Kong and they would make contact with him there."

"This is what I find puzzling," Naomi says. "According to what you've told us, Jonny Bing was cooperating with this woman spy who acted as your translator. He was also partners with Professor Keener, so why couldn't Keener simply be induced to pass information through Mr. Bing?"

Ming-Mei says, "They felt it was important that Joe not suspect Jonny, or he would also suspect that the whole relationship with me was arranged for that purpose. Which it was, of course. Also Jonny told me he was always under surveillance, they were keeping an eye on him because he was Chinese-American."

"A Chinese-American deeply invested in a company developing a secret computer system for the Pentagon."

"Yes, exactly."

"And you remained in Hong Kong for about a year?"

"Thirteen months."

"Why did you return?"

"Because he never came to visit! They couldn't get over it. The colonel made sure I kept sending video clips of Joey, to induce him into visiting, but eventually it became clear that for him the video clips were enough. He loved seeing the pictures but it didn't make him want to visit us in person. So then the decision is made, and I am to return to U.S.A. We are to live in a very nice condo Joe has purchased in Arlington. At first I refuse, and that's when the colonel makes it clear exactly what my situation was."

"They threatened to take the baby."

Now it's Ming-Mei's turn to look shocked. "How did you know?"

"Because that's the logical choice. The baby gives them leverage over you, even if it hasn't yet worked with the professor."

"I had no choice. But it turns out to be maybe the best thing I did. Because Joey does get to know his father a little bit, for a little while. And that's when he discovered music."

"Music?" I ask, piping up from the peanut gallery.

"Did you not know? Like his father my son is a genius. Not a science or math genius, a musical genius. In other ways Joey is normal, he is a regular little boy who likes to have his mi ma hold him and fuss over him and tickle his tummy and read him stories. But what his father did, he played some classical music on a CD, and Joey got so excited—he was two years old at the time, a toddler—that his father went out and bought a little piano keyboard, with special child-size keys. It was like watching magic happen. His father shows him how to hit two keys, an octave apart, and Joey right away starts using six fingers, three on each hand, to make simple chords. He liked it so much it made him laugh. By the time he's three he's making up his own music. He's spending so much time at his keyboard, playing for hours, that I'm worried, but his teacher tells me not to worry, this is the way it is with true musical prodigies, you can't keep them away from the music, it's opening up whole new worlds and they want to explore."

"Professor Keener's birth parents were both musicians," Naomi points out. "You're a singer, and therefore musically inclined. I'm not really surprised that music is in the boy's DNA."

"That's what Joe said," Ming-Mei says, nodding eagerly. "He said, 'on my side it skipped a generation.' It helped both of them, I think. Joe still didn't want to pick up Joey, but the music was a connection. He was fascinated by Joey's progress, and very pleased, very proud."

"Okay, let me see if we understand the chronology," Naomi says. "On your second visit you and Joey stay at the Arlington condo for about a year and a half, is that correct?"

Ming-Mei nods firmly. "Yes."

"And then, abruptly, you return again to Hong Kong. Why was that?"

"The excuse, my grandmother has taken ill. In reality, both my grandmothers died long ago. The colonel was by then very eager to get Joe's cooperation. They thought he had bonded so much with his son that he would surely visit us in Hong Kong, where they could spring their trap and make him share secrets. I was not to send him videos or emails, if he wanted to see Joey he would have to come to us. And six months later, he did."

"What happened, exactly?" Naomi says, a little too casually. Those familiar with her technique pick up the signals—she's about to bore in, shaking out something crucial to the case.

"Everything went wrong," Ming-Mei says with a sigh. "That was the beginning of the end. At first it was very nice—he was so glad to see Joey, so amazed by his musical progress—by then Joey was starting to read music, and practicing some of the simpler Mozart sonatas. He came every day to watch and listen, and seemed to me to be as happy as I had ever seen him. Then one day he comes and I can see right away that he's very upset. Some Chinese men came to his hotel and threatened him in some way, or said something that made him suspicious. He has decided that I am part of this conspiracy and I don't admit it, but of course he's right. Suddenly he's looking at me like he looks at everybody else in the world, like I'm not quite there."

"He knew?"

"He knew something was wrong. He became very angry and left us and went back to the U.S.A."

"So they tried to recruit him but he refused to cooperate."

Ming-Mei nods. "The colonel was very angry, too, and at first she tried to blame me. But they had bugged my apartment and they went over the audiotapes, which proved that I never said anything to make him suspicious. So they came up with another plan. And this was the most cruel thing of all. This is my curse, which has come back to haunt me."

"You pretended that Joey was kidnapped," says Naomi, glancing around to make sure we're all paying strict attention.

"Yes. Yes, I did." Ming-Mei weeps freely, her lovely cheekbones glistening with tears. "That's what I pretended. And then it really happened."

"Please explain," Naomi says, as if for our benefit. "The timing and sequence of this is, I believe, crucial to any possible recovery of your son."

Ming-Mei sniffs, but doesn't attempt to blot away the tears. "It was the colonel's idea, but I obeyed. I knew what I did was evil. I let Joe believe that little Joey had been taken from the mall. That the authorities believe he had been stolen to be sold as a replacement child."

"But Joey wasn't stolen *then*."

"No. He was fine. I told him he had to stay with his piano teacher for a few days, for special lessons, and he was very enthusiastic. Of course, his father came to Hong Kong, very upset, and he did everything possible to find Joey."

"He hired private investigators to search for the boy."

"Yes, but that was all part of the plan. They used their own people. They led him to the mainland and told him if he didn't cooperate, Joey would never be seen again. He called me from Beijing, so upset I can hardly understand what he is saying. Of course the call is being monitored, but he doesn't care. He says he has failed, because he has no secret to share. He would give them anything they want, but he has nothing to give. Then the call is cut off and that's the last I ever heard from him."

"He had no secrets to share."

"That's what he said, and I believed him."

"That was a year ago. When was Joey really kidnapped?"

Ming-Mei takes a deep breath, apparently determined to keep it together, no matter how difficult the subject matter. "Three weeks ago. As usual I took him for his piano lessons, but when I go to pick him up, he's already gone. I find his teacher tied to a chair in her practice room. Three men came to take him away, moments before I arrived."

"Could she identify them?"

Ming-Mei shakes her head. "Only that they were *sai yan,* Western. And that they were very quick and efficient, like soldiers."

The confession concluded, Naomi sits back and surveys us, satisfied that we've all been sufficiently impressed by the revelations. "Gatling's men," she concludes. "I'd stake my life on it."

Midnight on the roof deck. Apparently I'm not the only one who can't sleep, because there's a red glow bobbing when I get there. Jack Delancey, having himself a fine cigar. Then I hear murmuring and realize he's not alone. Teddy, in his dark clothing, fully blended into the night.

"Sorry," I say. "Didn't realize this roof was occupied."

"Don't be silly," Jack says. He makes a welcoming

gesture. "Join us, please. I was trying to explain to young Ted about the Benefactor."

"Oh?" I sink into a chair, glad of the breeze, which is wafting the smoke elsewhere.

"He was surprised, shall we say, that our mystery guest could be so easily summoned."

"I doubt it was easy," I say.

"My point exactly. Just because the boss didn't leave the residence doesn't mean she wasn't working the case, and working it hard. I've also been suggesting that, tempting as it might be to peek behind the curtain, it would be a mistake to try and identify the Benefactor."

"I believe we all signed contracts to that effect."

Teddy pipes up, "No, no, I wasn't looking, not like that. Just speculating."

"Maybe an ambassador, he was thinking," says Jack, taking no position. "Or someone from the Justice Department."

"Maybe," I say. "Or maybe an eccentric billionaire using us as his giant game of 'Clue.'"

Teddy makes a noise that sounds suspiciously like a giggle. "That would be cool. Are there secret passages in the residence?"

Jack clears his throat.

I say, "As a matter of fact, there are."

I like it that he doesn't ask where. In the dark I can almost feel his young mind racing. It'll give him something to do, other than obsess on the identity of the person who makes this all possible, and who obviously has the power to move a game piece halfway around the globe.

"Busy day tomorrow," Jack says, standing up. "The boss has plans."

"If you don't mind, I'll stay for a few minutes," I say when the two men get up to leave.

Measure of Darkness
======================

"Suit yourself."

"Good night, Miss Crane. I mean Alice."

"Away with you both."

The lights of the city usually have a calming effect, as if some grand purpose is being illuminated from within, but tonight the calm part isn't working. I keep thinking about helicopters hovering silently, painting targets on a screen, and men in black masks, and an assassin's bullet crashing into the residence, and a few minutes later I hurry down to bed, if not to sleep.

Chapter Forty-Five

Monster Man in the Electric Night

Kathy Mancero has a weapon and a plan. She would have preferred a baseball bat, but none being available she had finally, after many frustrating, nail-breaking hours, managed to pry a length of two-by-four from the inside of a closet. It will have to do. As to her escape plan, it all depends on Joey.

"You want to get away from the bad man?" she'd asked him.

"Yes, please," he'd answered without hesitation.

"I want you to play your music without the headphones on, so we can all hear it, can you do that?"

"Mozart," the little boy had said. "I want to play Mozart. Sonata no. 1 in C Major."

"Good. Lovely. When I say, you unplug the headphones and turn up the volume."

Night has fallen. The time has come round at last. Kidder is up there, she can hear the dull thump of him moving around on the first floor of the guest cottage. She imagines him getting a beer from the fridge as he settles down to watch the ball game, and the thought of baseball makes her long for an actual bat, one she can wrap her hands around. A Louisville Slugger would be ideal, but the length of two-by-four will simply have to do. She knows from studying Randall Shane's exploits that things are never perfect, that in order to save a child's life it is sometimes necessary to use what is close to hand.

Clear thinking and a willingness to act, that's what matters most.

Kathy adjusts the overhead lighting, bringing the corners and edges of the room into shadow. She positions a standing lamp to one side of Joey's keyboard, so that his sheet music will be illuminated, as well as the boy himself. Like a spotlight on the stage, it will draw attention to the eye and provide the necessary moment of opportunity. Or so she hopes, most desperately. It will just have to work, she has no other options.

Kathy positions herself to the left of the door, just beyond the inside radius, and leans the two-by-four against the wall. Not wanting to distract Joey from his task. She doesn't want him looking at her when the door opens, that's essential.

"Just read your music and play. Look at the keyboard, not at me."

Sturdy little hands poised above the keys, he says, without looking at her, "We're going to run away and find my real mommy?"

"Yes, sweetie, that's the plan. Go ahead."

At first she thinks something is wrong, that the boy has somehow contrived to turn on a recording. Up until now he's always played with the headphones on, for himself alone, and therefore she hadn't been exposed to his skill level. She'd been expecting something childlike, precocious and cute, perhaps, but childlike. There's nothing childish about what emerges from the keyboard speakers. The sonata, composed by Mozart in the nineteenth year of his life, begins simply, a slow, almost waterlike trickle of notes. Light, graceful, haunting. There's something of a melancholy waltz about the melody, which yearns to turn and pirouette up through the scale. And yet there's none of that oom-pa-pa beat of the waltz. Instead it slowly builds in complexity, touching and rising like a butterfly sampling ascending blossoms.

She's so mesmerized by the sound emerging from those small hands, by the contrast of his fierce concentration with the clear, contemplative beauty of the music itself, that she almost fails to react when Kidder opens the door.

"I'll be damned," he says, chuckling, all agog at the boy. "It really is you."

Joey never hesitates. He keeps playing as Kathy steps out from behind the open door, swinging for the fences. At the very last moment Kidder turns toward her, having sensed something, but the hunk of wood connects with back of his skull and he falls to the floor with a guttural sigh.

"Joey! Now!"

The little boy abandons his keyboard without a backward glance and runs to her, taking her outstretched hand.

Run, run, run.

No thinking, only running. Up the basement stairs, through the house and out into the night, the little boy keeping up with her, his short legs pumping, not a sound out of him. A glance shows Joey's eyes as big as silver dollars. He may be only five years old but it's obvious he knows the stakes, knows his life depends on getting away from the bad man, the monster man.

Keys.

The thought of keys hits her like a stab wound in the guts, stops her in her tracks, bending her over. Keys, damn it! That was part of her plan. Knock Kidder out, search his pockets for car keys, gate keys, whatever keys might be useful. And yet as soon as he'd gone down, his eyes rolling back, the instinct to flee had been overwhelming. What if he woke up and grabbed her by the neck? He'd kill her with his bare hands and Joey would be next.

Stupid, stupid, stupid. She should have kept beating him with the two-by-four, but she'd been so terrified that she'd dropped the weapon after the one hit. Dropped it like it was burning her hands. Shane would have made sure. He'd have tied the bad guy up while he had the chance. She'd thought of that when escape was still in the planning stages, couldn't find any rope, but Shane would have made do somehow, he'd have ripped up sheets or found some clever way to neutralize the enemy. Killed him only if absolutely necessary because Randall Shane had rules about things like that.

"Run, Mommy!" Joey screams. "Don't stop!"

The boy urging her to keep moving before the monster in the basement wakes up.

They run together, into the darkness, moist grass under their feet. He called me Mommy, she thinks, and it pleases her. Not that she has any illusions about a happy ending that would let her keep the boy. No, he has to be returned to his real mother, that's what will make this right, what will make her time on earth worth living. That's what Stacy wants her to do, looking down from heaven. That's the only thing that makes sense, as to why she's been left behind. To do this, exactly this.

The big house, a shingled mansion, rises against the dark sky, a great hulking shadow of high peaked roofs and gables. Beyond that, as she recalls from a single glimpse on the day she arrived, is a sandy dune of beach grass, a rocky shoreline, the sea. Somewhere to the right of the big house is a long curving driveway that joins the main road. They have to get there, to the main road, and without a car—keys! keys!—they'll have to do it on foot.

What she can't recall is how far it is to the next house. Are there normal houses in the area, or are they all unoccupied mansions? What she wants, of course, is a door to bang on, some kind stranger who will take them in, call the police.

The guest cottage where they've been held hostage is something like a hundred yards from the main house, no more than that, surely, but at night, under a cloudy sky, it seems much farther, more perilous. The ground uneven under their feet, tripping them up. Bushes and hedges looming, making it difficult to judge distance. Rather than stumble, Kathy slows them both to a hurried walk as they approach what must be the edge of the property. They've crossed some sort of transition. Her feet detect gravel. Then, suddenly obvious, an eight-foot chain-link fence. Not metal-colored but something darker, green perhaps, to make it blend into the landscaping, which it certainly has done.

A fence never figured into her plans. She hadn't noticed a fence when they first came to the property. How could she have missed it? Stupid, stupid, stupid. Shane would be tearing the chain link from the posts, utilizing his great strength and the leverage of his long arms. All she and Joey can do, find some way around it, or over it. Could the boy climb the links? Is he strong enough to pull himself up and over the fence? Can she push him somehow and then get over the top herself?

Kathy reaches out with her left hand, intending to

grasp the chain and give it an experimental tug. A hot blue spark, big as a glowing softball, arcs from the fence to her hand. The voltage knocks her to the ground, into the big nothing of the deepening darkness.

Joey starts to cry.

Chapter Forty-Six

When the Scurry Time Is Here

Morning finds us fifty miles to the northeast on a perfect summer day. High thin clouds, glorious sunlight. Everything sparkling, the world alive and breathing. But not everybody's happy.

"I don't like it," says Jack Delancey.

"Your concern is noted," Naomi says. "We'll be fine, won't we, Alice?"

"Totally," I say. "If the son of a bitch tries to torture us I'll tie his shoelaces together."

"I'm serious," Jack says. "I saw what they did to Milton."

"And if something goes wrong you'll come to our rescue, just as you did for him."

"That was sheer luck. I happened to be in the right place at the right time. You can't count on a thing like that."

"Certainly I can," Naomi says. "That's why I hired you in the first place."

Jack's a pretty smart guy, and knows when the argument has been lost. He grunts unhappily, but he puts the car in gear and steers us over the quaint little bridge onto the island of New Castle, in the *live free or die* state of

New Hampshire. Anyhow, that's what it says on the local license plates. Live free or die. Which I have always assumed had something to do with the state not having income taxes or sales taxes, until Naomi corrects me. Dates from the Revolutionary War, and Patrick Henry vowing to give him liberty or give him death. Whatever, upon crossing the bridge we've entered an enclave of the wealthy, a small, tidy oceanfront village of multimillionaire estates built tight up against the Atlantic shore. The sea visible here and there through gaps between the old colonial homes. Lighthouses, a harbor, a few sleek sailboats bracing in the wind. A postcard home: dear mom, if we win the lottery I want to live here, please.

At Naomi's direction, Jack drops us off a hundred yards or so from our destination. There's a sidewalk and, kid you not, a white picket fence holding back the blooming azaleas.

"Maybe we should be wearing bonnets," I say. "Carrying baskets of flowers."

"I'm sadly lacking in bonnets," says Naomi. "Try to be shy. We're supplicants, begging the lord of the manor."

"Yes, my liege."

She snorts and shakes her head. We advance through a picket gate, latch it behind us and follow a white gravel path that slopes down a slight hillside toward the harbor. *Crunch, crunch.* I decide to walk on the grass, which is probably against the rules, but so what, we're here to beard the lion in his den. And quite a den it is, too. A colonial governor's not-so-humble mansion, no doubt rebuilt from the stone foundations up, but looking authentic, from the narrow clapboards to the great brick chimneys that seem to bristle from the cedar-shingled roofline, marking a fireplace in nearly every room. Windows glinting with handcrafted panes of glass, and a delicate trellis of heirloom roses arching over the entrance.

"Don't look, but we're under observation."

"Don't look where?"

"To the left, by the low hedges."

Naturally I look and spot a big bruiser in a blue blazer. Try saying that fast. He's wearing sunglasses, has an earpiece with a microphone wand drooping alongside his strong, clean-shaven jaw. Standing vigilant with legs apart and hands behind his back.

I wave, he waves back.

"Alice!" Naomi hisses.

"What? You think we're not supposed to notice he has his own personal Secret Service? I'm just being polite."

"You're flirting."

"Not my type."

"What is your type?"

"I no longer have a type. I'm typeless."

We've reached the entrance, climbed the steps. She rings the bell. Sounds like we've activated Big Ben for a count of two. I'm expecting a butler, or at the very least a French maid, but much to my surprise the door is answered by the man himself. Taylor Gatling, Jr., big as breakfast and favoring us with his billion-dollar smile.

"'Morning, ladies. Ms. Prescott, I presume? Welcome to Langford House."

Naomi introduces me as Ms. Allen, which happens to be my mother's maiden name. We're supposed to be from the Colonial Dames, scouting out Langford House for the possibility of a tent auction to raise money for a historical preservation fund. But that's just to get us in the door. On the ride up to New Hampshire Naomi called the deception our "Trojan Horse" and I pointed out that she was mixing historical metaphors, and that the real Co-

lonial Dames would take umbrage, had they but known.
I pointed out, quite helpfully, that unless Naomi was of
lineal descent of an ancestor who lived and served prior
to 1701 in one of the original thirteen colonies, she would
not be eligible for membership. Boss lady had responded
with a raised eyebrow worthy of any dame, period. Even
one whose ancestors somehow forgot to sign the Mayflower Compact.

"Tour first and then coffee in the garden, how does
that sound?"

"Splendid," says Naomi.

I can't resist adding, "Wicked good."

Oops. That stops Gatling in his tracks. He gives me a
sly look. "Really?"

"My family is kind of backwoods colonial, if you
know what I mean."

He seems keenly and genuinely amused. "I believe
the term is 'Swamp Yankee.'"

"That's us. Very swampy."

Behind him Naomi is looking daggers, but sometimes
I really can't help myself. Besides, I can tell he likes it
because he addresses his tour remarks mostly to me.
Pointing out the various rooms, all of which seem to feature hand-printed wallpaper and lots of fancy doodads
on the trim that he calls "flourishes," which we have to
pretend to admire. There are window boxes with upholstered seats and Indian shutters—to keep out the Indians,
apparently—and various hutches and "cupboards," which
are little cubbyholes where the servants slept—and a fab-
ulously formal dining room with an elaborate candelabra
that was a gift from some king or other. In the kitchen
he shows us a really enormous fireplace equipped with
a number of iron doors for baking breads. I point out
they'd probably work for pizza, which gets more daggers

from boss lady, although Taylor Gatling continues to find me ever so amusing, to the point of admitting that some of his less illustrious ancestors were themselves "very swampy."

Ho, ho, ho, we're having such a jolly good time that it's easy to forget our host is maybe guilty of ordering abduction, torture and possibly murder, and that at the very least he'd frightened Milton Bean to within an inch of his life. I for one have no intention of drinking his coffee, given his penchant for chemical interrogation. Luckily there's no need to pretend because just as the coffee is served—our host actually fetches it himself— Naomi gives me a nudge, indicating that she's about to drop the pretense and get down to business.

We've just been seated in a lovely garden overlooking the harbor. Birds are flitting about, bees are prowling the flower blossoms. It's all very civilized. Gatling pours. "Ms. Prescott? Miss Allen? Cream, sugar?"

Leaving her cup untouched, Naomi clears her throat and says, "Actually, Mr. Gatling, I have a confession. We're not from the Colonial Dames and we're not here to discuss a fundraiser."

Gatling lowers the coffeepot, gives us a tight smile and sits back in his authentic colonial chair. "Ah. And I was so enjoying this. Wanted to see how far you'd push it."

"You know who we are?"

He shrugs, as if not the least concerned, and very pleased with himself. "Naomi Nantz, private investigator, and her trusty sidekick Alice Crane. Or maybe I should say her 'wicked good' assistant. You look surprised. Facial recognition software. Not the stuff you have access to. The good stuff that can identify a suspect from a drone altitude of twenty-six thousand feet. As it happens you were identified by a stationary camera that monitors every vehicle crossing the New Castle bridge."

Naomi recovers her cool aplomb. "So you know why we're here."

"Haven't a clue," he says. "The facial recognition software doesn't read minds. That's an entirely different process."

"Enhanced interrogation?"

"A misleading term, don't you think? Could mean almost anything."

"I'm here for the boy, Mr. Gatling. Joey Keener. I'm here to make a deal for his safe release. Whatever it takes."

As he welcomed us into his house Gatling's eyes had been a lively blue. Now they're chips of gray ice. "No idea what you're talking about."

"We're not wired, Mr. Gatling. Not even cell phones. Scan us if you like."

He shrugs. "You were scanned as you came through the front door. That's not the point. I've nothing to do with any person called Joey Keener."

"You've been running a rogue espionage operation targeting Professor Joseph Keener. Therefore you know about his little boy."

Gatling lifts his cup, sips rather deliberately. "If you're asking me if I'm aware that Keener, who may well have been a traitor, had an illegitimate child with a Chinese national, the answer is yes. It would have been irresponsible not to know, since my company provides security at QuantaGate. But that's the extent of my knowledge. Where the child might presently be located is no concern of mine, although I hope it is well, as I would hope for any child, everywhere. Children are the future, don't you agree?"

Naomi stares out at the beautiful harbor, where seagulls hover in the breeze like some perfect mobile, as if attached by invisible wires. She turns to our host, speaking with utter calm and complete confidence.

"Here's my offer, Mr. Gatling. If the boy is released unharmed my investigation will cease. Any intelligence we've gathered and developed will be destroyed. Your connection to this case, including your probable culpability in the abduction, torture and framing of Randall Shane will remain, at most, a matter of speculation, although not by me or my associates. All we require is the safe release of the child. Nothing else matters. That's my offer, I suggest you give it due consideration."

"You must be joking."

"I assure you, I am not."

"You sound like you think you're infallible, Miss Nantz. Let me assure you of something. You're not. You're very much mistaken. I had nothing to do with the murder of Joseph Keener, and I have absolute proof that would stand up in any court of law."

"If you're referring to the items planted in Randall Shane's motel room, those are easily refuted."

Gatling puts the cup down and leans forward, and for the first time radiates a kind of physical menace, without so much as lifting a finger. It's just there, palpable. This is a man who knows how to kill. "You think you know something but you don't."

"Please enlighten me," Naomi says.

He twitches in his seat and for a moment I think she's gotten to him. Then he reaches into a trouser pocket and retrieves a vibrating cell phone. Text message, apparently. Whatever he sees on the screen displeases him. He stands up and jerks his chin at the manicured pathway that leads to the exit.

"Get out," he says, cold as the berg that sank the *Titanic*. "Now. Or you'll be taken into custody."

He lifts the cell phone to his ear, turns away and gestures to the bruiser in the blazer, who has been lurking in the rhododendrons.

We dames know how to scurry when the scurry time is here.

Chapter Forty-Seven

All the Way Home

For the first ten miles or so, Naomi doesn't say a word. She's in the back, brooding, while I ride shotgun, peeking at the side mirror to see if we're being followed. Yes, there are many vehicles behind us, including a convoy of freight trucks, but nothing jumps out. We've cleared the tollbooths on 95, heading south, when I finally decide to break the silence. "That went well. We really left him shaking in his penny loafers."

Naomi stares out the window, ignoring me. Which totally gets on my nerves.

"It was amazing, Jack," I say. "You should have seen us. We strapped him to an antique ironing board, stuffed his mouth with an authentic seventeenth-century dishrag and applied water. Two cups and he was begging for mercy. Confessed he had Joey locked in the servant's cupboard. That's why we're heading back to Boston, to get a locksmith."

"Hush," Naomi says quietly. "I'm thinking."

Nuts. Those happen to be the only two words that will stop me. When Naomi Nantz says she's thinking she's not kidding. Her brain is working the problem, running the possibilities, looking for a way in.

So I shut up for thirty miles.

"I believe him," she finally says.

"Bernie Madoff? O. J. Simpson? Glenn Beck?"

She ignores me, and directs her comments to Jack. "He said he had nothing to do with the murder of Joseph Keener, and that he has absolute proof to that effect."

"Okay," says Jack. "But what makes you believe him? Gut reaction or facts on the ground?"

"That's what I'm trying to determine," she says. "We know the following about Taylor Gatling, Jr. He was pushing to have Professor Keener investigated by a legitimate agency, and when that failed he took it upon himself to put Keener under surveillance. Because he has reason to want revenge on Randall Shane, we assume that he was complicit in planting evidence that made Shane the prime suspect in the professor's murder. That's an assumption not yet established as fact. On the other hand, it's a virtual certainty that Gatling's men took Shane and subjected him to enhanced interrogation. But why? If they knew Shane to be innocent, what could they possibly learn from him? And if the purpose is to frame him, why not leave him to be arrested, why complicate the situation with an airborne abduction in broad daylight?"

"So you're saying you don't think Gatling had Joey abducted?"

Let her try and ignore that one. She can't, and she doesn't.

"No, I'm not saying that" she says, leveling her eyes at me. "Gatling is a seeker of power. It's highly probable that he had the boy kidnapped in Hong Kong and brought here, to give him some sort of leverage. I just don't know for what purpose, precisely."

"Maybe it started out as a plot to implicate the great

Randall Shane in a kidnapping," I suggest. "Turn the hero into a villain, make it look like his whole life was a lie. And then the professor gets killed and framing Shane for the murder is an extra."

"I'll buy that," Jack offers.

"Then you are both ignoring facts in contravention of the premise," Naomi says. "Evidence was planted in Shane's motel room in advance of him discovering Keener's body. That can only have occurred if the plot to frame him was under way before Keener was executed."

"Maybe the facts are wrong."

"Facts are facts, Alice," she reminds me. "Inconvenient as they may sometimes be."

"Well, somebody famous said facts are the hobgoblin of little minds," I retort.

"Ralph Waldo Emerson. And what he said referred to a foolish consistency, not facts."

"Okay. So maybe we're being foolishly consistent."

"Emerson's idea was that we should all avoid conformity and find our own way. He was urging us to be self-reliant."

"Know-it-all," I say.

"I wish I did know it all," Naomi says, sounding plaintive. "If I knew it all, we wouldn't have been trying to shake the suspect's cage, and Joey Keener would already be safe and sound."

Not another word from her, all the way home.

Chapter Forty-Eight

God Who Made the Stars

By the time Gatling arrives in Prides Crossing he's in a full-blown rage. His anger is directed not only at the man called Kidder, but at himself for hiring the screwup in the first place. He'd known Kidder since they'd both served in special ops, and he'd been an oddball even then, but it was a useful kind of strange. The man simply had no compunction about breaking the law when ordered to do so, which had come in handy on more than one occasion. But Gatling sees that it had been a mistake to take him on as a civilian freelancer. Whatever competence Kidder had in the military has diminished over the past few years, along with any sense of discipline. He no longer follows orders, has no respect for the chain of command. He thinks he knows better, he makes threats, and now, finally, a screwup so huge that it's beyond mind-boggling, and might actually put Gatling and his entire organization at risk, despite all his connections, all his precautions.

Gatling screeches the van to a halt, jams it in Park and turns off the motor. Kidder meets him in the driveway, shambling out of the open bay of the garage like some oversize garden gnome wearing, absurdly, a black wool watch cap pulled down over his ears. Plus his eyes look wrong.

"Woo!" Kidder huffs, clapping his hands together. "That didn't take long. When was it I called you? Last week?"

Gatling speaks through clenched teeth. "Less than an hour ago, you moron. What the hell happened?"

"Ha! Wish I knew!" Kidder grins. There are flecks of blood on his teeth. "There was beautiful music and then I saw God."

"What the hell are you talking about?"

Kidder sidles up close. His breath is putrid, powerfully bad. "You know who God looks like? He looks like you in a bad mood. Are you in a bad mood, Junior? Huh?"

Gatling grabs Kidder's right arm and squeezes. Sees the pain light up the man's eyes. "What did you do? Speak, or so help me God."

Kidder smiles that weird smile, that's his only outward physical reaction to Gatling's pincerlike grip on his forearm, which has to hurt like hell. "Didn't I just say you were God? So what's your problem? You're all-powerful, right? You can fix things."

"What do I have to fix? What happened here? And why are you wearing that stupid hat?"

In answer Kidder peels up a corner of the hat, using his left hand, awkwardly. Revealing a mass of clotted blood and hair. "You tell me," he says. "I really want to know."

Kidder leads him through the garage, into the cottage and down into the basement lockup. He points at the floor, where a pool of blood has coagulated into a dark mess. "That's where I woke up. Last thing I remember, I was watching the ball game. Pedroia got a single, he's on first. I'm thinking the little bastard always gets on base, how does he do it? And then I wake up with my head stuck to the floor. I mean it was like my skull was welded to the floor. It made this really scary sound when I tore myself loose. Like my brains had leaked out or something."

Staring at the floor, feeling sickened by the loss of control, Gatling snaps, "That's blood, not brains, you idiot. Your brains, such as they are, are still in your skull. You were hit from behind with that piece of two-by-four," he adds, pointing.

Kidder giggles horribly. "I knew you were God. The all-seeing, the all-knowing. So what happened next? Your humble servant tore himself loose from the floor. Then what?"

"Are you crazy? I can't play this game. We haven't got time for this."

Kidder fumbles at him, pawing, his expression strangely gleeful. "Your humble servant crawled up the stairs and out into the yard. There were stars in the sky. They say that stars are like the sun, only farther away, but I never believed that. Stars are where God poked pin-holes in the night. And the light that shines through, the little twinkles? That's you. God himself."

"You're insane."

"You made me. Whatever I am, that's on you."

"Don't touch me," Gatling says, jerking away.

"This is my confession, God. I crawled up the stairs and went out into the shiny night and I found him. The boy. He was in one corner of the yard and when he saw me he started waving, that's how I noticed him. Hard to see with all the blood in my eyes, you know? That's how it is for us humans, we don't see in the dark too good when our brains have been spot-welded to the floor. So the little brat makes it easy for me to find him. Isn't that odd? He can't get away because of the fence, but still you'd think he'd try to hide."

"What are you talking about? What fence? And where's the woman?"

"Just a little old electrified fence. Why would you notice? Stuff like that is beneath God's interest. It was supposed to be powered from a twelve-volt battery, like a cattle fence, but I did a little rewiring, hooked it up to the household current with a hundred-amp breaker. That's enough to kill us normal humans, but somehow she must have got around it. The breaker was tripped. She got away. Left the kid behind and took off. Told me all about it, the little brat."

Gatling is incredulous. "If this was last night she could be on her way back here with the cops any moment. Why didn't you call me when it happened?"

Kidder, amused, says, "Gee, God, you must have been too busy listening to all those prayers, huh? Too busy to notice what was happening to me. Otherwise you'd know I crawled up the stairs and went out and found the kid and locked him in the closet, and then I passed out again."

"Show me," Gatling demands.

Kidder leads him to a bedroom closet. The bi-fold closet door doesn't lock, so the door has been blocked shut by a heavy bureau. Gatling lends a hand and they both shove the bureau out of the way, Kidder dusting his hands melodramatically and saying, "Hoo-ha! Everything's easier when God's on your side."

Gatling studies the closet door and frowns. There's nothing he likes about the situation, but he knows what has to be done. The building will have to be burned to the ground, to destroy any evidence of the kidnapping, but first he has to take care of the boy, who is himself the most damning piece of evidence. Gatling reaches into his back pocket, snakes out a plastic Ziploc bag, holds it to his side. With his left hand he sweeps open the bi-fold door.

Crouched in the corner, small hands covering his eyes, is Joey Keener.

"Come out of there, little man," Gatling says softly, soothingly. "It's okay, you're safe. I'm the good guy."

He takes an ether-soaked rag from the plastic bag and holds it to the boy's mouth until he stops struggling.

Chapter Forty-Nine

Wicked Bad

The first Naomi Nantz case I ever worked involved a teenage girl, a movie star and a nationally known wacko-religious cult that will remain nameless in these pages because I really hate finding rattlesnakes in unexpected places. At first I didn't believe a word of the girl's story, touching, as it did, on midnight visits from extraterrestrial beings, but Naomi was somehow able to cut through all the spin and special effects (mostly created by the movie star) to the core of truth about what really happened. It's like the average person—me for instance—when confronted by the impossible, sees exactly that, the part that couldn't possibly be true, and can't get around it. Whereas Naomi sees behind the impossible, and is able to make cognitive leaps that to this day boggle my little mind.

Case in point, the strangely encoded message that arrived about ten hours after we returned from our failed mission to rattle Taylor Gatling's gilded cage. Naomi is in the command center with Teddy, all screens blazing, the two of them sifting databases for clues on where Gatling might be hiding a five-year-old boy. They're working from a fifty-mile radius of Boston, in light of the fact that Joey and Mrs. Mancero were filmed on Harvard Bridge, within sight of the MIT dome. Compiling cross-references to buildings and properties that may have any connection to Gatling, his company, his extensive business contacts and his circle of friends.

Teddy has a satellite map up on the largest screen, with red dots indicating possible locations. This seems to include most of southern New England.

"Exclude business locations," Naomi suggests. "Try residential properties owned by anyone who has ever crossed paths with Mr. Gatling."

Teddy does so at the stroke of a key. If the dots were pimples the poor screen would have a very bad case of acne. "Why exclude business locations?" he wants to know. "A lot of these involve warehouses and storage facilities."

Before Naomi can explain, every screen in the command center goes blank.

"What the hell?" says Teddy, his voice rising an octave or so.

The largest screen, the one that had been dedicated to the satellite map, starts to glow blue. Then a white dot begins to bounce along the middle of the screen, as if to an unheard musical beat. Teddy, eyes bugging, is frantically jabbing at various keyboards, to no effect.

"Wait," Naomi says softly.

The dot finally settles in the middle of the screen, condensing and expanding in a way that reminds me of a beating heart. *Bah-bump, bah-bump.*

"Now," she says. "The escape button, top left."

Teddy deliberately depresses the escape button. At first nothing happens. And then the pulsing dot expands and changes, morphing into an image of a young girl in a frock-style dress. Not a photograph, an illustration of some kind. Looks familiar, but I can't place it.

Naomi chuckles, shaking her head. "Clever man," she says.

"Clever who, and what does it mean?"

"That's Alice from *Alice in Wonderland*. The original 1865 edition, illustrated by John Tenniel. Apparently you made an impression on Taylor Gatling, Alice. He's saying hello."

"Ridiculous," I say, folding my arms, preparing to be stubborn. "What makes you think this is him? And what could it possibly mean?"

"I conclude that it is Gatling because he has the ability to do this. It can't be a coincidence that we've been hacked within hours of confronting him."

"Hey, look at that," Teddy says. "Her mouth is moving."

"Click on her lips," Naomi suggests.

Teddy clicks and the image of the young girl vanishes, replaced by a blinking password entry. "Any ideas?" he says. "It could be anything."

"Not anything," Naomi points out. "There's a blinking cursor and eleven blank spaces."

"So?"

"Password prompts don't usually include clues about how many characters are required. And this came from Alice's mouth." She turns to me. "Therefore I conclude that the password is something you said."

"That narrows it down to about a million words a month, if you count all those conversations I have with myself."

"I'm curious," Naomi says, evenly. "Why are you so resistant to the idea that Mr. Gatling prefers to communicate with you, rather than with me?"

"Because I loathe the man. It looks like he had a child kidnapped for his own political purposes, which is disgusting enough right there. Plus he's smug and preening and so...so... I don't know, macho."

"You're repulsed by machismo?"

"His version, yes."

"Interesting. Maybe Mr. Gatling is attracted to women who revile him. But that's neither here nor there. The image of Alice speaking is conclusive. Therefore the eleven blank characters represent a word or phrase uttered by you, in his presence."

I shrug. "I said a lot of things."

"Yes, but what utterance did he remark on? A few come to mind. 'Swamp Yankee' is twelve spaces, so that doesn't work. And 'backwoods colonial' is out," she says, before pausing to muse for a moment. "Teddy, try this: 'wicked good.'"

He keys in the letters, hits Return.

The password entry space vanishes and is instantly replaced by a video play-bar on the bottom of the screen, with icons for play, pause, fast-forward and stop, and a digital clock that begins counting as a slightly grainy nighttime image forms out of the darkness.

"Stop right there," Naomi says, and when Teddy hesitates—apparently fearful that he'll lose the video enclosure—she reaches out and taps the keyboard herself, freezing the image.

"How did you do it so fast?" I ask, incredulous. "What led you to 'wicked good'?"

"Logic. Rather obvious, actually. We can discuss the finer aspects of deductive reasoning later. Right now I want Jack Delancey, the quicker the better."

As it happens Jack is already in the residence, specifically downstairs in Mrs. Beasley's breakfast nook, fueling himself on her French press coffee while he makes phone calls to various sources. He joins us in the command center in exactly the time that it takes him to bound up the stairs.

"What have we here?" he asks, focused on the big screen. "If I'm not mistaken, that's the Keener residence. Taken with some sort of night-vision camera. High quality, from the look of it."

"Play," Naomi commands.

The scene doesn't change, even though the clock is ticking off the frames. Professor Keener's home on Putnam Avenue, as seen from a slight angle that covers the front porch as well as part of the south-facing side of the house. Obviously, from the steadiness of the scene, the video camera had to have been mounted on some sort of tripod or steadying device. The windows are dark, as if the house itself is sleeping. A minute ticks by. Lights flare onto the front porch and I hold my breath, but it's only headlights from a passing vehicle.

"My guess, this is a remote," Jack says. "An operator would have instinctively panned toward the light."

"We know Gatling had Professor Keener under surveillance," Naomi says. "Remote cameras make sense. Probably automatic feeds."

"Right there," Jack says, pointing.

The guy has good eyes, I'll grant him that. He's the first to spot an approaching visitor, screen left. A male of average build, seen from the back as he emerges from the dark of the sidewalk to the slightly more illuminated area of the front porch. The pool of lesser darkness is apparently the result of an unseen streetlight. Whatever the source, the night-vision camera is sensitive enough to show that he's wearing jeans, sneakers, windbreaker and a ball cap.

"Pause," Naomi instructs, and this time Teddy obeys. The image on the porch freezes. "Ring any bells?"

Jack shrugs. "Not yet. I'd say young rather than old. Slender rather than fat. Male rather than female."

"Note the time stamp," Naomi says. "It could be faked, of course, but it corresponds to the day Keener was killed. 05:10. Military time for 5:10 a.m."

"A further observation," Jack says. "Whoever that is on the porch, it's not Randall Shane."

"Continue," Naomi says.

We watch the visitor ring a doorbell, wait. A light comes on upstairs.

"Oh man," Jack says. "Makes me want to shout out 'don't answer the door!'"

But he does answer the door. We follow his progress as lights come on, and less than a minute after the bell was pushed, the door opens.

"Freeze," says Naomi. "Now try zooming in."

Teddy makes a face, sucking his teeth. "What if I screw up? We could lose the whole thing."

"Nonsense. This has been sent to us because he wants us to see it. Just try the normal zoom, centering on his face."

It works. Teddy sighs with relief.

"Do we all confirm that the man at the door is Joseph Keener?"

We do. The video continues. Keener opening the door wider, the visitor stepping into the hall, the door closing behind him.

"I wonder if they had a camera inside," Jack says.

I'm hoping there was no inside camera. It's sufficiently horrible as it is—I really don't need to see an actual snuff film, thank you very much.

"Are we going to sit through this or fast-forward?"

Jack wants to know when nothing happens for another sixty seconds.

"Patience," Naomi says. "We watch every frame. It can't be long."

Long depends on what you're waiting for. In this particular case, five minutes seems to be an eternity. Finally it happens. No sound—there's no audio track—but a distinct flash of light from the ground floor, no doubt from the kitchen area.

"God rest him," Naomi says.

Ten seconds later the front door opens. The man—the killer—steps out, one hand shoved into his windbreaker pocket, the other reaching up to tug down his ball cap.

"Freeze and zoom," Naomi says.

"I'll be damned," Jack says. "I've seen his mug shot. That's Micky Lee. Aka Mr. Baked Alaska."

Chapter Fifty

The Luckiest Guy in the World

Even though I'm a head taller and longer of leg, I still have to run to keep up with Dane Porter. The petite attorney power-walks her way through life, elbows pumping. We're rocketing through the halls of MGH to bring the good news to Randall Shane, who has just been proven innocent of murder to our satisfaction, if not yet to the D.A.'s. There's still a uniformed officer outside his door, and Dr. Gallagher, making notes on her chart, wants a word before we enter.

"It's a good news, bad news kind of deal," the young doc says, glancing down at her charts. "The good news is, Mr. Shane is recovering faster than we ever expected, considering the physical and mental trauma he sustained. The bad news is, because he's so much better they're pushing to have him transferred to the Middlesex Jail."

"Old news," Dane assures her. "The real killer has just been identified. The D.A. will come around once he's had time to digest the latest evidence."

The doctor breathes a sigh of relief. "I knew he couldn't be guilty after I checked him out on Google. Do you know he's rescued something like twenty kids?"

"We were aware of that, yeah," Dane says with a grin.

"They offered him a TV show, *Kid Finders USA*. The big guy turned it down, told them to leave him alone, let him do his work. Can you imagine?"

Inside the suite we find Randall Shane sitting up in his chair, massaging the thick plastic band of the ankle monitor. Looking, as his doctor implied, pretty darn chipper for a man who had been tortured half to death not so long ago. In addition to radiating health he also looks faintly embarrassed, possibly as a consequence of being gushed over.

"Hey, big guy."

That's Dane Porter, popping through the door like a gorgeous little cuckoo expelled from her clock.

"Did you know that's what they call you, your fans? I mean the medical staff. The Big Guy. I need to be more formal, being an attorney, so I'm thinking maybe of going with The Large Dude."

"Please don't."

"Wouldn't dream of it," Dane says, effervescent with good tidings. "Shane you are and Shane you shall be. Did Dr. Gallagher happen to mention Tommy Costello is getting a little antsy? She did? Well, we're here to put your mind at rest. We just received evidence, physical evidence, that's going to result in all charges being dropped. Maybe not today, but in the next few, that's guaranteed." She makes a sweeping gesture in my direction and says, "Alice? Tell him the wicked good news."

When I tell Shane about the surveillance video that identifies the shooter he shakes his head and says, "Who the hell is Micky Lee?"

"He may have been an acquaintance of Jonny Bing, the entrepreneur," I say. "We're running that down. We're assuming this was a hired hit, but we don't yet know who did the hiring or why, exactly."

Dane says, "The point is, you're off the hook, or soon will be. Plus there have been some interesting developments. One of whom just happens to be drop-dead gorgeous."

Over the course of the next ten minutes, the attorney tells him, very succinctly, about the extremely large-caliber bullet fired into the residence, as well as the arrival of Michelle Chen, also known as Ming-Mei, her triad background as the mistress of a dragon head and the real circumstances of Joey's abduction.

"So that's what happened," Shane says when the summation is complete. "That's why everything changed. The kid was being bounced between the two sides, both trying to get leverage on his father. Chasing the dream of a functioning quantum computer. You say your boss is convinced that Gatling is the one who had the boy lifted from Hong Kong? She's absolutely sure about that?"

"Ninety-nine percent," I say. "Naomi Nantz never goes a hundred. Ninety-nine is as good as it gets."

"And she thinks he'll do the right thing and have Joey released?"

"If he can find a way not to be implicated, why not? With the father dead, the son is no longer leverage, if ever he really was. Taylor Gatling isn't overburdened with conscience, but he's not a psychopath. At least, that's our thinking."

"Hope you're right," Shane says uneasily. "Gatling may not be a psycho, but he has a few of those on the payroll. Believe me, I know."

"Sorry."

"Don't be. If Kathy Mancero *was* duped into taking care of Joey, she'll do everything in her power to keep him safe. I'm clinging to that. She may not look it, but she's tough," he says, looking suddenly exhausted.

"Naomi is confident we'll have a location in the next twenty-four hours," I promise him.

"Good. Good. You know the one thing that strikes me as odd?" Shane says thoughtfully. "That shot through the window? Sounds to me like someone was testing the system. Probably watching to see who responded and how fast."

"You think?"

"Tell Nantz if it happens again to be very, very careful."

"Consider her told. Listen, we have to get back to the ranch," Dane says, repositioning the strap on her purse. "We're expecting a stampede of lawmen and that's going to make our boss very antsy, to say the least. You hang tight, okay?"

"Will do," he says, yawning. "Thanks for everything."

The good news having been properly and thoroughly delivered, we head back to the residence. Dane doing her power-walk and me jogging to keep up.

Shane drifts off, dreaming about a good day. Amy is an infant, three months old, the quintessential bundle of joy, and he and Jean have decided to take her to the lake, her very first visit to a body of water bigger than a bath basin, and she's pointing at the birds, ducks and seagulls, and making cooing noises because apparently she thinks all birds are pigeons, and Jean is happily reading a book and Shane is just sitting there with his big feet in the sand, feeling like the luckiest man in the world, even though he knows how it all will end, he's still the luckiest guy in the world because he got this much and them, and the happy day will always be there, somewhere in time, even if he can only visit in his dreams.

"Wake up," someone whispers, shaking his sore shoulder.

He opens his eyes. A nurse leans over the bed, fussing to wake him with her right hand because her left is wrapped in gauze, which strikes him as odd.

"It's me, Kathy Mancero," she says, her desperate eyes locking on his. "We haven't got much time."

Chapter Fifty-One

A Man Who Would Walk through Fire

Having the residence invaded by felony detectives is hard enough to take once, let alone twice. But that's exactly what happens. I'm the one who gets the call from the hospital and has the excited caller repeat the message twice before relating the stunning development to Naomi Nantz, who takes it like a slap in the face.

"Randall Shane *escaped?* That can't be right."

She takes the phone from my hand without so much as a please or thank-you and has the caller repeat the story for a third time. Then she drops the phone back in my hand and, muttering darkly, marches down the hall to lock the door to the command center.

"No one gets in there, do you understand? No one. We'll deal with them in the library. I will not have the command center infiltrated by strangers."

At least she puts the key in her pocket. For a moment there I thought she might swallow it.

Less than an hour ago the hordes of lawmen—three, actually, two from Cambridge and one liaison officer from Boston—left in possession of the downloaded surveillance tape, promising to share the new evidence with their respective superiors. Now they're back with reinforcements including a special FBI detail commanded by Assistant Director Monica Bevins, who looks like she's eaten a bad shrimp. Or maybe a dozen bad shrimp.

"Tell me you didn't have anything to do with this," are the first words out of her mouth.

"I'm as surprised as you are," Naomi counters.

"Really?" the big FBI agent says. "Because I'm not that surprised."

"No? Elucidate, please," Naomi urges.

In response Bevins folds her arms and leans back in the chair, remaining more or less silent. As if she's here because her presence is required, rather than because she has any particular enthusiasm for the interrogation. The questioning comes from the felony detectives, who seem to have taken Shane's escape personally, and who are more than ready to blame Naomi Nantz, even if they have no particular proof to offer.

"You're wasting your time and, even more important, my time," she says. "I've told you that we had nothing to do with Shane escaping. That's all you need to know. And even if he did leave the hospital without notification, so what? The charges against him were about to be dropped."

"The charges *haven't* been dropped and maybe now they won't be," the Cambridge detective reminds her, not even trying to keep the smirk from his voice. "Besides, this is a separate matter. If a man escapes from prison and proves his innocence he's still guilty of escaping."

Naomi gives him a dismissive look. "Is that the best you can do, threaten us with a movie?"

"Excuse me?"

"You just described *The Shawshank Redemption*. I sincerely hope your investigations are not being informed by fiction."

Embarrassed, he retorts, "Yeah, well, the surety bond you posted has been forfeited. You're on the hook for a million bucks and a charge of aiding and abetting, if we have anything to do with it."

"We'll see about that." Naomi turns to Dane. "Hold them off. Do whatever it is that lawyers do."

"I'm not a miracle worker," Dane says, sounding slightly abashed.

"Yes, you are. I can think of at least four examples."

Which leaves Dane speechless, a kind of miracle in itself.

For the next twenty minutes the cops harangue us from a number of directions, none unexpected, given the circumstances, before grudgingly admitting they have no proof of our complicity in Randall Shane's escape.

"The man tore off his ankle monitor. Do you have any idea the kind of strength that takes?" one of the Boston detectives notes. He sounds awestruck. Awestruck and at the same time aggrieved because his men were responsible for keeping the prisoner in custody. "Obviously he can kill with his bare hands."

Naomi says, "As I understand it, the guard at the door wasn't killed. Is the injury serious?"

"Choke holds can kill."

"I seriously doubt it was a choke hold. My guess is Shane pressed the guard's vagus nerve," she says, touching the nape of her neck instructively. "If done correctly pressure on the vagus nerve will induce a brief blackout."

"You're making excuses for him?"

"Not at all. Be assured that if Shane contacts us, we will contact you."

"Damned right you will. If you don't, it's a felony violation and you can be sure the D.A. will prosecute."

"Jack? If you have any theories about where Shane

might have fled, please share them with these gentlemen."

Jack has been fidgeting silently—he's no doubt anxious to get into action mode—but he knows how to play the game and does so, lying like a pro. "No theories," he mutters. "Shane lives in upstate New York. Maybe he went home."

In all of this Monica Bevins remains strangely reticent. Confronted with Naomi's conclusion that Taylor Gatling is somehow deeply involved, she merely grunts. More of a snort, really. As if she has knowledge she can't share, or doesn't fully understand herself. "Obviously he'll be attempting to find the missing child," she says. "That's what Shane does. My question is, why now?"

"We got pictures of a female leaving the hospital in his company," the Boston detective points out.

Bevins stirs herself to ask, "Have you identified her?"

"Not yet, but we will."

The fact that the FBI assistant director doesn't spill the beans—she has to suspect, as we do, that the female in question is Kathleen Mancero—is telling. Whatever Bevins is up to, it doesn't involve sharing with Boston or Cambridge police, both of whom are keenly interested in apprehending Randall Shane, the sooner the better. But when the moment comes, when they all get up to leave and she could make an excuse to stay behind, she doesn't. All she does is give Naomi a loaded glance and say, "It's out of my hands, do you understand?"

When the group of angry law enforcement types are finally out the door, I bolt it behind them and hurry back to the command center, where the door has been unlocked and activities have already resumed. "What did she mean by that?" I demand of boss lady. "That you would understand?"

Naomi shrugs. "I think I do. Voices have spoken, orders have been given or alluded to, and the result is that she can't touch Mr. Gatling. As we already knew, he has friends in very high places."

"Friends who'll let him get away with kidnapping a child?"

She shrugs, as if to say that is the way of the world. "Friends who have made fortunes hitching themselves to his star. Friends who must be aware that as a civilian he made decisions to target and kill suspects in Afghanistan. At least one of those targets turned out to be a school, for children most likely, and yet the investigation was squelched and his contract was not terminated."

"*This* child is an American citizen."

"Obviously the life of one particular child has not made a difference, in respect to those covering for Gatling and his enterprise. They have already established themselves as men lacking in conscience or they wouldn't have allied themselves with him. That much must be obvious by now to you. Shall we all get back to work?"

There's something in her manner that warns me off from any further discussion. Naomi Nantz is truly angry, and when that happens I've found from past experience that it's best to bury the wisecracks and let her concentrate on the case. She takes her seat, but does not turn immediately to the screens where Teddy is already hard at work, fingers flying over the keyboards like some mad composer. "Jack? Your impressions?"

Jack Delancey has slumped into a seat looking thoroughly discouraged. "The shit has hit the fan. If Mancero has taken the risk of approaching Shane in the hospital, something must have gone badly wrong."

"Do we know it's her?"

"Not yet. They've confiscated the data from the hospital surveillance cameras. But who else could it be?"

"No other confederates leap to mind?"

"No. And why would he call in someone? It's not like he needed help overpowering the guard. No, the only thing that makes sense is that something happened, she got separated from the kid or whatever and she went to Shane for help."

"And in your estimation he would render assistance, even if it put him at legal peril?"

"Are you kidding? The guy would walk through fire."

She nods, satisfied. "Then we agree. He'll be going after Mr. Gatling."

Jack says, "Absolutely. I should head back up to Cow Hampshire, stake out this scumbag Gatling. See if Shane has the same idea."

"Not tonight," Naomi says, very firmly. "Need I remind you that we are, all of us, under deep surveillance? They expect you to lead them to Shane. We must confound that expectation, however much we might want to assist our friend. He will contact us when he sees fit. Until then, I suggest we stand down and let him do his thing. With the exception of Teddy, who will maintain vigil in the event Shane makes contact, I advise you all to get some sleep. I have a feeling tomorrow is going to be a big day."

Chapter Fifty-Two

All They Need

"I'm worried about the gun," Kathy Mancero says, staring at the motel room door. "Not having one, I mean."

Shane, his sore and swollen ankle wrapped in hot towels, considers the problem. "Guns can be useful," he says. "If we need one, we'll get one."

"How?"

"Leave that to me. First things first."

There's no need to be more specific than that. They both know that their first and only task is finding Joey. Shane notes that Kathy Mancero's need is so deep in this regard that it radiates from her body like a fever. She has described the circumstances of her separation from the boy in very nearly the same terms that she used when speaking about her missing daughter, as if some vital part of her soul has been freshly amputated. Recounting how she had fled the basement with Joey and had then been knocked down by a massive electrical shock that had left flash-point burns in her left arm. She describes the sensation of falling into unconsciousness as dying, and how when she came back to life, hours later, she was somehow under a thick, bushy hedge at the corner of the property, with no memory of how she got there. If she had crawled to the hiding place, she has no memory of it.

"All I remember is this vague sense of a child lying next to me, breathing into my face and whispering, 'Mommy, Mommy, wake up.'"

In her semiconscious state Kathy had believed it was her daughter, come to take her to heaven at last. Had longed for it to be so. But then she heard Joey calling out, from another corner of the property, and knew in her heart that his had been the voice begging her to wake up. She was injured but alive.

"He must have helped me get behind the hedges, out of sight. I can't remember that part. All I know is, I woke up to the sound of Joey's voice, from the opposite side of the yard. I almost called out to him. But something stopped me. Some instinct, I guess, because I certainly wasn't thinking clearly."

Whatever made her hesitate, silence had saved her. From her hiding place under the hedges she had seen Kidder stagger by—it was daybreak, how had that happened?—and then she heard him howl in rage, a horrible animal sound, and she had tried to crawl out, anything to distract him from Joey. Because she knew with a terrible sickening thud exactly what the boy was doing. By calling out he was offering himself, saving her from Kidder, like a little bird drawing a predator away from the nest.

"It was almost as bad as Stacy dying, watching that monster grab Joey and take him back into the house and shut the door behind him."

She had stayed there under the hedge, regaining her strength, and had managed to crawl to one of the windows, but could see nothing of Kidder or the boy—he must have taken him back down into the basement.

Scrabbling back under the hedge she'd rooted around in the dirt until she uncovered a fist-size rock.

"Killing size," she tells Shane, with no inflection in her voice. "I intended to kill him when I got the chance, which is what I should have done in the first place, to protect Joey."

Except it hadn't happened that way. As she waited, poised to strike, a van had pulled into the driveway and Kidder had come out through the garage and she was powerless to act, all she could do was watch and listen as Kidder and a younger man had argued, and then the younger man had gone into the house and emerged with Joey, the precious child unconscious but with his little hands and feet twitching in a way that convinced her he was still alive, and the new man had put the boy into the van and driven away.

Her eyes burning with the intensity of her need, Kathy says, "That's when I put the license plate number on my arm. Because I might forget it, and then we'd never find Joey."

Shane winces, aware that she scratched the tag number directly into the burned area on her arm, where it shows up white against the singed flesh.

"A few minutes later Kidder drove away and I started to run back into the house—I was going to call 911—and that's when the house exploded."

Some sort of incendiary device had been detonated—possibly something as simple as a natural gas line—and Kathy had fled through the open gate before the fire engines arrived, and made her way down the beach to the next big oceanfront estate where, miracle of miracles—she took it as a sign from God—she had found a silver Volkswagen Beetle in the garage of an unoccupied mansion, the ignition keys hanging on a hook inside the garage door, and she had driven the miracle car into Boston and found him where he lay in his hospital bed, the only man in the world who could help her put things right.

Shane is not a man of faith, not her kind of faith anyhow, with its certainty of heaven, but he knows that whatever is keeping this woman alive depends on recovering Joey Keener. Not because she intends to keep him—the only child she has ever wanted is the one she can no longer have—but because she needs to return the boy to his rightful mother, restoring balance to the world, and that portion of her soul that has been torn from her by grief.

He's got a few things he wants to even up, too. After that there will be time enough to treat physical maladies like burned arms and ankles bruised by tearing away electronic monitors. Bodies heal with time. Souls require something else again.

"There's a Best Buy at the mall," he tells her. "First exit off the traffic circle. Buy the cheapest laptop they have in stock. Just make sure it has Wi-Fi. I'd do it myself but I'm, ah, more noticeable."

There will be a manhunt under way, he's sure of that. His description and image will already be circulating, but there's a chance that she hasn't yet been connected to his escape. It's a chance they'll have to take.

"I'll have to use my card," she warns him, standing up. "We're out of cash."

"The card will be fine. By the time it's posted you'll be out of the mall, back on the road. If the owners weren't in residence at that estate you stumbled into, there's a good chance the car hasn't been reported as stolen yet. There's nothing to connect you to the vehicle."

"But they'll know we're here, in this area. The card will tell them."

"They'll already know that much. If the cops haven't figured it out, Naomi Nantz has. Whatever happens will be in the next twenty-four hours. That's all we need. One last day."

Chapter Fifty-Three

Too Many Guns

When the whole thing blew up with my fake husband—not that I knew he was fake at the time—I had to resort to sleeping pills. There was no way I could run the office of a busy dental practice without sufficient sleep, and no way I could stop the mad whirl of self-recrimination in my head whenever it hit the pillow, not without assistance from those helpful little pills. Fortunately the brand my doctor prescribed were not physically addictive, but even so I'm not really a pill popper by nature, and threw away the bottle soon after taking the job with Naomi and moving into the residence. Something about the 1200-thread-count bedding must have worked, because I'm almost always able to sleep, no matter how tense and involving the case.

Not tonight. I know it without even trying. And there's no way I'm going to take a pill and risk being groggy in the morning. So that's why I'm once again wandering around the residence after midnight, still fully dressed, and wishing I could take a stroll around the block to settle my nerves. That's not a possibility, not with half the Boston cops and probably the FBI parked outside our door. A nighttime tour of the residence always involves a visit to Naomi's Zen garden, which exudes peace even to us nonbelievers. The cool shadows of the room, with its vaulted ceiling and subdued lighting, have always appealed, even if I would never dare draw a rake through the sand like Naomi is doing at the very moment I enter, aware that I'm intruding on her privacy.

"Join me," she says.

"You're raking," I say. "That means you're thinking."

Her shoulders lift. "I'm always thinking. This is just another way of getting there. Sit, relax."

I sit. Relaxing is not an option.

"Meditation might help," she suggests.

"No, thank you."

"I wasn't offering to teach you. Although I could put you in touch with an excellent instructor."

I turn to her, puzzled. "Don't you mean like a monk or something?"

She chuckles softly. "I'm not a Buddhist, Alice. But I do find meditation useful, and I have great respect for certain aspects of the religion."

"Oh," I say, flummoxed. Just when I think I know what she's thinking, it turns out she's thinking something else. "What aspects?"

Naomi is considering her reply when a window explodes.

We're both on our feet almost before the sound stops echoing. There was no gunshot, only the sound of bullet-resistant glass shattering, pretty much exactly as it did the night before, and I'm up and running, heading upstairs because that's where the safe room is located, and there's nothing like the noise of high-powered ammo to make you want a nice safe place to hide.

I'm not the first to arrive. That would be Mrs. Beasley, arrayed this evening in an ankle-length dressing gown.

She says not a word, but her expression communicates a sense of disgust, that such an inconvenience could be allowed to occur two nights in a row.

"Teddy!" Naomi shouts behind me. "To the safe room. Follow the drill, please. The alarms have already sounded."

"It was Jack's room again," Teddy says, clearly terrified. "But he's here this time."

"I'll check on Jack. Alice, you get Ming-Mei."

Our Chinese visitor has been given the largest of the guest accommodations. I pound on the door and call her name but there is no reply, so I have to use the pass key and let myself in. It's way less than a minute since the glass shattered and the alarms went off, but it seems much, much longer.

As I wake Ming-Mei in her bed she sits up befuddled—apparently she does not share my reluctance for sleeping pills—and she has to remove the foam earplugs from her ears before I can make myself understood.

"We may be under attack. Follow me, please."

She has the good sense not to ask questions and follows, wearing only a light T-shirt that seems to emphasize her diminutive size. Approaching the safe room at a run—our international guest is fleet of foot—I'm greatly relieved to see Jack Delancey standing there, big as life.

"Hit the ceiling, just like last time," he's telling Naomi. "Had to be fired from ground level. Lucky for me I wasn't looking out the window."

"Indeed," says Naomi. "Everybody in, quickly!"

But when the door to the safe room is shut, bolts engaged, and I finally have time to take a breath and count heads, Jack is not among us. And when I insist that the door be opened and he be admitted, Naomi insists otherwise. "Jack will take care of Jack. He's very competent when it comes to self-defense. He's very competent, period, as you must know."

"What's going on?" I demand. "Why did we violate protocol?"

Naomi holds up her hand, calling for silence. "Leave it for now," she says softly. "When the all clear comes, as it soon will, it is crucial that none of us mention that Jack remained outside this room after the alarm sounded."

So we wait. A minute or two passes. I can't help noticing Teddy noticing Ming-Mei in her little thin T-shirt. Noticing the astonishingly beautiful woman the way a starving man notices a T-bone steak grilling on the other side of a restaurant window. Because poor Teddy knows he's on the other side of the glass, at least I hope he does.

After five minutes or so a green light blinks, indicating the all clear from Beacon Security. At a nod from boss lady I release the magnetic bolts on the heavy steel door and swing it open. The Beacon Security chief nods politely, then makes his report. No surprise, it's a repeat of last night's incident. No one broke in; the alarms were tripped by a heavy-caliber lead slug shattering a window in Jack's room. "I don't know what to tell you," the security guy says. "Someone is using you for target practice. Obviously, stay away from the windows. And I'm going to suggest that we post armed guards in the vicinity. Maybe we can catch the perp in the act, if he tries again."

Naomi is dubious about the efficacy of that. "We're already under surveillance by at least two law enforcement entities. If they didn't see anything, your men are not likely to."

He shrugs. "Up to you."

The Beacon Security men dutifully file out, and each is logged exiting the residence. In the resulting silence I decide it's time to escort Ming-Mei, who is visibly trembling, back to her guest suite.

"A moment, please," Naomi cautions.

The delay is explained, at least partially, when Jack appears in the hallway, finger to his lips. He says something to Teddy, too quietly for me to pick up, and our young hacker looks hopeful. Why that should be I can't imagine until it becomes clear that he's been instructed to take Ming-Mei back to his room instead. "Lock the door and stay in there," Jack whispers. "Come out for no one but me, okay?"

When they're gone Jack turns to me with a grin and says, "Can you sound like her? Like Ming-Mei?"

"Are you serious?"

"Just fake it, that may be good enough."

"What are you talking about?" I hiss.

"Pretend you're her. Just for five minutes."

"But I can't—"

"Sure you can," he says, taking my arm and guiding me in the direction of the guest suite.

He reaches behind his back and removes a handgun from his belt. Again with the finger to his lips. I don't necessarily trust Jack Delancey with all things, but as it so happens I do trust him with my life. So I stop resisting and follow his lead.

Naomi is trailing behind us, and damned if she isn't armed as well, with a .38 Smith & Wesson Airweight, small and light enough for her slender hands. She's not exactly a gun enthusiast, but a while back we all received a few hours of training at the firing range, under Jack's tutelage, so my first thought is, what about me? What about a weapon for me? How about sharing with your friends? My next thought is how to avoid getting caught in a cross fire. What the hell is going on? And if it's going to get dangerous, how come we're not donning body armor? Not that we have any body armor, but still, the thought occurs.

We're outside the guest room where Ming-Mei has been staying.

"Say something," Jack whispers, his lips so close to my ear that I can feel the warm pulse of his breath. "Try to sound like her."

This is more embarrassing than having to stand up in front of everybody at speech class in ninth grade—did I mention I had a slight lisp at the time, since corrected?— but with a sense of here-goes-nothing, I attempt to speak in a very slight but very cultured Chinese accent, with British overtones. The best I can do is drop *r*'s and pitch my voice slightly higher. I end up sounding vaguely Polish.

"Thank you ve'y ve'y much. You're a big strong man, Mistah Jack."

Jack scowls—obviously he thinks my impression sucks—and gestures for me to open the door. "You'll be fine, Ming-Mei. It was just a false alarm," he says, a little too loudly. "If you need anything, ring the buzzer."

I open the door. Nice digs, nearly as nice as mine, but with a trace of perfume that isn't my thing, not at all. The bed is rumpled from when I roused her, and her clothing is strewn about. Hadn't noticed that, either, what with all the excitement. Nor do I have any idea what Jack has in mind—he and Naomi have slipped into the room behind me, and taken up positions in opposite corners. Jack gestures for me to shut the door. Actually, if there's going to be gunplay I'd just as soon leave, but that doesn't seem to be part of the plan.

Very carefully Jack gets down on his knees and looks under the bed. He shakes his head. Naomi has moved to get an angle on the open bathroom door. She silently slips inside and quickly returns with a shake of her head.

Jack gestures at me, making a yawn. He wants me to yawn? Am I supposed to yawn in Chinese or what? Follow-up gestures indicate that I'm supposed to be preparing for bed. We'll never win at pantomime if we can't do better than this.

The pair of them, Jack and Naomi, raise their weapons in unison and point at the closet door. Jack edges closer, keeping to an angle, and presses the latch, swinging the door open. As befits a proper guest suite, it's a sizable walk-in closet. And standing there with a creepy grin on his face is a man I've never seen before.

A big, rangy guy with a wool cap snugged down over his ears, rapper-style, and crazy dare-me eyes, and a great big gun in his hand.

"What do you know," he says. "Mexican standoff. Or is it Chinese?"

Chapter Fifty-Four

Into the Night

"Bang," says the man in the closet. "You want to go that way? You shoot me, I shoot her?"

By *her* I'm supposing he means Naomi, only because I'm slightly farther away, cowering in plain sight.

"Put the gun on the floor and place your hands behind your head," Jack says.

The man in the wool cap gives us another loony grin, as if delighted that Jack is playing along. "Spoken like a real lawman. But here's the thing, sunshine. I've got a gun and you've got a gun and I hate to say it, but mine is bigger than yours. You have, let me see, a nine-mil for the gentleman and a .38 for the lady. Nice firearms. Quality. But the gun in my hand is a Kahr PM45, nineteen ounces fully loaded, which means I can hold it all day long. And the nice thing about a large-caliber bullet, all it takes is one shot. I'm aiming at the lady's torso, but even if I wing her in the arm or leg she'll bleed out in less than a minute. So why don't we go in the other direction? Put your guns on the floor and place *your* hands behind your head."

"Never going to happen." Jack is adamant, and his eyes are subzero.

"Thought you might say that. Here's the real deal. I'm coming out, so you better back up or I'll shoot my way through you. And I will not hesitate."

The man strides out of the closet. We all back up, keeping the same distance. Naomi's gun is starting to waver. I know from the shooting range that keeping a handgun level is a lot harder than it looks. Tie a two-pound weight to your wrist and see how long you can hold your arm out. Not long, even if you're bracing.

"Hey, this is great," the man says, moving us backward. "Let's use the momentum. Keep rolling. Or die. Your choice. Personally I could care less. Always wanted to die in a shoot-out, and tonight is as good a time as any."

Maybe you had to be there, but there's never any doubt about his personal interest in death. Which, believe me, is even more convincing if the man in question looks like he was turned on a lathe from hardened steel and smells like he's been eating raw hamburger left out in the sun. I know about the bad breath because as he slips forward, accelerating the pace, daring us all to die in an exchange of variously sized bullets, he reaches out his left hand, snake-strike quick, and grabs hold of my neck.

In the same motion he somehow slips behind me, all in that one sly movement, like a conjuror's trick. And his gun ends up jammed under my chin.

"Don't look so embarrassed," he says to Jack. "I've done this before. More than once. And you know what? I'm not even going to ask you to lower your weapons. Take a shot if you think you can take me down without hitting my new pal here. No? Then keep moving. I do enjoy the company."

My knees don't seem to be functioning, but that turns out not to be a problem, because the man wraps his arm around my waist, lifting me effortlessly. With the business end of the snub-nose buried under my chin I don't even fantasize about struggling or fighting to get free.

He makes Jack and Naomi go down the stairs backward, which he apparently finds very amusing. Jack is really, really angry, looks like he's going to snap off his own teeth he's so pissed, and Naomi has an expression I've never seen on her face. Fear. She's trying to mask it, probably for my benefit, but there it is. She fears for my life.

The man with my life in his hands backs them all the way to the ground floor, to the rear fire exit. He swings me around like a rag doll and puts his back to the door.

Jack and Naomi are only a few yards away, still armed. Jack is still trying to find a shot that won't risk killing me, too, but he looks discouraged.

"You're good folks, I can tell that," says the man who has the gun to my head, sounding oddly jovial. "You know why? Because you chose life."

"What do you want?" Naomi says. "Why go to all the trouble of breaking into the residence?"

I can feel him laughing inside, which is nearly as terrifying as the gun under by chin. "It wasn't any trouble," he says. "I thought New Mommy might be visiting and I wanted to give her my regards."

"New Mommy?" Naomi asks, puzzled.

"The skinny bitch with the two-by-four. She's not here, obviously, but I'll find her. Bet on it."

He pushes backward through the door, carrying me out into the night.

It's not like I think about death a lot. Not my own death. That stays buried away in the back of my mind, a dark little shape to be taken out and examined as rarely as possible. We're all short-timers with specific but unknown-to-us expiration dates, we know that even as children, so what's the point of dwelling on the fact of our own mortality? Bummer, man. But when I do have occasion to contemplate the end of me, I figure I won't go easy. Not the type. I'll be one of those who rage against the oncoming light, fighting to stay behind.

Or so I thought. As it turned out in this particular circumstance, in the arms of death himself, I was strangely docile. A voice inside was saying, this is it, you've come to the last moment of your life, try to be calm because the last thing you want—your very last desire—is to leave without your dignity intact. Don't let fear turn you into something less than you are. Don't let your last moment be one of terror.

So when the steel god of death tosses me aside and slips away, into the shadows, I remain where discarded, as numb as if I'd been wrapped in cotton batting.

Jack finds me a block from the residence. I'm sitting on the curb hugging my knees to my chin without a thought in my head. Just being.

"Alice, I'm so sorry."

A moment passes before I can speak. Several moments. "You did the right thing," I finally manage to say. "I'm alive."

Chapter Fifty-Five

Whatever He Does for Fun

Daybreak finds Gatling in his home office in New Castle, setting up the operation at a discreet remove. Using third and fourth parties, none of whom have known connections to GSG, or to him personally. The operation is fraught with risk—they always are—but he finds himself responding to the challenge. In days of old a good cavalry officer rode to the sound of gunfire. Something of that remains, although in his particular case, given all of his powers and connections, the gunfire is likely to be in the form of a subpoena, rather than a hail of lead. As to the real thing, he's been there, thank you very much. He knows what it is to melt himself into a mountainside as enemy snipers rain fire, bullets fragmenting inches from his head, and, all things considered, he prefers the current situation.

Having determined that a charter jet will be touching down within the hour, and that a fuel truck will be standing by at precisely the right moment, Taylor Gatling, Jr., grants himself a five-minute juice break. The hand-squeezed OJ is chilled to his preferred temperature, waiting on the shelf in the fridge under the office bar. He's bending over to fetch it when the door opens. A door he distinctly recalls locking. He freezes in position, the most vulnerable parts of his body crouching behind the thickness of the bar, and then relaxes and stands up when he sees who it is.

"You're kind of cute when you're bending over," Kidder says.

"Don't you ever knock?"

Kidder holds up an electric lock-pick gun and pulls the trigger, making it spin. "Amazing little gizmos," he says. "Only thing that stops 'em is a keyless dead bolt. The only thing more effective is a fifty-caliber bullet."

"You're late," Gatling says.

Kidder shrugs, and Gatling notes that he seems not the least concerned with any timetable. Idiot. He's still wearing the wool cap, which Gatling suspects has scabbed to the back of his head. His eyes, always weirdly blank somehow, have gone seriously strange. Sign of a concussed skull, perhaps. Not a concern, long term, because, frankly, the man's time is just about up. Gatling hasn't arrived at the precise scenario, there are a couple of interesting options, but this particular threat is getting his ticket punched in the next forty-eight hours. After an enhanced interrogation has revealed whatever pathetic backup plans the nutball's put in place. In the interest of containment, Gatling will have to take charge of the interrogation himself, but that's not a problem, he has the skill set. Been there, done that.

"You're sweating and you stink," Gatling says.

"I love you, too."

"Not that you appear to care, but your mess has been cleaned up. Even if the woman goes to the authorities with some wild tale there will be no proof, no evidence. Her mental history will make any investigation unlikely."

"What are you saying?" Kidder says with a sly grin. "You finally offed the little brat?"

Gatling looks repulsed by the suggestion. "Of course not. We're not baby-killers. Not on purpose, anyhow. No, no, the flight has been arranged. He's going back to China, where he will be hidden in plain sight. There are thousands of families eager to adopt. He'll be given to some nice, hardworking peasant family in a remote province on the mainland."

"Oh yeah? I heard half-breeds end up in state orphanages. Nobody wants 'em."

Gatling shrugs, "Whatever happens, it will no longer be our responsibility."

"Out of sight, out of mind, eh? I like the way your brain works, Cap. Always have. But you're dreaming if you think New Mommy is going away."

"Who?"

"That chick you hired to nurse the brat."

"I told you, with her mental history no one will believe her."

"So that's why you picked her? On account of her medical record?"

"You know I did." Gatling doesn't like where this is going. He shouldn't have to discuss tactics with a grunt.

"Just so you know—I wouldn't want to keep you out of the loop, Cap, no sir, that's not my style—I dropped by the Nantz house to check on New Mommy. Figured she might go there."

For a long, stunning moment Gatling is at a loss for words. "You *what?*" he finally says.

"Aside from anything else, the bitch knows what I look like. I can't have positive IDs walking around in the world."

That's not entirely true, nor his reason for invading the

Back Bay residence. It's more that he can't let a woman get the better of him; the thought is insufferable, and makes the wounded back of his skull pulse with anger. As a matter of fact, not to be shared with his boss, he didn't enter the Nantz residence in disguise and there are now at least three more people who have a pretty good idea what he looks like. He's thinking, once he extracts sufficient funds from Gatling, that a little face surgery may be in order. He's always wanted to look like George Clooney—why not?

"I don't know what to say," Gatling says carefully, hiding his own spike of anger.

"Done and dusted, nobody home."

"So they don't know you gained access?"

"Not a chance," Kidder lies.

"Okay, I think we're done," Gatling says, pausing to finish his juice.

"Done? Really?"

"Take a shower, Bob. Feel free to use the facilities. And for God's sake, peel off that filthy cap. It makes you look demented."

Kidder appears to find the insults amusing, and makes no move to leave. He keeps hitting the trigger on the lock-pick gun. It makes a screechy little noise that has him smiling. "Since you're so calm and everything, I'm assuming you haven't heard the latest news."

Gatling is thinking that he has a gun in his desk drawer, fully loaded of course—what's the use of a gun if it isn't loaded?—and he could take care of the problem right this very minute. Except for the mess. No, better to wait, find his moment. "What news?" he says, not really interested in anything Kidder has to say.

"Randall Shane is in the wind."

"I knew that five minutes after it happened," Gatling

says dismissively. "A physically and mentally damaged man wanders away from custody. So?"

"He's coming for the kid, Cap."

"Not a problem. He won't know where to start."

Kidder seems to be amused by his nonchalance. "You had him on the premises. You think he can't find his way back?"

Gatling shakes his head. "He's not a homing pigeon. Shane had no idea where he was being detained, believe me. And any connection he or Naomi Nantz have made to this organization is strictly theoretical. She came right here to my home and made demands, can you believe the nerve? But she was bluffing. She hasn't got anything tangible, just a suspicion, and we're going to keep it that way."

"Are we? That's nice."

"Fancy a trip to Sichuan?"

"Can't say I do."

"Too bad. Because that's your final assignment. You'll handle the drop-off, and when you get back you and I are going to have a discussion about your severance package. It will be generous. You can retire and make crush videos, or whatever it is you do for fun."

"That your idea of a kiss-off?" Kidder smiles, clicking his front teeth together.

"I think we've outgrown each other, Bob."

"Crush videos? If I didn't know better I'd think you were trying to hurt my feelings."

"I wasn't aware you had any."

"Oh," Kidder says. "That hurt."

He's thinking that between here and China, accidents can happen. He intends to make sure the brat never has a chance to identify him. Gatling may not want a dead child on his conscience, but Kidder doesn't suffer from that particular weakness. Murder can be fun, if you give it half a chance.

Chapter Fifty-Six

Good Enough for Alice

Maybe there are people who can sleep soundly after having a gun put to their head. I'm not one of them, and if the previous sentence is ungrammatical, blame it on edgy insomnia.

So at four-thirty in the morning, having showered more than once to get the stink of creep off me, I'm wide-awake and brushing my teeth when I hear the *rat-tat-tat* of a certain distinctive knock upon my bedroom door.

"Ah," says Naomi. "You're up. Good. Dress quickly and meet us in command."

"Us" turns out to be Naomi and Jack. It's clear that our senior investigator hasn't been to bed at all and is eager to get on with whatever mission he's been assigned. His "tell" isn't subtle—he keeps glancing at his wristwatch.

Boss lady, attired in one of her full-length silk kimonos, looks similarly determined. "Less than fifteen minutes ago Randall Shane made contact with Jack, using a throwaway phone. We have to assume the call was picked up by one of the national security agencies, because all calls are run through their filters. So that's a given. Whether or not the raw data has been tagged or identified is unknown, but we have to assume that Mr.

Gatling and his associates have access to the data banks, or can tag certain calls and callers. No doubt we are on his list. Shane spoke in a code familiar to Jack, but the mere fact that he made contact indicates an assumption that we intend to provide assistance, so there isn't much time."

"Time for what?" I ask.

"Providing assistance, of course. We need your help. Are you willing to risk the legal exposure?"

Without hesitation I say, "Yes. Count me in."

Naomi nods, satisfied. "You'll accompany Jack to the rendezvous point and remain there, reporting to me as events unfold. I can then take whatever actions I deem necessary."

"We're going to help Shane get Joey, right?"

"That's the plan. You are to remain with the vehicle or nearby, is that understood? Keep your cell off unless you have to use it. It's a virtual certainty they'll be attempting to trace our movements."

"The FBI or Gatling's people?"

"Probably both."

"You really think the FBI is assisting in a kidnapping?"

"No, absolutely not. But their security has been compromised. Anything they learn about this case is being passed on to GSG. Monica Bevins said as much, suggesting we're on our own, and we must take her at her word. Now go, and Godspeed."

As we hurry down the hallway it's obvious Jack isn't really cool with having me along, but orders are orders.

"What's the problem?" I ask.

"Nothing personal. I'm just not sure it makes sense to expose you to felony charges if the thing goes sideways."

"You're concerned for my well-being?"

He shrugs. "Yeah."

"That's sweet. So what kind of code did Shane use?"

"Not a code, exactly. Verbal shorthand. We used to use it on open frequencies, in case bad guys had a scanner. You'd be surprised how many do. The call was very brief and to the point. 'Mind your p's and q's.'"

"That's it?"

"Emphasis on p's. That would be Pease International Tradeport. He'll be expecting us within the hour."

On the way down to the garage Jack opens a gun safe, hands me a Smith & Wesson Airweight that's identical to the weapon Naomi was wielding for last night's festivities. Also a box of .38 ammo that feels heavier than the gun itself.

"Fine for me, but what about you?"

He snorts. "I'm already carrying, and that's for Shane. 'Q' is code for a throw down. He was letting me know he needed a weapon."

We get into his Lincoln Town Car and strap up. Jack's a pest about seat belts. Before he turns the key he gives me one last out. "By picking up that gun you're already in the act of aiding and abetting an escaped prisoner. It would be a whole lot safer to stay here and assist Naomi."

"It wasn't safer last night."

"Good point," he concedes. He thumbs a button on the visor and the garage door lifts.

Standing there, blocking our view, is a big beefy guy in a Massachusetts State Trooper uniform.

"Ah, shit," says Jack. "You've got the gun. Get it to Shane. No delay. No time to clear it with Naomi, understood? I'll make sure she knows what's going down. You just make sure that—"

Before he can finish the car door is yanked open and

the big trooper "assists" Jack from the vehicle. "Mr. Delancey? You'll have to come with me."

"What's the charge?"

"The charge is, get in the cruiser and don't speak until spoken to."

"Like that, huh?"

"Captain Tolliver wants a word."

As he's being jammed into the cruiser Jack catches my eye and croaks out, "Don't hesitate, go!"

And then the cruiser screeches down the public alley, leading our lead investigator away.

Let me tell you, driving a Lincoln Town Car is like piloting a boat. Not that I've ever piloted a boat of any kind, but you get the idea. Big and wide and gliding along the highway like a battleship with an uncertain navigator at the wheel. There'd been such urgency in Jack's request—right away, no delay, don't hesitate—that I resisted the temptation to return to boss lady for a consultation. She'll know soon enough and time is of the essence. By the time the cruiser clears the alley I'm headed in the opposite direction, doubling back through a few side streets, and then slipping onto Storrow Drive with fingers crossed, hoping I haven't picked up a tail.

As to the precise rendezvous location, all I know is that Taylor Gatling's company is headquartered at the Pease International Tradeport. That's where Milton Bean had been threatened with torture so it makes sense that Shane would be checking out Pease in his hunt for Joey Keener. And if he's doing so in the company of the woman who had originally helped kidnap the boy, or at the very least helped care for him, then he—they, Shane and his accomplice—quite possibly have current information on the boy's whereabouts.

Fortunately for me, Jack's ride has a built-in GPS. A female-sounding navigator who rather snippily directs me to go north on Route 95, which I do manage, although not as efficiently as Miss Snippy would have liked. Using the cruise control—the boat comes with every option—I keep it to just a teensy bit over the maximum speed limit, so as not to attract attention from the highway patrol, and settle in for the fifty-minute journey.

All the while wondering if I'm doing the right thing. Not so much worried about legal repercussions—there's always hope that Dane can sort those out—but doing the right thing for Joey. Maybe we're wrong about the FBI being compromised and we should bring them in, use all that manpower and tactical advantage. Naomi could be wrong about that, we all could, but it's not my call. So I decide to leave the option to boss lady, who is no doubt already factoring in what happened to Jack, considering all the possibilities. Possibilities I probably can't even imagine, not being a genius with a brain that recalls every little thing.

It boils down to this. Jack Delancey thinks it's important that Shane be supplied with a weapon. And that, ultimately, is good enough for me.

Chapter Fifty-Seven

Faith

The birds are going nuts, making so much noise I feel it like a pressure in my ears. All of them shrieking, *Over here! There's a human over here!* Or maybe they do this every morning, regardless of intruders. I wouldn't know. The last time I went camping I was still married—or thought I was—and the experience involved a lovely little bungalow in the Berkshires. Paid for by me, of course, although I didn't know that at the time. Still, Girl Scout I'm not. Girl Scouts would have bug spray, in addition to nutritious cookies—I'm suffering from a distinct lack of breakfast—and I resent donating blood to the local mosquito swarm, however needy they may be.

The navigator turns out to be useful but limited. It guides me to the Tradeport, no problem, but for whatever reason it can't seem to come up with Gatling Security Group World Headquarters. Maybe it's been blocked or shielded, like other high-value security targets. Or maybe I just failed to find the right screen on the smug little GPS. Whatever, in the end all I've got to guide me is my recollection of Jack's description of where he was when he rescued Milton Bean. Something about a nature trail running alongside a huge airfield. The Tradeport is, after all, built around a former U.S. Air Force base with a runway big enough to land the space shuttle—if we still had one, that is.

I located the runway—really, it can't be missed—and by following the signs found a trail marked, no surprise, Nature Trail. The only trouble, as soon as I ventured away from the paved road I somehow misplaced the trail part. The vast expanse of the airfield is in sight, just beyond the thick leaves, but I'm left thrashing around in the thick underbrush, trying not to panic because the birds, damn their little shrieking beaks, are going to give me away.

And that, of course, is exactly when my cell phone starts twittering. I'd turned it back on when I left the car, hoping Naomi will text me with something useful, but swear to the god of SIM cards that I left it on vibrate. Honestly, the rotten little Nokia seems to have a life of its own. I fumble around in my purse, nearly dumping out the Smith & Wesson, and flip open the phone. It is, as I expected and hoped, Naomi Nantz herself.

The message is succinct, and maddening, because she doesn't wait for my reply.

"I'll make this quick," she says. "Jack is on the way. He says don't do anything foolish, wait for backup. And turn off your phone. If I can see you, they can, too."

Then she hangs up. What I want to do is throw the phone all the way back to Boston. Instead I turn it off and remove the battery for good measure. The idea that I might be a little green blip on somebody's screen is un-nerving to say the least.

I'm thinking, come on, Jack. Hurry. I messed up bad. I can't find Shane, hell, I can't even find myself. Rescue me and I'll let you call me "doll" anytime you like.

That's when a very large hand clamps over my mouth and drags me down into the bushes.

Randall Shane, big as life. Bigger.

"Who the hell are you?" he wants to know, his voice a husky whisper. And then he relaxes his grip. "Oh yeah, I remember you from the hospital."

I explain about Jack getting delayed and sending me ahead with a gun.

"Have you got it?"

"In my purse."

The big guy slips the Airweight and ammo out of my purse, but doesn't seem overly enthusiastic.

"You wanted a bigger gun?" I ask.

"No. I wanted Jack Delancey."

"Sorry, it's the best we could do."

He nods grimly and whispers, "Kathy? Come on out."

His accomplice emerges from the ferns, smeared with dirt and looking not at all happy to make my acquaintance. I barely recognize her as the woman on the bridge with Joey. She's lost weight—she can't be a hundred pounds soaking wet—and her eyes have sunk back in her skull. Haunted eyes that burn with a feverish intensity.

"You trust her?" she hisses.

Shane shrugs and says, "Yeah, I guess."

I'm tempted to make a wisecrack about the less-than-enthusiastic endorsement, but they both look so exhausted, so anxious and on edge that I can't bring myself to say anything but, "How can I help?"

"You know any first aid?" he wants to know. "Kathy has a bad burn that needs attending to."

"Forget it," his scrawny little companion says. "Not until we find Joey."

The burn on her arm is festering. The pain must be

unbearable—the top layer of skin has burned away from wrist to elbow—but she makes no complaint. When I mention that, knowing Jack, the Town Car might have a kit in the trunk, she adamantly refuses to accompany me back to the vehicle. "Not until we find Joey," she insists, repeating her mantra.

"She scratched her arm, made it worse," Shane says.

The remark seems to make her eyes shine even more brightly. "It worked, didn't it?" she says. "That's what counts."

He brings me up to speed. Explains how Kathy was made to think she was working with Shane, protecting the boy, and how she eventually figured out that she'd been duped and that Joey was in danger. She had risked her life attempting to escape with Joey and when it had all gone wrong she found Shane and begged him to help her find and save the boy.

"She saw Taylor Gatling loading Joey into a van," Shane says, in an admiring tone. "According to the plate number the van was leased by GSG, Gatling's company, right here at the Tradeport. I don't care how many Pentagon big shots he has on his side, or how invulnerable they've made him feel, when they understand the evidence against him they'll throw him to the wolves. Kathy's prepared to testify."

She nods, affirming, but insists, "Save Joey first."

"Absolutely," Shane agrees.

"You know why I know he's alive?" she says, directing the question to me, or maybe to the world, such is her intensity. "Because when they brought him out of the house his little hands twitched. That was a sign to me, a gift from God. I know he's alive because God told me so and we're going to save him and give him back to his real mommy, and whatever happens after that, none of it matters."

"Okay..." I say.

"They drugged him with something but he's alive," she insists. "If they wanted to kill him they'd have left him there and burned him up in the fire, but they didn't, they didn't, so I still have a chance, I can still do it, I can make it okay."

I look down at where she's gripping my arm with both hands and she apologizes and lets go. Shane gives me a very sober look, as if to say he hopes she's right but can't be sure. He measures his words with care. "We're working on the assumption that the kid survived. From Kathy's description of the situation, Gatling is operating in something of a panic, making decisions on the fly. He has to take the boy somewhere, so it makes sense he'd come here, to a location where he believes he's in complete control. Either to hold Joey in one of his secure facilities, or possibly to transport him to another, safer location."

"You think we should notify the local cops or the FBI?"

He shakes his head, a firm no. "From what Monica told me, Gatling has ears everywhere. And even if he doesn't get tipped off, the FBI won't come in on tippy-toes, that's not the way they roll. If he suspects they're making a move he might do something drastic."

According to Shane, he and Kathy have been out here since well before dawn, surveilling the buildings, bunkers and hangars that make up Gatling's kingdom, all readily visible across the wide expanse of runway. So far they haven't seen the white van, or any activity that looks out of the ordinary.

"I was hoping Jack could make a play from the other side, flush them out."

"He's on his way."

Kathy crawls through the foliage for a better view and almost immediately calls out, her voice urgent.

We both join her at the edge of the runway, where the early-morning light is already baking the acres of concrete.

"Over there," she says, pointing toward one of the GSG hangars. "Just drove up. Is that a fuel truck?"

"It is," Shane says, sounding impressed.

"When they flew me to Hong Kong to pick up Joey, we stopped to refuel along the way. The trucks were like that. There's a driver in the truck, see? He's waiting. Means a plane will arrive soon."

"You're good," he says. "Anything else?"

"I still don't see a white van."

"Probably already destroyed, or at the very least being thoroughly cleaned and detailed. Gatling is very careful. That's how he's gotten away with it so far."

"He wasn't being careful at the cottage," she points out. "I've been going over it in my mind, everything that happened, and I don't think it was part of the plan, him coming to fetch Joey. He was angry and upset."

"Because you'd messed things up by clobbering his lackey."

"That's the other thing. Whatever he is, Kidder isn't a lackey. He despises Taylor Gatling."

"And you're thinking maybe we can use that?" he says, treating her as he might a colleague.

"Maybe. Somehow."

That little exchange makes me understand why Shane allowed her to come along. He believes that she has earned the right to risk her life if that's what she wants to do. Maybe he understands because, according to everything I've heard about him, he's been indulging a save-the-child-at-all-costs impulse for years. Having a greater purpose is apparently what saved him from a suicidal madness of grief and loss, and he isn't about to deny Kathy Mancero a similar opportunity to redeem herself.

And me, normally not that much of a risk-taker, I'm along for the ride. A bit frightened—okay, I'm terrified, way out of my comfort zone—but nevertheless glad to be of help. Even if all I did was bring a man a gun.

"Jet," Shane says softly, pointing into the sun.

We freeze in place until the midsize plane touches down. As the jet slows and taxis down the long runway, the driver gets out of the fuel truck wearing overalls, an orange vest and sound mufflers covering his ears. He uses a pair of orange wands to guide the jet within range of the fuel truck, fifty feet or so from the hangar. The engines wind down.

"Let's do it," Kathy says, obviously eager to be on the move.

Shane touches her uninjured arm. "Hold position," he says firmly. "Don't move until we have a visual on Joey. If he's there. If the jet is for him."

"He's there."

She sounds so certain.

"You see him?"

She shakes her head, the light of a true believer blazing in her haunted eyes. "God led me to this place. Just as he led you."

And really, what can you say to that? We watch silently, intently, as the jet refuels. At no time does the aircraft open a hatch or lower stairs. Which I find strange. In my limited experience of flying on private jets, the pilots like to get out and kick the tires, go through their checklists and so on. And when, finally, the refueling has been completed, the man in the orange vest returns with a small tractor. He hooks up to the front wheel of the jet and begins the slow process of pulling it toward the hangar.

As the superwide hangar doors begin to lift, yawning open to the dimness within, Kathy Mancero suddenly gets to her feet. "That's it," she announces. "They want the plane under cover when they bring Joey out."

Shane takes issue. "Sorry, hey, but we still don't know for sure the kid is there."

"You don't," Kathy says adamantly. "I do."

She breaks free of Shane's restraining touch and runs. Heading along the edge of the woods, aiming for the hangar, as fast as she can go.

We have no choice but to follow.

Chapter Fifty-Eight

Everything She Has Ever Feared

Kathy runs instinctively, choosing an angle that will make her approach unseen to anyone who happens to be inside the hangar. If there are other guards in place they've not made themselves known, and she sees the intentional lack of witnesses as yet another signal that something terrible is about to go down. The ground crew had been limited to one. The pilots have yet to exit the plane, as if to make sure they never register on surveillance tapes, or because they suspect their mission is somehow shameful. And now the refueled aircraft is being dragged into the darkness of the hangar, as if complicit in some terrible act best concealed from the world of light.

All signs that the time for bad things has come.

Shane and the other woman may not quite be able to see it, but the meaning is clear to Kathy. It has been revealed. Her belief that she's being guided, that she has a purpose, a role to play, is absolute. The pain of her wound is as nothing. All that matters is Joey, who, in her desperate foolishness, she helped abduct in the first place. Now she's being given a chance to put that right, to return balance and love to the world and, in her own mind, to confirm the existence of heaven.

Kathy runs like the wind, feeling light and strong and filled with an exhilarating sense of joy. She has no fear because everything she has ever feared has already come to pass. Her heart is open, her eyes are clear. She knows absolutely that her blessed daughter, Stacy, watches and approves, rooting for her to help the little boy with the music in his hands.

At some point, as if letting her feet find the way, she cuts across the wide expanse of the runway, heading for the north side of the hangar. A high wall of gray corrugated metal. It is there that she believes she will find Joey, there that he will be saved. She believes that in that same miraculous moment she, too, will be saved, and nothing on this earth will stop her from trying.

Chapter Fifty-Nine

When the Music Stops

Randall Shane, doing his best to keep up—his long legs should easily be outrunning my own—seems to have come hard up against the limits of what his damaged body can deliver. We're barely out of the woods when he doubles over, clutching his left knee, and wobbles to a halt. Through a grimace of pain he says, "Torn ligaments. Sorry. I can walk but apparently I can't run."

He reaches into a trouser pocket, retrieves the snub-nosed .38 Smith & Wesson and places it in my hands. "Fully loaded," he cautions. "Concealed hammer, double-action. Pull the trigger all the way and it fires."

I accept the weapon, feeling about as confident as a first-day medical student being dropped into the middle of brain surgery. That one time at the range I had managed to empty a five-shot cylinder without hitting the target.

"I may be the worst shot in Boston," I warn him.

"Then consider yourself armed and dangerous. Go. I'll try and catch up."

"The woman is crazy, you know."

Shane shakes his head. "She's not afraid to die. That's

not the same thing as crazy. I'll be right along. Please, just go, do what you can."

What the hell. Maybe this is the day I get to be a hero, or to help one out. I slip the little snubby in my waistband and bolt across the wide concrete runway, following the skinny gazelle with the crazy, wonderful light in her eyes.

Probably no more than a few hundred yards, but it feels like miles. Not because the running is hard—I have adrenaline to spare—but because it's so exposed. I feel like a big fly on a windowpane, waiting for the swatter to splat me. But if there's anybody watching, they give no sign, no shouts or sirens, and I reach the hangar wall unimpeded.

Pausing for just a moment to catch my breath, aware of the heat radiating from the corrugated steel. Kathy Mancero, poised at the far end of the hangar, beckons me forward. Eyes still so intense I can barely meet her gaze.

"You've got the gun?"

I reach to my waist, prepared to hand it over.

"No, no, keep it. I'd be afraid of hitting Joey. Just cover me."

Great. I'm hoping Shane gets here fast. I'm keenly aware that without the necessary skill, and the willingness to use it, a handgun isn't much more than a prop. I make a silent vow to sign up for more firing-range lessons, as many as it takes. Hoping that it won't be too little, too late.

From inside the hangar we hear the creak and moan of the huge doors lifting, steel on steel, bucking and grinding. A noise that will surely cover our footsteps as we edge along and find the outside corner of the massive building.

"Inside," Kathy whispers, her breath strangely cool as it brushes my ear.

Before I quite understand, she ducks into the shadows just inside the hangar.

There's nothing for me to do but follow. My heart slams like a two-year-old in full tantrum. I'm aware of a mass of cooler air, the chill of shadows hushed within the hangar. Crouching, I attempt to make myself small as the jet passes into the interior, the end of the wing only yards away, being smoothly pulled by the little tractor. My eyes gradually adjust—the interior illumination does little to pierce the vast dimness of the hangar—and realize, with great relief, that I haven't been spotted because there's nobody to see me, or, for that matter, Kathy, who continues to slip along against the wall, finding cover as she goes. There are no security guards, no ground crew or mechanics, no one but the gleaming jet and the man on the tractor, whose back is toward us.

When the jet is fully inside the hangar, the man on the tractor climbs off and removes his noise-muffling head-gear, revealing a wool cap pulled down to his ears.

Him. The guy from the closet. The home invader who put a gun to my head.

Kathy recognizes him, as well. She slips back to me, close enough to grip my arm and whisper in my ear. "That's Kidder. Joey can't be far away."

She seems exhilarated by the thought, almost giddy with purpose. I'm about to suggest that maybe we should make a plan, coordinate our efforts, but my eager companion has already moved on.

I slip behind a waist-high chest of mechanic tools and peek around the corner. This Kidder dude has his back to us. He seems to be talking to himself, shaking his head, as if in an argument with himself. Then I spot the slim microphone wand extending from beneath the wool cap and realize he's equipped with a Bluetooth headset. He's talking to someone, taking orders or arguing, or both. Whatever, he seems frustrated, not in complete control, and that gives me a little more confidence. Maybe we can pull this off, after all. Assuming the boy is nearby— though I've seen no sign of him yet.

As Kidder turns in my direction I pull back behind the tool chest. Trusting the dimness to hide me. Not that Kidder has given any sign of awareness that he's under observation. He seems to be concentrating on his headset.

"What?" he says, his voice echoing in the vast interior. "Repeat? Well, why didn't you say so?"

His posture tense and angry, he reaches up to thump on the tail section of the jet. A moment later a hatch opens and a stairway begins to unfold. I expect someone to descend—a pilot or possibly a flight attendant—but no one emerges. Apparently there's no one in the passenger compartment, or if there is they're not revealing themselves to Kidder, who stands below the stairway, shaking his head in frustration.

"Idiots," he mutters. "Do I have to do everything myself?" Then, louder, into the headset, "Are you ready for the package or not? Okay, fine. Whatever you want. It's just us chickens out here, so have a little patience."

The man with the wool cap and the deeply aggrieved attitude climbs back on the tractor and retreats into the gloom. The only sound in the vast hangar is the electric whine of the tractor motor, and the small hard wheels spinning along the concrete floor.

Part of me wants to leave the protection of the tool chest and run after him, waving the gun and demanding Joey, but my best instincts tell me that would be futile.

That would be giving up my best weapon: the element of surprise. Have patience, wait until you know where the boy is and that you can make him safe. So I remain in place, watching as the little tractor closes in on a white panel van parked deep in the shadows at the rear of the hangar.

Kathy, appearing out of nowhere with a suddenness that nearly stops my heart, hisses, "That's it. The same van that came to fetch Joey, there's no doubt."

"We should wait," I say. "Let him bring the boy to us. Then we get the jump."

Adding, in my own mind, and let's hope Shane is here by then, he'll know what to do.

"Bring him to us," Kathy repeats, as if mulling it over. "Okay, that makes sense."

Kidder gets off the tractor, opens the rear door of the van, blocking our view. When he gets back on the tractor he has something with him. As he emerges from behind the van he's towing a little low-bed trailer, the kind they use to transport luggage. On the trailer is a crate, of the size that might be suitable for a medium-size dog.

The whine of the tractor begins to sound like a high-pitched scream, but still we wait. I'm keenly aware that we have to choose our moment, that our timing has to be perfect and that Kidder is quite possibly armed.

Kathy Mancero, with that oddly cool breath, whispers, "I've got this," and slips away on all fours, crawling around the back of the tool chest.

I've got this? What does that mean?

Before I have time to explore the thought, it happens. As Kidder swings the tractor around the wing of the aircraft, Kathy explodes from behind the tool chest, launching herself into the air, a missile aimed at a monster. As she collides with the muscled hardness of his body, her arms tighten around his neck, pulling him off the seat with the forward momentum of her hundred pounds of bone and grief.

They land on the concrete, a tangle of limbs, Kidder spitting curses.

"Stop right there! I've got a gun!"

That's me, holding the .38 in both hands and trying to look like I know what I'm doing.

Kidder takes one look at me, grins like a lunatic and flips over so that Kathy's skinny body is between him and the gun.

"Take your shot, sweetheart!" he chortles.

Giggling. Like he thinks this is fun. But the crazed giggle abruptly stops as Kathy rips off his wool cap and grabs a fistful of clotted hair. The back of his head is one big scab. She slams his head down with all her might and his nose smacks into the concrete.

Kidder yelps, an animal howl of rage. He outweighs her by about a hundred pounds and in an instant she's bucked away by his vastly superior strength. She flies through the air for several yards and lands flat on her back with her left arm behind her, stunned or worse.

Measuring my distance carefully—deathly afraid he'll find a way to take the gun away from me—I shuffle closer, bellowing, "Hands in the air! I'll do it, I'll pull the trigger!"

Kidder, up on his knees, gives me a sly grin, like he'd been hoping it would come to this. "I know you," he says. "My friend in the bedroom. Bet I made you wet your little pants."

"Put your hands behind your head and lace your fingers together!" I demand, borrowing a familiar, if amalgamated, line from just about every cop show ever seen on TV.

"Anything you say," he says, feigning agreement. His hands remain in front of him and his smile is taunting, daring me to fire.

"Uh," says Kathy. "Uh."

The poor woman has had the breath knocked out of her, at the very least. Her eyes are unfocused and her left arm looks wrong, as if maybe the landing jarred it out of its socket at the shoulder. Despite what has to be excruciating pain she smiles oddly and with her good arm she points upward. Something flits through the air high above us, something that emits a soft, sad cooing.

Mourning doves in the great steel rafters, under the curving roof of the hangar. When I glance back again Kidder has halved the distance between us. Still on his knees but much, much closer.

"Stop!" I scream, tightening my crouch, re-aiming the .38. "Not another inch!"

He grins and actually backs up a foot or so. "Have you ever fired that thing?" he asks conversationally. "It takes like a two-pound pull on the trigger. Harder than you might think. And the barrel is going to jump, that's guaranteed. I've seen people miss from three feet away and we're like, what, six whole feet?"

"Shut up."

Kathy has managed to get to her feet, her bad arm dangling. Her eyes have started to clear and it looks to me like she's going to be okay, assuming we can get her to a hospital in the very near future.

Her mouth starts to open, but before she can get a word out a deep male voice booms through the hangar.

"Kathy! Alice! I've got him! You did it!"

Keeping one eye on Kidder, I turn my stance slightly and find Shane, the big man himself. Panting from his efforts but with an immense grin on his face. He's ripped open the dog crate and has a small boy in his arms, unconscious but clearly alive.

Joey.

Kathy cries out with joy, her whole face glistening with tears. She limps toward Shane and the boy, wounded but unvanquished. It's a beautiful sight, and I'm close to tears myself. But I can't quit now. The gun, even grasped in both hands, is starting to get heavy.

Kidder, humming to himself, shuffles closer, marching on his knees with his arms swinging, tick tock, like a child playing at soldier.

"No," I say, finger squeezing. "No!"

Grinning, Kidder says, "You know what's funny?"

"Shut up and grab the floor."

Kidder looks like he's going to comply, and then his eyes roll up and his body convulses and he grabs at his chest. It's a convincing move, he sells it, and for just that one moment I almost believe he's going into cardiac arrest. Until, a millisecond later, his right hand emerges from a fold in his orange overalls, holding a shiny pistol. Which swings not toward me, but toward Shane and Kathy and the unconscious boy.

"Screw it," Kidder announces. "The little brat is coming with me."

Several things happen all at once. I pull the trigger. The gun jumps in my hand like something alive, and a red splat emerges from the side of Kidder's neck.

He grimaces, as if shrugging it off. He extends his arm and fires at Shane and the boy.

In the exploding confusion that follows, one thing remains clear in my mind: a vision of Kathy Mancero throwing herself at Kidder, cutting off his angle and taking a bullet in the center of her chest.

So fast I can't react, can't stop it, can't change what happens.

Next thing, a flat, metallic snap coming from behind me. Another shooter heard from. And then Kidder is down with a round red hole in the center of his forehead and a death grin imprinted on his collapsing face, and Jack Delancey is racing up to say, "Sorry I'm late," and taking the gun from my shaking hand and making me sit on my butt because he thinks I'm going to faint, which is ridiculous.

I do faint, but only for a moment. And when my vision clears Shane and Jack are crouching over Kathy. Two tough guys looking as tender as angels. Shane with the little boy in his arms, assuring her that Joey is okay, he'll be fine as soon as he wakes up, and his mother is on the way, and she did it, she did a great good thing.

"You took the bullet, love," he says, "so that he might live."

The other thing I'm absolutely positive about: as the light faded from her eyes Kathy Mancero looked up at the cooing doves and smiled.

Chapter Sixty

Best Done Alone

Whatever moral complexities may have been exposed by recent unfortunate events, Taylor Gatling, Jr., remains a man of principle. He still empties his own spittoon, and that's exactly what he's doing one fine evening in August, a couple of months after that mess at the hangar, the one he was adroit enough to avoid. He tips the brass spittoon over the railing, hears the fine, satisfying flush of it galumphing into the river below and thinks not for the first time that he's the luckiest man in the world. Not that he hasn't made his own luck, not that he doesn't deserve to enjoy all the wealth, all the toys, but still. One must make time to smell the roses. Or in this case a salty whiff of the white-capped sea. Best done alone, which is why he's closed the boathouse to his little circle of handpicked members. Much as he enjoys the company of his card-playing cronies, he's decided that for the rest of the month he'll have the place to himself. Getting his thoughts in order, recharging his batteries, planning his next move. Because for sure he hasn't given up on the business of keeping the country safe for right-thinking patriots like, well, himself and a few select others, worthy and vetted.

He's smiling, content with his situation, his mission, as he returns to the relative darkness of the boathouse. The thing about being here alone, he doesn't have to turn on any lights, he can enjoy the passing evening by looking out at the harbor with eyes unpolluted by unnatural light.

He puts his spittoon in the appropriate place by the card table and is about to help himself to a little something at the bar when he jumps about a foot in the air.

"Where the hell did you come from!"

"Oh, sorry, our bad."

Bart and Bert, better known as the B brothers, the fraternal twins who work on the domestic drone program. Couple of local woodchucks, like to put on their countrified Down East accents. Ayuh, bubba, flannel shirts and logger boots, the whole bit. Normally Gatling finds the brothers amusing company, but this is beyond the pale, walking into the boss's private club, his personal refuge, it just isn't done. He's about to say so, striking the right tone of executive aggrievement, when he recalls locking and bolting the door to the boathouse. Of course he did, so his pals, his posse, wouldn't be tempted to drop by, despite his admonition not to. Which means the brothers must have jimmied the lock somehow, and that means—

Gatling feels the tip of a blade against his sternum and looks down to see the glint of a deer-gutting knife. "Bart? What's going on?"

"Nothing to worry about, boss. By the way, it's Bert."

"Fine. Bert. What's that your brother's got?"

The other brother has a bulky black velvet sack slung from his shoulder. It's not so dark that he can't see they're both smiling at his predicament, the damned ignorant woodchucks. Gatling has a small but distinct sense of what might have brought them here, and he's confident he can work things to his advantage, given his powers of persuasion and his unlimited checkbook.

"Sorry about the interruption," Bert says. "Me and Bart, we're here to give you notice."

"Give me notice?"

"We got signed by another club, just like ballplayers," Bart says proudly, speaking up for the first time. He shifts the sack on his shoulder, at ease with himself and whatever it is he's doing.

"Supposed to be a secret," Bert confides. "But it can't hurt to tell a guy like you, with all your connections. The DIA, and they gave us a signing bonus, too."

"Defense Intelligence? What unit?"

"One you never heard of, because it's like ultra-ultra secret and brand-new."

"Oh, I seriously doubt that. Not that you've been offered jobs, no, no, that makes sense, a couple of talented boys like you, but I'll bet you dollars to donuts I know the unit."

"He's betting us donuts, Bert."

"Ayuh. We like donuts."

The lightness of the exchange convinces Gatling that he can turn them, and he's deciding what, exactly, to offer the brothers when Bert bumps a chair into the back of his knees, forcing him to sit down.

"Sorry, Mr. Gatling, you're a cool guy and everything, but you messed up wicked, that's what they told us."

Gatling's spit has dried up but he manages to ask, "How so?"

"We don't know exactly. Above our pay grade. But something Kidder did. Some files he sent to this certain web address at the Pentagon? Got a lot of very powerful folks all agitated. Decisions got made. And the result is, we got signed by the new unit."

"Boys, I've got more money than God. You can have it all. Most of it."

Bert grins. "Keep back just a tiny little for yourself, huh?"

His brother Bart unslings the sack from his shoulder, loosens the drawstring and removes a shotgun. Even in the dark Gatling recognizes the weapon and knows what it means. A little squirt of urine wets his underpants and he clenches, telling himself he's better than this, he won't soil himself.

"This is the exact same Purdey your dad used," Bart says. "Kind of sad."

"You really expect me to shoot myself?"

"No," says Bart. "But we can make it look that way."

They do.

Chapter Sixty-One

Almost Perfect

Okay, here's how I feel about what went down. If only I'd pulled the trigger a heartbeat sooner and a little more to the right. Jack says I shouldn't let myself think that way, but I can't help it. Just because Kathy Mancero died doing a great good thing doesn't make it right that she's no longer in the world. I mean, it's a miracle that she managed to save both Joey and Shane, and maybe me, too, because it turns out that Robert James Killdeer had been trained as a sniper, and was notably adept with a pistol, and as you know, I'm not and probably never will be.

That was Kidder's real name, Robert James Killdeer, and there's ample indication that he was employed by Gatling Security Group, although no direct evidence, none that we can find, proving that Taylor Gatling, Jr., personally knew what Killdeer was up to within the company. Before he took his own life, apparently out of shame for what he'd allowed to happen, Gatling claimed that both the kidnapping of Joey Keener and the execution of Jonny Bing were parts of a rogue operation directed by Killdeer alone. Everything in the records points that way. That's the maddening thing. Gatling may be gone, but the company lives on, doing pretty much what they've been doing all along. Unfortunately there doesn't seem to be much we can do about that. The Pentagon is the Pentagon and money is money, and Naomi says I just have to accept the fact that some things can't be fixed, because justice, like humanity itself, is never perfect.

All we can do, she says, is the best we can. Which brings me back to me missing my shot and Kathy sacrificing herself. Shane thinks it means something that she died with a smile on her lips, secure in the knowledge that Joey was safe, but I'm not convinced. Dead is dead. I wish I believed in heaven the way Kathy Mancero obviously did, but I don't. If God wants to pay me a visit, explain how all the bad and terrible things in the world are part of the cosmic plan, the door is always open, and I'm willing to listen. Until then, I'll stick with believing the greatest miracle of all is life itself, and hope that will be enough to sustain me.

Just so you know, Kathy had made her wishes known to an estate lawyer in Olathe, Kansas, and her ashes are to be scattered over a playground in Kansas City, where she and little Stacy had happy times. Shane has promised to make it happen, even though there's some ordinance about remains being dispensed in public places. We all figure any kid that comes in contact with a molecule of Kathy Mancero will be the better for it, no matter what the rules say.

As to the Randall Shane legal situation, that gets a little more complicated every day. He's been released, no longer an active suspect in Professor Keener's murder, but may eventually face charges for escaping from custody, should D.A. Tommy Costello be willing to endure the bad publicity for punishing a genuine American hero. For the moment, the million-dollar bond remains in effect, which, as Dane Porter says, tends to concentrate the mind, meaning we have to tie up the loose ends.

It's great—fabulous—that Joey has been reunited with Ming-Mei—believe me, there wasn't a dry eye when that little scene unfolded, but the question of who killed who, and why, is still up for grabs. Naomi has strong views on the matter, but the D.A. has yet to sign off on the theory that the man who ordered the hit on Professor Joseph Keener was, in all probability, the late Jonny Bing himself. Turns out—and this was well hidden, so deep that even Teddy had trouble finding it—Mr. Bing's entire fortune was in peril. On paper he was still a billionaire twice over, but it turns out Jonny was obsessed with chasing higher-than-normal interest rates and had invested hundreds of millions in offshore certificates of deposit with Sir Allen Stanford, the Texas swindler and cricketer, and when all the phony dust settled, Jonny Bing came up close to empty. For the last year or so the lucrative development contracts for QuantaGate had been his only source of revenue, and the prospect of the company admitting defeat and closing up shop may have been more than he could face. Maybe he was desperate enough to kill a man he undoubtedly had once called a friend. Or maybe his fellow travelers in the Chinese espionage business, who had helped him snare Keener in the first place, decided to end his involvement in single-gated photon communication, the impossible-to-hack quantum computers that are the current Holy Grail of cybernetics.

Whatever happened, we know from the anonymous surveillance tape that the man coming out of Keener's house minutes after his murder was a thug and triggerman well-known to Jonny Bing. Did Bing really order the hit? Apparently that's one of the sordid little details that will never be known to civilians like us.

Forget it, Alice, it's Chinatown. Jack actually said that to me. He loves those old movies, does dapper Jack.

And what about Taylor Gatling, Jr.? Did he really kill himself or did he have help? It may not make any difference to the late Mr. Gatling, but I really want to know, Chinatown or not. I'm the chief factotum around here and would like to set the record straight. Call it housekeeping if you like.

Naomi says, in her maddeningly remote way, that I need to develop more patience, and that despite our best intentions, sometimes the bad guys get away with it, even after they're dead and buried.

Oh, speaking of bad guys getting away with it, consider the case of that snake-in-the-grass Glenn Tolliver. At this point I can barely stand to write the creep's name, so I'm just going to include a transcript of Piggy's last interview with Jack Delancey, duly recorded at Cigar Masters without the Pigster's knowledge. Such undisclosed recordings may be against the privacy laws, but as Piggy himself might say, in his ever-charming way, tough titty.

JACK: Hey. Looks like you started without me.

TOLLIVER: Hope you don't mind. Couldn't resist the Padron. [sound of puffing, groan of pleasure] Ah! Scotch tonight, though, not the cognac. Figured your boss would spring for the single malt, considering.

JACK: Yeah? Considering what?

TOLLIVER: My continued cooperation.

JACK: Oh yeah. That.

TOLLIVER: You sound a bit snippy, my son. What's got you down? I hope it's not having to shoot that low-life Killdeer. You did the world a favor, Jack. You should stand proud on that one.

JACK: I'm fine with that. Just wish I'd hit him sooner. I'd have been there in time if you hadn't decided to haul me in for questioning that morning.

TOLLIVER: Can't be helped. How was I to know?

JACK: Naomi has a theory about that. Gatling's outfit picked up Shane's cell phone call to me, from his end, and let you know.

TOLLIVER: [laughing] That's crazy talk.

JACK: Is it? Quite a coincidence, you having me picked up minutes after Shane called requesting backup.

TOLLIVER: That's all it was, a coincidence.

JACK: Really? My boss has a theory on that.

TOLLIVER: Full of theories, ain't she?

JACK: Yeah, and this particular theory is, if something impossible is supposed to have occurred, look very deep, because the impossible doesn't happen. That's why it's impossible.

TOLLIVER: Very profound. Almost as deep as that old wisdom dude in *The Karate Kid.*

JACK: Excuse me?

TOLLIVER: Pat Morita. Popular character actor. Probably croaked by now. Great movie.

JACK: We're discussing movies?

TOLLIVER: Don't get your boxers in a twist. Have a malt. Relax. Damn, these are great cigars!

JACK: As I was saying, we looked deep. And guess what we found?

TOLLIVER: Go on, astound me.

JACK: The bloody shirt. It was completely impossible for Shane to have returned to his motel room and left the bloody shirt behind, because by the time he got back to the motel it was already under surveillance.

TOLLIVER: So you say. But they found the shirt on the premises, so I guess it wasn't impossible.

JACK: The motel was under surveillance by your men. Dispatched by you, as it turns out.

TOLLIVER: Sure. Just passing the word from Homeland. You knew that already.

JACK: There was no word from Homeland. The order

originated with you. You dispatched your men to stake out the motel, and you went in with a warrant when it arrived. You were the first one through the door. The first one to discover the bloody shirt. Which, as we've already established, was impossible. Therefore we're left with one really unpleasant conclusion: you planted it, Piggy.

TOLLIVER: Hey, son, watch your mouth. And that's bull, about planting the shirt. Why would I do a thing like that?

JACK: Don't ask a question you don't want answered, Piggy, my boy. My brother. My son. You planted the shirt—handed to you by one of Gatling's operatives, I'm guessing, because they had the professor under surveillance and were the first to be aware of his death, and because Gatling couldn't pass up a chance, a gift, at revenge on Randall Shane. Or maybe they gave you a vial of the victim's blood, and you used that on an item of Shane's clothing. However you did it, you risked a felony conviction because you'd applied for early retirement so you can take a job with, drum roll, Gatling Security Group.

TOLLIVER: You'll never prove none of that. It's just a bullshit theory cooked up by some private investigator.

JACK: She didn't make up the part about you retiring to take a high-paying job with GSG. Right there in your jacket. You put in your papers a month before Keener was killed.

TOLLIVER: So? No crime in that. It's all legit. I got a daughter, a smart little angel, she deserves to go to a good school.

JACK: She deserves an honest father. Too bad she didn't get one.

TOLLIVER: Screw you, Mr. Fancy Pants.

JACK: She deserves someone who didn't try to frame an innocent man, for money. Who didn't, in effect, delay the return of an abducted child to his rightful mother.

TOLLIVER: I never did that!

JACK: Sit down before you fall down, you big fool. Sure you did. Your actions helped Gatling put Shane out of commission. Left to his own devices, Randall Shane would have recovered Joey Keener while he was still being held in Prides Crossing, and at least one and possibly two human beings would still be alive.

TOLLIVER: No way. You can't lay that on me.

JACK: I just did. Have a nice retirement, Piggy. I hope your little girl gets into a good school, I really do.

TOLLIVER: You'll never prove it!

JACK: I'm not going to try. Why bother? You're already dead to me.

TOLLIVER: Jack, come on.

JACK: The tab is in your name, by the way. I made sure of that.

You have to admire the style. That whole "you're dead to me" thing reminds me why I'd never want to get on the wrong side of Jack Delancey. And unfortunately it's true that we can't prove Piggy planted evidence, even though he was the only one to have the opportunity. Dane Porter has explained the difficulties, no doubt she's correct in the legal sense, but still it irks, knowing a high-ranking officer betrayed his oath and got away with it, and caused incalculable harm in the process.

It burns me, it really does.

Naomi says I need to cultivate a belief in karma. She invites me into her studio one afternoon to chat while she attempts her daily watercolor, and so far it is going remarkably well. The watercolor, I mean. It's just an average still life, a Chinese vase with flowers, but she's getting the light just right, a beam of late-afternoon sun that catches one particular blossom, a white lily, making it look illuminated from within.

I'm holding my breath, hoping for once she'll accept the inevitability of imperfection she mentioned and let the pretty little painting survive.

"Piggy will find his own karma," she says, wetting her softest brush. "Think of it this way. He gets the money, and whatever further corruption his new career provides, and we get the music."

"The music is good," I say.

Mozart trills airily from the soft echo chamber of the Zen garden, the next room over from the studio. The keyboard kid is practicing under the watchful, grateful

eye of his mi ma. The mother and child have been offered sanctuary until Naomi can set them up with a new
life in the homeland, the U.S. homeland. We're thinking New York, Los Angeles or San Francisco, where it
will be easy for a talented Eurasian boy to blend into
the local culture and also have access to the best music
teachers. No rush, though. It's a treat to have them in
the residence, especially Joey, who is really something
special, even aside from his genius for music. He knows
what happened to Kathy, and mourns her in his own way,
which includes writing a long, lyrical piece he's calling
"Brave Lady Sonata in C Minor." She'd love it, I'm pretty
sure. It's beautiful and sad and brave, just like she was.

Naomi says, "Taylor Gatling found his own karma,
too. If not in this life, then in the next."

"He's coming back as a cockroach."

"If that's his karma," Naomi says, amused. "Which
of course we can't know."

"Apparently you're coming back as a fortune cookie."

Naomi puts down her brush and laughs so hard her
eyes tear up. Blotting away the wetness with a tissue she
says, "You're a treasure, Alice. You keep me centered,
do you know that?"

"Don't go all gooey on me, boss lady."

"No chance," she says. "I don't do gooey."

Naomi Nantz peels the gorgeous watercolor from the
easel, holding it up to the light, as if to compare to the
real thing.

"Almost perfect," she says.

Then she tears it up.

* * * * *

The chilling tale of a parent's worst nightmare, by acclaimed author

CHRIS JORDAN
taken

No parent believes it can happen to them—their child taken from a suburban schoolyard in the gentle hours of dusk. But, as widowed mother Kate Bickford discovers, everything can change in the blink of an eye.

Opening the door to her Connecticut home, hoping to find her son, Kate comes face-to-face with her son's abductor. He wants money. All she has. And if she doesn't follow something he calls The Method, the consequences will be gruesome....

> "Jordan's full-throttle style makes this an emotionally rewarding thriller that moves like lightning."
> —*Publishers Weekly*

Available now wherever books are sold.

MIRA™

HARLEQUIN®
www.Harlequin.com

MCJ2468R

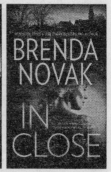

NEW YORK TIMES BESTSELLING AUTHOR

JACI BURTON

Before the Special Forces hero has even unpacked
his bags from twelve years of active duty, he's
embroiled in murder—corpses bearing the brutal
trademark he's seen only once before—on the
worst night of his life.

The last time Detective Anna Pallino saw
Dante Renaldi, they were in love. Now, he's linked
to a string of fresh homicides and a horrible assault
that Anna survived only thanks to him.

Anna wants to trust Dante. But as the bodies and
the coincidences stack up, Anna has to decide:
Is the man she owes her life to the same one
who wants her dead?

THE HEART OF A KILLER

Available wherever books are sold.

REQUEST YOUR FREE BOOKS!

2 FREE NOVELS
FROM THE SUSPENSE COLLECTION
PLUS 2 FREE GIFTS!

YES! Please send me 2 FREE novels from the Suspense Collection and my 2 FREE gifts (gifts are worth about $10). After receiving them, if I don't wish to receive any more books, I can return the shipping statement marked "cancel." If I don't cancel, I will receive 4 brand-new novels every month and be billed just $5.99 per book in the U.S. or $6.49 per book in Canada. That's a saving of at least 25% off the cover price. It's quite a bargain! Shipping and handling is just 50¢ per book in the U.S. and 75¢ per book in Canada.* I understand that accepting the 2 free books and gifts places me under no obligation to buy anything. I can always return a shipment and cancel at any time. Even if I never buy another book, the two free books and gifts are mine to keep forever.

191/391 MDN FEME

Name _____ (PLEASE PRINT) _____

Address _____ Apt. # _____

City _____ State/Prov. _____ Zip/Postal Code _____

Signature (if under 18, a parent or guardian must sign)

Mail to the **Reader Service:**
IN U.S.A.: P.O. Box 1867, Buffalo, NY 14240-1867
IN CANADA: P.O. Box 609, Fort Erie, Ontario L2A 5X3

Not valid for current subscribers to the Suspense Collection
or the Romance/Suspense Collection.

Want to try two free books from another line?
Call 1-800-873-8635 or visit www.ReaderService.com.

* Terms and prices subject to change without notice. Prices do not include applicable taxes. Sales tax applicable in N.Y. Canadian residents will be charged applicable taxes. Offer not valid in Quebec. This offer is limited to one order per household. All orders subject to credit approval. Credit or debit balances in a customer's account(s) may be offset by any other outstanding balance owed by or to the customer. Please allow 4 to 6 weeks for delivery. Offer available while quantities last.

Your Privacy—The Reader Service is committed to protecting your privacy. Our Privacy Policy is available online at www.ReaderService.com or upon request from the Reader Service.

We make a portion of our mailing list available to reputable third parties that offer products we believe may interest you. If you prefer that we not exchange your name with third parties, or if you wish to clarify or modify your communication preferences, please visit us at www.ReaderService.com/consumerschoice or write to us at Reader Service Preference Service, P.O. Box 9062, Buffalo, NY 14269. Include your complete name and address.

SUS11

CHRIS JORDAN

31258	MEASURE OF DARKNESS	___ $7.99 U.S.	___ $9.99 CAN.
32468	TAKEN	___ $6.99 U.S.	___ $8.50 CAN.
32471	TRAPPED	___ $6.99 U.S.	___ $8.50 CAN.

(limited quantities available)

TOTAL AMOUNT	$_____
POSTAGE & HANDLING	$_____
($1.00 for 1 book, 50¢ for each additional)	
APPLICABLE TAXES*	$_____
TOTAL PAYABLE	$_____

(check or money order—please do not send cash)

To order, complete this form and send it, along with a check or money order for the total above, payable to MIRA Books, to: **In the U.S.:** 3010 Walden Avenue, P.O. Box 9077, Buffalo, NY 14269-9077; **In Canada:** P.O. Box 636, Fort Erie, Ontario, L2A 5X3.

Name: _____
Address: _____ City: _____
State/Prov.: _____ Zip/Postal Code: _____
Account Number (if applicable): _____
075 CSAS

*New York residents remit applicable sales taxes.
*Canadian residents remit applicable GST and provincial taxes.

www.Harlequin.com

MCJI211BL